CRAWFORD SMITH

# Jackrabbit

SWEET
WEASEL
WORDS
sweetweaselwords.com

First published by Sweet Weasel Words 2019

First edition

ISBN: 978-1-7332699-0-2

Cover art by Kenneth Huey
Editing by Jennifer Huston

This book was professionally typeset on Reedsy.
Find out more at reedsy.com

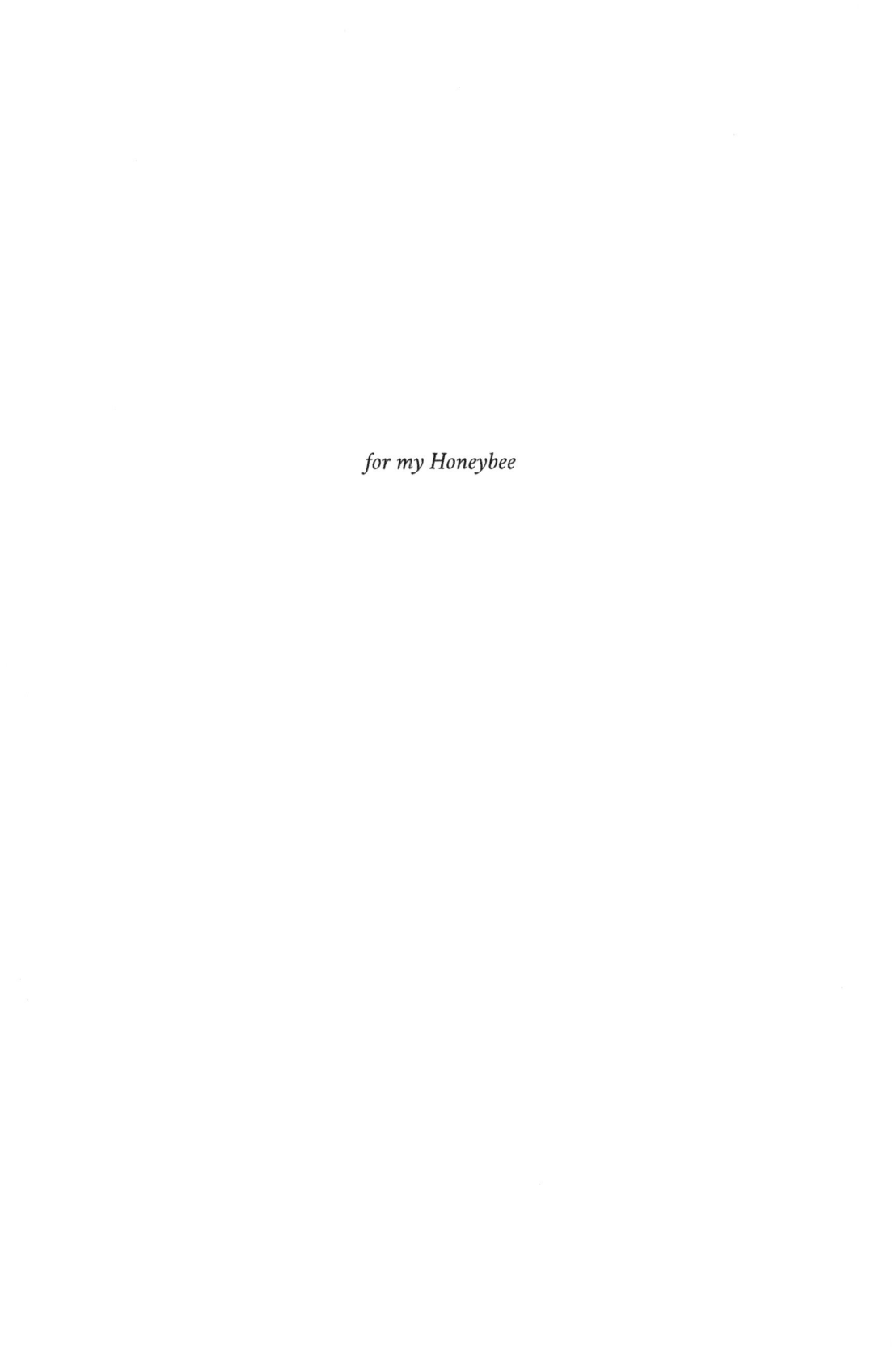

*for my Honeybee*

# Acknowledgement

Special thanks for all who helped make this book a reality. I'm indebted to Jess Truhan, Kim Smith and Klint Finley, who all provided valuable feedback. Also, love to my wife NancyAnne Smith who did likewise, as well as putting up with my overall ridiculousness. Thanks to Jen Huston for her superb editing job. And a special tip o' the hat to Ken Huey for his wonderful cover art.

Special appreciation to my eighth grade history teacher Earl Lucius, who started me down this path nearly forty years ago when he handed me a copy of *Dillinger: Dead or Alive?* and said, "You should read this."

# PROLOGUE

## McNeil Island Federal Penitentiary
## January 1969

I was there. I was right there in the middle of it all.

Who I am isn't that important. My folks saddled me with the name Alvin. Some people call me "Old Creepy," but never to my face. Most of my friends just call me Ray. Don't worry about that, though. This isn't my story; it's the Jackrabbit's.

Back in late 1933 and '34, the country was in the middle of a crime wave like no one had ever seen. The United States was deep in the Depression, and a lot of folks blamed rich people and the banks for screwing everything up. Gangs roamed the Midwest, robbing banks and kidnapping rich bastards, and the common folks ate it up. They saw it as just deserts for those who had taken their livelihoods, their savings, their homes.

I was in the thick of things back when it was front-page news. I got falling-down drunk with Pretty Boy Floyd. I shot the shit with Machine Gun Kelly. Bonnie and Clyde bummed cigarettes off me. God, those two stank. I don't think they ever took a bath.

And of course, I knew the Jackrabbit.

I met him shortly after he waltzed away from the lockup at Crown Point. We got along pretty well, but it's not as if we were best friends. We would run into each other at the Green Lantern Saloon in Saint Paul from time to time. And we were both there for that horrible mess with Red Hamilton in Aurora.

By the time I met him, the Jackrabbit was already a celebrity. Everybody knew his name, had seen his picture in the papers, and followed his exploits on the radio and in the newsreels. After Crown Point, he got even more famous. Hell, there were Hollywood stars that would've given their right arm to get that sort of press. He was what people nowadays would call a superstar.

The only person I can think of who even came close to the Jackrabbit was Jesse James. The Jackrabbit loved it when the papers started calling him "the modern-day Jesse James." Jesse was a boyhood hero of his. In the end, I think the Jackrabbit surpassed Jesse in celebrity. Hell, how many newsreels was Jesse James ever in?

What made the Jackrabbit and Jesse James both so popular was the whole David-versus-Goliath thing. Regular people thought that by breaking the law, these outlaws were getting back at the legal robbers, the exploiters, the big-business crooks who would never be punished. Both Jesse James and the Jackrabbit had that unholy mixture of criminality and public adoration. It's a volatile combination, and, in the end, it brought them both grief. It killed Jesse James. As for the Jackrabbit . . . well, I'll get to that part later.

Most of the gangsters who were front-page news back in late '33 and '34 didn't live to see 1935. The era of what one historian called the "Jackrabbit Days" lasted barely eighteen months. I was one of the few who managed to survive. I'd like to think it's because I was a little bit smarter than the rest, but I know I'm just bullshitting myself. If I were so damn smart, I wouldn't be spending my days sewing collars in a prison shirt factory.

Thirty-three goddamned years. That's how long I've been behind bars. Yeah, yeah, I know—it beats the alternative, right? Still, that's a long time to cool your heels. It gives a man a lot of time to think and to hear things.

There are a lot of forms of currency when you're in lockup: cigarettes, skin mags, candy, and, of course, information. I've had over three decades to get my hands on plenty of all those things. Over this glacier-like span of time, I've heard a lot of stories, some true, some not. It's actually pretty easy to pick out the grains of truth from the staggering amount of bullshit you hear in prison. You know what they say, anything that sounds too good to be true usually is.

Between what I've picked up in the yard and the stuff I already knew from having been in the thick of things, I've got a pretty good handle on the true story of the Jackrabbit. I'm not sure what compelled me to write it all down other than plain ol' boredom. Sure, I've got my own story to tell, and maybe one day I will. You can bet your ass I won't do *that* until I'm free and clear of this stinking pit . . . if that ever happens.

I guess I'm starting to ramble now, but no matter. There's a guy in D Block who used to work for a big publisher in New York. For a carton of smokes and a couple of girlie mags, he says he'll clean up my writing and make it look professional. I'll keep some of it just the way I wrote it, though. Just to remind you that it's authentic, and I know what the hell I'm talking about.

This is what really happened to the Jackrabbit.

# CHAPTER ONE

**Crown Point, Indiana**
**March 3, 1934**

E d Saager didn't see the three men with guns come into the garage. He was up to his waist in the engine compartment of a Chevy, cursing at the engineers who had decided to put the generator so far in the back. He didn't want to be working on a Saturday, but he needed the overtime. With the economy in the dumper, any opportunity to earn a few extra bucks was welcomed.

Even if Saager had noticed the armed men enter, he wouldn't have thought much of it. The Lake County Jail was just a block away. The infamous John Dillinger had been brought in following his arrest in Tucson the week before, and the entire neighborhood was an armed camp. Extra deputies had been put on shift. A Farmers Trust vigilante group roamed the town with hunting rifles and shotguns. Sheriff Holley had even called in the National Guard to help prevent Dillinger's gang from breaking him out of jail. The guardsmen set up machine guns and sandbags on the front lawn of the jail to repel any rescue attempts. The sight of men toting firearms in downtown Crown Point was not unusual right now.

Sheriff Lillian Holley had plenty of reason to worry about a breakout attempt. Dillinger had already been involved with several successful breakouts. A few months prior, he'd helped arrange a major breakout from the Michigan City pen in Indiana where ten cons had fled into the pouring rain. Shortly after that, he was arrested again, and his gang busted him out of jail in Lima, Ohio, brutally killing Sheriff Jess Sarber in the process.

Dillinger had started his criminal career the way a lot of hard-luck cases do—as a small-town troublemaker who fell in with a bad crowd. In 1924, at age 20, he'd been arrested after he and an associate beat and robbed a grocer in his hometown of Mooresville, Indiana. He was sentenced to ten years at the state pen in Michigan City, despite being promised leniency for pleading guilty.

His experience in prison was essentially an advanced course in felony. He quickly took up with seasoned criminals like Homer Van Meter and Handsome Harry Pierpont, who taught him the finer points of bank robbery.

Dillinger was paroled after nine and a half years and immediately set about putting his new criminal knowledge to good use. He conducted a string of robberies throughout Indiana and Ohio. His first major bank robbery was the New Carlisle National Bank in Ohio. During the robbery, he nimbly vaulted over the six-foot-high teller's cage and made off with ten grand. His clean getaway left the police scratching their heads. For his teller-cage athletics and his speedy getaway, the local paper dubbed him "the Jackrabbit." The nickname stuck.

At first, the Jackrabbit's exploits only made the local papers then a few regional ones. But the Lima breakout catapulted the Jackrabbit and his gang into the national spotlight. They increased their notoriety by robbing more banks and even raiding police stations for weapons and bulletproof vests.

Eventually, the law caught up with the Jackrabbit and his gang in Tucson. Handsome Harry and two others were sent back to Ohio to stand trial for Sheriff Sarber's murder. Instead of going to Ohio with the rest of his gang, the Jackrabbit was flown to Indiana to answer for a bank robbery in East Chicago where he'd fatally shot a police officer named O'Malley. Reporters and newsreel crews mobbed him as the police brought him off the plane. It was America's first media circus.

Crown Point had been in a state of frenzy ever since. At first Ed had found it exciting, but, after a while, the presence of armed men in uniform had become more of a petty annoyance. He hoped that all the fuss would be over soon.

The first thing that made Ed realize something was amiss was the silence. The local postman, Bobby Voss, was in the habit of hanging out at the Main Street Garage and shooting the breeze after finishing his rounds. Bobby was a regular chatterbox, and Ed rarely paid much attention when he was flapping his gums. Bobby had been blathering away about the White Sox, but now he'd gone totally silent.

Wondering what had suddenly turned Bobby mute, Ed looked up and saw the three men standing right by him. One—who looked very nervous— was wearing a sheriff's deputy uniform. The other two were wearing rain slickers and carrying Thompson submachine guns. One was a huge Negro, and the other was a white guy with a high forehead and slicked-back hair. He looked a little like Humphrey Bogart, the latest Hollywood star.

"Say, pal," said the Bogart look-alike. "What's the fastest car in here?"

Ed hooked a thumb at a car in the back of the garage. "I guess it would be that Ford V8 back there."

The man cracked a crooked grin that twisted up the left side of his face. "You'd better come with us," he said.

"Look, fellas," said Ed. "I'm pretty busy here. I don't have time to join some posse, OK?"

"You'd better do what he says," said the deputy. "These guys aren't fooling around."

The Bogey double pointed his gun at Ed and nodded. The grin crept further up his face. "Deputy Blunk is absolutely right," he said. "We're not fooling around. And we're all going to take a little ride in that hot rod Ford."

The realization hit Ed like a ten-pound sledgehammer. The man in front of him was the country's most famous outlaw. The Jackrabbit had broken out of jail—again!

Ed held up his hands. He looked around and saw that Bobby Voss and the rest of the mechanics in the garage were doing the same. "O-OK, OK, sure," said Ed. "Whatever you want. Do you want me to drive?"

"No, you get in the back with Mr. Youngblood there," said the Jackrabbit, nodding toward the Negro. "Deputy Blunk is going to drive, and I'll keep an eye on him."

Ed led the men back to the Ford. He realized that he should be frightened to death, but the whole thing seemed surreal—like he was having a dream or watching a movie.

They piled into the car and pulled out into the rainy winter morning. Amazingly, the street was empty. The Jackrabbit had broken out of jail and made it past the armed camp in front without attracting any attention whatsoever. They had barely gone half a block before the Jackrabbit said, "Blunk, stop the car. Roll down your window."

Blunk did as instructed. Over the drumming of the cold rain, the sounds of muffled cries and yells could be heard from the direction of the jail.

"Ha! Ha!" barked the Jackrabbit. "They're still in there! No one's come to let them out yet! I must've locked up twenty of those mugs—guards, trustees, even the warden! OK, Deputy, let's blow this town. Drive slow, though; I don't want to attract any attention."

The car rolled sedately through the center of Crown Point. As they rolled down Main Street, they passed the First National Bank. The Jackrabbit eyed it with a smile. "Y'know, I oughta just knock over that jug right now," he said. "That would be a hoot! The Jackrabbit breaks out of the 'escape-proof' Crown Point jail and robs the bank on his way out of town. Think of the headlines!"

Deputy Blunk shot him an alarmed look. He missed a red light and almost collided with a produce truck. The Jackrabbit jammed his Tommy gun into the lawman's side. "God dammit, Blunk!" he snarled. "Watch where you're going! If you get us into a wreck, you'll be the first casualty, I guarantee it!"

"OK, sorry, sorry," stammered Blunk. "I'm just a little nervous, y'know. Where do you want me to go?"

"No need to be nervous," assured the Jackrabbit. "We're all friends here. Just some good buddies out for a ride. What road leads west from town?"

"Eightieth Avenue is up ahead," said Blunk. "It turns into the Lincoln Highway outside of town."

"No good," said the Jackrabbit. "Too obvious. There'll be roadblocks all over it before too long. We'll find another way. Look, up ahead by those train tracks, there's a gravel road. Turn left there."

Following back roads and gravel tracks, the car slowly made its way out of town and through the countryside. Ed cut a glance at Youngblood sitting beside him. He seemed enrapt in the passing scenery. The muzzle of his machine gun sagged toward the floor. Ed started to relax. Maybe he would get out of this alive, after all.

"Hey, you, mechanic," said the Jackrabbit. "What's your name?"

"S-saager. Ed Saager."

"Well, Saager Ed Saager, is there anything about this car that would make it stand out? Anything they could use to spot us?"

"Well, there's a red light on the right front fender."

The Jackrabbit turned, his eyebrows raised in astonishment. "You mean to tell me this is a *cop* car?"

"Uh, yeah. Actually, it belongs to Sheriff Holley. She just bought it."

"Ha! Ha! Oh, that's rich!" cried the Jackrabbit. "That's almost as good as knocking over the bank! Making my getaway in the sheriff's own car! Blunk, pull over."

The Jackrabbit bounded out and twisted off the telltale police light. He wound up and sailed it way off into the cornfield on the side of the road. It looked to Ed like he could throw a pretty mean fastball.

"Well, that takes care of that," said the Jackrabbit as he got back into the car. "No distinguishing characteristics. Let's go."

They continued through the barren Indiana countryside. There were practically no other cars on the road. Outside of St. John, they approached what looked to be a roadblock, but it turned out to be a road crew. "Just another bunch of WPA loafers!" laughed the Jackrabbit.

A few minutes later, Blunk misjudged a curve, and the car slid off the muddy road into a ditch. "Don't kill me!" cried the terrified deputy. "It was an accident! Honest!"

"Don't worry," said the Jackrabbit. "No one's going to catch up with us out here."

They piled out of the car and took a look. The rear wheels were mired in the swampy ditch by the side of the road. "OK, Mr. Mechanic," said the Jackrabbit. "Glad we brought you along. Now get this car back on the road.

I'm sure Mr. Youngblood here will be glad to lend you a hand."

Ed was grateful to have something to occupy his attention. He was beginning to worry what would happen to him at the end of this ride. The Jackrabbit seemed like a nice guy for a dangerous criminal, but Ed couldn't help but think of the cop he had allegedly killed in East Chicago. He wondered if he would soon meet the same fate.

"There are some chains in the trunk, I think," Ed said. "But this might take some time."

"Not to worry," said the Jackrabbit. "What's time to me?"

It seemed like an outlandish statement coming from the man who had just become the most hunted fugitive in the country. The Jackrabbit gazed out over the cold, flat landscape, and whistled "California, Here I Come!"

With the aid of a two-by-four, Ed and Youngblood managed to lever up the Ford and get the chains on the rear wheels. The Jackrabbit watched them idly, still whistling. Deputy Blunk stood a few paces behind him, nervously smoking a cigarette.

"Hey, Ed," said the Jackrabbit. "I'll bet you're wondering how I escaped from the escape-proof jail, huh?"

Actually, the question hadn't occurred to him. He was too busy wondering if he was ever going to see his family again. "Uh, yeah!" he said, trying to sound enthusiastic. "I'm sure everybody's going to be asking about that soon."

The Jackrabbit reached into his pocket and pulled out a small wooden object. "Look at this!" he said proudly. "I made it myself!"

In his hand, the Jackrabbit held a small wooden replica of a pistol. It was crudely carved and had the words "Colt 38" scratched into the side. "Carved it out of a bed slat and used shoe polish to darken it," said the Jackrabbit. "I fooled all those screws with it!"

Behind him, Deputy Blunk snorted.

The Jackrabbit turned to him. "Shut your head, Blunkie! You know I've got the real thing now." He lifted the Thompson toward the deputy, who raised his hands and took a step back.

"I think we can get the car out now," said Ed, trying to defuse the situation.

"OK," said the Jackrabbit. "Let's go!"

They pulled back onto the country road and were soon zipping along at a high rate of speed. "Hey, this thing can really move!" commented the Jackrabbit. "It even has a radio. How about some music?" He turned on the Motorola slung under the dash. Gene Autry was warbling "The Last Roundup."

"C'mon, fellas, you know the words," said the Jackrabbit. "Sing along! 'I'm headin' for the laaaast roundup . . . gonna saddle Old Paint for the laaaast time and riiiiiiiiide. . . .'"

The fugitive vehicle zoomed through the countryside, a chorus of cowboy music coming from within. "Get along little dogies, get along, get along, get along little dogies, get alonnnng. . . ."

Just outside Kreitzburg, they passed a small wooden sign that said, "Now Entering Illinois. Welcome!"

"Hey, didja see that?" said the Jackrabbit. "We're out of Indiana. Good riddance, I say! Things are going to start turning around for me now!"

They drove for a few more miles, and then the Jackrabbit told Blunk to slow down. He stuck his head out the window and seemed to be looking for something. "OK, this'll do," he said. "There's no telephone lines. Nobody will be able to report this. Pull over Blunk. Everyone out."

Ed felt his guts turn to ice. This was the end of the ride. If he was going to be shot, it would happen here.

"Well, fellas," said the Jackrabbit. "Sorry to do this to you." He reached into his coat pocket.

"Here it comes," thought Ed. He felt his knees start to quake and fought to stay upright. If he was going to die, then he meant to die on his feet. He was so focused on keeping from falling over that he didn't notice the Jackrabbit was waving a pair of dollar bills in his face.

"Here's a few bucks for carfare," said the Jackrabbit. "Sorry I can't spare any more. I took up a collection at the jail before I left, but they were a little tight. Ha! Ha!"

In a daze, Ed took the offered cash. He looked at it idiotically. The Jackrabbit was holding out more money to Blunk, but the deputy just shook his head.

"C'mon, Mr. Youngblood, let's make tracks," said the Jackrabbit. "The big city awaits. You'd better hunker down in the back. You kinda stand out, y'know." The two crooks climbed back into the car, and the Jackrabbit stuck his head out the window. "Thanks again, boys! See you in the funny papers!" The Ford pulled away in a cloud of dust.

"Well, what do we do now?" asked Ed.

"What do you think?" said Blunk sourly. "We start walking."

# CHAPTER TWO

**Chicago, Illinois**
**March 3, 1934**

"I don't know!" shouted Art O'Leary. "I'll get back when I get back!" He slammed the apartment door behind him, cutting off his wife's complaints. This scene had become all too common in the last few months with Grayce frequently nagging him about his long and irregular work hours.

He hurried down the rain-slicked sidewalk. The Loop was mostly empty on this dismal Saturday morning, but he had to be at work early. Big things were happening at Lou Piquett's law office.

Art was forty years old and as Irish as a Dublin fistfight. He had a round face, thin lips, and cold, blue eyes—a face made for fighting. Art knew this all too well, so he tried to compensate by cultivating the air of a well-educated sophisticate. Despite having only a high-school education, he learned to enjoy classical music, highbrow literature, and fine wines. He was likewise fond of well-tailored clothes, and on this rainy morning, he was sporting a natty gray camel hair overcoat and a matching fedora.

He yanked the hat down over his forehead to thwart the rain and walked faster, muttering to himself. He hated these scenes with Grayce. She was always riding him about how much time he spent at work and how little money he brought home. She didn't seem to appreciate that things had changed since the stock market crash in '29.

Art O'Leary was a self-made man. He'd fled his family's Iowa farm and ended up in Chicago selling stocks and bonds. He was successful in the securities business and had made many useful connections. He'd had a comfortable life until the Crash wiped out nearly all of his savings. Soon, Art was working his network of contacts for any job he could find.

He'd eventually been introduced to a lawyer of dubious reputation named Louis Piquett. Piquett represented a wide variety of underworld figures. The Depression had forced many otherwise honest citizens into a life of crime, and a lot of new criminals were not very good at it. Consequently, Piquett had more work than he could handle and was in the market for an able assistant. Art was a perfect fit. Suave, self-assured, and well-connected, he helped Piquett as investigator, assistant, bagman, and all-around man Friday.

Art was grateful for the work, although Grayce didn't seem to understand that working as the assistant to a crooked lawyer was quite different from being a big shot at a brokerage. The pay was meager and irregular, and the hours were long and unpredictable. It had been even worse since Piquett had signed on his latest client.

Art reached the office on Wacker Drive and went up to the second-story office. He was not surprised to see his boss hunched over his desk working through a stack of paperwork.

"Anything yet?" asked Art.

"Not yet," replied Piquett. "Have patience, it's still early. Is everything all right? You look a bit frazzled."

"Just sparring with Grayce again," Art said. "She doesn't like my working hours."

"Not to worry, man," said Piquett. "Once we get our visitor squared away, we'll both be able to take it easy for a bit."

Art doubted it, but he knew it was pointless to argue with his boss. He was, after all, a trial lawyer and quarrelsome as the devil. Lou Piquett was fifty years old with a bulbous nose and an unruly shock of gray hair that he tried to keep brushed back from his high forehead. He had a booming baritone voice that he put to good use in the courtroom when hassling prosecutors and browbeating juries.

Piquett had recently scored his greatest coup by convincing Public Enemy Number One John Dillinger to retain him as counsel shortly after his incarceration at Crown Point. Piquett had immediately gone to work representing his celebrity client with a vigor and voice that grabbed headlines across the nation.

Piquett's efforts on behalf of his star client went beyond mere courtroom dramatics. He'd dispatched Art on a number of shady errands on behalf of the Jackrabbit. Art had traveled to the World's Fair on the south shore of Lake Michigan to meet up with an Indiana judge and hand off a briefcase full of unmarked bills. The day before yesterday, he had traveled to East Chicago to deliver a small, heavy package to a detective named Martin Zarkovich. He had no idea what was inside. It was all just part of the job, and Art knew better than to ask questions.

He had just started paging through the business section of the paper when there was a sharp rap at the office door. "Holy moly! Is he here already?" Art asked.

"No, I imagine it's just Ms. Frechette," said Piquett. "Get that, will you?"

Art opened the door to reveal a petite, attractive woman in her mid-twenties. She had dark eyes and hair and wore a great deal of makeup. Her threadbare cloth coat and matching hat somehow managed to emphasize her pretty face—she was a true Depression cutie. Her name was Billie Frechette, and she was the Jackrabbit's girlfriend. "Has anything happened yet?" she asked.

"Not yet," replied Art.

"Fear not, my dear," said Piquett. "It is still quite early. I'm certain that we'll get word soon. In the meantime, please make yourself comfortable." He indicated a chesterfield at the back of the office.

They watched the minutes creep by. Nearly two hours later, the phone rang. After a terse conversation, Piquett slammed down the receiver and grinned. "There was just a news flash on the radio," he announced. "The Jackrabbit has escaped!"

Billie squealed and jumped up, dancing around the room. Art blew out a breath of pent-up tension. He and Piquett had been working toward this for weeks now. "Too bad we don't have a radio," he said.

"No need for a radio," replied Piquett. "I can go straight to the source." He picked up the receiver again and instructed the operator to put him through to the Crown Point jail. "Hello? Warden Baker? This is attorney Louis Piquett in Chicago. Is there any truth to the news reports that my client broke out of jail? . . . Was anybody hurt? . . . Good, that's very good. . . . He didn't leave a forwarding address, did he? . . . Yes, he is a hell of a client to have. . . . Thank you, Warden. Good day."

He hung up and said, "It's true. He got away clean!"

Surprisingly, Billie burst into tears. Art gave Piquett a quizzical look.

"What's the matter, my dear?" asked Piquett.

"They'll kill him for sure, now!" wailed Billie. "Now that he's out, they'll gun him down like a dog! I just know it!"

"Now, my dear, that's just balderdash," said Piquett. "Your boyfriend is untouchable. He cleared out of that jail like nobody's business, and they didn't lay a finger on him. We'll take good care of him. The police won't find him, trust me."

Piquett produced a bottle of cognac, and they toasted the Jackrabbit's newfound freedom. The booze got right on top of Billie, and in no time she was snoring loudly on the sofa. Piquett and Art busied themselves getting ready to receive their client.

After making a few telephone calls, Piquett got up and shrugged on his overcoat. "Come on, my dear," he said, shaking Billie's arm. "Let's go meet your beau."

With some difficulty, Art and Piquett got Billie upright, downstairs, and loaded into Piquett's huge Lincoln. Piquett drove off, and Art went back upstairs and continued perusing the papers. An hour later, the phone rang again.

He snatched up the receiver. "Piquett Law Office."

"Hiya, Art!" said a familiar voice. "Where do I go?"

"Four thirty-four Wellington Avenue. We'll meet you there."

The line went dead, and Art headed off to the rendezvous.

\* \* \*

The address on Wellington was the apartment of Piquett's part-time secretary, Margie. When Art arrived, a bad drama was already playing out. Piquett, Billie, and the Jackrabbit were huddled in the hallway in front of Margie's door. The door was cracked open to show an inch-wide segment of Margie, who was clearly not happy with the situation.

"You didn't tell me who you wanted me to put up!" Margie argued. "I had no idea you meant *him!*"

"My goodness," said Piquett. "I believe you are overreacting just a tad, dear."

"Hogwash!" said Margie. "I am willing to do many things to help you out, Louis Piquett, but this crosses the line! I will NOT have that man in my house!"

The door slammed shut, followed by a series of rattles and clicks as locks were locked and chains were chained.

Piquett turned. "Not to worry, friends," he said. "Just a minor change of plans. Please follow me."

They trooped down to the lobby, and Art strolled out to the sidewalk to make sure the coast was clear. After he gave the high sign, the rest of the group sidled out. "OK," said Piquett. "We can go to my sister's place at Addison and Southport. Art, you take our guests in your car and follow me. I'll go up first and get everything squared away then come get you. OK? Let's go."

Billie and the Jackrabbit climbed into the back seat of Art's car. "Better keep your heads down," he told his passengers.

"Not a problem," said the Jackrabbit.

Art scanned the area for police as Piquett's huge Lincoln pulled into traffic. Art could feel the tension in his shoulders. Things were already starting to feel a little dicey to him. He wasn't surprised that Margie had balked at harboring the fugitive Jackrabbit. In a matter of hours, every cop in the country would be looking for him. She had always been a little high-strung anyway.

Up ahead, Piquett's Lincoln cruised along sedately, carefully following the speed limit. Art continued to scan the area for cops. After a few minutes, he began to relax. He was afraid Margie might have panicked and called the police.

"Whew. . . . Sorry about the mix-up," said Art. "Not to worry, though. I'm sure Lou's sister will put you up."

He got no response other than a muffled giggle from the back seat. He glanced at the rearview mirror but could not see his passengers. Billie's leg appeared and kicked upward. Her shoe flew off, thunked off the ceiling, and disappeared. There was more giggling.

"Everything OK back there?" asked Art.

"Just fine," came the Jackrabbit's muffled voice. "Just keep driving, OK?"

The giggles became heavy breathing then moans. The air inside the car became humid and fragrant. Art cracked a window and muttered to himself, "Get a room, huh?"

"Don't need one," laughed the Jackrabbit. "Your back seat's big enough. Ha! Ha!"

Art shrugged. After all, the guy had just gotten out of the lockup. Art would probably be doing the same thing if their situations were reversed.

As they approached Addison and Southport, Piquett's car pulled to the curb in front of a brick apartment building. Art drove half a block past and parked. Things in the back seat were going hot and heavy and clearly weren't going to end anytime soon. Art got out of the car and leaned against the rear door, trying to block the view. The car was rocking heavily on its springs now, making it difficult to look casual. For a moment, he was irked at the Jackrabbit's lack of subtlety. After all, he was supposed to be keeping a low profile. On the other hand, who would believe that the notorious criminal would be having sex in the back seat of a car on a busy street in the middle of a big city?

Piquett appeared from the apartment building with a wide grin on his face. He walked up to the car and thumped on the roof. "Come on you two. Knock it off and let's go!"

The Jackrabbit's head appeared in the window. "Hiya, Lou!" he said.

"Perfect timing!"

"Put your pants back on, and let's get going," said Piquett. "My sister has kindly offered you the use of her apartment. She's going to spend the weekend at her friend's house. You'll have the place all to yourselves."

"Gee, that's swell," said Billie. She squirmed around to get her underwear on straight. "Did you see where my shoe went?"

Piquett led the group up to an apartment on the third floor of the building. His sister had apparently already cleared out. Piquett gave them a quick tour. "OK," he said. "Now that things are settled, there's some business to take care of."

"I know," agreed the Jackrabbit. "C'mon, honey." He grabbed Billie by the hand and led her to the bedroom. In short order, squeaks and moans filled the apartment.

"Holy cow!" said Art. "That guy just doesn't quit!"

"I guess they don't call him 'Jackrabbit' just because of his fast getaways," said Piquett. "Let's go get an egg cream."

When they returned twenty minutes later, the couple was still at it.

"Hey, is this billable?" asked Art with a smile.

"My boy, *everything's* billable," replied Piquett. "You should know that by now."

The jouncing and caterwauling from the bedroom reached a crescendo then abated. A couple of minutes later, the Jackrabbit emerged, straightening his tie and grinning like a madman. "Well, that takes care of business," he said. "Now let's talk about money. Ha! Ha!"

"Indeed," said Piquett. "That is truly a topic of interest to me, especially considering the legal fees that have accrued to this point."

"Don't worry, Lou," said the Jackrabbit as he patted the attorney on the back. "I appreciate everything you've done for me, and I'll get you the money as soon as I can."

"I have no doubt, my boy," said Piquett. "And I will do whatever I can to facilitate your return to your chosen profession."

"Ah, Lou, you're the best lawyer a fella could ask for," said the Jackrabbit. "I need to get to Saint Paul to meet up with Van Meter and Nelson. It's time to rob some banks!"

# CHAPTER THREE

**Saint Paul, Minnesota**
**March 4, 1934**

H omer Van Meter was restless. He paced. He sat down, thumbed through a newspaper, put it down, stood back up, and then paced some more.

"What the hell?" he muttered to himself. He hadn't even felt this restless before his big trial, the one that sent him to the Michigan City pen for a ten-to-twenty-year stretch. He'd felt this way ever since he'd gotten back from his scouting mission in Sioux Falls that morning.

Homer had grown up on a hardscrabble farm outside of Fort Wayne, Indiana. He hated it there and fought with his father constantly. When he was twelve, he swiped a handful of cash from the cookie jar and took off for the promise of Chicago.

The waiter and bellhop jobs he found there were low paying and miserable. Hanging out in the low-rent hash houses and speakeasies, Homer hooked up with a rough crowd. Before long, he tried his hand at petty larceny then bigger things like stealing automobiles. When an attempted train robbery in Crown Point went sideways, Homer wound up at Michigan City.

In prison, the convicts were grouped together based on their crimes. The murderers had their own clique. The con artists hung together. The rapists were universally despised. Homer fell in with the robbers and stickup men. He wound up running with a group that included notorious robbers such as Handsome Harry Pierpont and Red Hamilton. He also took up with a little-known crook named John Dillinger, who had yet to earn the nickname "Jackrabbit."

In the pen, Homer was a clown. It was a defense mechanism he had developed as a child to cope with his alcoholic father. He knew if he could get the old man to laugh, he might avoid a beating. A kind word might turneth away wrath, but a good laugh worked better. In the unfamiliar and terrifying prison environment, Homer's clowning went into overdrive. His antics won over the other prisoners—except for Pierpont, who thought he was an asshole. His behavior also really pissed off the guards; it garnered Homer special abuse from the screws and a lot of time in solitary. But that was OK—he could take a beating and didn't mind being alone. Besides, the hard time helped earn him more respect out in the yard.

He and Dillinger got on exceedingly well. Dillinger had a pretty wicked sense of humor himself and always laughed at Homer's antics. The two soon became fast friends and often talked of the heists they would pull together once they were out of the pen.

Surprised by a knock at the door, Homer nearly upset the table jumping up from his chair. He swung open the door to reveal the twisted grin of his old prison comrade.

"Hiya, Van! Great to see you!"

The two hugged, and over the Jackrabbit's shoulder, Homer saw a petite dark-haired girl smiling shyly.

"Hey, who's the twist?"

"Van, meet Billie. She's my heart and soul."

Homer stared at Billie. She was very pretty, and he felt a twinge of jealousy. Homer had never really been what you'd call a whizbang with the ladies. He was thin and lanky and had knobby, oversize hands—the hands of a farm boy. His face was plain and rawboned. Handsome Harry liked to joke that Homer's mug looked like a rubber sack full of doorknobs.

He bowed in what he imagined was a very courtly manner. "So pleased to meet you, m'lady," he said in a horrible English accent. He reached out to take her hand, but she drew back.

"What is *wrong* with him?" she giggled. "He's weird!"

"Don't worry, doll," said the Jackrabbit. "That's just Van being Van."

Homer put on a happy grin, but Billie's reaction stung. It figured. He never knew how to deal with women—at least the nice ones.

"Look, baby doll," said the Jackrabbit. "We've got some business to discuss. Why dontcha go down to the coffee shop around the corner and get a sandwich or something?"

"Whatsamatter, don't you trust me?" she pouted.

"It's not that. It's just the less you know, the less danger you'll be in."

"Yeah," added Homer. "We're just trying to look out for you."

Billie shot him a mistrustful look and scooted out the door.

"Sorry about that," said the Jackrabbit. "Billie's a swell kid, but she's had a tough life. It takes her a while to warm up to new people."

Homer waved him off. "Not to worry, old pal. It's just good to see you again. Damn good!"

"Same here. I can't thank you enough for helping arrange my, um, early release. Ha! Ha!"

"Don't thank me," said Homer. "You can thank Nelson. He's the one that bankrolled the whole thing. He's awful keen to have you in his gang. He's got some pretty big jobs lined up. Wants some experienced people to help get the big moola."

"Well, I'm all for that," said the Jackrabbit. "But the word on the street is that he's a little off the track. What's the skinny on this guy? Is he a good egg, or is he gonna blow up the second things get a little hinky?"

"He's all right, man. Yeah, he can be a little high-strung—especially if you call him 'Baby Face' to his baby face. But, look, he cut me in for some big jobs without hardly even knowing me."

Homer had initially met Baby Face Nelson a few summers before at a gangster hangout on the shores of Lake Michigan. Then he'd hooked up with him through a mutual acquaintance shortly after his parole from Michigan City. Nelson had invited him to join his gang right before a very lucrative bank job in Minnesota. He'd been part of the gang ever since.

"Guess I can't fault the guy," said the Jackrabbit. "If it weren't for him, I'd still be cooling my heels in the Crown Point can. When am I gonna meet him anyway?"

"Not today. He's off somewhere getting us some wheels for the next job. Eddie Green'll be by soon to discuss the lay. He's an ace jug-marker, got an easy bank in Sioux Falls. Says it's worth a quarter mil, easy."

"Hot cha! That's a fat jug, Van!"

Homer felt a strange tightness in his throat as he looked at his friend. "Man, it is good to see you," he said. "Really good. It just feels, I dunno, weird. . . ."

"It's because we're finally on the outside," said the Jackrabbit. "For the first time, there's not some damn screw hassling us or bars on the fuckin' windows. All that shit we talked about doing when we finally got out—we can do it now! We'll grab the world by the balls, Van!"

"Better than the other way around. I don't wanna wind up back in the joint, man. I really don't. I'd almost rather go straight, y'know?" Homer was astounded to hear these words coming out of his mouth. The idea of going straight was as foreign to him as getting elected president of the United States or winning the World Series. Sure, it sounded great, but really it was impossible.

"Ha! Ha! You gotta be kiddin' with that talk," said the Jackrabbit. "Besides, we're not gonna get caught. That's behind us. We're not gonna make the same mistakes as before. We're gonna get rich! That Lamm Method really works! I've tried it!"

The Michigan City pen was basically a graduate school in crime. Homer and the Jackrabbit had both studied at the feet of an ex-Prussian Army officer who called himself Baron Lamm. Lamm advocated running a bank robbery like a precision military operation. The target was to be carefully studied with notes taken and plans drawn. Detailed escape routes, called "gits," were drawn up with multiple options for escape noted to the nearest tenth of a mile. Above all, the operation was to be strictly timed. When the time was up, the gang was to leave the bank regardless of the amount of money they'd grabbed.

Homer jumped up and began strutting stiff-legged around the room. "Planning! Planning! Planning!" he cried in a thick German accent. "You cannot have enough of ze planning, ya!"

"Ha! Ha! That's perfect, Van! This is really gonna be a great job."

"Red's in on it too," said Homer. Red Hamilton had been another member of their clique back at Michigan City.

"Red too! Damn, that's great! It's like Old Home Week. This is the job we always dreamed of back in lockup."

Homer felt that tightness around his throat again. He thought back to his early days in Chicago and how alone and miserable he'd been. Even after he'd started making friends in the city, he'd always felt like a lone wolf. It wasn't until he'd met up with the Jackrabbit and Red in prison that he really felt like he was part of something bigger, something almost like a family. Now that they were on the outside and getting ready to work together, he felt an unaccustomed sense of acceptance and gratitude that was so strong he started to choke up. He thought about saying something to the Jackrabbit but held his tongue. There were some things you couldn't say, not even to your closest friend.

At the door, two sharp knocks, a pause, then three quick ones.

Homer's hand twitched toward his shoulder holster then relaxed. "It's just Eddie," he said. He opened the door to admit Eddie Green. Eddie had squinty eyes and big, jug-like ears—a face that was made for trouble. Behind him stood a short woman with bright red hair and a lot of eye makeup.

"This is Eddie Green and his wife Bessie," said Homer. "I'd like you to meet the Jackrabbit."

Eddie and the Jackrabbit shook hands while Bessie eyed him critically. "So this is the world-famous Jackrabbit," she said. "Huh. I thought you'd be taller."

She turned to Eddie. "I don't like the looks of him," she said. "He's gonna be trouble. I can tell. *Big* trouble."

Eddie rolled his eyes. "Stifle it, OK Bess? He's our guest, and he's gonna help us make a lotta dough."

Bessie gave the Jackrabbit the stink eye and muttered to herself.

"Look, let's get down to business, why don't we?" suggested Eddie.

The Jackrabbit jerked his chin at Bessie. "You think that's a good idea with your, uh, wife here?"

"Hey, Buster," spat Bessie. "I'm not just some dumb skirt, OK? I'm in this as much as any of you assholes. Me and Eddie work as a team. You got a problem with that, you'd better just hit the fuckin' road!"

"Whoa, whoa!" said the Jackrabbit, holding up his hands in mock-surrender. "Sorry, sister! Don't get your bloomers in a bunch!"

This brought another blast of cursing from the tiny redhead. It took Eddie a minute or two to calm her down. Finally, she stomped into the bathroom and slammed the door behind her.

"Sorry about that," said Eddie. "She gets that way sometimes. She's a good egg, though—does a lot of the legwork for us. She's already found you a good place to stay over on Lexington. She'll be fine."

"Yeah, great," said the Jackrabbit. "So what's the deal? Van tells me you've got a fat jug lined up in Sioux Falls."

"Yep. Security National Bank and Trust. Every Tuesday around noon, they get a shipment of cash. Payroll for the local quarry. Between that and their other assets, I make it at least two hundred thou, maybe more."

The Jackrabbit gave a low whistle. "That's real good. Who else is in on this caper?"

"Nelson and Tommy Carroll are back in Chicago lining up some transportation. You'll get to meet them both tomorrow. Me and Red Hamilton are in on it too."

"Hey, this sounds all right," said the Jackrabbit. "I just want you guys to know how much I appreciate all of this. Not just cutting me in on this heist but also all the stuff you did to get me out of the hoosegow."

"Don't thank me," said Eddie. "That was all Nelson's doing."

"Well, I look forward to thanking him in person."

They spent the next hour reviewing the notes Homer had made in Sioux Falls: the street map, a detailed layout of the bank, and a meticulous git that covered three separate ways out of town. Bessie emerged from the bathroom and watched warily but didn't say anything.

"Boys," Eddie said. "I think we're on to something hot here. Now that we got this gang together, we're gonna do big things, I just know it!"

25

"Damn straight!" said the Jackrabbit. "Now let's go have us a little fun, eh? I bet Billie's getting bored. I'll go around the corner and get her, then let's do up the town."

Homer put the plans back in their hidey-hole, then they collected Billie and spent the rest of the evening drinking and dancing at the Green Lantern Saloon.

# CHAPTER FOUR

**Sioux Falls, South Dakota**
**March 6, 1934**

At twenty minutes past two, a dark green Packard sedan pulled up in front of the Security National Bank and Trust. The handful of people on the street took scant notice of the car. They were hunched into their coats against the icy wind, heads down, walking quickly. Spring was only a few weeks away, but South Dakota was still tightly in winter's grip.

Homer Van Meter and a slender young man with blond hair and a pudgy, boyish face sat in the front seat. The young man's real name was Lester Gillis, but he called himself George Nelson. The newspapers called him Baby Face, although he hated the nickname. John Hamilton, known to his friends as Red, was behind the wheel. Red was also called Three-Fingered Jack because he had lost two fingers on his right hand playing chicken with a train when he was eight. He had a blocky, chinless face that wore a perpetually blank look.

From the back seat, the Jackrabbit watched the street with an anticipatory grin. Squeezed in next to him was Tommy Carroll. Tommy had been a boxer, and his movie-star good looks had been roughened around the edges from the beatings he'd taken in the ring. Rounding out the group was Eddie Green, who peered nervously out the back window.

All of them except Red exited the car and walked calmly toward the entrance to the bank. Tommy Carroll stepped aside at the front door, scanning the street as the four others entered the bank.

As soon as they were in the door, Eddie Green reached into his coat pocket, pulled out a stopwatch, and set it running.

"Go," he said conversationally.

There were about thirty customers inside the bank. At a table in the center of the room, a uniformed cop stood filling out a deposit slip. Eddie nudged Homer and nodded at the cop. The two veered away and began walking swiftly toward the unsuspecting police officer.

Just before they reached him, Nelson threw open his coat and brandished a Thompson submachine gun. "All right, this is a stickup!" he hollered. "Everybody get on the ground!"

The cop by the table looked up in surprise just as Green wrapped his arm around his neck. Homer pulled the cop's gun from its holster, reversed it in his hand, and brought the butt sharply down on the cop's head. Green released him as he slithered to the floor.

With this, the other people in the bank finally realized that an actual robbery was in progress. A woman screamed and was cut off by a murderous look from Nelson. Homer waved his gun at the openmouthed crowd of customers. "All right, folks, you heard the man," he said. "Get on the floor now, and nobody gets hurt!"

Suddenly, an alarm began to ring, the harsh clang bouncing off the marble walls and plaster ceiling. The sound drove Baby Face Nelson into a rage. "I'd like to know who the hell set that alarm off! Who?" he snarled as he paced up and down in front of the teller cages. "Which one of you bastards did that? If you wanna get killed, just make another dumb move like that!"

The Jackrabbit strolled up to the man-high teller cage, reached up, and casually vaulted over to the other side. A murmur of amazement went through the crowd. "It really *is* him," said a man on the floor. The Jackrabbit removed a pillowcase from his jacket and began scooping cash into it. Homer joined him while Eddie hung back and covered the door.

The Jackrabbit went over to a pretty young teller who was cowering in her cage. "Pardon me, miss," he said pleasantly. "I was wondering if you might direct me to the bank president?"

At that moment, a man in a gray three-piece suit emerged from an office in the back. "What in the world . . . ," he began.

"That's him," said the teller.

The Jackrabbit pulled out a .45 pistol and waved it under the president's nose. "I want you to open the vault now, Mr. Banker."

"B-b-but I can't," stammered the man. "I-I don't know the combination!"

The Jackrabbit half-turned and delivered a sharp kick to the man's rear end. "Then get me someone who does!" he shouted.

"Mr. Dargen does!" cried the president. He pointed at a middle-aged teller standing behind the cages with his hands in the air.

"Mr. Dargen, open the vault and make it snappy!" ordered the Jackrabbit. "We haven't got all day. What's our time?"

Eddie Green consulted his stopwatch. "We got two minutes thirty!" he shouted from his post by the door.

Dargen came out from behind the cage and began fumbling with the vault combination, his hands shaking wildly. After three tries, he managed to get the lock to disengage, then he pulled open the heavy door. Homer scooted in and began loading up his sack with cash.

There was a gunshot from just outside the front door. "Everything OK out there?" yelled Eddie.

"Starting to get crowded out here!" came Tommy's voice from outside. "But it's OK . . . I got it under control!"

"Shit! There's a cop!" yelled Nelson. He climbed up on one of the tables to get a better view of the motorcycle cop who was dashing down the sidewalk. He raised his Tommy gun and fired a blast through the window. Roses blossomed across the motorcycle cop's uniform, and he went down.

"I got one!" crowed Nelson. "I got one of 'em!" He danced a little jig on the table.

The Jackrabbit shot Homer a quizzical look. Homer shrugged. This sort of behavior was pretty typical of Nelson—the guy was as high-strung as an over-tuned harp.

Homer joined the Jackrabbit in the vault and began scooping bills into his sack. He pointed to a second door. "Open that one too!" he told Dargen.

"I-I can't!" said the terrified teller. "It's on a time lock!"

"Bullshit," said Homer. "You open that damn thing right now!"

While Dargen fumbled hopelessly with the time lock, an elderly man came into the lobby from an upstairs office. Oblivious to his surroundings, he strolled through the besieged bank lobby lost in thought.

"Hey you!" shouted Nelson. "You! Old man! Hey! HEY!"

The man paid him no attention.

Baby Face Nelson let loose a prolonged burst from his machine gun that shattered the window above the old man, showering him with broken glass. He looked around, stunned, finally realizing what was going on. His briefcase dropped to the floor with a loud smack.

"Get on the floor, asshole!" screamed Nelson. The old man carefully lowered himself to the marble tiles.

Nelson ducked behind the teller cages and began picking up the cash that Homer and the Jackrabbit had missed. Inside the vault, the Jackrabbit continued to stuff money into his bulging pillowcase.

"Thirty seconds!" yelled Eddie. "Round up a traveling party!"

Nelson finished scooping a mound of singles into his pillowcase. He brandished his gun at the tellers behind the cage. "OK, boys and girls, time for a little trip. Get out from behind there and line up by the door." He herded the tellers from their cages in the direction of the front door.

"Time!" yelled Eddie. "Time to go!"

The Jackrabbit and Homer emerged from the vault, their pillowcases stuffed full of cash and bonds. Dargen and the bank president followed sheepishly behind, unsure what to do.

"Everybody up!" the Jackrabbit told the patrons who were cowering on the floor. "You're leaving with us. Normally, I don't like getting lost in the crowd, but today I'll make an exception! Ha! Ha!" He and Homer began herding the crowd to the front door.

The four robbers gathered by the door in a bunch. "Stay close," the Jackrabbit told the group of tellers. "You won't get hurt. They never shoot civilians. Just don't try to run away, and we won't shoot, either. OK, away we go. You citizens go first, then we come out with the tellers. Step lively now!"

The knot of people squeezed through the front door. Outside was an amazing spectacle. Despite the cold, nearly a thousand people had gathered to watch the bank robbers make their getaway. They were gathered in the street in a huge cluster, hanging out of windows up and down the street, lined up on the roofs, peering over the parapets. Tommy Carroll had four policemen lined up against the front wall of the bank and was covering them with his Thompson.

"You're throwing a party out here, and you didn't invite us!" said the Jackrabbit.

"I didn't realize I had this damn many friends!" said Tommy.

Nelson turned and fired off another volley of machine-gun fire through the front window of the bank. The crowd shrieked and shrank back but did not disperse. This was the most exciting thing to happen in Sioux Falls in ages, and no one wanted to leave just when things were getting interesting.

The robbers and their human shields sidestepped to the Packard, where they arrayed the tellers on the running boards. The gang rolled down the windows and grabbed their hostages so they couldn't make a break for it. Red started up the Packard and slowly pulled out. The crowd parted to let them through.

They had only gone a block when there was a loud whipcrack, and the car shuddered. A plume of steam shot from the front of the Packard.

"Son of a bitch!" exclaimed Red. "They shot the radiator!"

"Dumb bastards!" said Homer. "Can't they see we've got civilians?"

"We won't be able to get far," said Red. "Do you think we should stop and get another car?"

"Hell no!" said Nelson. "Keep moving! If I see some bastard with a gun, I'll plug him!"

"George is right," said the Jackrabbit. "Let's keep moving while we can. Once we're away from the crowd, we can stop and grab another car."

Still hissing steam, the Packard slowly made its way down 14th Street. Homer fed Red directions from the git he had put together during his scouting mission. "Two tenths of a mile, take a left by the red brick apartment building . . . through the stop sign, one tenth of a mile to the bakery . . . then make a right." The car wove its way through the town toward the outskirts.

The gangsters had their hostages gripped tightly so they wouldn't make a run for it. A quarter mile from the bank, they stopped and released one of the tellers.

"What about the rest of us?" asked one of the women. "We're freezing out here!"

"Sorry, ma'am," said the Jackrabbit. "We're gonna need you to accompany us a little further. You can get in here with us."

The woman curled her lip. "I don't think it would be proper for us to do that!"

"Quit your yapping, you dumb broad," grumbled Nelson. "Get in, stay out—doesn't matter to me!"

Reluctantly, the women climbed into the car, sitting on the laps of their captors. "Excuse me, ma'am," the Jackrabbit said. He reached between the legs of the woman who was perched on his lap and came up with a handful of roofing nails from a box on the floor. With a wide grin, he flung them through the window where they scattered on the road behind them. "Let's roll, Red," he said.

They hadn't gone far before Eddie Green noticed that they were being followed. "We've got at least two cars behind us," he announced. His observation was punctuated with gunshots. Behind them, a sheriff's deputy was leaning out of a patrol car firing his revolver.

"Fuck!" screamed Nelson. "Let 'em have it, Tommy!" Carroll twisted around and fired a burst out the rear window. The women screamed, and the police cars dropped back out of sight.

A few miles later, the Packard's engine began to cough and sputter even harder. "We're not gonna get much farther," announced Red.

The Jackrabbit checked out the back window. "I don't see anyone following us," he said. "This is as good a place as any. Pull across the road here."

The big car's engine gave a final wheeze and cut out just as Red turned it to block the road. "OK, kids, everybody out," said the Jackrabbit.

As they piled out of the disabled Packard, a drab green Dodge sedan approached, headed toward town. It slowed, and an elderly farmer poked his head out the window and asked, "Car trouble?"

"Not anymore," said Eddie, thrusting his gun in the farmer's face. "Get out!"

The old man paused for a second then launched himself from the car and dove into the cornfield across the road.

"OK, let's move it," said Nelson. "I'll transfer the loot. You guys shift those gas cans over." He began hauling the stuffed pillowcases from the Packard and stashing them in the back seat of the Dodge. The Jackrabbit and Red began transferring five-gallon gas cans from the Packard.

"What about us?" asked one of the tellers.

"That Dodge is too small," said Homer. "Much as we like having you sit on our laps, ladies, I'm afraid we must say goodbye."

"I suggest you follow that guy," said Eddie, gesturing with his Thompson to where the farmer had disappeared into the withered cornstalks.

"Aw, nuts," said the Jackrabbit. "Looks like we just can't shake these friends of ours." He pointed at the road back to town where the two sheriff's cars had just crested a rise.

"Let's go, boys," said Red. "Time to get while the gettin's good."

They began piling into the farmer's Dodge, except for Nelson, who stood screaming in the road. "You goddamn coppers, you don't learn, do ya?" he shrieked. "Well, maybe this will teach you! Sons of bitches!" He opened up with his Thompson, emptying the entire 100-shot drum in less than twenty seconds.

"Will you get in here, dammit?" hollered the Jackrabbit. He leaned out of the car and hauled Nelson in by the shoulder.

Homer winced. He had worked with Nelson long enough to know that he despised being ordered around, especially with physical force. Fortunately, the bantam gangster was still too stoked to care. "Didja see that?" Nelson asked. "They turned and ran like little girls! Buncha chickenshit bastards!"

"They sure did, George," said the Jackrabbit. "Now who has the git?"

33

\* \* \*

It was dark by the time they got back to Eddie Green's place in Saint Paul. They moved quickly and quietly, transferring the pillowcases of cash into the apartment before any neighbors had a chance to notice.

"Well, fellas, it looks like payday!" said Red.

"Might as well start counting it now," said the Jackrabbit. He reached for one of the pillowcases, but Nelson smacked his hand away.

"Hell, no!" snarled Nelson. "I'm counting the money, not one of you birds. This was *my* heist, and *I'm* gonna count the loot. Any of you got a problem with that?"

"Gosh, no, George," said the Jackrabbit. "You go ahead and count it, and we'll stand right here and watch." He turned to Homer and held his index finger next to his right eye. It was an old piece of prison sign language meaning, "Watch him; he may be dangerous." The Jackrabbit stood back and leaned on the wall, his hands hanging loosely by his sides.

Homer nodded and sat down in a chair in the corner. He unbuttoned his coat in case he needed to go for his shoulder holster. It wasn't impossible to think that Nelson would just shoot everybody to avoid having to share the take.

But Nelson was playing fair. He sat on the floor in the middle of the room happily counting the money into six stacks he piled between his spread legs. He looked like a demented little boy on Christmas morning. When he was done, each man had nearly $8,000 in cash.

"The rest here is for J. P. Chase," said Nelson, indicating a small stack of bills he had held aside. "For expenses—guns, ammo, gas, and a little for his trouble, OK?"

"Sounds good to me, George," said the Jackrabbit. "I want you to know how much I appreciate you cutting me in on this." He cut his stack and handed part of it back to Nelson. "Here's a partial repayment for the dough you spent getting me out of Crown Point. I'll get the rest to you as soon as I can. I'd give you more now, but I need to pay the lawyer to try and keep Handsome Harry and the boys from going to the chair. I'm the reason they're in that jam."

"Don't worry, pal," Nelson replied. "There'll be another chance to make some more dough real soon."

# CHAPTER FIVE

**Chicago, Illinois**
**March 7, 1934**

D oris Rogers had a teensy hangover. She'd been out the night before and had perhaps a bit too much to drink. It was an easy thing to do nowadays. Ever since Prohibition had been repealed last year, the booze had been flowing like water over Niagara Falls—especially in Chicago. It was a town that liked a drink, as did Doris.

The hangover was actually a little pleasant. Just like her date the night before. Still, it wouldn't do at all to appear incapacitated at work. With times the way they were, any sort of job was hard to find. This was particularly true of a good-paying position like the one she held. Fortunately, there was a café in the office building that served strong coffee. She checked her wristwatch. There was enough time to grab a quick cup of Joe and still punch in on time.

Doris stepped off the El train, hurried up West Adams Street and entered the Bankers Building through the massive Art Deco entryway. After a quick cup of industrial-strength coffee, she checked her reflection in the chrome finish of the napkin dispenser. Her brown hair was long and tied back from a face that sported a generous smile and wide-set blue eyes. She made a minor adjustment to her lipstick and went up to the office.

She took the elevator to the nineteenth floor and hustled down the hall to a pair of frosted-glass doors stenciled with the legend: "Bureau of Investigation, United States Department of Justice." She went inside, punched the time clock, and went to her desk. The office was mostly empty, but Doris was not surprised to see the light on in her boss's office. She liked to get into the office early, but her boss was almost always there before her.

Her boss, Melvin Purvis, was the special agent in charge (SAC) of the FBI's Chicago field office. Both Mr. Purvis and Doris were new to Chicago. She had worked as his assistant when he was the SAC of the field office in Birmingham, Alabama. Two years ago, he'd been tapped by J. Edgar Hoover to head up the Chicago office—a plum assignment for the twenty-nine-year-old agent. Mr. Purvis had surprised Doris by asking her to work for him in Chicago. She surprised herself by saying yes.

At that point, Doris's life had been in a state of chaos. Her marriage had disintegrated with frightening speed, leaving her with a one-year-old son and limited means of support. There was a small settlement from the divorce, but she knew that she wouldn't be able to live independently on that alone. She soon realized that Mr. Purvis's offer was one that she shouldn't pass up.

Besides, she didn't have any strong ties to Birmingham; most of her family was in the Midwest. It seemed like a good idea to put some distance between herself and her ex-husband. Fortunately, she had an uncle and auntie in Chicago who would be happy to look after little Charlie while she was at work—and when she socialized.

At first, she had felt intimidated by living in Chicago. The city was big—a lot bigger than Birmingham and certainly a lot bigger than the town in South Dakota where she'd grown up. She also felt stigmatized by the divorce. As a working single mother, she felt very much alone and very much afraid of judgment.

However, after about a month of living in Chicago, she realized that nobody was really that concerned. If she'd stayed in Birmingham, she knew that she'd forever be the subject of whispered gossip and poorly concealed pity. Doris had gone so far as to concoct a cover story about why her child's father was no longer in the picture. However, she'd never had to use it. In Chicago, people had better things to do than concern themselves about the background of the new gal with the lively little boy.

The realization was enormously liberating. She'd felt a spectrum of possibilities open up to her that she'd never imagined. Free from the pressures of a failing marriage, Doris began to really enjoy her job. She also began to think about a career. She'd gotten a business degree from a small college in South Dakota, but she'd always figured it was just a bauble that would help her land a husband. Now she realized that she was no longer destined to be a housewife for a big-shot husband. For the first time, she realized that her future was wide open.

Mr. Purvis stuck his head out the door of his office. "Ah, Ms. Rogers," he said. "Glad you're here. I'm expecting a very important call from the director. I'll need you to put it right through to my office."

Melvin Purvis was a slight man with delicate facial features and a head of wavy brown hair that he wore swept back from his forehead. Born and raised in South Carolina, he had the appearance and manners of a southern gentleman. He also had a mild southern accent that became markedly more pronounced when he was excited or angry.

Purvis had joined the FBI after graduating from the University of South Carolina law school and had quickly risen through the ranks by making quite an impression on FBI Director J. Edgar Hoover. In quick succession, he was made SAC of the FBI offices in Oklahoma City, Cincinnati, and then Birmingham.

"I'll be sure to put the call through as soon as it comes in," Doris said.

Mr. Purvis gave her a quick once-over. "Are you feeling all right this morning, Ms. Rogers?" he asked. "You look a little peaked."

"I was just up late with a case of the sniffles," she said. "But I'm feeling much better now, thank you."

A brief look of concern flitted across Purvis's smooth features. Doris fought the urge to fidget. Sometimes Mr. Purvis's investigative instincts were a bit much—he seemed to have the ability to sense any sort of evasion. "Well, I guess that's all right," he said. "I'll be waiting for that call." Then he disappeared back into his office.

Doris busied herself getting ready for the day as agents began to filter into the office. It was a large open bull pen with government-issue wooden desks arranged in a large square. Each desk contained a green blotter and black telephone—and absolutely nothing else. No pictures or personal items were allowed on the agents' desks. In the evening, one of Mr. Purvis's assistants went through the bull pen to make sure all the desks were in absolute order. Any infraction—personal items on the desk, food crumbs, or even a blotter not squared with the desktop—was grounds for disciplinary action. More than one violation would result in a dismissal. The same went for clocking in. Agents who showed up even a minute late were reported to headquarters. The director was known to take a personal interest in agents who did not report to work on time.

Behind the bull pen was a row of offices. Mr. Purvis's office was closest to the door, and Doris's desk sat right outside it. Next to that was the records room, which was zealously guarded by an ancient woman named Helen. No one—not even Mr. Purvis—was allowed to go into the records room without being directly supervised by Helen. In the far corner of the office was the interview room, where suspects were questioned. The interviews were often quite vigorous. More than one suspect had to be physically carried from the room after his "interview."

As the hands of the clock crept closer to nine, more agents filed in the front door, punching the time clock just inside. Doris was keeping an eye out for an agent named Johnny McLaughlin—her date the night before—whom she wasn't exactly looking forward to seeing. In retrospect, Doris might have let things go a little bit too far with him. She was still trying to find her way with her romantic life. That was another liberating realization that came with her move to Chicago—she could date again. Although "again" was a bit of a stretch since her ex-husband, C. B. Rogers, had been her high school sweetheart. They had married early, and little Charlie had come along soon after. Now she felt like she could make up for lost time. She could relax and date around and actually have the independent social life she'd missed out on by marrying so young. Of course, with her newfound freedom came the propensity for making mistakes. For all the talk about modern women in the so-called Jazz Age, Doris found there were a lot of double standards that young women still had to watch out for. Doris liked to have a good time, but she was still aware how easy it was to get a reputation as a chippie—especially given that she was also a divorcée.

Being aware of how she was perceived was especially important when working for the FBI. Director Hoover held all the Bureau's employees to the highest of standards. Frankly, Doris doubted whether she would even be working there if she hadn't been hired before her divorce. Certainly, the Bureau would take a dim view of a divorced secretary fraternizing with the agents. She had already dated three agents in the Chicago office and had made it clear to each of them that if they blabbed about their dates, it would be that last of them.

Besides, Doris felt that dating the agents was her business and should be of no concern to Hoover or anyone else for that matter. She had the right to run her personal life as she saw fit, as long as it didn't interfere with anybody's job. Doris sighed. It wasn't as easy being a modern woman as it appeared in the movies.

Five minutes before nine, Johnny McLaughlin came through the door and clocked in. Sure enough, he made a beeline for her desk. "Hey Dore," he said with a broad grin. "How are you feeling this morning?"

"I'm quite well, Agent McLaughlin," she said. "I hope you are likewise well."

A confused look flitted across his face. "Say, what's the story, morning glory? I thought we . . . you know . . ."

Doris sighed. "I'm sorry, Johnny," she said. "I *did* have a swell time with you last night—"

"That's more like it!"

"It was fun," she continued, "But I don't think you should read too much into what happened between us. We went out, we had a few drinks, and we . . . um . . . enjoyed ourselves. Can't that be enough?"

He looked crestfallen. "Yeah, I guess so," he said. "Does this mean we won't be going out again?"

"No, not at all," Doris replied, although she knew it wasn't really true. Johnny McLaughlin seemed a little too needy for her tastes. She might go out with him one more time to avoid hurting his feelings, but that would be it.

"Well, that's the bee's knees!" said Johnny. "How about tomorrow night?"

"Sorry," answered Doris. "I'm taking my little boy to the movies. Maybe some other time."

"OK," said Johnny. "That's just fine." He headed off to his desk, whistling.

The telephone exchange on Doris's desk lit up. It was the call from Washington that Mr. Purvis had been expecting. She patched it through to her boss's office . . . then she counted to ten, carefully lifted the receiver, and began to listen in.

Doris was devoted to Mr. Purvis, so she was conflicted about listening in on his conversations. She owed him a great deal and was thankful, but she was also more than a little worried. He sometimes seemed to be in over his head with the responsibilities heaped upon the Chicago field office. Doris felt it was her responsibility to help and support her boss in any way possible. In order to do that effectively, she had to know what was actually going on. Mr. Purvis trusted her enough to allow her to compose and even sign letters in his name. Certainly, he wouldn't mind too much if she kept tabs on his conversations with the director. After all, it was for his own good. In her mind, she needed to know what was going on in order to help him. It was her responsibility and her job. And she took her duties very seriously.

Doris felt like she was on the front line of a war—one in which lowlifes and criminals like the Jackrabbit were assaulting the very foundations of American democracy. Mr. Purvis had actually sent Doris on a stakeout once. The Bureau had been looking for a crook named Verne Miller and had traced him to an apartment in downtown Chicago. By odd coincidence, Doris had met Miller before—he'd been the sheriff of the small town in South Dakota where she'd grown up. Doris stayed with the stakeout team and identified Miller, but he shot his way out of the building and escaped. Nevertheless, Doris was thrilled to be part of the confrontation. Ever since then, she had thought of herself as more than just a mere secretary. Compared with the criminals they were up against, a little harmless eavesdropping seemed meaningless.

". . . violation of the Dyer Act," Director Hoover was saying. "I don't like it, Mel, but at this point, I have little choice. This Jackrabbit character is grabbing too many headlines. We have to go after him *now*! The attorney general made that very clear to me today."

"I understand," said Mr. Purvis. "I will do my best to bring the Jackrabbit to justice. I'm just concerned about resources . . ."

"You'll have all the resources we can get for you. Don't worry about that."

"I'm not worried at all, sir. I have faith that justice will prevail. I suspect, however, that it would prevail much more quickly if I had a few more men. After all, we have a lot of men dedicated to the Kansas City investigation, as well as the Hamm and the Bremer kidnappings."

"Mr. Purvis, I am well aware of the unsolved cases still on the Chicago office's books," said Hoover acidly. "Perhaps if some of those were cleared up, you would be able to focus properly on the Jackrabbit case!"

Doris winced. Mr. Purvis was already busy with three high-profile cases. Now the director was getting ready to pile the Jackrabbit case on top of those. Doris didn't understand why the other field offices couldn't take over some of the caseload.

The Kansas City shooting was a big deal for the Bureau. In June 1933, the FBI was transporting an escaped bank robber called Jelly Nash back to Leavenworth prison. At the Kansas City train station, three men wielding machine guns ambushed the agents. They killed an FBI agent named Caffrey, along with three police officers and Nash himself. The newspapers had dubbed it the "Kansas City Massacre." Director Hoover had made capturing the perpetrators of the Massacre a top priority.

On top of that responsibility, there were also two high-profile kidnappings to contend with. Brewery owner William Hamm had been kidnapped and released after a $100,000 ransom was paid. A few months later, the kidnapping of businessman Edward Bremer had netted a $200,000 ransom. Despite an intensive regional investigation, there were no major leads in either case.

"Look, Mel," said Hoover. "This is a big deal. This Jackrabbit is giving the Bureau—indeed all of American law enforcement—a black eye. As you know, I've been working hard to get the Bureau past its corrupt history to make it the nation's premier law enforcement agency. Now is a crucial time. The attorney general is pushing Congress for a number of bills that will give the Bureau a lot more power and a lot more funding.

"Unfortunately, the Jackrabbit is getting way too much attention from the press. They treat him like he's some sort of modern-day Robin Hood. It's disgusting, absolutely disgusting! I've heard stories about crowds in movie theaters cheering for him during the newsreels. Cheering! For a thieving, murdering rat! We need to crush this vermin! *You* need to crush him, Mel!"

Doris noticed the slightest of pauses before Mr. Purvis answered. "I . . . I understand, sir," he said. "I will not fail you."

"I certainly hope not. I wouldn't expect you to. Mel, you are my golden-haired boy. If you bring me the Jackrabbit, the world is yours. Make me proud, son. Make the Bureau proud."

"I will, sir."

Doris gently replaced her receiver and went about straightening the piles of paper on her desk. She couldn't avoid feeling a little bit shady when she listened in on Mr. Purvis's discussions with the director. She reminded herself that she was just helping her boss in a tight situation.

In a few minutes, the light on the telephone exchange went out, and Mr. Purvis stuck his head out of the office door. "Ms. Rogers, please come in here and bring a pad," he said. "We have quite a bit of work to do."

# CHAPTER SIX

**Saint Paul, Minnesota**
**March 31, 1934**

omer Van Meter pulled his new car to the curb and killed the engine. He sat for a moment, surveying the neighborhood around the Lincoln Court Apartments. Not many people were out and about on this cold, gray Saturday morning. A few cars moved on the streets, but the sidewalks were deserted. Errant flakes of snow drifted among the skeletal trees that lined Lexington Avenue.

Homer leaned up and checked his reflection in the rearview mirror. He was wearing a brand-new suit and a spiffy homburg hat. He really liked the homburg. He'd always had trouble finding a lid that looked good with his horsey face. Most hats made him look like a farm boy playing dress-up. This homburg, however, really made him look sharp.

He'd gone on a spending spree after the latest heist. In addition to the new clothes, Homer had also sprung for this hot new Ford V8. He liked the new car smell and the huge engine under the hood. The car could really move! The only problem was the light green color. Baby Face Nelson sneeringly called it "monkey-puke green." This burned Homer, but he knew better than to say anything to Nelson about it.

Baby Face had been in a foul mood after the last heist in Mason City, Iowa. The Mason City job hadn't gone as smoothly as the one in Sioux Falls because Homer had somehow overlooked an armored guard booth while he was casing the bank. Located high above the entrance to the lobby, it was easy to miss. Homer and the rest of the gang first became aware of it about thirty seconds after they entered the bank, when the guard inside fired a tear gas grenade into the middle of the lobby.

Fortunately, the guard's gun jammed after the first shot. Eddie Green sprayed the booth with bullets from his Tommy gun, but the guard was protected by bulletproof glass. Then a gray flannel hero lobbed another tear gas grenade into the lobby from the mezzanine, further complicating matters. Next, a crafty teller locked himself into the vault, thwarting Red Hamilton's attempt to haul off $200,000 in large-denomination bills. To top it all off, both the Jackrabbit and Red had been wounded as they made their way out of the bank. Fortunately, the wounds were minor, and they had gotten away clean.

Baby Face was livid after Mason City. Sure, they had gotten away with over $50,000, but it was well short of the quarter million they would have netted if they'd been able to get into the vault. Nelson was also pissed about the tear gas, and when he was unhappy, he made everyone's life miserable.

He even threatened to kick Homer out of the gang for the guard booth fuckup. This sent Homer into a deep funk. The thought of being cast into the outer darkness after finally hooking up with his old pal was paralyzing. He knew he couldn't make it on his own—he didn't even want to try. The spending spree had helped lift his spirits a little, but not much.

Baby Face's mood got even worse a few days later when the newspapers began reporting that the Jackrabbit had been involved with the Sioux Falls and Mason City heists. His notoriety skyrocketed yet again, and the papers were soon running headlines about the advent of the new "Jackrabbit Gang."

"God dammit!" Nelson raged. "It's the fucking 'Nelson Gang'! This is *my* gang, these are *my* heists! If it weren't for me, there wouldn't be *nothing*!"

"Sure, sure," soothed the Jackrabbit. "Don't worry about it, George. We all know you're the boss. These newspaper guys don't know the real score. They're just a bunch of lunkheads."

Everyone was relieved when Baby Face took his family off to California a few days later to let things cool down. Despite his unhinged and violent behavior, Nelson was a devoted family man. He spent as much time with his wife and two young children as he could. While the Nelsons went off to visit sunny California, the rest of the gang holed up in their apartments in Saint Paul.

The main hangout was the Lincoln Court Apartments. The Jackrabbit and Billie were sharing a place with Red and his girl, Pat Cherrington. There'd been a big party there last night. When Homer went back to his apartment around midnight, the party was still going strong.

By noon, Homer figured that everyone should be up and around, so he got out of his new green Ford and crossed the street to the apartment building. Out of habit, he scanned the area before going inside. He noticed a man reading a paper inside a blue Hudson parked across the street. "Stakeout?" Homer thought. Possibly. But more than likely it was just some poor jerk trying to stay out of the cold. Homer decided that he'd check on him in a few minutes. Other than that, the area was deserted. The wind began to pick up, and Homer suspected they'd be in for more snow soon.

He went into the main entrance and tromped up the stairs to the third floor. As he came into the hallway, he noticed two men in business suits standing outside the door of the Jackrabbit's apartment.

"Oh shit!" thought Homer. This was definitely a raid. He spun on his heel and walked quietly back to the stairwell.

"Hey, you!" said one of the men. He was wearing a gray fedora with a colorful feather. "You! Who are you?"

"I'm a soap salesman," said Homer. "I sell soap."

"Where's your sample case?" asked Fedora Man.

"It's out in my car."

"Yeah, do you have any identification? Let's see your identification, pal!"

"That's out in the car too. How about I just go get it?"

Without waiting for an answer, Homer turned and walked quickly toward the stairwell. He heard a shout behind him and broke into a run. He rushed down the stairs, shiny new shoes clattering on the marble steps. When he was halfway down, he heard someone run through the third-floor doorway. Homer practically leapt down the final flight of stairs.

Just past the bottom of the stairway, a small alcove led to a utility room.

Homer ducked into the alcove and yanked the .45 from his shoulder holster. Who the hell *were* these guys? What the hell did they think they were doing? The bastards! Homer could feel his heart hammering in his chest. A red ring crept in around his vision as he got angrier and angrier. He'd teach them to bust in on their hideout!

Homer had always had a problem with his temper. It was what got him in trouble with the law in the first place. He was normally a pretty happy-go-lucky guy. Sometimes, though, if he was startled or threatened, he would just lose control. The first time it happened had been when he was in fifth grade. One of his classmates, a snotty kid named Charlie Smales, was giving Homer a hard time because of his secondhand clothes. Charlie would never have that problem; his family was well-off by Fort Wayne dirt-farmer standards. Charlie kept ragging him, calling him "the world's ugliest scarecrow." Homer's vision was soon clouded with red, and he just . . . lost control. When Homer realized what he was doing, Charlie Smales was flat on his back with a compound fracture of his arm. Homer couldn't remember exactly what had happened.

He wasn't exactly sure of what was happening now. His breath came in sharp jerks. The crimson ring around his field of vision grew wider and wider.

The footsteps came clattering down the stairs. In a moment, Fedora Man appeared in front of Homer's hiding place.

"You want some identification?" shouted Homer. "Well, here ya go, motherfucker! Identify *this*!" Homer squeezed off three quick shots.

Fedora Man rushed out the front door of the building with Homer following close behind. The snow was falling in earnest now. Homer chased Fedora Man across the lawn in front of the apartment building, firing as he went. The shots kicked up little puffs of snow from the lawn. Fedora Man did a quick buttonhook and disappeared around the corner of the building.

Homer charged after him. He tore around the side of the building where Fedora Man had disappeared. Fedora Man was waiting for him, down on one knee in a shooter's stance, his revolver pointed right at Homer's head. Homer quickly backpedaled, just before he felt a slug brush by his nose.

Another gunshot zoomed over Homer's left shoulder. He looked and saw the man from the Hudson charging up the sidewalk, revolver drawn. Clearly, it was time to get out of there.

As if to affirm that conclusion, a prolonged burst of machine-gun fire emanated from inside the building. Homer charged back to the apartment entrance and flung himself behind one of the brick columns that supported the portico. He reached around the column and fired off three quick shots from his .45, the recoil snapping his wrist back each time.

He hazarded a peek around the column but could see no sign of Fedora Man or the man from the Hudson. Good. He snapped off three more shots just to be safe then hurled himself through the front door of the apartment building.

Every one of the gang's hideouts had multiple exits; it was a requirement for any place they rented. Homer sprinted through the stairwell and down a short hall to a little-used back entrance. The gang, of course, used it all the time.

In fact, it was clear that someone had just been through there because fresh bloodstains dotted the snow near the back door. The cherry-red blotches ran from the door to a detached garage. Homer looked up to see the Jackrabbit's car fishtailing crazily down the alley. The rear end of the car slewed around and slammed into a telephone pole then disappeared around the corner.

Homer turned and ran in the opposite direction. There was no point trying to get back to his car—the cops would be all over Lexington Avenue in a few minutes. But he was no good at hot-wiring, so he would have to hijack a vehicle.

At the end of the alley, Homer stopped to look up and down the street. No cars or people were in sight. With the snow starting to fall harder, Homer turned toward downtown and began running again. Behind him, he heard sirens muted by the mounting snow.

Homer knew he had to get out of the neighborhood—fast. He was the only thing moving on the streets, and pretty soon, the area would be crawling with cops. He kept hustling down the snowy street, hoping a car would come by that he could flag down.

Half a block ahead, a horse-drawn coal cart clopped into the middle of the intersection. It certainly wasn't the fastest transportation, but Homer couldn't afford to be picky. He sprinted to the cart and vaulted nimbly into the seat. Two men in threadbare coats and ratty woolen caps sat there openmouthed.

"Hiya, fellas!" greeted Homer. He held open his coat to reveal his holster. In the cold air, steam and smoke rose grimly from the holstered gun. "Let's all be quiet and play nice, and Mister Pistol will stay in his holster, OK?"

The two men nodded vigorously.

"That's good," said Homer. "Now, I'm in a bit of a pickle here, fellas. You see, my wife's about to give birth, and I need to get downtown right away to get to the hospital."

The two men looked at each other and shrugged. The older man, who was holding the reins, slapped them down. The ash-colored horse strained forward, and the cart began to move.

Homer could hear more sirens, but they didn't seem to be getting any closer. He hoped the Jackrabbit had been able to get away. There hadn't been too much blood in the snow, but it wasn't anything to sneeze at, either.

As the cart neared a main road, Homer could see cars moving cautiously through the curtain of snow. Realizing that his clothing made him stand out a bit, he tossed his homburg hat to the floorboard, snatched the cap from the man beside him, and jammed it down on his head. His dressy coat was still noticeably different from the coal men's garb, but with the way the snow was falling, they'd all look like snowmen before too long.

The sirens grew louder.

"Hey, can't this rig move any faster?" asked Homer.

The older coal man shrugged as he said, "She's an old horse."

Homer was a farm boy, and the horse looked healthy enough to him. He snatched the reins from the old man and gave them a brisk snap. "Yah!" he hollered.

Sure enough, the horse moved out at a respectable trot. Before long, they passed Grand Avenue, and Homer began to get his bearings. When he judged that he was within an easy walk of Eddie Green's apartment, he hauled back on the reins and brought the horse to a stop.

"Well, fellas, this is my stop," Homer said. "You guys have been good sports." He dug out a wallet and held out a ten. "For your trouble."

The coal men just stared at it. After an awkward moment, Homer shrugged his shoulders, returned the bill to his wallet, and began to stroll off. "Well, fellas," he said, "don't take any wooden . . . wait a minute . . ."

He dashed back to the cart. The coal men shied back, but Homer only reached onto the floorboard to retrieve his hat. He tossed the cloth cap back to the older man and pulled the homburg snug on his head. He nodded with satisfaction. It was so hard to find a hat that suited him.

# CHAPTER SEVEN

**Saint Paul, Minnesota**
**March 31, 1934**

Bessie Green slumped at the bar of the Green Lantern and took a knock from her old-fashioned. She wasn't nursing her drink, but she was nursing a grudge. Ever since the Jackrabbit had shown up, things had absolutely gone to shit. She knew it was going to happen, but regardless of how much she'd screeched at Eddie, he had dismissed her, which only made her angrier.

She glared at Homer Van Meter, who sat at the other end of the bar drinking a beer. Normally, she was pretty fond of the lanky gangster, but today she wasn't in the mood for playing nice. "You're a fuckin' moron, Van Meter, you know that?" she snarled. "An absolute moron! You barely escape from a shoot-out, and you go straight to our apartment! Never mind that there might be a truckload of cops tailing your skinny country ass! Shit, why don't you just nail up a sign outside that says 'Gangster Hideout'? I'm sure my idiot husband wouldn't mind!"

Homer glanced over at her and slumped a little further, but he said nothing. Bessie dumped the rest of the drink down her throat and signaled to Pat Reilly, the Green Lantern's bartender, to make her another.

The Green Lantern Saloon was one of the busiest drinking establishments in Saint Paul, but it certainly didn't look that way from the street. A dingy "Closed" sign hung askew in the front door. On the other side of the dusty windows, a few neglected tables and chairs were scattered around a cramped serving area. The place looked like it hadn't been used in years.

Despite its dilapidated appearance, the Green Lantern served as the epicenter for the underworld community in Saint Paul. It was run by Harry Sawyer, who was one of the most well-connected men in town. Criminals visiting the city would "check in" at the Green Lantern. Sawyer required them to pay a fee and promise that they would not kill, rob, or kidnap anyone within city limits. Sawyer would assign the visitors a place to live and tip them off if one of his many police informants learned of an imminent raid.

Sawyer also operated as an all-purpose criminal concierge. He could hook you up with whatever you needed, such as a good attorney, or a way to unload hot jewelry and stolen bonds. He also operated as a sort of bank. He would keep sums of cash in the Green Lantern's huge safe—for a small fee, of course.

There was a heavy pounding on the door. Reilly scuttled across the room, checked the peephole, and unbolted the door to admit Red Hamilton, his girl Pat Cherrington, and her sister Opal. Pat was a petite redhead who had once been a nightclub singer. But apparently, she had robbed the gene pool because Opal had not inherited any of her sister's good looks. She was thick-limbed with a broad posterior, which prompted the gang to call her "Mack Truck."

Red quickly spotted Homer. "Jesus, Van!" he exclaimed. "Have you heard? They raided our place!"

"Heard?" said Homer. "I was there! Walked in right in the middle of that mess. Had to shoot my way out. The Jackrabbit and Billie got away, but looks like one of 'em took a bullet."

"Shit. It was a lucky thing we weren't there," said Red. "Me and the girls had just gone out for some cigarettes and breakfast. We saw those two guys in suits going in and decided to drive on by. When we came back, the place was crawling with cops."

The door to the alley slammed open and in strode Harry Sawyer, the proprietor of the Green Lantern. He was about forty-five with a large jowly face and a droopy nose that made it look like his face was sliding off his head.

"What the hell, boys?" said Harry. "Heard there was a bit of trouble over at the place on Lexington."

"'Bit of trouble,' my ass!" Homer shot back. "We're lucky we didn't all get nabbed! Why didn't you warn us we were about to get raided? What the hell are we paying you for?"

"Easy there, tough guy," scolded Harry. "I just found out myself. It wasn't the police, it was the Feds. They took one of the Saint Paul cops with them, otherwise I'd be reading about it in the papers just like you. I don't know much more, just that everybody got away."

Ten minutes later, there was another pounding on the steel door. Pat Reilly looked out the peephole then opened the door to let in the Jackrabbit and Billie. The Jackrabbit had a bloody bandanna tied just below his right knee. He was limping heavily, and his pale forehead was glistening with sweat.

Bessie felt the bile squirt into her throat. "If it isn't the fuckin' man of the hour!" she spat. "The big-shot celebrity gangster who's bringing trouble down on all of us!"

"Watch your mouth!" hollered Billie, her dark eyes ablaze. "He's the one that got shot, you know."

Bessie ran a hand through her shock of bright red hair. About the only person she disliked more than the Jackrabbit was his girlfriend. Bessie gave her a nasty look and said, "You're the one who'd better watch your mouth, you Chippewa chippie!"

"Just shut up, both of you!" said Eddie. "I need to think!"

"It's about damn time you did some thinking," muttered Bessie. Eddie could be a real wimp sometimes, but Bessie loved him madly. She'd had a rough life until she met Eddie. He was the first man who actually seemed to respect what she said and listened to her ideas. He basically had taken her on as an equal partner in his criminal enterprises. Of course, the rest of the gangsters couldn't know that. As far as most of them were concerned, a wife or a girlfriend was just a "moll"—a bit of fluff for recreation when the job was done. Billie was one of the worst kinds, a flighty birdbrain who wouldn't be able to fend for herself if it weren't for her hot-shit fella. Bessie glared at her then ordered Reilly to make her a sidecar.

"Jesus," Homer said to the Jackrabbit. "Are you OK? I can't believe they actually tagged you."

"Just a flesh wound," said the Jackrabbit. "And that dumb feeb didn't shoot anywhere near me. I shot myself . . . ricochet. I'll be OK."

"No, you won't!" wailed Billie. "You're not OK! You need to see a doctor!"

"Yeah, she's probably right," agreed Eddie. "We'd better take you to see Doc May. I've known him for years; he's a stand-up guy." He began pacing. "Did you leave anything incriminating at the apartment? Any addresses, phone numbers?"

"Probably," said the Jackrabbit. "We had about two minutes from being in bed to blasting our way out of there. Billie threw a few things in a bag, but everything else is still there."

"Damn," said Eddie. "We're going to have to move fast. You fellas can't go back to your places, and we're going to have to clear out of our apartment too."

"Oh, that's just swell!" said Bessie. "That's just what I need!"

The whole deal with the Jackrabbit was stuck in her craw. She'd known that having him around was going to be trouble, but it didn't matter. She'd complained loudly to Eddie, but the decision wasn't Eddie's, it was Baby Face Nelson's. Of all the gang members, Nelson was the one that she wouldn't mouth off to. The guy was a purebred psycho. Bessie had no doubt that he'd shoot her dead if she bitched at him when he was in a bad mood. The thought of her powerlessness over the situation made her even angrier. "Eddie, I told you this son of a bitch was going to land us in hot water! Didn't I? Hell, yes!"

"Can it, sweetheart," chided Eddie. "There'll be plenty of time for that later. Homer and Red, you oughta just get outta town right now. Take what you have and head back to Chicago. I'll get the Jackrabbit to a sawbones and get him patched up."

"Guess I'm riding with you, Red," said Homer. "Can't go back to get my car now. Damn. I just bought it last week."

"Just be glad you got away," said Red. "Let's get going."

"Yes, don't worry about a thing, boys," said Eddie. "I'll take care of things here. Homer, I might be able to get some people into your apartment to clean up before the cops get there. You just get going and don't worry. You can always get in touch with me through Harry. I'll handle things on this end, no problem."

"No problem, my fat ass," grumbled Bessie as she signaled Reilly for another drink.

*  *  *

The next day, she rode with Eddie to pick up Van Meter's stuff. He had sent a trusted housekeeper to go clear the apartment of incriminating evidence. He was now swinging by the housekeeper's place to pick up the things that had been recovered. It was an easy enough errand, but something about it made Bessie very uneasy. She insisted on riding with her Eddie and chewed his ear off on the ride over.

"If you had a lick of sense, you would turn this car around and leave town right now," she said. "But I know you don't have a lick of sense, which is why I'm telling you this. Do you hear me?"

"Oh, for Chrissakes, Bess! I'm just going to pick up Van Meter's suitcases, then we'll be gone. It'll take all of two minutes."

"That's all it would take for them to put you in cuffs! *If* you're lucky!"

"Look, I'll just go get the suitcases from Leona, and we're gone."

"Just how well do you know this woman?" demanded Bessie. "How do you know they haven't gotten to her?"

"I've been using Leona Goodman for years. She's rock solid." Before Bessie could mount another attack, Eddie slid out of the car and slammed the door behind him.

She watched him cross the street to the dingy clapboard house with a droopy front porch. He hammered on the skewed frame of the front door. No answer.

Bessie felt her stomach start to knot up. Something wasn't right.

Eddie knocked again. Another pause. Just as Bessie was about to get out of the car to drag her lunkhead husband back, the door to the house swung open. For half a second, Bessie saw the profile of a rotund Negro woman in a black maid's uniform. She shoved a suitcase into Eddie's arms and slammed the door. Eddie turned from the door with a quizzical look on his face.

A bright lance of fear slid into Bessie's guts. "RUN, YOU IDIOT!" she screamed. "DROP THE FUCKING SUITCASE AND RUN!"

He did, and as it thunked to the packed earth of the yard, Bessie heard a muffled yell from the house and the crash of breaking glass. The front of the house exploded with gunfire. Eddie staggered, and blood erupted in great gouts from his forehead and stomach. He flopped face-first into the street and didn't move.

"EDDIE! NO!!!" Bessie jumped from the car and rushed to where he was lying, a pool of blood spreading beneath his body. He groaned and tried to move.

"Eddie, no! Eddie, don't move!" Bessie wailed. She knelt down beside him. From inside the house, a half dozen men in suits came rushing out, pistols and machine guns drawn. "You cocksuckers! You killed him! YOU KILLED MY EDDIE!"

One of the men shoved her aside and knelt down next to her husband. "Good. He's still breathing," he reported. He and another man rolled him over. There was a huge divot in the side of his skull, and beneath the pulsing blood, Bessie could see the yellow glimmer of bone. There were two holes in his chest, and his shirt was soaked through with blood.

"DON'T TOUCH HIM! YOU LEAVE MY EDDIE ALONE, YOU MOTH-ERFUCKERS! I'LL KILL YOU! I SWEAR, I'LL KILL YOU ALL!"

She hardly felt it when they jerked her arms behind her back and slapped on the cuffs.

# CHAPTER EIGHT

### Chicago, Illinois
### April 10, 1934

Doris knew something was up as soon as she stepped off the elevator. The hallway on the nineteenth floor of the Bankers Building was jammed with reporters. Over the course of the last several months, Doris had become accustomed to the presence of newspapermen in the hallway almost every day. Today, however, was the worst she had seen it.

A tubby man in a dirty raincoat noticed her and rushed over. Doris couldn't remember his name, but she knew he worked for the *Chicago American*. "Is it true that there has been a major arrest in the Jackrabbit case?" he asked breathlessly.

"How should I know?" asked Doris. "I just got here. You probably know more than I do!" Other reporters noticed her and began to crowd around, shouting questions. She marched resolutely down the hall to the office, clamoring newsmen trailing behind her as if she were some sort of Pied Piper.

When she got to the door, she spun to face the raucous mob of reporters. "I told you, I don't know anything about any arrests!" she shouted. "If it's true, I'm sure Mr. Purvis will make a statement soon. Now, if you'll excuse me, I have work to do."

"How about if we just follow you inside and find out for ourselves?" demanded the reporter from the *American*.

"You know that's not how it works," said Doris. "You can stay out in the hall, and we'll give statements when we can, but you can't come inside."

"Why not?" said the reporter. "This is public property. Tax dollars are paying for it. How about if we come inside anyway?"

"How about you get a federal obstruction of justice charge?" snapped Doris. She'd never liked the mob of reporters that camped in the hallway, but lately they had been especially aggressive and obnoxious. "Now, you boys just relax, and someone will come out with a statement soon." She slipped through the door and slammed it behind her.

Inside the office, it was just as chaotic. There was an excited hum of activity throughout the office. Agents ran back and forth. Most of the activity focused on the interview room. As she watched, an agent named Carter Baum hustled by with a desk lamp in his hand. Baum was in his late twenties and had movie-star good looks and wavy hair swept back from a high forehead.

"Agent Baum!" Doris cried. "What on earth is going on?"

"Haven't you heard?" Baum said. "We got her! Billie Frechette! We got the Jackrabbit's girlfriend!"

"What? When?"

"Just last night! Agent Purvis made the collar himself!"

"What about the Jackrabbit?"

"No dice," said Baum. "Frechette says he was in the bar, too, and that he'd just walked away when we came in. I'm sure she's lying, though. No matter—we'll get the truth out of the little chippie soon enough!" He hefted the high-intensity desk lamp then hurried off toward the interview room.

Doris sat down at her desk. Before she could get settled, the door behind her swung open and Mr. Purvis shuffled out. He looked exhausted, with huge circles under his eyes and sweat stains under the arms of his shirt.

"Ah, Doris, thank goodness you're here," said Mr. Purvis. "I believe I'm going to need all the assistance I can get today."

"You should have called," said Doris. "I would have been glad to come in early."

"Well, that's all right," said Mr. Purvis. "At least one of us will be reasonably well rested today."

"There's a hungry pack of reporters out in the hallway. They practically mobbed me on my way in. I told them that someone would come out and give them a statement."

"That can wait," said Mr. Purvis. "Right now, I've got a more important audience to attend to. Please put me through to Director Hoover's office in Washington as soon as you have a chance."

"Right away, sir."

Mr. Purvis glanced at the interview room where questions were being shouted. He turned and retreated into his office while Doris began the process of connecting Mr. Purvis's line with Washington. Once the connection was made, Doris waited a bit, then carefully lifted the receiver on her desk.

". . . newspapers are saying that the Jackrabbit was in the same room as you," growled Director Hoover. "And he just walked right by you without so much as a glance."

"Sir, that is simply not true!" protested Mr. Purvis. "I'll admit that he may have been watching from outside the bar, but it is not possible that he was inside. I was there. I know what he looks like, believe me. I've studied all the pictures."

"Be that as it may, that's what the newspapers are saying, and that's what I have to deal with. Recent events have not cast the Bureau in a very good light, and that worries me. That worries me quite a bit, Melvin. It's about time we had a break in this Jackrabbit case."

"We're working on that right now," said Mr. Purvis. "I'm optimistic that we'll get a great deal of useful information from her."

"Good," said Director Hoover. "We need to show some progress—and quickly. Those congressmen are all over me, the newspapermen are all over me. I've had egg on my face since he got away in Minnesota, and let me tell you that I don't like it one bit. We need to get the Jackrabbit! We need to find out where that rat is holed up. You need to wring whatever information you can from this Frechette woman. I'm counting on you, Mel."

The conversation continued for a few more minutes, and then Doris carefully replaced the receiver. She was typing out some overdue correspondence when Mr. Purvis emerged from his office and went into the interview room. He was only there for a few minutes, undoubtedly passing on the encouragement from the director to the agents inside. When he left, she could hear shouting inside the interview room followed by a peal of feminine laughter. She heard a loud *smack,* and then the laughter abruptly cut off. An agent named Harold Reinecke came out of the interview room scowling and cursing.

Doris didn't like Reinecke; he was rude and a bully. That was OK for some of the suspects who went into the interview room, but this was a woman. There was no reason for anyone to hit her.

Doris tried to tune him out, but Reinecke kept shouting. "They were in Mooresville! They spent a day and a half at the family farm for Chrissakes! Just waltzed right in and had a picnic then drove away! Jesus!"

Carter Baum tried to hush Reinecke, but it was too late. Doris looked over at the door to the hallway. Reporters clustered around the door, peering in the window like little boys peeping through a knothole in the girls' locker room. They were all scribbling furiously. When Reinecke realized what he had done, he disappeared back into the interview room. The reporters in the hallway dashed off to the pay phones down the hall.

Doris's sense of unease deepened. Without really thinking about it, she abruptly stood up from her desk and marched into Mr. Purvis's office. As usual, her boss was scribbling notes in a notebook. His tiny, perfect copperplate script filled the page from margin to margin. Without looking up, he said, "May I help you, Ms. Rogers?"

"How long has she been here?" Doris demanded.

"What? Who?"

"The Frechette woman, of course. How long has she been here?"

"We brought her in about nine last night," Mr. Purvis answered. "Why?"

"Has she had anything to eat?"

Mr. Purvis looked startled. "Why, I don't think so. Perhaps the agents who are interviewing her have given her some food."

Doris thought that was unlikely. If Reinecke was smacking her around,

60

he probably wasn't providing any comestibles. "I think I should go get her something to eat," Doris offered.

"Yes, that would be fine. I could use a bite to eat too. I've been in here just as long as she has, you know."

"I doubt you've had people screaming at you all day."

Mr. Purvis gave her a sharp look and opened his mouth to respond. Instead, he just sighed. "This is a difficult job, Doris. By all means, you can get a sandwich for our guest, and pick one up for me as well."

Doris went to the café on the ground floor and picked up some sandwiches. When she went into the interview room, Agent Reinecke and his partner Murray Faulkner were shouting questions at Frechette, not even waiting for a response.

"What did you do with the loot from the Mason City job?"

"Where is the Jackrabbit hiding? We know you know where he is!"

"Is Red Hamilton still alive? Did he help out on the Sioux Falls job?"

Reinecke finally noticed Doris standing in the doorway. "What do you want?" he grumbled.

"I've brought a sandwich for Miss Frechette," Doris responded.

"*Miss* Frechette? This chippie doesn't deserve such courtesy—or any food."

Doris glared at the agents. "Mr. Purvis told me to bring her a sandwich. If you have a problem with it, you should take it up with him."

The agents glowered but said nothing.

Doris looked at the object of their attention. She was small and dark-skinned. There was a lot of pancake makeup on her face that Doris could tell was covering up an embarrassing complexion. She was dressed in clothing that was expensive and looked new. It didn't seem to suit her, though. She looked like a little girl that had been playing dress-up with a well-off auntie's wardrobe. Above all, she looked exhausted. There were huge dark circles under her eyes—eyes that showed fear but also defiance.

Doris handed Frechette the sandwich and marched back into Mr. Purvis's office. "The way you're treating that woman is disgraceful!" she announced. "She's been here for what, over twelve hours now? She's had no rest, no food—why, she probably hasn't even been allowed to answer the call of nature!"

Mr. Purvis looked up from his desk. He looked nearly as tired as Frechette. "What should I do, then?" he asked.

"Let me take her to the women's room. She can use the facilities, clean up and maybe get a little rest."

"I suppose," said Mr. Purvis. "But only for an hour."

It wasn't much, but it would have to be good enough. Over the protests of Reinecke and Faulkner, Doris led the woman down to the restroom. Fortunately, they didn't have to go past the slavering pack of reporters in the hallway to get there.

In the ladies' room, Doris had Frechette sit on the leather divan by the door while she fetched her a glass of water. She drank it down quickly, and Doris got her another. It disappeared just as quickly. "Thank you," she said. "Can I go . . . use the facilities?"

"Of course," said Doris.

She was in there for a long time. "Hardly a surprise," thought Doris. "The poor thing's been in the interview room for a long time."

When Billie came out of the stall, she said, "Thank you. You've been so kind. Those men in there . . . I don't think they even listen to me. They just shout and shout." She sighed. "I don't even know your name."

"My name is Doris. Your name is Evelyn, right?"

"Yes, but you can call me Billie. Everybody does."

"Tell me, Billie. You seem like a nice girl. What are you doing mixed up with a criminal like the Jackrabbit?"

"He treats me right," said Billie. "He's a good man. Things are tough now for people, but they've always been tough for me. I grew up on a reservation in Wisconsin. Things were always tough there. It wasn't any better when I came to Chicago. Never enough to eat, never knew if I'd have a roof over my head.

"When I met him, he just seemed so . . . carefree. He doesn't worry about money; he just likes to have fun. We always go out dancing or to the movies. Best of all, he treats me right. He never yells, never hits. Not like a lot of men. We just have so much fun together."

Doris didn't know what to think. In the newspapers, the Jackrabbit was made out to be a ruthless villain, a heartless man who would thoughtlessly kill or destroy to get what he wanted. Some papers soft-pedaled him and made him out to be a modern-day Robin Hood who took on the greedy banks that had bankrupted so many families. Either way, Doris had never thought of the Jackrabbit as an ordinary man with ordinary interests.

"Try to get some sleep, dear." said Doris.

Billie yawned widely. "That sounds good. It feels like I haven't slept in a hundred years." She curled up on the couch and was snoring within two minutes.

Doris sat on the edge of the sink smoking a cigarette and watching Billie. She felt confused. The woman before her was touted as almost as dangerous as the Jackrabbit. But clearly Billie was no vicious gangster's moll living only to assist a bloodthirsty killer. She was just a vulnerable and lonely person trying to get by in a hard world. Doris thought of her hardscrabble upbringing in rural South Dakota and wondered how many bad decisions really separated her from Billie Frechette.

Once the big hand had made a full sweep of the clock, Doris gently shook Billie's shoulder. The woman woke with a cry.

"Time to go, dear," said Doris.

"No, no!" cried Billie. "Don't make me go back in with those men! I'll tell you anything you want, just don't make me go back!"

"I'm sorry," said Doris. She gritted her teeth and led Billie back to the interview room.

The rest of the day dragged on, and Doris's mood got darker as the shadows grew longer. There were no more smacks or cries from the interview room, but it bothered her to think of Billie in there with Reinecke and Faulkner. She kept her head down and focused on her work, willing the clock to speed up.

Shortly before it was time to go home, an agent named Allan Lockerman strolled up to Doris's desk and leaned against it. Allan was tall with wavy brown hair swept back from a high, intelligent forehead. He was handsome and polite, but right now, Doris didn't want anything to do with him. She just wanted to go home and have a brandy.

"What can I do for you Agent Lockerman?" she asked.

"Can you believe it, Doris?" he said. "We got her! We're just one step away from the Jackrabbit!"

"That's wonderful," said Doris flatly. "You should be proud of yourselves."

"Say, what's wrong? Are you feeling OK?"

"I'm just fine," said Doris. "Now, if you'll excuse me, I have some work to finish up before I leave."

"I'll excuse you," said Allan. "But only if you'll have dinner with me tomorrow night. I know a great little Italian place. You'll love it."

Doris eyed Allan warily. Going on a date was the last thing she wanted to think about right now. On the other hand, he wasn't asking her to go out *now*. Besides, he was cute. "Tomorrow night? I'm sorry, I have plans then. Some other time, perhaps?"

"Oh, OK," said Allan. "Whenever you feel like it, Doris."

"I'm sorry," said Doris. "I can't really think about my social life right now. I really just want to go home and rest."

"Yes, of course," said Allan. "It's been a long day for everybody."

"*That's* the truth," said Doris. She thought of Billie sweating it out in the interview room. Who knows how much longer they would keep her in there.

An hour later, Doris headed home with her head hung down. She ended up having two brandies after she got there but still had a difficult time falling asleep.

# CHAPTER NINE

### Saint Paul, Minnesota
### April 13, 1934

"You won't get shit outta me," snarled Bessie Green. "Whaddaya got on me, huh? Harboring? That's a year, tops. That's fucking nothing, you flat-footed bastard."

The FBI agent looked at her indifferently. They had been going through this for four days now, trying to get information out of Eddie Green's wife. The interview room consisted of four windowless cinder block walls, a scarred metal table, and a number of mismatched wooden chairs.

The agents had kept her in this room with only an occasional trip to the restroom. They had been working her in pairs—nearly around the clock—without success. It was wearing thin, though. Bessie could feel her hold on reality starting to slip, and it scared her.

"You sure you don't want to cooperate?" the agent asked hopefully. "It'll make things easier on you if you do."

"Ah, go fuck yourself," said Bessie. "I don't know jack shit, and even if I did, I wouldn't tell you shitheels."

"Suit yourself," said the agent. "If you're not gonna talk to us, then you can talk to Clegg."

"Yeah, you do that," said Bessie. "You go get your big shot Clegg, see if I care. I'd rather talk to him anyway. I'd rather talk to a pile of dog shit than you two jackoffs."

The agents shrugged and left the room. Bessie slouched in her chair. It was difficult keeping up the tough-girl front. She was tired and scared. She'd barely had four hours of sleep in as many days, and it was starting to wear her down.

Even worse than the fatigue was the fear. She knew that they really couldn't do anything to her, but she was worried about her Eddie. And there was her other one . . . but she didn't want to even *think* about him.

The door opened, and a short, rotund man strolled in. He wore a three-piece linen suit that was at least twenty years out-of-date and a straw boater with a narrow brim. He removed the hat and gave a semiformal bow from the waist. "Good mawnin', Miz Green," he said in a syrupy Mississippi drawl. "And how are we today?"

Bessie regarded him blankly. "I don't know about you, buster, but I feel like a shit sandwich without the bread."

The man looked at her goggle-eyed for a moment then burst out laughing. "Ah-haw-haw-haw! Ah say, Miz Green, you *do* have a way with words! Do you mahnd if Ah sit down?"

"It's your goddamned show, Inspector Clegg. Do what you want."

"Actually, it's *Assistant Director* Clegg, as Ah b'lieve you well know." He pulled a chair around the side of the table and sat down next to her. "Ah don't stand much on fawmality, though. You can call me what you please, just don't call me late fo' dinnah! Ah-haw-haw-haw!"

Hugh Clegg had shown up here at the Saint Paul FBI field office two days after Bessie had been arrested. The agents had initially terrified her with the threat of his arrival. They made him out to be a monster, a heavy who would beat the truth out of any suspect no matter how tough they might be. As J. Edgar Hoover's handpicked second-in-command, Clegg had been sent to Minnesota to clean up the FBI's mess after the fuckup at Lincoln Court Apartments.

Bessie had spoken with him three times before this. The agents always made Clegg out to be a brutal inquisitor, as if having him take over the interrogation would be a form of punishment. However, Clegg turned out to be an amiable southern pepper pot—agreeable and easy to talk to.

But Bessie wasn't fooled. She wasn't going to let his easygoing demeanor lull her into spilling the beans. Still, she'd rather spend time with him than the run-of-the-mill goons they'd had interrogating her. At least Clegg was interesting. His style was to just get her talking about trivial things like the weather. Before she knew it, he'd have very subtly steered the conversation around to the price of Tommy guns on the black market or the relative merits of the Hudson Terraplane versus the Ford V8 for a getaway car. He was wily that way, and Bessie rather enjoyed the game of trying to figure out exactly what Clegg was after and how best to turn the tables on him.

Today, however, he was in no mood for preliminaries. "Miz Green, Ah know that *you* know where the Jackrabbit hightailed it off to," he said. "Why don't you just go ahead and tell me? It will save everyone a lot of trouble—especially you."

This directness was off-putting, and Bessie stuttered for a moment before slipping into her dumb-broad routine. "How the hell should I know? Nobody tells me squat, Inspector Clegg. I just do the dishes and look pretty, right? Just a dumb moll."

Clegg fanned himself with his hat even though it was chilly in the interrogation room. "Aw, Miz Green, we both know that's not true," he said. "You are *not* just some 'dumb moll.' You're quite an enterprising woman. Ah know quite well that you've managed or owned several nightclubs around this area. That's a very complicated business. Ah'm very impressed, Ah must say."

"Not me," she countered. "They just had me put my name on the paperwork. I just washed dishes and served drinks."

"Uh-huh. Ah see. That's not too surprisin', Ah guess. That's pretty complicated stuff, runnin' a business, keepin' the books. Pretty hard fo' a woman, Ah think." He tipped her a wink. "'Specially if theyah's more than one set of books. Am Ah right?"

Bessie ground her teeth. She wasn't going to let him bait her this way. Sure, she had run a couple of clubs for Harry Sawyer and had, in fact, owned one outright. It alarmed her that Clegg had somehow figured this out. Still, it was best to keep him guessing—never admit to anything.

Clegg crossed his legs, stared off into space, and began whistling tunelessly.

Abruptly, he turned to her and said, "Where the hayull is the Jackrabbit? Ah know that *you* know. Eddie told us so."

"I don't know jack shit, Inspector. All I know about the Jackrabbit is what I read in the papers. Just like you." She smirked as she saw the subtle dig sink in.

"Just lahk me," he repeated softly. "No, Miz Green, the Bureau knows consid'rably mo' than what appears in the papers, Ah assure you."

"Well, that's just fine and fuckin' dandy," said Bessie. "In that case, why don't you just ask Eddie? Why are you bothering me?" Every time Eddie's name came up during these sessions with Clegg, Bessie's stomach took a lurch. He just looked so awful lying in the street in front of that rotten woman's house. She was surprised he'd survived at all, much less for ten days. He was probably weak, scared, and incoherent. There was no telling what he might say or how accurate it would be.

"Ah'm afraid that Eddie Green will not be of much fu'ther use to our investigation." Clegg looked at her sadly. "Ah regret to info'm you that he passed away early this mawnin'."

Bessie felt something shift and break inside her. She had been with Eddie for nearly a decade, had loved him more than she thought was possible for her to love nearly anyone—except her other. Deep down, she knew that he was dead, had known it from the moment she'd seen the blood burst out of his forehead on that dirty street. Her stomach filled with acid and her mouth began to work soundlessly. With a mighty effort, she got her emotions under control. She loved Eddie and would miss him horribly, but she was damned if she was going to show it in front of this flat-footed cracker bastard.

"Ah'm terribly sorry," said Clegg. "Ah truly am."

Bessie's mind raced. She had been holding on to the information about the Jackrabbit as a bargaining chip, hoping to use it to negotiate down Eddie's sentence. That didn't matter now, but she wasn't going to give Clegg or anyone else the benefit of her knowledge.

She really didn't give a rat's ass about the Jackrabbit or any of his pals. She knew he was going to be big trouble the moment she'd met him. She'd hated having him turn up in Saint Paul and hated that Eddie had decided to help him out. It's not as if he'd had much choice; it was Baby Face Nelson's idea to bring him on board. Once he'd decided that, the deal was done. There was no way Eddie—or anyone else in Saint Paul—would've crossed Nelson. The man was too dangerous.

Right now, however, she wasn't worried about Nelson, and she certainly wasn't worried about the Jackrabbit. They were both relative newcomers to the goings-on in the Saint Paul underworld. It was all her other friends and associates that were on her mind. She had been dialed into the Twin Cities criminal scene for many, many years, and she knew where a lot of the bodies were buried—both literally and figuratively. Likewise, a lot of people had the goods on her. She couldn't afford to be thought of as a fink, couldn't be known to be cooperating with the Feds. Sure, this Clegg seemed pretty decent, but he was still a fucking cop. Now that she couldn't help Eddie, there was no reason to cooperate.

She looked up at Clegg. He was staring at her with a strange mixture of empathy and contempt. Also, he seemed to be waiting.

"Don't take this the wrong way," said Bessie. "But why don't you just go fuck yourself, huh? My Eddie's gone, and you and the rest of you shitheels were the ones responsible. Fuck you, fuck your Bureau, fuck your bullshit, and *especially* fuck J. Edgar Fuckin' Hoover!"

Clegg cut his eyes away and nodded as if he'd been expecting this response. "That's what Ah thought you'd say."

"Good. Then let's quit fucking around, huh? You're getting nothing from me, not now, not ever, so just go do what you think you have to do, put me away for harboring or whatever else you think you can make stick. It's nothing to me. A year? Two years? Nothing. I can do that time without batting an eye."

"There is one more thang you should know, Miz Green. We know about Buddy."

Bessie felt a chill rush through her body. How the fuck had they found out? Over the last fifteen years, she'd gone to great lengths to make sure no one would find out about Buddy—that he would never be connected with her illegal activities.

His name was John, but everyone called him Buddy. He was Bessie's son from her first marriage. When her marriage had fallen apart, Buddy had gone to live with his grandparents in California. As Bessie slowly got involved with shadier and shadier people in the Midwest, she'd determined to keep her son out of it. She only spoke with him or saw him once or twice a year, and then she was very careful not to let anyone know what she was up to. Even Eddie hadn't known about Buddy. Or had he? Regardless, the FBI had found out.

"Ah know this is very difficult for you. Ah'm sorry it's come down to this. He seems like a fahn boy. It'd be a shame to have to upend his life, now wouldn't it?"

A thousand curses boiled up in Bessie's mind, words and phrases that would have made a sailor blanch. Her pulse raced, and she could feel the sweat coating her palms. Her breath came in short, harsh gasps.

"All we want is the Jackrabbit, Miz Green. We're not interested in anythang else."

Her mind spun. Could she trust Clegg and the rest of these FBI bastards? Probably not, but what choice did she have? If she didn't cooperate, they'd drag her sweet, blameless son into the sordid mess of her life. She just couldn't have that.

"You only want to know about the Jackrabbit?" she asked. "Nothing else, right?"

"That's all we care about Miz Green. Whatever other, um, business activities you may have been involved in are of no interest to us."

"And you'll leave Buddy out of this? He's never done anything wrong! He has a future, dammit!"

"Ah give you my word as a gentleman that yo' son will not be involved in any way."

There was the slightest of hesitations, then Bessie nodded. "All right," she said. "I'll tell you everything I know about the Jackrabbit."

# CHAPTER TEN

### Chicago, Illinois
### April 16, 1934

"Thirty-two west and sixteen north. Four o'clock." That was the abrupt telephone message Art O'Leary had received at the office earlier in the morning. The caller had hung up without elaboration.

Art checked his watch. It was nearly four now. He hurried across the northern edge of Humboldt Park. He hoped he had it right—he'd interpreted the message to mean that the meet was the 3200 block west and the 1600 block north. This worked out to be the intersection of North and Kedzie, at the northwest corner of the park.

A beige Hudson Terraplane sat at the curb, just past the park entrance. Behind the wheel sat a man with a large-brimmed hat. Another man sat in the back. The man behind the wheel leaned over and turned his head toward Art then tugged on the brim of his hat. Art did the same. It was the underworld sign that one wasn't being followed.

The man behind the wheel leaned over and pushed open the passenger's-side door. Art hesitated. He couldn't be sure who was in the car, couldn't be sure who it was who had called with the cryptic message. Art assumed that it was the Jackrabbit. Suddenly, it occurred to him that this could be some sort of setup. He knew the Chicago Police had set up a Jackrabbit Squad, run by a brutal old bull named John Stege. Maybe they had decided to play hardball with him.

The man behind the wheel motioned impatiently toward him. Art suddenly wished that he'd brought a gun. Well, too late now. He'd just have to deal with the situation as it unfolded.

Not for the first time, he realized he was in pretty deep. It hadn't started out that way, though. When he'd signed on with Piquett, he knew he would have to deal with some shady situations. The problem was that they just kept getting shadier and shadier.

Art was just a regular guy trying to support his family. Times were tough, and he had lost almost everything in the stock market crash. Despite Grayce's nagging, he loved her—and the kids—deeply. He'd do anything for them, but lately he'd begun to wonder where the line was between providing for his family and putting himself in mortal peril.

Now, however, was not the time for philosophical introspection. He shrugged and slid into the passenger seat of the Terraplane.

The man behind the wheel pulled the hat down even lower on his head and turned his face away. Art started to turn around to see who was in back, but a voice from the back seat barked, "Eyes forward, smart guy!"

Art's stomach shriveled—it was a trap! He looked desperately out the window. The safety of Humboldt Park was just a half dozen steps away—if he could make it that far without catching a slug in the back. He'd started to reach for the handle when the man behind the wheel whipped off his hat.

"Hiya, Art!" cried the Jackrabbit.

"Jesus Christ!" said Art. "You scared the crap out of me!"

The man in the back seat guffawed loudly.

"Art, I'd like you to meet a good friend of mine," said the Jackrabbit. "This is my old pal Red Hamilton."

Art turned and shook Red's hand. He couldn't help but notice the two missing fingers.

"Look, Art," said the Jackrabbit. "You have to help me do something about Billie. It's driving me mad knowing that those lousy Feds have her. We went to a bar to meet a friend of Billie's. I dropped her off and went to park the car. As soon as I'd pulled to the curb, I saw a dozen cops rush into the bar. Someone had ratted us out. When they took her away, I cried, Art. Sat right here behind the wheel and bawled like a baby. You and Piquett have to help me get her out!"

"I'm sure Lou would be glad to represent her—"

"No, no, that's not what I'm talking about," the Jackrabbit interrupted. They're going to have to move her from Chicago to Saint Paul for the trial, right? That's when we hit 'em! Shoot 'em down and get her outta there!"

"Whoa, whoa, whoa!" said Art. He could tell the Jackrabbit was distressed. He also knew the gangster was prone to rash and grandiose plans. It was the same when he was in Crown Point. The Jackrabbit had concocted an escape plan that involved dynamiting the jail. It had taken Art and Piquett a great deal of effort to talk him out of it. "Look, I know you're upset—" Art began.

"Upset ain't the word for it!"

"I know, I know. But we don't know when or where they're moving her, of if she's even still in the city. For all we know, she might be halfway to Saint Paul right now. We can't do anything rash, anything that might endanger her. Right?"

"Yeah, right," said the Jackrabbit sullenly.

"OK, then," said Art. "Lou will take the case, and I'm sure he can get her off. We'll handle this all aboveboard and legal. It's really the only option we have. OK?"

"OK."

"Finally, someone who can talk some sense into him!" exclaimed Red. "All week long, he's been talking about raids and armored car assaults and stuff. It's been nuts!"

The Jackrabbit reached into his coat and pulled out a fat sheaf of bills. He tossed it onto Art's lap. "There you go, Art" he said. "There's five grand to put toward Billie's defense and toward the money I owe Piquett. I know he'll give you your cut too."

Art wasn't so sure about that. He briefly considered taking a bit off the top to cover his own costs but quickly decided against it. He didn't want to get on the bad side of the Jackrabbit *or* Lou Piquett. They were both too dangerous.

He'd just to have to impress on Piquett that he hadn't been paid in a long time. Art's wife was riding has case worse than ever about the long hours he was working and the short pay he was bringing home.

"There's one more thing I want you to check out for me," said the Jackrabbit. "I want you to ask around and find a good plastic surgeon. One who does good work and knows how to keep his mouth shut."

"Are you serious?" asked Art. Reconstructive surgery had come a long way since the end of the Great War, but it was still primitive. Art had heard numerous horror stories about underworld plastic surgery disasters.

"Yeah, I'm serious," answered the Jackrabbit. "I just want to be a regular guy. I'm tired of running all the time. I'm tired of having my face all over every newspaper."

"Bullshit!" laughed Red. "You *love* it! You have a damn suitcase full of newspaper clippings!"

"Not anymore," countered the Jackrabbit. "The lousy cops got it with the rest of my stuff at the apartment in Saint Paul."

"Oh yeah, that's right," recalled Red. "Just don't pretend that you don't like it. Hell, you buy five or six newspapers every day just to see if your name's in 'em. And don't even get me started about the damn movie newsreels."

"Oh yeah, the newsreels!" said the Jackrabbit. "Have you seen the latest, Art? After I went back to see the family in Mooresville? Oh, man, were the Feds steamed about that! I made 'em look like a bunch of monkeys! After that, a studio sent a newsreel crew down to the farm to interview my old man. He said a lot of nice things about me—more than he ever told me to my face, that's for sure."

"And you're really ready to give up all of this movie-star stuff, huh?" questioned Red.

"Hell, yes!" the Jackrabbit replied adamantly. "In a minute! Really, Red. Sure, this is all a hoot, and I'd be lying if I said I didn't get off on seeing my name in the papers. But I really just want to settle down, stop running. Find a house with Billie and just be a regular person, you know?"

"Somehow, I just don't see it happening," said Red.

"You need to get your eyes checked then," said the Jackrabbit. "But first things first. I need to get a new mug. Can you help me, Art?"

"Yeah, I guess so," said Art. "I'll ask around to see if there's anyone who can do that kind of work. I'm sure Lou knows someone. I'll find out and get back to you soon."

"Well, I'd like it to happen soon," said the Jackrabbit. "But it doesn't have to happen today. We're going to be taking a bit of a vacation, see, just until the heat dies down. Baby Face found us a place in northern Wisconsin. Line it up for two weeks from now if you can."

"I'll see what I can do," said Art.

"Hope this turns out better than your last 'vacation,'" snorted Red. "Things didn't turn out so well for you in Tucson." Red had avoided being caught in Tucson because he'd been in Chicago recovering from wounds from the ill-fated bank robbery in East Chicago.

"Ha! Ha! No, it won't be anything like that," said the Jackrabbit. "This is someplace out in the middle of nowhere. We can just relax and not worry about anybody hassling us."

"Sounds like a good idea," said Art. "Probably the best thing for you right now."

"Absolutely," said the Jackrabbit. "Just a quiet rest in the ol' Northwoods."

# CHAPTER ELEVEN

## Manitowish Waters, Wisconsin
## April 20, 1934

H omer Van Meter had been driving down the forest highway
for several hours now. The farther they got from Chicago, the
better he felt. He was a country boy at heart, and life in the city
sometimes made him nervous. This had been especially true lately, since
the shootout in Saint Paul and the heat that followed. Everyone in the gang
was hit hard by Eddie Green's death. Getting out into the Northwoods for
a little relaxation was an idea that Homer welcomed wholeheartedly.

"Are we almost there, baby?" asked Marie Comforti from the passenger
seat. Marie was a tall, slender brunette who had deep brown eyes and an
easy smile. She'd been Homer's on-again, off-again girlfriend for nearly a
year. Lately, they had been on-again—in a big way. Homer was very happy
to have her along on this trip.

He was happy to have her, period. Marie was a real looker, and what's
more, she genuinely seemed to like him. Homer was almost giddy whenever
she was around, like he was high on laughing gas. What was a nice girl like
her doing with a goon like him? He didn't know, and, honestly, he didn't
care.

Most of the time anyway. Underneath the pleasant euphoria that came
from being with Marie was the dark certainty that it was just a matter of
time before she came to her senses and ditched him. This vague notion
made him uneasy and angry. Most of the time, he was able to keep these

thoughts tamped down tight, but they were still there, circling like hungry sharks beneath the dark surface of his consciousness.

Those thoughts were far away today, though. He grinned and looked over at Marie. She was smiling out the window and stroking Rex, the Boston terrier pup Homer had bought her.

Pat Reilly, the bartender from the Green Lantern Saloon, was in the back seat. The gang decided to bring Reilly along as a general errand boy and gofer. Reilly's job was to take care of anything that involved interacting with the public. The rest of the gang had mug shots in every post office in the country; it was best if an unknown like Reilly did the shopping and fetching. Everyone else could just take it easy.

"Almost there right now," Homer told his passengers as he turned left onto a driveway. They soon passed under a wood-and-concrete arch bearing the name Little Bohemia Lodge.

They cruised through a forest of tall hemlock trees. Patches of snow were scattered throughout the woods. Even though it was almost May, it was still quite chilly in northern Wisconsin. The driveway opened up to a large dirt parking lot in front of the lodge.

Little Bohemia Lodge was a sturdy two-story structure. The ground floor was made of stout logs while the upper story was whitewashed wooden siding. There was another small cabin beyond the main lodge, and beyond that, a sparkling lake a quarter mile wide.

"It looks like we're the first ones here," said Homer. "I wonder where Nelson is." The entire gang had rendezvoused in the town of Fox River Grove back in Illinois. They left in three cars spaced about thirty minutes apart. Nelson left first with Tommy Carroll and their wives Helen and Jean. Homer followed, and the Jackrabbit, Red Hamilton, and Red's girl Pat Cherrington trailed behind.

A nightclub called the Crystal Ballroom was the rally point in Fox River Grove. It was owned by a character named Louis Cernocky, an old associate of Nelson and Piquett. Cernocky made the arrangements for the gang to stay at Little Bohemia and had given Baby Face Nelson a letter of introduction. He assured the gang that it would be a quiet, out-of-the-way location for them to lie low and get some rest.

Homer pulled his car to a stop in front of the stone arch that marked the entrance to the lodge. Around the side of the building, two collies in a pen began barking maniacally. Homer got out and stretched his legs. It felt good after spending so much time behind the wheel.

Marie and Reilly got out of the car. Marie cast a worried glance at the raucous dogs in the pen. "Do you think it's safe here for Rexie?" she asked.

"Yeah, sure," Homer reassured her. "Those dogs are fenced up. Just keep the little fella away from them, and he'll be fine."

Homer glanced around the parking lot, unsure what to do. There was still no sign of Nelson, and he was the one with the letter of introduction. Homer shrugged. He could handle this. "You guys stay right here," he said. "I'll go see if anyone's home."

He went through the entrance into a wood-paneled lobby. Inside, a round, middle-aged man was lackadaisically polishing the front desk. The owner, Homer figured. Cernocky had told them his name, but Homer had forgotten it.

"Hello!" said Homer brightly. "You must be—"

"Emil," said the man. "Emil Wanatka. What can I do for you?"

"My name's Wayne," said Homer. "Wayne Huttner. I'm a friend of Louis Cernocky."

"Lou?" said Emil. "How's that old bastard doing?"

"About the same, as far as I can tell," said Homer. "Look, I've got a bunch of business associates on their way, and we need a place to stay. We're on our way to Duluth to see about opening a clown college."

"A clown college?"

"Did I say, 'clown college'?" said Homer. "I meant a shoe factory. I always get those two mixed up." Emil looked nonplussed.

"Anyway," continued Homer, "we're going to need lodgings for a day or so. For ten people, give or take."

"Ten people?" Emil's wary look was replaced with an expression of unalloyed greed. Homer could practically see the dollar signs popping up in his eyeballs. "Yes, of course, we can accommodate your party. However, some of them will have to stay in the cabin, and it will take a little time to get all the rooms ready. I hope that's not a problem."

"Not a problem at all," said Homer. "I'll just take a little look around the grounds."

"Sure. Sure thing," said Emil. "I'll get those rooms ready right away. Be sure to take a look at the lake too. Best fishing in Wisconsin, and we have boats available at very reasonable prices."

"Not for me, thanks. I get seasick just taking a bath," said Homer "Say, those dogs of yours aren't dangerous, are they?"

"No, they're real friendly; they're just loud."

"Well, I hope they won't keep us up at night."

"No, they're very quiet at night," said Emil. "I'll just go and get those rooms ready now."

Homer strolled back outside and told Pat and Marie to wait in the parking lot for the others. He started walking the grounds, keeping an eye out for potential threats and good escape routes.

Behind the lodge, Little Star Lake sparkled in the midday sun. Homer could see a number of cabins on the other side of the lake. Presumably, there was a way to get back to the main highway from them. It would be a good way to get out of the area if something happened. Better yet, the path around the edge of the lake was lower than the rest of the landscape. A short but steep slope separated it from the lodge's parking lot. Homer stumbled down the hill and was pleased to note that he could barely see the parking lot from the edge of the lake. It was the ideal escape route.

The rest of the property wasn't as nice. The area between the lodge and the main highway was thickly covered with trees and underbrush. While this provided good concealment from the highway, it was almost impossible to walk through. As he was forcing his way through the bushes, Homer heard another car come in from the highway. He found his way back to the driveway and walked to the lodge.

The Jackrabbit's car was pulled up next to his. "Hiya, Van!" said the Jackrabbit. "Any idea where Baby Face is?"

"No idea," said Homer. "I just got here about half an hour ago. No sign of

Nelson or his car."

"I'm sure he'll be here soon," said the Jackrabbit. "What about our accommodations?"

"I talked with the owner," said Homer. "Maybe they're ready by now."

Emil's dogs were barking like crazy. The Jackrabbit strolled up to the pen where they were running back and forth and yapping like maniacs. The Jackrabbit squatted down and held out his hand to the collies. They sniffed his hand and immediately quieted.

"See?" said the Jackrabbit. "They just want to be friends. Now let's see about those rooms."

Sure enough, Emil had prepared the rooms. The gang unloaded their luggage and reconvened in the lobby just as another car pulled into the parking lot. They had never seen it before, but when it came to a stop by the lodge, Baby Face Nelson jumped out. His face was as red as a beet.

"Where the hell have you been?" asked Homer.

"Goddamn Wisconsin drivers!" spat Nelson. "Can't drive for squat. This bastard rammed me, and I had to get another car. It wasn't my fault!"

"What do you mean?" said Nelson's wife, Helen. "He wouldn't have hit you if you hadn't run that stop sign!"

The rest of the gang gaped in astonishment. Baby Face's wife hardly ever made a peep. To have her openly contradict her husband was unheard of. There was a moment of silence, and then everyone burst into laughter.

Everyone except Baby Face. "Aw, shut your traps, all of ya!" he spat. "I've had a helluva trip and just want to relax. Where's the owner of this dump?"

They went into the lodge and found Emil. Nelson handed over his letter of introduction from Cernocky then tore it to pieces when Emil had finished reading it. He seemed like he was starting to relax until he was informed that the rooms in the lodge were full.

"We have the cabin for you," said Emil. "It's very nice and will sleep four quite comfortably."

"Cabin!" roared Nelson. "I don't wanna stay in no fuckin' cabin! I'm in charge here! I should have the good room! You read the letter! *I'm* in charge!"

"Too bad, George," said the Jackrabbit. "Maybe it'll teach you to drive more carefully next time!"

"Aw, cram it, pal!" hissed Baby Face.

"Look, George," said Tommy Carroll. "This cabin don't look too bad. It's right by the lake, see? If the cops do show up, it's the best place to be. Easy to defend and close to an escape route."

Eventually, Nelson consented to staying in the cabin. Emil summoned a bartender to help him and Tommy carry their bags.

"Jeez, these things are heavy," said the bartender. "Whaddaya have in here? Lead bars?"

"Mind your own goddamned business, kid," snapped Nelson. "You'll live longer."

Homer hoped that Baby Face would take his time unpacking. The atmosphere was a lot more relaxed without him around.

The gang spent the rest of the day lounging around the bar, drinking and playing cards. Baby Face returned after a while, and he was in a surprisingly good mood. He bought round after round and tipped heavily. The mood was light and relaxed. It was a welcome change from the tension in Chicago.

"Hey, Emil," said the Jackrabbit. "How 'bout some grub? I'm getting a little hungry."

"We normally serve dinner at five thirty," said Emil. "People will begin showing up around five. I'm sure I can get my wife to cook you up some steaks, though."

"Wait," said Homer. "People are going to be coming here to eat?"

"Yes, there will be a few tonight," said Emil. "But Sunday night it'll *really* be busy. My Dollar-a-Plate Sunday Dinner is very popular. Y'see, I just bought this place three years ago, got a huge mortgage. I'm one of the few places around here that stays open year-round. I have to pay the bills, right? The bar and the dinners help with that."

Homer wasn't happy about the situation. This was supposed to be an out-of-the way retreat. He didn't want to worry about every rube in the countryside piling in for a cheap chicken dinner.

"Glad you mentioned it," said Red Hamilton. "We'll just eat now and stay

81

out of your hair when your guests arrive."

They sat down to a steak dinner that Emil's wife, Nan, prepared just for them. She was a skinny woman with a pinched face and a suspicious expression. After they ate, the gang retired to their rooms before the regulars showed up for the evening meal.

Fortunately, there weren't very many of them, and they didn't stay very long. By the time the gang began to filter back in, there were just a few lumberjacks drinking in the bar. Eventually, the lumberjacks left, and the Jackrabbit talked Emil into a game of five-card stud.

As usual, the famous Jackrabbit luck was in effect, and he ended up winning most of the hands. At one point, the pot grew to thirty-five dollars, and the betting and bluffing became intense.

Homer had a crap hand, and he was never any good at bluffing, so he threw his cards in as soon as the betting got heavy. Eventually, it came down to the Jackrabbit and Emil.

"OK, Emil, my boy," said the Jackrabbit. "I call. Show me what you got."

Emil laid down his cards. "Two pair, jacks and kings."

"Ha! Ha!" said the Jackrabbit. "Good, but not good enough. Full house." He laid down his hand—queens over threes.

Emil tossed down his cards in disgust. "You have the luck of the devil!" he said.

The Jackrabbit leaned far over the table to rake in the pile of cash. His jacket fell open to reveal the twin .45s in matched shoulder holsters. Homer saw Emil's eyes lock on the guns and widen.

"Well, fellas, I'm beat," Emil said. "Off to bed."

"Hey, what's the rush?" said Tommy. "It's still early."

"N-nope," said Emil. "Not for me. I'm bushed." He pushed back from the table and scuttled out of the room.

"I'd better go after him," said the Jackrabbit.

Homer followed them down the hallway that led to the kitchen. The Jackrabbit grabbed Emil by the elbow. "Say, Emil, what's wrong?" he asked. "You look like you've just seen a ghost."

"I-I think I just figured out who you are," stammered Emil.

"Is that going to be a problem for you?"

"L-look, I don't want no trouble. Every cent I have is tied up in this place. I can't risk it getting shot up or something. I got a family to worry about."

"Hey, there's not going to be any trouble," said the Jackrabbit. "No risk, no shooting. Your family will be fine. We just want to rest up for the weekend, then come Monday we'll be on our way. We'll pay triple the going rate too."

"*Triple?*" said Emil. "Well, I guess that will be OK then."

Having defused the situation, Homer and the Jackrabbit returned to the bar. The gang played a few more hands of cards, but nobody's heart was in the game. The game broke up a half hour later. Homer went up to the room he shared with Marie, but he had a hard time falling asleep. The Little Bohemia Lodge was not as restful as he had hoped.

\* \* \*

The next morning, the gang met in the lobby to discuss the situation.

"There's too many damn people coming and going from this joint," said Baby Face. "We need to keep an eye on who shows up, who's using the telephone. There needs to be one or two of us keeping an eye on things at all times."

"Yeah, I agree with you there, George," said Homer. "This place is a little hinky for me. I need to send Reilly to Saint Paul to pick up some cash from the Green Lantern, so he won't be around to stand guard."

"Hey, do you mind if Pat goes along?" asked Red. "She ain't feeling too well. Lady problems. I'd like her to see a doctor."

"Yeah, sure," said Homer. "I actually don't like the idea of being without my car, but I really need the cash that Sawyer's keeping for me. Maybe after that we could see about finding a quieter place to stay—like Union Station!"

Reilly and Pat headed out to Saint Paul in Homer's brand-new Ford. The rest of the gang tried to relax, but it was impossible. The air of leisure they had enjoyed the previous afternoon was long gone. Homer spent most of the morning pacing around the lobby, fretting and muttering to himself. Shortly before noon, the Jackrabbit came down from his room.

"Hiya, Van! How's tricks?"

"Too goddamn tricky, if you ask me," said Homer. "This whole deal stinks. There's too many damn people around this place. That Nan Wanatka doesn't want us here, that's for sure. And half the county's going to be showing up tomorrow night for the damn buck-a-plate dinner."

"Yeah, I know what you mean," said the Jackrabbit. "This isn't what I was hoping for, either. I think after Reilly and Pat get back from Saint Paul, we should shove off. I'd feel better being back in the city."

Baby Face Nelson strolled up. "You keepin' an eye on things, boys?"

"Yeah, George," said the Jackrabbit. "We sure are. But this doesn't feel right to me. Too busy. There's people in and out of here all the time."

"Shit . . . here comes another one now," said Nelson. "Van Meter, go find out who that is."

Emil's dogs began barking as a beat-up brown Chrysler pulled into the parking lot. "Stupid dogs," muttered Homer. He went to look for Emil to ask him if he knew who the driver was.

"It's my brother-in-law, Henry," said Emil. "My nephew is having a birthday party this afternoon. There'll be some family members around and about."

"That's just swell," said Homer.

Henry was skinny and hatchet-faced like his sister. Nan rushed from the kitchen to meet him as he walked in the front door. "Henry!" she cried. "I'm so glad you're here. We bought too much meat for the weekend. You should take some of it to cook at the party. Come on!"

She practically dragged Henry to the kitchen. Homer followed along to keep tabs on their conversation. They were having an intense discussion right outside the pantry door.

"Will your friends be coming along to Eddie's birthday party?" asked Nan.

"I don't know," said Henry. "I was going to give them a call on my way to the store."

"Well, you better get going then."

"OK," said Henry. "Say, I left my cigarettes at home. You don't happen to have any, do you?"

Immediately, Nan produced a pack from her apron and thrust it into Henry's hands. "Here you go. I just opened it. There should be plenty."

Homer thought this was odd. It was as if she'd been expecting the question. Well, maybe the guy was just a mooch.

Henry turned to leave, and Homer faded back to the lobby. There was no further discussion of the meat that Nan supposedly wanted to give away. Homer slunk into an armchair and watched as Henry climbed into his rattletrap Chrysler and drove off. Baby Face was right—Nan was up to something. He would have to keep a close eye on her.

But first, he went upstairs and made sure all his stuff was packed. He had the feeling they would have to leave Little Bohemia Lodge in a hurry.

# CHAPTER TWELVE

**Chicago, Illinois
April 22, 1934**

D oris wasn't especially surprised to get a call from Mr. Purvis just before lunchtime telling her to get into the office right away. These sudden weekend calls to the office were not unusual. Still, there was something in his voice that made it sound like this was more than just the standard fire drill. He hadn't explained—just told her to get in there *now*—and then hung up the phone.

As the El train clattered through the Loop, she wondered if Bessie Green had finally given them some useful information. After the Jackrabbit and his gang had gotten away from the apartment in Saint Paul, there had been a burst of optimism when Bessie had agreed to talk. She had provided some useful information, but it had become outdated in a hurry. The agents raided a number of apartments used by the Jackrabbit Gang, but by the time they got there, the occupants were long gone.

More troubling were stories that had surfaced about Bessie's husband, Eddie. He had been gravely wounded in Saint Paul and had lingered in the hospital for more than a week without passing on any useful information. Now, some of the newspapers were saying that he'd been shot in ambush, and agents had drilled him in the back without giving him the chance to surrender. Just as unsettling were reports that FBI agents had impersonated doctors and nurses in order to coax information from the dying man.

Doris didn't know what to make of these reports. She knew quite well that newspapers were not above publishing gross exaggerations or outright lies in order to sell a few extra papers. On the other hand, she knew very well that the bureau could be heavy-handed when it came to dealing with suspected criminals. She was no fool about what went on in the "interview room."

Previously, she hadn't much cared. These people were criminals and thugs who wanted to destroy the American way of life. If they got caught by the good guys, then they got what they deserved. But lately, she wasn't so certain about that. Ever since her conversation with Billie in the ladies' room, she'd begun wondering more and more about people who had accidentally been caught up in a big mess. If one encountered a bad circumstance or made a poor choice, things could just go downhill quickly with no way to get off the ride.

Doris couldn't afford to let such thoughts cloud her judgment now, though. There was something big going on today, and Mr. Purvis needed her help. She just hoped that things would be resolved as peacefully as possible. She squared her shoulders and pushed through the front door to the office.

It was like walking into an armed camp. Agents ran back and forth, holding pistols, rifles, and other weapons. Two agents were handing out bulletproof vests. Boxes of ammunition and packs of cigarettes were being doled out like candy at Halloween.

As Carter Baum hurried past, Doris grabbed him by the arm and asked, "Carter, what is this? What on earth is going on?"

"They're in Wisconsin!" shouted Baum. "Someplace called Manitoba or something!" He dashed across the bull pen and began rummaging through a seldom-used closet.

More agents showed up, some still tying their ties as they dashed through the door. Mr. Purvis came in shortly after Doris, still buttoning his shirt and adjusting his tie.

"What is it? What's going on?" she asked.

"It's the Jackrabbit," said Mr. Purvis. "We've gotten a tip thayut he's holed up at a fishing resort in Wisconsin. We can git him! We hayve him trapped!" He was flushed and his southern accent was much more noticeable.

"What can I do?" asked Doris.

"Raht now, Ah need you to find me an airplane," said Mr. Purvis. "Staht calling the airlines at the municipal ayahport. We need a charter that will take us to . . ." he consulted a scrap of paper, ". . . Rhinelander, Wisconsin."

Doris got on the phone and started calling the airline desks. On her third try, she got lucky: United Air Lines had a plane available at thirty-five cents a mile. Doris told them to fuel it up, and the passengers would be there in less than an hour.

After that, she was making nearly constant calls to FBI headquarters in Washington and the field office in Minneapolis. Another group of agents from that office were heading toward Rhinelander as well. After twenty minutes of frantic calling, she hung up the phone and stopped to rest.

Carter Baum pulled up short in front of her desk, face plastered with a goofy grin. "Can you believe it, Doris? I think we'll finally get him this time! I can feel it!"

"That's great, Carter! I hope you get him. How did you find out where he was?"

"Well, they're staying at a hunting lodge upstate. The owner's wife got suspicious and smuggled out a message to her brother in a pack of cigarettes. The brother knows a deputy at the US Marshall's office here in Chicago. Mr. Purvis spoke to him directly. He's 99 percent convinced that it's the Jackrabbit staying there—him and his entire gang. We can put the whole bunch out of commission!"

"That would be great!" Doris exclaimed. "I just hope nobody gets hurt."

"Quit your worrying, Dore. This is going to be a cakewalk. Finally, I'll get to see some excitement!" He looked around and leaned closer to Doris conspiratorially. "You know, when I first applied to the Bureau, I thought it was just going to be a bunch of boring desk work. I just wanted a job until the economy picked up. Then I'd go back to Milwaukee, get a position in a law firm there, and settle down. I never thought this job would be so . . . so thrilling. It's like playing cops and robbers for real!"

Doris started to say that this was no game, but someone cut her off. "Who's got the dratted key to the heavy weapons locker? Carter?"

"Harry has it!" yelled Carter. "I think he's in the interview room!" Carter sprinted off toward Harry's last known whereabouts without looking back. "He looks just like a little boy running off to recess," Doris thought.

She sat down and took a deep breath. A sickly feeling was growing in the pit of her stomach. The agents seemed so excited and happy, but she didn't share their enthusiasm. This was serious business. Every day, the newspapers had an account of the violent misdeeds of the Jackrabbit and his gang. Now the agents—her boys—were going to confront them. She just hoped that the whole thing would be over quickly and with minimum bloodshed. She wanted her boys to come home safely.

Mr. Purvis stepped out of his office, took a look at the bedlam, and checked his watch. He took a deep breath and yelled, "Make haste, men! We need to be on our way in fahve minutes! No mo'! Now move!"

Doris winced; it always surprised her to hear her normally soft-spoken boss bellowing like a bullfrog. Across the room, a brief cheer went up as the heavy weapons locker was opened. "Take 'em all, fellas!" Doris heard Allan Lockerman yell. "Empty that son of a bitch out!" Doris suppressed a grin.

"Agent Lockerman!" hollered Mr. Purvis. "You ah an agent of the Federal Bureau of Investigation! You do not use such language, regahdless of the circumstances!"

"Yes, Chief! Sorry, Chief!" Allan said. Doris noticed him concealing a little smirk, as if the teacher had reprimanded him for cutting up in class.

Allan saw her watching him and hurried over to her desk. Despite the turmoil in the office, he seemed like he was keeping calm. "So, Doris," he said. "It looks like I've got a little business out of town. When I get back, I'd really like to take you to that Italian place. What do you say?"

"Yes, that sounds wonderful," said Doris. "You just be safe and come back, OK?" Once again, she realized that her agents were really going into a dangerous situation. There might actually be gunfire! She was much less concerned with future social engagements and more concerned with boys like Carter Baum and Allan Lockerman coming back unharmed.

"Don't worry, Doris. Everything will be fine, you'll see." He gave her a wide smile then headed off to the ammunition locker.

Soon, the epicenter of the roiling mob began moving toward the door. It seemed like every man was carrying an armload of weapons and equipment. Mr. Purvis oversaw the departure of the two carloads of agents who would be driving up and carrying most of the gear. He would be flying in the United charter along with nine other agents.

He shrugged on his overcoat and turned to Doris. "Perhaps you should go home and get some rayust," he said. "It will take us several hours to get to Rhinelander then at least another hour to get to this lodge. At that point, Ah'll need you at your desk to relay messages to Washington, if need be. Until then, trah to get some sleep. Lord knows none of us will be able to."

"Are you feeling all right, Mr. Purvis? You look a little peaked."

"Oh, Ah'll be fine once we get to Wisconsin." He lowered his voice to a whisper. "Ah'm going to let you in on a little secret, Ms. Rogers."

"What's that, sir?"

"Ah'm scared silly of flying."

# CHAPTER THIRTEEN

### Manitowish Waters, Wisconsin
### April 22, 1934

"There go those goddamn dogs!" said Baby Face Nelson. Emil's collies were going berserk again. The dogs had been doing so all weekend, but the members of the gang were so jumpy that they'd been unable to get used to it.

"It's nothing," said the Jackrabbit. "They probably just saw a bird."

The gang had convened in the bar for a meeting. They'd been waiting all afternoon for Reilly and Pat Cherrington to return, but there was still no sign of them. They'd had an early dinner in anticipation of a quick departure. Now, hours later, there was still no sign of the two. The gang had lain low while Emil's famous Sunday dinner was underway. At this point, there were only three lumberjacks left drinking in the bar.

"Look, something's happened to them," said Tommy. "We can't wait around forever."

"I don't know," said Homer. "Let's give 'em just a few more minutes, but then we should cut out." In truth, he was worried. He was concerned about getting his new car back, but mostly he just wanted to get the hell away from Little Bohemia. The tension had been cranking up all weekend, and he was about ready to jump out of his skin.

"We've been waiting all goddamn day for 'em," said Baby Face. "Screw 'em. They can look after themselves."

"What do you think?" Red asked the Jackrabbit.

"Uh, I think we've hung around here as long as we should," said the Jackrabbit. "I'm in favor of hauling stakes."

"Damn straight," said Baby Face. "I'm gonna go get my stuff." He stomped off toward the cabin.

The three lumberjacks got up from the bar and headed out the door. Homer wasn't sorry to see them go. He would be glad to be gone himself. "Hey," he said. "Who are me and Marie gonna ride with? Don't make us ride with Nelson. I don't wanna get in a wreck with that loon behind the wheel."

"Don't sweat it, Van," said the Jackrabbit. "There's plenty of room in my car. We'll be gone like a cool breeze in no time."

From outside, the dogs started barking again—this time louder than ever. This was followed by the rattling report of a Tommy gun being fired then a firecracker string of pistol shots.

"Jesus!" cried Homer. "Too late! It's a raid!"

Tommy threw himself down behind one of the front windows and raised his head just far enough to see. "Holy shit!" he said. "There's a bunch of guys with guns out there! They just shot the shit out of those lumberjacks!"

"OK, we gotta move fast," said the Jackrabbit. "Red, get the girls into the basement. The rest of us better get upstairs and get our typewriters."

Homer followed Tommy and the Jackrabbit up to the rooms. The Jackrabbit ducked into his room, which faced out back. Homer's room was across the hall, facing front. He hunched over and scuttled into the room to retrieve his Tommy gun from under the bed. He crept up to the window and hazarded a peek outside.

In the corner of the parking lot, a beat-up Chevrolet coupe was riddled with bullets. A bunch of men holding Tommy guns and pistols were standing around the car. A man was lying next to the coupe, not moving.

"Goddamn cops!" cried Homer. He smashed out the window glass with the muzzle of the Tommy gun and sent a long burst of rounds toward the men. They returned fire immediately. Homer jumped back out of the way and dashed into the hall.

Just then, the Jackrabbit emerged from his room. "Nothing out back," he reported. "We can get onto the roof from my room. Then we jump down and make a run for the lake."

"Look, I'm gonna go back to the cabin," said Tommy. "See if George needs any help."

"It's your funeral, brother," said the Jackrabbit.

As Tommy rushed down the stairs, he passed Red, who was on his way up from the basement. "The girls are safe," he reported.

"Good," said the Jackrabbit. "Let's go."

They scrambled out the window and skittered to the corner of the roof. It was an eight foot drop to the ground, but fortunately there was a large pile of snow below. They dropped down and stumbled to the edge of the lake.

From behind them came a sustained burst of machine-gun fire, and then Baby Face's voice: "Hah! Ya like that ya bastards?"

"Holy crow!" said Red. "That little psycho is actually *enjoying* this!"

"Never mind him," said the Jackrabbit. "He can sink or swim on his own. Let's move!"

They stumbled through the woods along the edge of the lake, trying to keep to the overgrown path. There was another round of firing from the lodge and then silence.

"The road should be right up here to our right," said Homer. They pushed through a cluster of bushes and found themselves standing on the edge of the highway. Headlights were approaching in the distance.

"Ah, I see our ride now," said Homer. He stepped up to the shoulder and stuck out his thumb. An ambulance zipped by, closely followed by a station wagon. Neither slowed down.

"You're too ugly to get us a ride," Red said with a laugh.

"Who the hell you callin' ugly?" demanded Homer. He was sensitive about his looks. His nerves had been on edge this entire weekend—especially since they'd just managed to slide out from an ambush. It seemed stupid to get mad at Red about some offhand remark, but he could see the red ring creeping around his vision. He took a few deep breaths, and it faded.

"Steady, fellas," said the Jackrabbit. "Let's check out that place across the road." He indicated a sign on the other side of the highway that read "Mitchell's Rest Resort Cabins." Lights could be seen beyond the trees.

The three gangsters trooped up the dirt driveway until they came to a large cabin. A tired-looking Model T pickup truck was parked beside it. A number of other smaller cabins sat farther back in the trees. Most of them were dark, but there were lights on in the main cabin.

"I'll handle this," volunteered Red. "Hang back a bit."

He marched up to the door and gave it a brisk rap. After a moment, an elderly man stuck his head out. "May I help you?" he asked.

"Yes, I seem to be lost," said Red. "Could I possibly trouble you for a glass of water?"

The old man hesitated. "Well, I guess so . . ."

Red shouldered past the man, marched across the room, and ripped the telephone from the wall. "OK, fellas!" he hollered to his companions.

The Jackrabbit and Homer followed Red into the cabin. The old man recoiled in fear. "My God, don't hurt us!" he said. "We'll do whatever you want. Please!"

"Are you Mitchell?" asked the Jackrabbit. "Is this your place?"

"Y-yes. Yes, it is," stammered Mitchell. "Do what you want with me, just leave my wife out of it. She's ill."

An elderly woman was reclining on a well-worn couch in the center of the room. She seemed unperturbed as she squinted at the men. "You wouldn't happen to be the Jackrabbit?" she asked.

A fractured grin spread up the side of the Jackrabbit's face. "You couldn't be more right, ma'am," he said. "Look, we don't want to harm a hair on your heads, Mr. Mitchell. We just need a ride. Does that truck run?"

"Naw," said Mitchell. "It hasn't started since last October, I reckon."

"Well, is there anyone else around here that has a car?" asked Red.

"Mr. Johnson, my carpenter, has a car," said Mitchell. "His place is just behind here."

"Let's go pay him a visit," said Red.

Johnson's door was answered by a sleepy-eyed man in a tattered bathrobe. He seemed confused by the sight of his boss and three strange men with guns.

"Sorry to bother you," said the Jackrabbit. "Mrs. Mitchell is very sick. We need a ride to town."

"You'd better do as they say, Johnson," said Mitchell.

"What?" said Johnson. "I don't understand?"

Homer was getting tired of these Northwoods hicks. He pulled out his pistol and stuck it in Johnson's face. "Look, it's simple," he said. "We get in your car, and you drive us where we want to go. If you do that, we won't shoot you. Get it?"

"Oh my God!" Johnson wailed.

They went down to Johnson's car. "Do you need me to come with you?" asked Mitchell.

"No, Dad," said the Jackrabbit. "You go tend to your wife."

As they climbed into the black Ford coupe, another prolonged burst of gunfire came from the south.

"I don't think that's coming from anywhere near the lodge," said Red.

"Sounds like it's coming from Koerner's," said Johnson.

"It's Nelson—gotta be Nelson," said Homer. "He got away from the lodge, and now he's starting a fight somewhere else. That boy is crazier'n a shithouse rat!" He was thankful that Baby Face hadn't come with them. His old benefactor was turning out to be a serious liability.

"What's in the opposite direction from Koerner's?" asked the Jackrabbit.

"The village of Manitowish Waters, and beyond that, the town of Mercer," said Johnson.

"Perfect," said the Jackrabbit. "Head for Mercer."

The tiny village of Manitowish Waters was dark and shut up tight. Mercer wasn't much better. The only open business was an all-night gas station. The black coupe cruised slowly by and came to a stop fifty yards past the station.

"Here's where you get out, Mr. Johnson," said the Jackrabbit. Johnson squealed and scampered from the car with his arms wrapped around his head.

"Here's a few nickels to call yourself a ride," called Homer. He tossed a handful of coins at the cowering man, who shrieked and rolled over into the snow.

"What a bunch of weirdos they have up here," said Homer. "Let's beat it."

# CHAPTER FOURTEEN

**Hastings, Minnesota**
**April 23, 1934**

"Oh shit!" said Red. "There's a cop car!"

It was shortly after dawn, and they had just driven down the corkscrew ramp of the Spiral Bridge that spanned the Mississippi River. They'd been driving all night to put as much distance as possible between themselves and Little Bohemia. After deciding that Chicago would be too hot, they were attempting to make it to Saint Paul.

The Jackrabbit craned around in his seat. He was riding shotgun; Homer was behind the wheel with Red squeezed into the middle. "I can't see them," said the Jackrabbit. "Maybe they were just looking for speeders."

Homer glanced in the rearview mirror. Behind them, a cattle truck lumbered into the lane, blocking the view behind them. "I can't see anything, either," he said.

"It's probably nothing," said the Jackrabbit. "Just drive casually."

With great effort, Homer managed to stick to the speed limit. He continually scanned the rearview mirror but couldn't see past the cattle truck. After a few minutes, it turned off onto a side road. It was clear behind them.

"I think it's OK," Homer reported. "I don't think . . . wait." A dot in the rearview mirror was growing rapidly. Something was coming up behind them—fast. "Oh shit! I think the cops are back!"

All of a sudden, there was an explosion as the rear window blew in. Homer managed to keep from swerving and hazarded a glance in the rearview mirror. The cop car was right behind them. Two cops were leaning out of the windows, brandishing rifles. There was the distinctive *ka-chow ka-chow* of a .351 automatic rifle. The car shuddered as the slugs punched into the trunk.

The Jackrabbit reached under his seat and came up with a Tommy gun. He emptied a drum through the back window. Red joined in with a .45 pistol, firing until the clip was empty. The cop car dropped back a few lengths then closed the gap again. The cops unleashed another barrage of gunfire. Homer hunched over the steering wheel, looking for an opening in the traffic ahead of them.

"Damn, they have us outgunned," said the Jackrabbit. "We need to get away from these bastards."

"There's too much traffic," said Homer. "I can't get around."

Another fusillade of bullets slammed into the car.

"We're getting pretty close to Saint Paul," said Red. "If we can just get past—AHHH! I'M HIT!"

Red slumped over. A red stain spread out behind him on the upholstery. "Ah, Christ, that hurts!" he said. "How bad does it look?"

"Ah, it's nothing," said the Jackrabbit. "You'll be dancing the Charleston by tonight." He locked eyes with Homer and gave his head a little shake. It was bad.

Homer spotted an opening in the traffic. He floored the accelerator and squeezed through a gap between a convertible full of teenagers and another cattle truck. There wasn't enough room for the cop car to make it. Having bought a bit of breathing room, Homer kept the pedal to the mat, trying to increase the gap between them and the cops.

Beside him, Red moaned. "Hang on, buddy," said the Jackrabbit. "We'll get you patched up."

Homer checked the rearview mirror again—no sign of the cops. Good enough, but he knew that it was just a matter of time before the police would be back. He had to find a place to turn off.

The highway made a broad, slow curve through a wooded area. Homer kept the accelerator down as far as he dared. Teetering on the edge of control, he could feel the tires almost ready to break free and send them cartwheeling into the woods. He desperately scanned ahead for a turnoff. Up ahead, the trees thinned and the road straightened out. There was a dirt road leading off to the right. Perfect.

"Hang on," said Homer. He hit the brakes and spun the wheel hard. The car skidded to the right and fishtailed violently. He frantically spun the wheel hard left then right again. The car straightened out and shot down the dirt road.

He ran the car down the road then stood on the brakes. Homer and the Jackrabbit were out the doors as soon as the car had come to a stop. They crouched down by the fenders, guns drawn. The only sounds were their harsh gasps and the sounds of birds in the woods.

Nothing happened.

At the end of the road, they could see traffic zipping by on the highway. No cars turned up the road after them.

"You ditched them," said the Jackrabbit. "Good job, Van! You're an ace wheelman!"

Homer felt an absurd swell of pride. Praise was something that he wasn't used to receiving.

A moan came from inside the car.

"Aw, shit," said Homer. "Red."

They rushed back to the car. Red was doubled over, his breath coming in harsh gasps. "How . . . how is it? Is it bad?"

"Nah, pal, it's nothing," said the Jackrabbit. "Couple of gauze pads and some surgical tape and you'll be right as rabbits."

"B-b-bullshit," sputtered Red. "I'm pretty messed up. I know it."

"Hey, don't worry," said Homer. "I seen guys get hit way worse than you, and they pulled through just fine." He hoped the lie didn't sound as obvious to Red as it did to his own ears.

"We can't just sit here jawing," said the Jackrabbit. "We've got to beat feet for the city. You think you can get us there on the back roads?"

"Sure thing," said Homer. "We'd better ditch the car, though."

"Right," said the Jackrabbit. "But first, let's put some distance between us and that highway. The cops will double back soon enough."

For the next hour, they cruised the back roads, working their way toward the Saint Paul city limits. Homer navigated the unfamiliar roads by the position of the sun and pure instinct. When they got close to a populated area, he pulled over to the side of the gravel road and got out.

Soon, a four-door Dodge approached. Homer stood in the middle of the road with his hand held up like a traffic cop. The car rolled to a stop. A young man sat behind the wheel. There was a young woman and a two-year-old boy in the back seat.

"Is something wrong?" asked the man.

Homer pulled out his pistol. "I'm terribly sorry to have to do this to you," he said. "But I'm afraid we need your machine."

"Roy?" asked the woman. "What's happening? Why do those men have guns?"

The Jackrabbit stepped up to the car. "You heard my friend," he said. "We're taking your car. We're taking you too. Get in the back seat, please, sir."

"Oh my God!" wailed the woman. "Don't hurt my baby!"

"Don't worry, ma'am," said the Jackrabbit. "We won't hurt anybody. We like kids. Van, you keep our new friends company. I'll go get Red."

The Jackrabbit managed to get Red transferred from Mr. Johnson's Chevy to the front seat of the Dodge. The back of Red's coat and pants were bright red with blood. The woman in the back seat screamed when she saw it.

"Don't worry about the upholstery, lady," said Homer. "The stains will come out with a little white vinegar."

Homer started the car and proceeded to zig and zag across country roads, all the time heading in the direction of the city. The Jackrabbit twisted around in the seat to chat with the hostages.

"So what's your name, pal?" he asked.

"R-roy Francis," answered the man.

"Well, Mr. Francis, I apologize for the inconvenience," said the Jackrabbit. "As you can see, we're in a bit of a pickle here."

There was no response, just heavy breathing from the back seat. Homer was afraid that one of the Francises would panic and do something stupid. He thought it best to try and distract them. "Where do you work?" he asked.

Mr. Francis seemed confused by this question. "I . . . I work for the power company," he said. "I'm on my lunch break. The baby wouldn't go down for his nap, so we thought we'd take a little drive to help him get to sleep."

"You're lucky," said the Jackrabbit. "You've got a good job and a nice family. I'd give anything for that."

"Johnnie?" said Red weakly. "I'm thirsty. Really thirsty. Can we get something to drink?"

"You bet, pal," said the Jackrabbit. "Van, better find a service station. We can gas up and get something for Red to drink."

A few minutes later, they approached a Texaco station. The Jackrabbit twisted around in his seat again. "OK, Francis family, we are going to make a quick stop now. Please don't cause any trouble while we do. I don't want to threaten you, but as you can see, we are desperate men." To emphasize this, he let his jacket fall open to reveal the pistol in his shoulder holster. Mrs. Francis gave a small yelp.

They pulled into the gas station, and the Jackrabbit popped out of the car. "Fill 'er up, buddy," he told the attendant. He leaned up against the passenger's-side door to block the view of Red bleeding in the front seat. While the tank filled, the Jackrabbit shot the breeze with the gas station attendant about the Cubs' prospects for the season.

"Say, you got any pop?" asked the Jackrabbit.

"Cooler's over by the front door," said the attendant.

The Jackrabbit sauntered over and retrieved two Nehis. Homer nervously watched the attendant, but the man wasn't paying any attention to the people in the car.

"What do I owe you?" asked the Jackrabbit after the tank had been filled.

"Buck ninety."

The Jackrabbit pulled out two singles and handed them over. "Normally, I'd tell you to keep the change," he said. "But you know how things are."

"Don't I just," said the attendant. He went back to the office.

The Jackrabbit leaned against the front fender, grinning at the sky and whistling "California, Here I Come." Homer marveled at his friend's cool demeanor. He had just escaped from a violent shoot-out and a car chase, and there was a bleeding man in the front seat. Yet here he was, whistling and waiting on ten cents change like he hadn't a care in the world.

When their business was concluded, he climbed back into the car, and they took off down the road. Ten minutes later, the Jackrabbit signaled Homer to pull over.

"OK, Francis family," said the Jackrabbit. "Here's where you get out."

"Thank God!" exclaimed Mrs. Francis. She practically leapt out of the car with the child in her arms.

"What about our car?" asked Mr. Francis.

"Sorry," said the Jackrabbit. "We're going to have to hang onto it for a little while longer. But look on the bright side: you and your family have a story that you'll be able to tell for the rest of your lives."

"I'd rather have the car," said Mr. Francis.

"Too damn bad," said Homer. He threw the car in gear and left the Francis family standing in a cloud of dust.

# CHAPTER FIFTEEN

### Chicago, Illinois
### April 23, 1934

T he nineteenth floor of the Bankers Building was like something out of a nightmare. The elevator opened onto a crowd of baying newspapermen. Doris pushed her way past the barking mob without responding to their questions and slid into the office.

Inside, the atmosphere was funereal. Doris had been at the office late the night before helping to relay the news from northern Wisconsin. None of it was good. First came the information that agents had accidentally opened fire on a car containing three civilians. One of the civilians had been killed outright, and the other two were wounded.

Then came the devastating news that Carter Baum had been shot and killed. Another agent, Jay Newman, had been severely wounded, as had a local police officer named Christiansen. The suspected killer was a hitherto low-level gangster called Baby Face Nelson.

Doris fell apart when then news of Baum's death had been called into the office. She barely kept herself together long enough to relay the news to Washington. Then she had gone home, leaving the telephone switchboard to the agents who had remained in the Chicago office.

Getting up the strength to come into the office this morning had been a herculean effort. She slumped into her desk chair and tried to focus on her work. The minutes dragged by like a funeral cortege.

Groups of agents filed into the office throughout the morning. At quarter to twelve, another cluster of exhausted-looking agents trooped in the front door. They were disheveled and downcast, their eyes glued to the floor. Johnny McLaughlin was among the group. He shuffled up to Doris's desk.

Doris tensed up. Johnny had asked her out a time or two after their first date, and she had politely refused. Still, he hadn't seemed to have gotten the hint. Doris hoped that he wasn't about to ask her out again, especially now.

"Is Mr. Purvis in his office?" Johnny asked.

"Yes, he is," said Doris solemnly. "But he's asked not to be disturbed."

"I can't blame him. What a disaster!"

"What in the world happened, Johnny? How could things have gone so wrong?"

"Ah, jeez, where to begin?" said Johnny. "It was a mess from the get-go. We rushed up there without any planning, without the right equipment. And without any leadership."

"Johnny, no!" said Doris. "You shouldn't say that about Mr. Purvis! That's insubordination!"

"I wasn't saying it about him—not exactly. The problem was that SAC Hanni from Minneapolis was there as well, and so was Inspector Rorer from D.C. Nobody really knew who was in charge. The Bureau threw everything but the kitchen sink at that place when the tip came in. We tore right up there, and things fell apart immediately. Those poor lumberjacks came out of the lodge, and we all thought it was the gang trying to make a break for it. I don't know who shot first, but it didn't matter. Carter had a Thompson, and he just raked that car from stem to stern. When he found out that he'd killed a civilian, he almost broke down crying."

Doris felt her blood run cold. It was one thing to get the awful news, but hearing the details made it much, much worse. She wished she could just blot it out—put her fingers in her ears and pretend it never happened. That wasn't really a possibility, though, because she wanted to know—she needed to know. Just the thought of Carter Baum made her throat close up, and she knew that tears wouldn't be far behind. Johnny looked like he might start crying himself. "Johnny, no," she said. "You don't have to—"

"Yes, I do Doris. This has been eating me up inside—it's been bad on all of us. Especially what happened next. Purvis saw how bad Carter was doing, so he decided to send him off on an errand to help ease his mind a little. He sent Carter and Jay Newman to a nearby telephone exchange to report what had happened. We're still not sure exactly what happened next, but somehow Baby Face Nelson got the drop on them. He killed Carter and wounded Jay and a local police officer. Then he stole their car."

"That monster!" hissed Doris. "I hope they hang him from a sour apple tree!"

Johnny didn't seem to hear her. "Back at the lodge, we just waited," he said. "We sat around until dawn, miserable and freezing cold. We thought the gang was still inside, and we just needed the car with the tear gas guns to show up so we could flush them out.

"When the car showed up, it didn't make a lick of difference. Those darn tear gas shells just bounced off the storm windows. They asked for a volunteer to rush the lodge with a regular tear gas grenade. I was one of the few there who wasn't married, so I raised my hand."

"Oh, Johnny, that's so brave!"

Johnny barked a bitter laugh. "Oh, yes, quite. When I tossed that grenade, I bravely flushed out three women and a busboy. We found out later that the entire gang had escaped just a few minutes after the shooting started. All of that mess—ALL of it—was for nothing."

"Don't say that," said Doris. "You didn't know."

"That was the problem, Doris. *Nobody* knew. Nobody knew *anything*. We didn't know how to get there, we didn't know the lay of the land, we didn't know any of the local law enforcement agencies, we didn't know that there were civilians in the car we shot to hell. We didn't know jack shit!"

Doris bristled. She could feel the wall she had put up against her emotions starting to crumble. She knew that Johnny McLaughlin and the other agents had gone through a hellish experience. There was a hollow look in Johnny's eyes that was alarming and a little bit scary. Reflexively, she said, "Agent McLaughlin! Watch your language! What if Mr. Purvis hears you? You could lose your job!"

Johnny shrugged. "I can think of worse things than losing my job. Such as taking three bullets in the throat like Carter did."

Doris slumped. She had resolutely avoided thinking about Carter Baum all morning. She felt the tears welling up in her eyes, and her vision started to blur. "Oh . . . oh, poor Carter! That poor man! I . . . I just can't. . . . Who's going to tell his family?"

"That duty will undoubtedly fall to our impeccable Special Agent in Charge," said Johnny. "It's the least he can do."

"Johnny—" Doris began, but McLaughlin held up his hand to silence her.

"I'm sorry, Doris. I'm not myself today. I'm not sure that I ever will be again." He turned and shuffled off to his desk.

Just then, the telephone rang. It was a call for Mr. Purvis from the director's office. She waited for a few seconds then discreetly lifted the receiver to listen in.

". . . utmost confidence, Mel," Director Hoover said. "You have my full support, make no mistake about it."

"Thank you, sir," said Mr. Purvis. "I know how bad this looks, and I take full responsibility. Some of the newspapers are already calling for my ouster."

"Pfah! The newspapers! They're just an impediment to us doing our jobs. I'd rather we didn't have to deal with them at all. Well, you needn't worry about them—that's *my* job. You just do your job and let me handle the press. In the meantime, just keep away from them."

"I'm not sure how I can do that, sir. They're lined up outside the office." Doris looked over her shoulder. It was true; the mob of reporters in the hallway was growing by the minute.

"Just don't say anything to them," said Hoover. "Refer them to headquarters. Your job is to catch the Jackrabbit, Mel. My job is to help you do your job. That includes handling those two-legged jackals that call themselves newspapermen."

"Yes, sir. I appreciate that."

"Good. I'll want a detailed report on my desk by first thing tomorrow morning."

"Yes, sir. Absolutely."

Doris gently replaced the receiver.

The rest of the day was spent in glum concentration on the tasks at hand. Doris tried to avoid thinking about what had happened to Carter Baum and the poor lumberjacks who'd been accidentally shot. Everyone in the office kept their heads down, moving slowly, not talking. The mood in the office had a tangible feeling of oppression. Doris found herself sneaking frequent peeks at the wall clock. It crept.

Later in the afternoon, another batch of agents slunk into the office, freshly returned from Wisconsin. They were the ones that started the rumor. It was no secret that some of the newspapers were calling for Mr. Purvis's removal. Now the rumor was that Samuel Cowley, one of Hoover's top aides, would soon replace Melvin Purvis. By the end of the day, it was being whispered all over the office: "Cowley is coming."

# CHAPTER SIXTEEN

### News of the World
### April 23, 1934

D aily *Globe*, Mercer, Wisconsin:

> "*The performance of the federal agents makes clear a need for a change in leadership as well as tactics. Melvin Purvis should be immediately relieved of duties, at least until the Jackrabbit is caught or killed. His behavior exemplified the stupid conduct of federal operatives, who failed even to contact local law enforcement to notify them that the Jackrabbit Gang was in the area. Had they done so, they would have been able to block the escape of the criminals merely by placing roadblocks on three bridges in the Star Lake area.*"

*Chicago American*, Chicago, Illinois:

> "*The performance of Mr. Hoover's Bureau of Investigation in handling the matter of the Jackrabbit has been appalling. The incident in Wisconsin illustrates this perfectly: three bystanders shot, one killed; one Federal agent killed, another wounded, and a local constable in critical condition. Despite this, none of the gang was apprehended, only a handful of their 'molls.' Unless the Jackrabbit and his associates are caught or killed real soon, Mr. Hoover's head will roll.*"

*London Express*, London, England:

*"When a community lets a pack of man-eating tigers dwell in its midst, it is easy for a lone wolf like the Jackrabbit to slip under the fold gate . . .*

*"The Roosevelt revolution, shaking up the whole structure of American government, has upset organized crime which fattened on corrupt officialdom.*

*"Capone had got that business down to a fine art. Nobody has followed him because conditions have been changed. In the present confusion of the economic crisis it is the lone raider type you would expect to flourish. Hence, the Jackrabbit."*

"Will Rogers Says," McNaught Syndicate newspapers:

*"Well, they had the Jackrabbit surrounded and was all ready to shoot him when he come out, but another bunch of folks come out ahead, so they just shot them instead. The Jackrabbit is going to accidentally get with some innocent bystanders sometime; then he will get shot."*

*Zwoelf Uhr Blatt*, Berlin, Germany:

*"No voice in America should be raised against the tenets of National Socialism as long as a deviate like the Jackrabbit is allowed to roam freely. The American government would be well advised to follow Germany's deep sense of responsibility and sterilize all murderers and the congenitally inferior. If such steps are taken, undesirables such as the Jackrabbit will cease to be a problem."*

*Evening Standard*, London, England:

*". . . all of the American continent has joined in the search for the Jackrabbit. Even some Red Indians joined the hunt today with bows and arrows.*

*"The hunt has extended across the Atlantic, following reports that the Jackrabbit had been sighted boarding a ship bound for the United Kingdom. Police in Glasgow and Liverpool have been instructed to search all vessels arriving from the United States and Canada in an effort to apprehend the notorious gangster."*

Flyer from the Willoughby Ford dealership, Milwaukee, Wisconsin:

*"Q: Will they catch the Jackrabbit?*

*A: Only when they get him out of a Ford V8!"*

*Kankakee Herald*, Kankakee, Illinois:

*"Police responded to reports that the Jackrabbit was in the Asher Hotel on Walnut Street barricaded in the dining room with a dangerous weapon. Upon their arrival, they discovered Mr. Davis Reynolds, of Muncie, Indiana. Mr. Reynolds—who bears a slight resemblance to the famed gangster—is a salesman of confections and was at the time distributing samples of his wares. The 'dangerous weapon' turned out to be a blunt knife used for cutting fudge."*

# CHAPTER SEVENTEEN

**McNeil Island Federal Penitentiary**
**January 1969**

Hi gang, Ray here. I'm still cooling my heels in McNeil, working my fingers to the bone with a pencil stub and a cheap piece of paper. Look, I'm gonna tell the next bit myself, because I was actually there, although I wish to hell that I wasn't. If I'd known what I was in for, I would have stayed the hell in Toledo.

At that point, at the end of April 1934, the federal heat was really on my gang because of the Hamm and Bremer kidnappings we'd pulled. Frankly, we were relieved when the Jackrabbit busted out of the pokey at Crown Point. That asshole Hoover shifted a bunch of his flatfoots from looking for our gang to looking for the Jackrabbit's, which made things easier for us.

Even though there weren't as many G-men on our tail, we still had to be careful. Me and and a couple of the boys were laying low in a Toledo whorehouse until things cooled down. The problem was that we were running low on dough. We couldn't just spend the ransom money because we knew the Feds had all the serial numbers and had the banks on the lookout for the bills. We had to fence it somehow.

The problem started with Joe Moran, this stupid quack doctor we knew. Moran said he could launder our ransom money for a 15 percent cut, so we decided to let him do the job. We knew that Doc Moran was a bit of an alkie, but we had no idea just how bad it really was. At point, we were desperate for clean cash, so we went ahead with Moran despite our misgivings. Looking back, it was one of the dumbest choices we ever made.

Sure enough, Moran screwed the pooch. He hired some of his rummy buddies to help move the money, and one of them slipped up. Before long, the cops had a bunch of them in custody.

I got a call from Volney Davis, one of our gang's most trusted members. He's really good in a fight, but he doesn't have much in the brains department. Volney and Dock Barker were sticking around the Chicago area, mostly so Dock could keep an eye on his Ma. Volney wasn't too smart, like I said, but he was a positive genius compared to Dock.

Anyway, Volney called me in Toledo and said the cops had nabbed Boss McLaughlin in connection with the Bremer ransom. That was bad news. McLaughlin was an old-time Chicago pol and was as crooked as a dog's hind leg. He was a good guy to know, but he also knew way too much about our gang—especially where our hideouts were. If the cops had him in custody, then it would only be a matter of time before he talked. Boss was a stand-up guy, but those rotten cops could make even the toughest guy sing like a canary.

So when I got the call from Volney, I jumped in my car and drove straight to his place in Aurora before he and Dock could do anything stupid. Unfortunately, by the time I got there, they already had.

When I walked into Volney's apartment, the smell of rotten meat hit me like a punch to the nose. The place was a horrible mess. There were piles of bloody sheets and towels all over the floor, and disinfectant powder was spread everywhere in a vain attempt to cover up the stink. It was like a slaughterhouse.

"What the fuck?" I said.

"Uh, yeah, Ray," said Volney. "We've had a, y'know, complication." He jerked his thumb at the kitchen table. The Jackrabbit was sitting there, and so was Homer Van Meter. They both looked like shit.

"Holy smokes!" I said. "That's about the last person I expected to find here." I shot a look at Volney, who had a hangdog expression on his face. We had enough problems already, and he had let the hottest outlaw in the country into our hideout.

"I'm sorry, Ray," said Volney. "I couldn't just turn 'em away. They didn't have no place to go."

Sure, he could have turned him away. I would have, but now that they were here, it didn't seem right to give them the boot.

The Jackrabbit got up and walked over, hand extended. "Sorry to impose on you like this, Ray, but there's nothing else we could do. Red took a bullet getting away from the Feds. It's bad."

I shook his hand. "Yeah, I can tell," I said. "I'd say it's good to see you again, but I wish it was under different circumstances."

"Yeah, I know. Sorry about this. We tried to find a doctor, but everyone else turned us away. Red's a goner, but we couldn't just abandon him. That wouldn't be right."

"Yeah, I know," I said. "Look, what's done is done. We got ourselves in a bit of a pinch here, as I'm sure you know. If Boss McLaughlin gives us up, there could be cops here at any time. It'll be good to have a few extra guns if things get dicey. So how's the patient?"

"Not good."

We went into the back bedroom where Red Hamilton was dying. I've been in some grim locations, but that room was the most awful place I'd ever been. There were more bloody sheets strewn around the room. The stink of gangrene was overpowering, and I had to fight to keep from losing my lunch. Red was stretched out on the bed. His skin looked like old newsprint, and there was a sheen of sickly sweat all over his body. His eyes were half open, and he was mumbling nonsense. "Tell Mama that Jamie left the barn door open. I'm gonna go get the good scissors." Stuff like that.

The guy was in awful shape, and I could tell right away that nothing could be done for him. I only knew the Jackrabbit and his pals from a few nights at the Green Lantern in Saint Paul, but we were all in the same boat. All of a sudden, I didn't feel so mad at Volney for taking them in. I'd like to think that someone would've done the same for me if I'd been in Red's shoes.

"Jesus, what a mess," I said. "So what the hell happened?"

"Well, we made a clean getaway from those feebs in Wisconsin," said the Jackrabbit. "But some cops spotted us as we were trying to get back to

Saint Paul. We got away, but Red took a slug in the back. We left him in an old mining shed near Platteville and cut down to Dubuque. Broke into a doctor's office to get some supplies. It helped, but not much.

"We knew we had to get back to Chicago to get some real medical help. I probably went through ten bucks' worth of nickels making phone calls. Nobody would even talk to me. Said I was too hot. Finally, I called Joey O'Brien at the Hi Ho Inn. He said he could hook us up with this Doc Moran, but he never showed."

"Yeah, I know," I said. "Moran's been too busy fucking things up for us."

"That's a tough break," said the Jackrabbit, but I could tell he didn't really mean it. I can't say I blame him, though. His old pal was going out badly. Dying a dog's death.

"Yeah, it's a tough life, ain't it?" I said.

"Well, at least Joey was able to get in touch with Volney here. He said we could use his apartment while we tried to find a doctor."

"I couldn't just turn 'em away," Volney repeated.

"No, you did the right thing," I said. Of course, it was too late to get Red a doctor. He was going to need a mortician pretty soon, though.

"Thanks again, Ray," said the Jackrabbit. "You guys are—"

"Get out here!" hissed a voice from the front room. It was Dock Barker, who had been watching out the front window. "This is it! They're coming now!" There was a mad scramble as everybody grabbed a gun and hustled into the living room.

I pulled out my .45 and rushed to where Dock was standing. "What's going on? Where?"

"Right there. That Hudson just pulled up. Right by those two guys on the corner. It's a raid; it's gotta be."

"OK, OK, just stay cool everybody," I said. "Jackrabbit, get by that window in the corner. Homer, you stay by Dock here. I'll take the other window. Volney, get by the back door in case they try to come in that way."

Once everybody was in place, I peered out the window. The two guys in the Hudson were chatting with the two on the sidewalk. If this was a raid, they were being pretty casual about it. "Keep calm, everybody," I said. "Wait for it."

The room was dead silent as we watched the men across the street. From the back room, we could hear the sound of Red's labored breathing. The seconds dragged by with painful slowness.

One of the men on the corner lit a cigarette.

"That's the signal!" said Dock. "They're coming! I'm gonna let 'em have it!"

"Don't do that!" hissed the Jackrabbit. "Wait 'til we're sure, Dock. Then we open fire."

I cut my eyes between Dock and the Jackrabbit. Dock could be pretty stubborn, even under the best of circumstances. I wasn't at all sure he'd listen to someone else, especially now. Dock tensed, and I was sure that he was going to open up with the Tommy gun.

"Dock . . . " said the Jackrabbit soothingly.

Dock's shoulders sagged, and the muzzle of his gun dropped a fraction of an inch.

"Everybody stay cool," I said.

The men on the street were oblivious. They just stood there chatting. After another minute or two, the one guy pitched his cigarette into the gutter. Then they all got into the Hudson and drove away.

"Christ on a crutch!" said Homer. "I thought that was it."

"Those dumb clucks don't know how close they came to getting' ventilated," said Dock. He seemed disappointed that there hadn't been a shoot-out. The guy could be trigger-happy sometimes, although not as bad as Baby Face Nelson.

"How's it look back there, Volney?" I asked.

"Can't see shit," came the reply.

"OK," I said. "I think we can all stand down, at least for now. Still, we oughta have someone watching the front and someone covering the rear."

For the rest of the night, we kept an eye out for cops, and Red drifted in and out of consciousness. Around midnight, he started to moan then scream. The Jackrabbit got a couple of morphine pills in him and sat talking to him until the drugs kicked in.

Around four o'clock we huddled around the kitchen table, trying to decide on our next move. We didn't want to stay any longer than we had to. We talked about just taking off and leaving Red for the cops to find. That way, he might be able to get some real medical help.

"No way," said the Jackrabbit. "If you guys want to leave, I'll help you pack. But I'm not leaving Red here to die alone or at the hands of the cops."

"Look, I don't like the idea of leaving him, either," I said. "But it's just a matter of time until Boss breaks down. It might be a week from now, or it might be this morning. We can't be sure."

"Look," said the Jackrabbit. "Let's give it 'til noon. If things haven't changed by then, me and Homer will load up Red in the car and try to make it to my dad's place. Let's just give it another couple of hours, OK?"

I thought it over. "Yeah, that's OK. I'm sure Boss can keep his lips zipped for another couple of hours. But after that, we've gotta scram."

A wan voice came from the back room. "Homer? Johnnie? Where are you?" Red was awake again. I followed the Jackrabbit and Homer into the terrible bedroom. He was awake and seemed more lucid than he'd been since I'd arrived.

"Hiya, sport," said the Jackrabbit cheerfully. "How's the boy?"

"Better. I'm thirsty, man. Can you get me something to drink?"

The Jackrabbit fetched a glass of water from the kitchen and watched Red try to drink it. Most of it went down the front of his sweat-stained shirt.

"What was going on?" asked Red. "I heard shouting earlier."

"Just a false alarm," said the Jackrabbit. "Nothing to worry about."

"Oh, good. How am I doing? You think I'll pull through? When's the doctor coming?"

"Oh, he'll be here any time, pal," said the Jackrabbit. He cut his eyes to me and Homer.

"Yeah," I said quickly. "Best sawbones in the state. He should be here any minute."

Red managed a sickly smile. "Good. Good. I was thinking that when I get better, everyone will think I'm dead, right? They'll just stop looking for me. Isn't that great?"

"Yeah," said the Jackrabbit. "That's good, Red. You'll be off the hook."

"Off the hook," Red repeated. "Maybe I'll go back to Sault Saint Marie and stay with my sister. I can be a mechanic. I was always good with my hands."

"You bet," said Homer. "I'll drive you there myself, buddy."

He started coughing, and a little bit of blood trickled out the side of his mouth. When he stopped, he cringed and said, "Ow. That hurts like a son of a bitch. When's that doctor coming?"

"Any minute, I'm sure," I said.

He seemed like he was going to go back to sleep, but then he started moaning and thrashing. Then yelling. Then screaming. He kicked off the filthy sheets, and it was all we could do to keep him from flopping off the bed. A fresh bloodstain spread across the mattress.

"Christ!" Homer hollered. "What can we do? What can we do?!"

"We need to try and shut him up!" I said. "We don't want the neighbors to call the cops!"

"I'll try to get some more pain pills in him," said the Jackrabbit, but when he reached for the bottle, one of Red's flailing hands sent it flying across the room.

"AHHHHHHHHHH! JESUS! JESUS CHRIST!" he screamed. "OH, MAMA! OH, JESUS! AAAAAHHHHHHHHH!"

Me, Homer, and the Jackrabbit were trying our best to hold him down. There was nothing else we could do. The smell coming off him was indescribable. I gagged but somehow managed to keep from puking.

Finally, the screams tapered off into a harsh, barking cough. Red's hands scrabbled furiously at the mattress, his head thrown back, mouth wide open. His eyes bulged out of his head. There was one final, pain-filled gasp and his eyes sort of filmed over. He slumped back into the mattress, and I swear to God, in that moment, his body seemed to shrink ever so slightly.

Red Hamilton was dead.

Dock and Volney stood just outside the doorway watching Red's final, horrible moments. For a minute or two, all five of us just stood there staring at his body. Finally, Homer said, "Well, at least he beat the noon deadline," and gave a half-hearted laugh. The Jackrabbit shot him a dirty look but said nothing.

"It's over," I said. "Now we have to think about what's next."

"We've got to get rid of the body," said the Jackrabbit. "We'll need some lye or something to burn off his hands and face."

"What for?" asked Dock. "If the cops know he's dead, then what the hell's it matter?"

"Don't be a dummy," I said. "If they think he's still alive, then every cop that's out looking for him won't be looking for us." Dock had to have these things explained to him. Like I said, he wasn't too sharp.

"Me and Homer will take care of Red," said the Jackrabbit. "We just need some tools and a place to bury him."

"I know a place down by Oswego where we can put him," I said. "There's a hardware store close by. They'll probably be open soon. I'll help you guys. Volney and Dock, you start cleaning up the place. We need to clear out of here as soon as possible. Right now, I'm going to have a smoke."

I'd seen a lot of hard action in my day, but the death of Red Hamilton was probably the worst. I desperately needed some fresh air and a chance to clear my head. I went out the back door and sat on the stoop at the edge of the apartment building's tiny, weed-strewn backyard.

I had finished about half of my Camel when I heard the door open and shut behind me. The Jackrabbit sat down beside me.

"Can I get one of those?" he asked.

"I didn't know you smoked."

"Well, I've been thinking of taking up a new hobby. This seems as good a time as any."

I flipped a cigarette out of the pack and held it out to him then lit it.

"Thanks," he said.

"That was a bad scene back there," I said.

"This is a bad business we're in."

We smoked for a while in silence.

"Tell me," I said. "We're both intelligent guys. How the hell did we end up here? I mean right here, right now?"

"I ask myself that every day," said the Jackrabbit. "Man, I really wish I had met you earlier, Ray. You and me, we're not like the others. Homer and Red are good guys. I'm sure Dock and Volney are too. But there's no way they would have ended up as anything other than what they are. Us, we might have had a chance if things had been even a bit different. We could have opened a law office. Wouldn't that have been something?" He barked a short, bitter laugh.

"Maybe," I said. I suppose it was possible . . . but not very.

"Do you believe in fate?" he asked.

"Just as much as I believe in anything else, I guess."

"That's what I believe. Fate. That's why we're here. We made one crazy decision and that was all she wrote. I didn't start out to be Public Enemy Number One, you know."

"Yeah, but here you are," I said. "Pictures in all the newspapers, all over the radio, newsreel features, the works. Don't try to tell me you don't like it."

He grinned that crazy lopsided grin. "Yeah, I like it. Maybe too much. But that's not what I'm saying. I didn't try to be this famous outlaw, it just sorta happened. It started with that job I pulled in New Carlisle last year when the newspapers went nuts about me jumping over the teller's cage. When I jumped up, I was just plain old Johnnie, but by the time I came back down, I was the Jackrabbit. One crazy move and a helluva lot of bad luck followed."

"Hell, man, luck ain't got nothing to do with it. Once we made that choice to pull out a gun and take someone else's money, there was no turning back. Nobody comes out of this game a winner. Nobody."

The Jackrabbit took a long pull on his smoke. "I don't believe that," he said.

"Really? Then maybe you're not as smart as I thought."

"Maybe I'm not as smart as you, but I think there's gotta be a way out of this game."

"Uh-uh. The only way out is the one that Red just took. That or rotting away in a cell somewhere."

"No," said the Jackrabbit. "Just between you, me, and the wall, I think I can knock it. I can see a way out."

"What, just go straight and be an average citizen? All law-abiding and home-loving? No fuckin' way. I can't do it, and neither can you."

"You don't think so?"

"*Hell*, no," I said, "And I'll tell you why. It's not the money, even though that's nice. It's the rush. You know what I'm talking about. That feeling when you're in a bank, and you've got everything under control. When you've got the money in one hand and your gun in the other and you're heading for the door. There's nothing to beat that feeling. *Nothing*. It's addicting."

"Yeah, that's true. When I'm on a job, I feel like I live more in those ten minutes than my old man lived his entire life. But I think there's other ways to match that."

"Like what? Become a cop?"

The Jackrabbit laughed. "You know, I've actually thought about it, Ray. I really have. But we both know that'll never happen. Still, there's other ways—like being a pilot . . . a barnstormer. That's got to be one helluva rush."

"Hmm . . ." I said. He had a point—that did seem like high-tension work.

I looked over at the Jackrabbit. He held the smoldering end of the cigarette between his fingers and was giving me that goofy twisted smile. Yeah, he was probably clever enough to give up the bank robbing business and take up barnstorming or some other high-risk occupation. But he was too addicted to his own celebrity. I always tried to keep a low profile, but the Jackrabbit didn't. He was more like a Hollywood movie star than a gangster. Even the best barnstormer in the world didn't get *that* much attention.

"You're a smart cookie," I said. "But I just don't think it can be done. We're both on a one-way street, and the end's just a matter of time."

"Wanna bet?"

"You're on." I said. "What's the wager?"

The Jackrabbit took a look at his stubby cigarette and said, "A pack of Camels. If I can go straight for a year and not get nailed, then you owe me a pack of smokes."

"Bet," I said. He held out his hand, and we shook on it.

"Well, we better get a move on," I said. "The sun'll be up soon, and we've got work to do."

We rolled up Red's body in a tarp and loaded it into the back of my car. It only took a half hour or so to get out to Oswego where there was an abandoned gravel pit that would suit our purposes. We stopped at a hardware store and picked up a couple of shovels and ten cans of lye. Digging the hole was tough, and the sun was high in the sky by the time we were finished.

We rolled Red's body out of the tarp and laid him faceup in the grave. His skin had already turned a sick grayish-green, like he'd already been dead for a couple of days. The Jackrabbit stood at the head of the grave and cracked open a can of lye.

"I hate to do this to you, old buddy," he said. "But I know that you'd do the same for me."

Overall, it was a pretty shitty eulogy.

The Jackrabbit poured the lye onto Red's face, and it began to bubble and hiss. We quickly dumped the rest, concentrating on the hands and face, then started shoveling back the dirt. Once the grave was filled, we threw the shovels into a nearby pond and drove back to Aurora.

The Jackrabbit and Homer didn't even stick around long enough to take a shower; they just tossed their gear in their bloody car and drove off. It was just as well. We had our own problems to deal with, and I was relieved when they had gone.

That was the last time I ever saw the Jackrabbit—but not the last time I heard from him.

# CHAPTER EIGHTEEN

### Homann, Indiana
### May 7, 1934

D etective Martin Zarkovich guided his Chevrolet down the rutted dirt road. He didn't like coming out to the boondocks. He was a city boy, and rural areas tweaked his city-cop sensibilities. There weren't enough escape routes, and there were too many opportunities for his suit to get dirty. He was wearing his white sharkskin, and it was always difficult to clean. Known around town as "the Sheik," Zarkovich took a great deal of pride in his clothes and appearance.

Zarkovich had been on the East Chicago police force for nearly twenty years. It used to be an easy gig. The East Chicago cops were known to be at least as crooked as their big-city counterparts across the state line in Illinois. Zarkovich thrived in the corrupt environment of the East Chicago PD. After nearly two decades, he'd built up quite a tidy little empire for himself. This mostly consisted of running a protection racket and taking kickbacks from the multitude of brothels and gambling dens in the city. Sure, there had been a few close legal scrapes and an indictment here or there, but generally, it was never a problem that a few well-placed bribes couldn't solve.

However, things had been getting tougher for him over the last year and a half. A Democratic governor had been swept into office on Roosevelt's coattails, and he'd immediately started making good on his campaign promises to clean up the corruption that was the hallmark of previous Republican administrations.

This zeal for reform extended to the East Chicago Police Department. There was now a new generation of cops on the force—a bunch of do-gooders. Zarkovich called them the "White Knights." He despised them, and he knew that the feeling was reciprocal. The worst was a detective named Lloyd Mulvihill, who made no secret of his desire to run Zarkovich off the force.

But Zarkovich couldn't worry about that now—he had other business to attend to at the moment. Unfortunately, it meant leaving the comfortable squalor of East Chicago and traveling out to the sticks. Homann was about as far off the beaten path as he could get and still be in his jurisdiction. It wasn't even really a town, just a few decaying cabins dotted around the extreme southwestern corner of Lake County. The Jackrabbit and Homer Van Meter had been hiding out in one of those cabins for the last week. Zarkovich had been charging them handsomely to do so.

He rounded the final turn on the dirt road and was surprised to see a red Ford panel truck parked next to the cabin. When he'd come out a few days earlier, only the Jackrabbit's nondescript Essex sedan was there.

Zarkovich didn't like surprises. He stopped and backed up to the tree line before getting out. He pulled his pistol out from under his immaculate jacket and scanned the area around the tumbledown cabin at the end of the dirt road.

"Hiya, Zark!" came the Jackrabbit's voice. "You alone?"

"Of course, I'm alone!" Zarkovich shouted. "Where's Van Meter? I know he's pointing a gun at me right now, and I don't like it!"

The Jackrabbit appeared from behind the cabin. "Stand down, Van!" he said. "It's just our landlord come to collect the rent!"

Homer emerged from a stand of brush next to the cabin. He was toting a Tommy gun. "I knew it!" said Zarkovich.

"Well, what the hell did you expect?" said Homer. "We knew it wasn't Avon calling!"

Zarkovich eyed Homer with distaste. Zarkovich thought he had too many loose screws, and his goofy demeanor concealed a dangerous and unpredictable personality. The Jackrabbit was rock-steady; you knew where you stood with him. But Van Meter was a loose cannon. He just rubbed Zarkovich the wrong way—and made him very nervous.

Zarkovich put his gun away and strolled up to the Jackrabbit and Van Meter. "Just checking in, boys. Everything hunky-dory?"

Homer scowled. "How can anything be wrong in a palace like this?" he asked, waving at the swaybacked shack. "I'd invite you in, but I'm afraid you'd need a tetanus shot."

"Hey, don't gripe about the accommodations," snapped Zarkovich. "It's better than you guys could do anywhere else, at any price. Speaking of which . . ." He held out his hand.

"Of course," said the Jackrabbit. "We're just . . ." He started coughing and pulled a handkerchief from his jacket to wipe off his lips. "Sorry, Zark. I seem to have caught a bit of a cold. This place is a little drafty."

"Hey, you wanted out-of-the-way," said Zarkovich. "This is as out-of-the-way as you can get and still be within an easy drive of the city. Nobody's going to come looking for you out here, I guarantee it. Of course, a guarantee like that doesn't come cheap." He wiggled the fingers of his extended hand for emphasis.

"Yeah, yeah, sure," said the Jackrabbit. He pulled a roll of twenties from his trousers and put it in Zarkovich's outstretched hand.

"Five hundred bucks a week for this dump!" complained Homer.

"Look, Chuckles," said Zarkovich. "Consider yourself lucky. You sure as hell ain't Public Enemy Number One, but your pal here is. Every cop in the world is trying to nab him, and I'm sure they wouldn't mind if they scooped up a small fry like you in the process."

Homer started to reply, but the Jackrabbit cut him off. "You're right, Zark," he said. "We're both grateful to you for helping us out. Right, Van?"

"Yeah, sure."

"We appreciate it," continued the Jackrabbit. "Right now, we need all the friends we can get."

"You won't find a better friend than me," said Zarkovich. "I know it's expensive, but you're hot. I gotta spread a lot of moola around to keep things cool." This wasn't entirely true. Zarkovich shared a cut of the money with Tim O'Neil, his captain and partner in crime, and that was about it.

"So what's the story with the new truck?" Zarkovich asked.

"You like it?" asked the Jackrabbit. "We're taking our show on the road."

"What the hell are you talking about?" asked Zarkovich. He didn't like the sound of this.

"We can't stand another day in Termite Terrace here," said Homer. "We've got a mattress in the truck. We're gonna keep moving around and sleep in the back."

"Whoa!" said Zarkovich. "Easy now, boys! I can't have you roaming all over the county. How am I going to keep you safe if I don't know where you are?" He had to quash this idea quickly. He couldn't have the most notorious criminals in the country on the loose on his turf, especially given the dangerous information that the Jackrabbit had on him.

Zarkovich had no idea that the Jackrabbit would end up being Public Enemy Number One. If he had, he might have been a bit more circumspect in his dealings with the fugitive. The two of them went back a ways, and over the last year or so, Zarkovich had collected a great deal of money for his extralegal support of the gangster.

First was the Crown Point breakout that Zarkovich had set up almost single-handedly. He had initially been reluctant to get involved with Piquett's planned jailbreak. The risk had been high, but so was the reward, so he'd agreed. Zarkovich bribed the judge and half the county jail staff. He'd also smuggled in a package with the fake gun *and* a real one. That alone was enough to put him behind bars for a long time.

Even more incriminating was the disastrous First National Bank job in East Chicago several months earlier. Zarkovich had set that up too. The bank's president had let it be known that he was not averse to having a misfortune happen to the bank. The robbers would take twenty or thirty grand, and the bank president could report a loss of two or three hundred thousand to the insurance company. It was a win-win: the robbers would get their loot, the bank would get its insurance claim, and Zarkovich would take a fat cut for putting it all together. Easy money.

Except it hadn't gone down easy. The two patrolmen who responded to the alarm were gung-ho White Knight cops. They either hadn't gotten word to steer clear of the robbery, or they didn't care. One of the cops, Bill O'Malley, drew down and shot the Jackrabbit point blank in the chest. Only his bulletproof vest had saved him. The Jackrabbit returned fire and caught O'Malley in the throat. The Jackrabbit and Red Hamilton made their escape as Officer O'Malley bled to death in the street.

If Zarkovich's involvement in that caper got out, it would mean serious shit—accessory to murder at a minimum. As with the Crown Point job, the Jackrabbit had too much information on him to allow him to sleep well at night. Zarkovich wasn't sure of what the long-term solution might be, but for the present, he wanted to keep the Jackrabbit close by. Besides, even though the gangster was a sizable liability, Zarkovich still hoped to squeeze a few more bucks out of him.

"You boys should trust me," said Zarkovich. "Look, haven't I always taken good care of you? Shit, if it weren't for me, you'd still be cooling your heels at Crown Point . . . or sitting on death row at Michigan City."

The Jackrabbit coughed, a long, staccato burst of hacking that shook his entire frame. "Yeah, Zark," he said. "I gotta hand it to you for taking care of things at Crown Point. On the other hand, I probably wouldn't have even been there if it weren't for that fuckup at the First National heist. You said it would be a cakewalk, and now I'm looking at a murder rap—for a cop no less!"

"Hey, that's all water under the bridge," said Zarkovich. "Let's not dwell on ancient history, eh?"

"Look, I never wanted to kill anyone. I just wanted to rob banks and spread the money around—like Robin Hood."

"Yeah, and I wanted to be a cowboy," said Zarkovich. "We don't always get what we want . . . especially in this racket."

"Look, we're not sticking around here," the Jackrabbit reiterated. "I've got it all worked out. We'll keep to this part of the county. Every morning, I'll leave a note saying where we'll be. I'll leave it under a rock at the base of the gate to that old cemetery on Black Rock Road. You know it?"

"Yeah," said Zarkovich. "But I'm not keen on you bouncing all over Lake

County. I don't like it."

"And I don't like staying in one place," countered the Jackrabbit. "I feel like a sitting duck. This way, we'll be harder to find. Besides, you'll still get your money."

"I dunno," said Zarkovich. "It's going to be more work for me. I'm going to have to charge a bit more in that case. Six hundred a week."

"Yeah, but you won't have to provide our luxurious lodgings," said Homer. "You should *cut* the price."

"OK, OK, we'll just call it even," said Zarkovich. He could see that Van Meter was going to be a pain in the ass. It wouldn't be a good idea to alienate these two. They just might take off, and Zarkovich needed to keep them on as short a leash as possible. Besides, five hundred dollars a week was an incredible amount of money; it was best to keep it coming in.

The Jackrabbit coughed again then wiped his lips. "Well, we're going to be leaving here pretty soon. Probably spend tonight somewhere off Dell Road. I'll drop a message tomorrow to let you know where we'll be next."

"Who else are you letting in on your little travel plans?" asked Zarkovich.

"I have to stay in touch with my counsel," said the Jackrabbit. "Especially with Billie's trial coming up soon. I go through O'Leary. It's too risky to contact Piquett directly."

"I guess that's OK," said Zarkovich. Art O'Leary was an all right guy, and he knew how to keep his mouth shut. Zarkovich had worked closely with him in setting up the Crown Point jailbreak. He wouldn't be a risk. "Just keep it to O'Leary, OK? And let me know where you'll be. I can't protect you if I don't know where you are."

"Your concern is touching," said Homer. Zarkovich suppressed the urge to belt him.

"Thanks again, Zark," said the Jackrabbit. "You'll be hearing from us soon."

On his way back to East Chicago, Zarkovich contemplated the unlikely longevity of the Jackrabbit. A jackrabbit was the wrong animal; the man seemed to have the extraordinary lives of a cat.

The problem was that the Jackrabbit continued to beat the odds—not only by pulling off the Crown Point breakout, but also by surviving the FBI shoot-outs in Saint Paul and Little Bohemia. Now the Jackrabbit was even hotter than before. Given the amount of press he was getting, someone was sure to spot him sooner or later.

However, unofficial "shoot to kill" orders had passed through the ranks of the law enforcement agencies—a directive from J. Edgar Hoover himself. All in all, Zarkovich figured the Jackrabbit's days were numbered. It made sense to keep collecting money from him and providing him with whatever protection he could—keep milking the cash cow before the inevitable slaughter.

Still, the whole setup was making him edgy. Between the White Knights and the notoriety that the Jackrabbit had attained, Martin Zarkovich felt vulnerable. If his connection to the Jackrabbit was exposed, there was no way he was going to be able to wriggle off the hook with just a demotion. He would end up behind bars—or worse. It felt like he had a tiger by the tail.

He removed a large silver flask from the glove compartment and took a long swig. He would feel a lot more relaxed once the whole Jackrabbit business was over with, one way or another.

# CHAPTER NINETEEN

**Chicago, Illinois**
**May 20, 1934**

A rt O'Leary pulled his car to the side of Garfield Boulevard and killed the engine. The rendezvous point was right outside Sherman Park, in the grimy area just south of the stockyards. Even with the windows rolled up, Art could smell the animal funk. It was overlaid with a burned garbage smell still lingering from a huge fire that had occurred there the month before. He hoped the Jackrabbit would show up soon so he could get away from the stink.

He didn't have to wait long. Soon, a red truck cruised slowly by then disappeared around the corner. A minute later, the truck pulled up behind his car, flashed its headlights twice, and pulled out again. Art started his car and followed.

They drove for miles, eventually crossing into Indiana and then heading south. Art thought he knew the area well, but after a few twists and turns, he was completely lost. All he knew was that they were deep in the sticks somewhere west of Cedar Lake.

Eventually, the truck pulled over to the side of the road. Art pulled up close behind it. He could see Homer Van Meter's grim face in the rear window.

Art grabbed a grocery sack from his back seat and climbed into the truck. The Jackrabbit was behind the wheel. He looked worn out—pallid and tired, as if he hadn't slept well in a long time. His nose was red, and his eyes had a feverish gleam.

"Hiya, Art," he said, his voice rough and hoarse. He started to say something else then launched into an alarming spasm of coughing that seemed to go on for a full minute. When it tapered off, he said, "Ugh, sorry about that. I seemed to have picked up a bit of a cold."

"Yeah," said Homer. "It's lucky we didn't both come down with pneumonia living out here."

"You bring the stuff we asked for?" asked the Jackrabbit.

"Yep. You'd better start with this." He reached into the sack and pulled out a bottle of cough medicine. "This is the good stuff. It'll cure what ails you."

The Jackrabbit snatched it out of his hand, spun the cap off, and drank deeply.

"Whoa, pal!" cautioned Art. "That stuff is chock-full of codeine, and who knows what else. Drink too much on an empty stomach and you might go to sleep and not wake up. Have you had dinner?"

"Oh, yes, of course," said Homer, "We had lobster and steak at the Ritz then stopped by a lovely little out-of-the-way place for some sorbet."

"What my companion is trying to say, in his own demented way, is that we've been living on lean rations," said the Jackrabbit. "I hope you've got more in that sack than just medicine."

"Oh, yeah," said Art. "Everything you asked for: corned beef, crackers, couple cans of soup, some sardines—"

"Quit yapping and hand it over, already!" grumbled Homer.

The gangsters ate like starving dogs. The truck itself was pretty animalistic too. A dirty mattress took up most of the interior, and dozens of empty cans were scattered around. It also reeked of a monkey-house funk that made Art wrinkle his nose. It was almost as bad as the stockyards.

The Jackrabbit finished wolfing down a can of corned beef and tossed the empty into the back seat. He reached down to the ignition but then paused before saying, "Whoa, Art, you weren't kidding about that medicine. It's really gone to my head. You're gonna have to drive."

"Sure thing," said Art. "Where are we going?"

"Doesn't matter. Just got to keep moving. That's pretty much how we live now. One of us drives, and the other keeps watch." They switched places, and O'Leary put the truck in gear and moved out. Occasionally, the Jackrabbit called out instructions about where to turn. Homer peered suspiciously out the back window, Tommy gun at the ready. As they traversed the rutted country roads, the empty cans in the back rattled around like lost souls.

Art marveled at how the Jackrabbit and Homer were living. It didn't seem that much better than being in jail. At best, they'd been reduced to living like Gypsies. He told them that, and they both laughed.

"Living like Gypsies," repeated the Jackrabbit. "By God, you make it sound almost romantic. Maybe we should start wearing scarves and bells, eh, Van?"

"I'm sure I'd look great in a hoop earring," Homer snorted. "Yeah, sure, let's make ourselves even more conspicuous."

"Maybe we can paint up the truck like a Gypsy caravan," said the Jackrabbit. "You know, mystical zodiac signs and stuff all over?"

"We could just ride right by the police station," said Homer. "It'd be hilarious!"

Art was starting to think that the two gangsters had gone stir-crazy in their rolling jail cell. "Uh, I don't know, boys," he told them. "Most of the cops I know don't have a sense of humor."

"Yeah, their flat feet hurt all the time," sniggered Homer. "Makes 'em grumpy."

Art twisted around in his seat, certain that he'd find Homer drinking from the cough medicine bottle. But no, he was just Homer being Homer.

"Oh, hell, I completely forgot," said Art. "I've got a note from Billie." Louis Piquett had been shuttling between Chicago and Saint Paul to try and get Billie out of jail on her harboring charge—or at least to get the sentence reduced. One advantage of Piquett's frequent trips was that the Jackrabbit and Billie could regularly exchange mash notes.

The Jackrabbit's eyelids had started to droop, but they snapped back open at this news. "What?" he exclaimed. "Why the hell didn't you say so earlier? Hand it over, man!"

Art pulled a sealed envelope out of his pocket and passed it over. "Sorry, buddy, I completely forgot. I was afraid you were going to die on me."

The Jackrabbit ripped the envelope open and scanned it avidly. It was two pages long, and Art could see the man's lips moving as he covered some of the passages. When he'd finished, he went back to the first page and read it again. He took another swig of cough syrup and read it a third time. When he finished, he looked over at Art and said, "Say, pal, you didn't read this, did you?"

"No, of course not," Art lied. He and Piquett read all the correspondence between the two, just in case they were planning to do something stupid. Back when Piquett had first started representing the Jackrabbit, the attorney had smuggled out a note to Billie that contained a detailed map of the jail, along with instructions on how the gang should blast their way in with dynamite. Piquett had been so alarmed by the contents that he'd conveniently "lost" the note. Fortunately, the Jackrabbit was so taken with Piquett's plan to smuggle in a gun that he never mentioned the dynamite scheme again.

Art could understand why the Jackrabbit wouldn't have wanted him to read it—most of it was pretty racy. A typical passage read, "O baby, how I want to feel yur big cock inside me and esplode and make me feel wonderfull agin." The rest of the letter was full of similarly sexy sentiments and complaints about how boring it was in prison. The only exception was a cryptic passage at the end that gave an address on North Sheffield Avenue in Chicago with the notation, "This is the last place Jimmy L lived. If hes not there than you can probly find him at Omallys tavern. I hop you can find him."

The Jackrabbit carefully folded the letter and tucked it away in his jacket, as if it were a valuable document like a will or a deed. To him, it probably was.

For the next four hours, they drove aimlessly around the woods and fields of southern Lake County. The Jackrabbit was alternately chatty and sleepy as the cough syrup took hold. At least the medicine seemed to be doing some good—his hacking cough had diminished, and he no longer had the demented, feverish look in his eyes. Art thought it would be ironic if the man that every law enforcement agent in the country wanted dead was brought down by an untreated cold.

Around midnight, Art realized he was the only one still awake. The Jackrabbit was snoring loudly next to him. Homer was conked out in the back of the truck, Tommy gun cradled in his arms. Art reached over and shook the Jackrabbit awake. "Say, buddy, I've really enjoyed the scintillating conversation, but I can't keep it up all night. I've got a wife and kids who expect me to come home from time to time. We need to find my car so I can go."

"What? Huh? Oh, yeah. Sorry, Art." It took the Jackrabbit a minute to get his bearings, but then he was able to direct Art back to his car. Amazingly, it was less than a mile away.

"Are you guys gonna be OK?" Art asked as he climbed out of the truck.

"Sure thing, pal," said the Jackrabbit. "We'll probably drive around for a few more hours then find somewhere to park when it starts to get light."

"OK, then," said Art. He started to close the door then stuck his head back in the truck. "Say, are you still interested in getting that plastic surgery on your famous face?"

"Hell, yes!" said the Jackrabbit. "Why? What have you got?"

"Piquett says he's got a line on a guy who can do the job. A doc named Loeser."

"Loser?" snorted Homer. "You're not going to let someone named Loser cut on your face, are you?"

"LOE-ser," said Art. "He's German. Ran into a little trouble with the government for narcotics. Did a stretch in Leavenworth. Still, Piquett says he's one of the best."

"Damn Art, why didn't you say so sooner?" the Jackrabbit said excitedly. "C'mon, you know I've been aching for a new phiz. Van's been thinking about it too. We're both getting antsy."

"Yeah, sure, I know," said Art. "But it's not going to happen tonight. And it'll cost you big. At least five grand each."

"Jeee-zus!" screeched Homer. "That's some long green!"

"Yeah, that's steep," agreed the Jackrabbit. "But consider the alternative." He gestured around the interior of the truck. "You wanna keep living like this?"

"Hell, no!"

"OK," said the Jackrabbit. "Make the arrangements, Art. What do we have to do?"

"Well, I'll tell Piquett it's a go. Loeser will probably need someone to assist him, but I've got a cousin with a little medical training and a lot of gambling debts. I'm sure he can handle it. The only other thing we need is a place to do the operation and for you to recover. I'm sorry, but your rolling penthouse suite here isn't going to cut the mustard."

"What, we're gonna have to live under a real roof?" said Homer. "I'd prefer one that didn't leak like a damn sieve, if that's possible."

"I'll tell Piquett that you're game," said Art. "I'm sure he'll be able to line something up pretty quick."

"Hot damn, Art!" cheered the Jackrabbit. "That's such good news that I'll forget about being mad at you for waiting to tell us. I'll be in touch in a couple of days, then I can get my brand-new face!" He threw the truck into gear.

"OK, boys," said Art. "I'll be talking to you soon. Just take it easy on the cough syrup—that stuff packs a wallop."

The Jackrabbit gave him a lemon-twist grin and drove off into the dark woods.

# CHAPTER TWENTY

### East Chicago, Indiana
### May 22, 1934

"Where the hell *are* they?" asked O'Neil.

"I don't know. Just calm down."

Martin Zarkovich and his partner Tim O'Neil sat at the corner table of the Pine Cone Inn nervously nursing their beers. They were waiting for word on a heroin deal that was going down in North Harbor. They'd spent a great deal of time setting it up.

This was new territory for them. Ever since Prohibition had been repealed the year before, the revenue from bootlegging had bottomed out. Of course, there was still money to be made from untaxed booze, but in Zarkovich's opinion, it wasn't worth the bother. Now that alcohol was legal again, the prices had gone way down. The repeal of the Volstead Act had been met with celebration around the country, but Zarkovich had recognized that it would put a significant crimp in his cash flow.

After considering his options and meeting with his Syndicate contacts in Chicago, he had decided to branch out into narcotics. It was a bigger risk, to be sure, but it also had a much bigger reward. Plus, the logistics were a lot easier. He could make more money on a shoebox full of heroin than he could on a warehouse full of beer. It seemed like a sensible decision.

"Where the hell *are* they?" O'Neil repeated. "They should have been here by now." His pointed face twisted with worry. He ran a hand through his thinning red hair.

"What the hell is your problem, Tim?" said Zarkovich. "We're safe. Even if something happens, they can't connect anything to us. We've got at least three levels of deniability between us and the poor sap that's running the package. Just relax."

"That ain't what I'm worried about," said O'Neil. "If I don't get my cut from this job, I'm gonna have some explaining to do to my bookmaker in Cleveland. I lost a bundle on that Carnera-Loughran fight, and the marker comes due next week."

"Serves you right for betting on Loughran," said Zarkovich. "Anybody with eyes in their head could see that Carnera was going to murder him. That's the problem with you micks—you bet with your hearts instead of your heads." He drained his beer and waved at the bartender, Tommy. The skinny Negro man quickly poured another draft and hustled it out to their table.

O'Neil checked his watch again. "Shit, they're over an hour late. Something must've gone wrong. We gotta do something."

"What do you want to do? Go down to the docks yourself and make sure the handoff got made?"

"Shit, Zark, I'm not *that* stupid. I just want to swing by Mitchell's Tavern and see if Sonny is there. If anyone knows what's going on, it's him."

Sonny Sheetz was the Syndicate capo for northern Indiana. Nobody made a big move in East Chicago without clearing it with him. Zarkovich suspected that Sonny wouldn't have much to say about the deal one way or the other. Still, if it got O'Neil out of his hair for a while, it would be worth it. "All right, go ahead," he told O'Neil. "But stay cool. Check with Sonny and come right back here. Don't do anything without letting me know, OK?"

O'Neil looked relieved. "You bet, o Sheik of Araby," he said. "I'll just find out what's going on and come right back."

O'Neil put on his topcoat and disappeared out the front door. Zarkovich took a long pull on his beer and glanced around the interior of the Pine Cone Inn. It was dark and dingy, just like every other bar in East Chicago. Through a complicated series of fake businesses and front men, Zarkovich and O'Neil owned the bar outright and used it as the base of operations for their sleazier business dealings.

Most of the bar's clientele knew to make themselves scarce when Zarkovich was holding court. Tonight, the bar's only other patrons were Tommy the bartender and a trio of old drunks who were too boiled to notice or care that the owner was in attendance.

Zarkovich took a cloth from his pocket and gave his two-tone wing tips a quick shine. They were his favorite shoes; he liked the way they complemented his plaid seersucker jacket. But a spot on the toe had been bothering him all evening. He hated unattended messes.

This got him thinking about the Jackrabbit. That situation was getting to be a big mess, and it would have to be attended to shortly. He'd managed to stay in touch with the fugitive gangster over the past two weeks, but it had been a major pain in the ass.

Every morning he drove out to check the drop at the Black Rock Road Cemetery. Every evening, he cruised the area indicated in the Jackrabbit's messages. Usually, they were vague, indicating the name of a country road or a nearby landmark and making them difficult to find.

He was getting more and more anxious about the Jackrabbit. He had America's most wanted criminal cruising the back roads of his turf every night with Homer Van Meter peering out the rear window with a Tommy gun in hand like some demented tail gunner. It couldn't continue.

For a while, Zarkovich had thought the two were just going to take their shiny red truck and clear out of the area. He had no idea why the Jackrabbit wanted to stick around the one city with the most cops looking to cool him and the most people who knew him on sight. It would make more sense to get as far away from Chicago as possible.

Zarkovich didn't try to make sense of the situation, though; he just wanted to make a few bucks from it. Despite his misgivings, he was happy to keep collecting 500 clams a week. All he had to do was keep steering the patrols and investigators away from whichever part of the county the gangsters were in on any given night. Easy money.

He knew easy money usually went by fast, and he knew he wouldn't be able to milk it forever. Pretty soon, the liability of the Jackrabbit's incriminating information on him would outweigh the cash Zarkovich was bringing in. It might not be too terrible of a tragedy if something unfortunate happened to the Jackrabbit and Van Meter. He was beginning to think that he might have to take care of them himself.

Zarkovich was putting the final spit shine on his shoes when the front door flung open. Closely occupied with his wing tips, he didn't look up. He figured it must be O'Neil back from his errand to see Sonny Sheetz. That had been quick.

The first indication that something was amiss was the way the three drunks at the bar suddenly made themselves scarce. They vanished through the front door in nothing flat. Tommy the bartender slowly lowered himself until his wide eyes were level with the bar.

Zarkovich spun around to see Lloyd Mulvihill and Marty O'Brien, the White Knight cops who had been dogging him. What the *hell* were they doing here? How did they have the nerve to just stroll into *his* bar as if they owned the place?

Zarkovich took a deep breath to steady his thoughts. "Well, well, well," he said. "If it isn't East Chicago's knights in shining armor. What brings the likes of you to a place like this? I figured you two would be at the St. Ignatius Bingo Night drinking whole milk and thinking pure thoughts."

"Did that last night," said Mulvihill. He was young—only twenty-five or so—but he looked like he was pushing fifty. His round face wore a perpetually pinched look, as if he'd just stepped in dog crap.

"Yeah, we had bigger fish to fry tonight," said O'Brien. He was small and skinny—Stan Laurel to Mulvihill's Oliver Hardy.

Mulvihill strolled over to Zarkovich's table. "Actually, Detective Zarkovich, we just stopped in for a little victory celebration. Y'see, we just intercepted a big shipment of narcotics up in North Harbor. A big win for the good guys, don't you think?"

Zarkovich's mind whirled. There was no way he could be directly connected to the heroin shipment. It was unlikely that the shit would splatter on his checked Glen Urquhart lapels. Still, the White Knights had *known*. There was a leak somewhere. For a split second, he wondered if O'Neil was the weak link, but then he dismissed it out of hand. He'd buried too many bodies with Tim O'Neil to think his partner had ratted him out. It had to have been some low-level East Chicago cop who felt he wasn't getting his share. Right now, the details didn't matter.

"Can you believe it?" said Mulvihill in mock astonishment. "Nearly a pound of uncut heroin coming into our fair community! As if bootlegging hadn't been bad enough, now these scumbags are bringing in narcotics. Can you believe the brazenness of those lowlifes?"

"Yeah," muttered Zarkovich. "Some people just don't know when to leave well enough alone."

"Well, we're putting 'em on notice," said O'Brien. "Starting tonight, we're going after those dirtbags in a big way."

"Wherever they are, and whoever they might be," added Mulvihill.

"Well, I expect that J. Edgar Hoover himself will soon be on his way to pin medals on you boys personally," said Zarkovich sarcastically. "Let me buy you a drink to celebrate your victory."

"That's mighty big of you, Detective," said Mulvihill.

"Not at all," Zarkovich replied. "Tommy, pour these heroes a shot of whiskey. The good stuff." The bartender rose up from behind the bar and started to pour the drinks.

"No thanks," said Mulvihill. "I've got to keep my head on straight tonight." He and O'Brien turned and headed toward the door.

"Well, thanks for the hospitality," said O'Brien. "We'll be seeing you."

"Oh, I doubt that," thought Zarkovich. "Believe me, you bastards will not see it coming."

He sat in silence for a moment then asked, "Did you leave that bottle out, Tommy?"

"Yes, sir, Mister Martin."

"Good. Bring it over here then lock up. We're closing up early tonight."

Zarkovich took a long swig from the bottle and contemplated his situation. It was not good. The White Knights had just raised the stakes astronomically. At first, Zarkovich had figured they were just going to try to get him fired.

Well, good luck with that. He had already survived two indictments with barely a scratch. But by messing up this heroin deal, they were hitting Zarkovich where it hurt—his reputation. He was known as the guy who could get things done smoothly. After tonight, word would get around that Zark wasn't as reliable as he used to be.

That wasn't the worst part, though. Not only had the White Knights screwed up his narcotics deal, they had the balls to come into his own goddamn place and brag about it. It was a declaration of war. The more he thought about it, the angrier he got.

"GOD DAMMIT!" roared Zarkovich. He slung the half-empty liquor bottle at a nearby column where it shattered with a satisfying crash. Tommy disappeared behind the bar like a diving U-boat.

As if it weren't bad enough having the Jackrabbit and Van Meter to chase after, now the White Knights were busting in on his territory and busting up his deals. It occurred to Zarkovich that there might be a way to use one problem to get rid of the other. The more he considered it, the more he liked it. He began to chuckle and then laugh uproariously.

Tommy's head appeared above the surface of the bar. "Is ever'thing all right, Mister Martin?" he asked.

"Huh? Oh, yeah. I think everything is going to be OK, Tommy. Now clean up this mess and get out of here. I have work to do."

# CHAPTER TWENTY-ONE

**East Chicago, Indiana**
**May 23, 1934**

"Make the call, asshole, or your bitch gets it."

To emphasize the point, Martin Zarkovich hauled off and delivered an openhanded blow to the Fink's face. His head rocked back, and blood began to dribble from a cut on his lip.

"OK, OK," sniveled the Fink. "I'll do whatever you want. Just don't hurt her."

The Fink's real name was Morris Finkelstein. He was skinny with listless brown hair and bloodshot eyes that bugged out of his sallow face. He was a half-bright, low-level con artist who'd been mooching around the periphery of the East Chicago underworld for over a decade.

The Fink was tied to a chair in the middle of a warehouse two blocks away from the Pine Cone Inn. On the far side of the room, Tim O'Neil leaned against a door. A faint whimper sounded from the other side.

Zarkovich crossed the room and dragged a small table and telephone back to where the Fink sat. He placed the phone decisively in front of the Fink then pulled out his service revolver and jammed it under the man's chin.

"You'd better not screw this up, dirtbag," Zarkovich snarled. "You'd better get it absolutely right, or we kill the bitch while you watch, then we kill you. You got that? So if you have any questions—ANY—about what you're supposed to say, you'd better ask 'em now."

"N-no, no . . . I got it, Detective," stammered the Fink. "You can count on me. I . . . I'm real good at this sorta thing."

Zarkovich figured that was about right. What he wanted the Fink to do was tell a lie, and the Fink lied a lot, so it shouldn't be a problem for him, even under duress.

In the days since the North Harbor heroin deal had gone south, Zarkovich and O'Neil had put in some serious detective work trying to figure out who'd tipped off the White Knights. Zarkovich had to tread carefully since the Syndicate boys from Chicago were mixed up in this. Dealing with Frank Nitti and his gang always made Zarkovich nervous. Nitti had taken over a few years ago when Capone had been sent away for tax evasion, and he was big-league. Zarkovich preferred being a big fish in the small pond of East Chicago. However, the proximity to the city of Chicago made interaction with the likes of Nitti and the Syndicate inevitable.

In the end, they'd concluded that the aptly named Fink had been responsible for Mulvihill and O'Brien getting tipped off about the North Harbor deal. He'd been employed as a lookout and had been made himself scarce right before the cops swooped in and seized the dope.

In the end, it really didn't matter if the Fink had squealed or not. It only mattered that he said the right thing on the telephone now. The Fink was disposable. Zarkovich had gotten that directly from mob boss Sonny Sheetz. He let it be known that if something unfortunate happened to the Fink, nobody in the Syndicate would be upset.

"All right, Fink," said Zarkovich. "Time to dance your ass off. Remember: red truck, Old Gary Road, half past eight. Got it, chump?"

"G-g-got it, Detective."

Zarkovich lit a cigar as the Fink nervously dialed the telephone. O'Neil watched the drama impassively from his post in front of the door.

The Fink put his hand over the receiver. "It's ringing," he said.

Zarkovich gestured impatiently with the cigar, and the Fink put the handset back to his face.

"Hello, Officer Mulvihill? It's me, Moe Finkelstein. Yeah, yeah, that's right—the Fink. . . . Look, I know this is pretty short notice and all, but I wanted to let you know that there's another deal going down, just like last time. . . . Yeah, yeah, different runners, but the same players behind it. . . . Uh-huh. They got pretty desperate when the first deal went bad, so I guess they're trying to make up for their losses. . . ."

The Fink had just removed the last remaining sliver of doubt that he'd tipped off Mulvihill to the North Harbor deal. Zarkovich looked up at O'Neil. His partner nodded and drew his thumb across his throat.

Zarkovich studied the Fink intently as he talked, looking for any telltale signs that he was slipping a warning or a code word into the conversation. The Fink looked suitably desperate, his bug eyes rolling and a sheen of greasy sweat spreading across his forehead.

"No, I'm not in on this one," the Fink continued. "But I got it on good authority . . . the best. . . . Yeah, yeah. Look, I wanna know if I'm gonna get the same price I did last time . . ."

The Fink winced and held the receiver away from his ear. Zarkovich could hear Lloyd Mulvihill screaming about cutting the Fink's balls off. Zarkovich suppressed a smile and took a few drags on the cigar.

"OK, fine, if you don't want to know—" said the Fink.

Another explosion of profanity came from Mulvihill.

"Right, right, OK. . . . The handoff is going to be further out in the country this time. They don't wanna run the same risk they did in North Harbor. . . . Yeah, yeah, out of everybody's way. It's about three miles south of Munster on Old Gary Road, just past the Cudahy meat packing plant. Half past eight tonight. The guys making the delivery will be in a red panel truck. You know, like a grocery delivery truck. . . . What? No, I don't know the license. Look, it ain't Lake Shore Drive. Any red truck you see on Old Gary Road is gonna be a safe bet."

Zarkovich decided that the charade had gone on long enough. The Fink had given a convincing performance, but it wouldn't be good to have him overdo the act. Zarkovich puffed his cigar until the end was glowing red then held it right in front of the Fink's bulging right eye.

The Fink took the hint. "Look, look, I gotta go now. Just remember, Old Gary Road, red truck, half past eight. . . . Yeah, right. Goodbye."

He hung up and sat breathing heavily. "Was that OK, Detective?" he asked.

"Oh, you outdid yourself, Mr. Finkelstein. Especially bugging him about the payment. A performance worthy of Clark Gable himself. What do you think, Tim?"

O'Neil clapped slowly three times.

"OK, I did what you wanted, Detective Zarkovich," said the Fink. "Now, will you please let my Honey go?"

"Well, I tell you, Fink," said Zarkovich. "I didn't think you had it in you. I was pretty sure we were gonna have to shoot you and her both. But after that inspired performance, I guess we'll let her go after all. Tim, let the bitch out."

O'Neil slid back the bolt on the heavy wood door and swung it open. A golden retriever bounded out and ran over to the Fink.

"Oh, my Honey!" burbled the Fink. "Oh, my sweet girl! Was you scared? Don't be scared. The bad mens won't hurt you."

"Don't be too sure of that," said Zarkovich. He yanked out his gun, jammed the barrel underneath the Fink's chin, and pulled the trigger. A gout of blood and brain tissue erupted from the back of his head and splattered across the dirty floor.

The dog yelped and ran into a corner.

"Swell," said O'Neil. "Another mess to clean up."

"You heard him," said Zarkovich. "He was the one that tipped off Mulvihill to the deal. He had to go."

O'Neil went to a closet in the corner of the room, pulled out a dirty blanket, and spread it out by the recently deceased Fink. "OK, sure, we can drop our friend here in the deep end of Cedar Lake," he said. "But what do we do about *that*?" He jerked his thumb at the dog that was still cowering in the corner.

"No problem," said Zarkovich. "I'll take her home with me. I love dogs."

# CHAPTER TWENTY-TWO

**Munster, Indiana**
**May 24, 1934**

The red truck pulled to the side of the road. It was an overcast evening, which added to the gloom of the wooded stretch of Old Gary Road. A chilly breeze kicked up, causing the late-spring leaves to flutter and chatter.

In the back of the truck, Homer Van Meter peered wearily out the windows and shivered. Even though summer was less than a month away, it was still plenty cold in northern Indiana. Homer had knocked out the rear window as soon as they'd gotten the truck. If there was a gun battle, he didn't want to waste precious moments blasting out the glass. He kept thinking about the running gunfight they'd gotten into while fleeing Little Bohemia. Sometimes he thought that if he'd been able to evade the cops, Red might not have gotten killed.

That was still a sore subject—one that he and the Jackrabbit danced around carefully whenever it came up. Homer knew that the Jackrabbit had taken Red's death very hard, and it was difficult for him to talk about it. Homer felt the same way. Ever since they'd buried Red, he'd been gripped by a sense of helplessness. His circle of friends was getting smaller, his options more limited. It felt to him like the wolves were closing in.

"Just what the hell are we waiting for anyway?" Homer asked for the third time that evening.

"You know as much as I do, pal," said the Jackrabbit. "Zarkovich left a note at the cemetery drop spot. He said to meet him on Old Gary Road past the meatpacking plant at quarter past eight. Said to be extra careful, but he didn't say why. That's all that was in the note. Do you want to read it again?"

"No, no," said Homer. He'd read Zarkovich's note three times. "I just don't like this bit about being extra careful? Why? Is someone on to us?"

"That Zark's a cagey one. He's probably just being cautious."

"Yeah, he's a little too cagey for my liking. I don't trust him."

"Hey, he's always treated us right," said the Jackrabbit. "No one else will touch us right now, but Zark's looking out for us."

"For five hundred a week, he'd better be. What the hell are we paying him for, anyway? That crummy shack was bad enough. Now we've got our own place to stay, and we're still forking over the dough. We'd be better off finding a place in the city."

"Zark's keeping the heat off us, Van. We've been out here for, what, two weeks now? Haven't seen so much as a Boy Scout patrol. That's not going to happen in Chicago."

"Well, at least we'd be able to get some decent food. I'm fuckin' sick of eating canned beans and crackers. The air in this truck is just one big fart. Besides, I'm starting to go stir-crazy. This isn't much better than sitting in a cell all day except the scenery outside changes."

The Jackrabbit was silent for a while before responding. "I don't think we'll be living out here much longer. I hope we'll hear from O'Leary soon. He'll set us up with a good plastic surgeon and a place to stay while we recover."

"What's this 'we' business, chum? I'm not letting anyone near my face until I see what they do to yours."

"Fair enough," said the Jackrabbit. "I just think . . . Hey, what's that?"

Homer peered out the rear window. "Car coming." He reached for his Tommy gun and thumbed off the safety.

"Stay cool," said the Jackrabbit. "It's just Zark."

"It'll be Zark when I can *see* that it's Zark. Until then, I'm gonna assume that it's J. Edgar Hoover."

"I think you *are* going stir-crazy. There's no reason—"

"What kind of car does he drive?" asked Homer. "A black Chevy, right? That's no Chevy; it's an Essex."

"Maybe he got a new—"

"Shh! This doesn't feel right!" Homer hefted the Tommy gun and aimed it at the approaching car.

"Yeah, I think you're right," muttered the Jackrabbit. He pulled out his .45 and scrambled to the rear of the truck to join his partner.

The car pulled up behind the truck and killed its lights. It took a moment for Homer's eyes to adjust from the glare. He could see the dull orange glow of a cigarette being smoked by someone in the passenger seat.

"Holy shit!" shouted Homer. "Two!" The red veil descended over his vision with startling suddenness. Without thinking, he pulled the trigger of the Tommy gun and sent a barrage of bullets crashing into the car's windshield. "Two! Two, dammit!"

"What?" cried the Jackrabbit. "What the hell do you mean 'two'?!"

"Two in the car! Shut up and shoot!" yelled Homer. He squeezed off another long burst. Beside him, the Jackrabbit began firing his pistol. The reports careened around the interior of the truck. Spent shells from the Jackrabbit's .45 caromed around the compartment, adding to the din. It sounded like a Chinese New Year celebration. They pumped rounds into the car behind the truck until they were both out of ammunition.

The silence was stunning.

Homer's ears rang, and his heart jackhammered in his chest. He could see the Jackrabbit's mouth moving, but he couldn't hear a word. The Thompson was a loud gun under normal circumstances, and in the confines of the metal-walled truck, it was deafening. Homer rubbed frantically at his ears as if to encourage them to start working again. Through the ringing aural haze, he thought he could hear the Jackrabbit's voice again.

". . . a whole lot of trouble . . ." the Jackrabbit was saying. ". . . the hell were . . . didn't know . . . talking about 'two'? . . . lost your mind?

"There were two men in that car," said Homer. "No way Zark would bring someone else out here. Not even that creepy O'Neil."

"Huh? Two men? Shit, we'd better make sure there are two corpses in there, or we're sunk."

Homer opened the back door and cautiously stuck out his head. Around them, the nighttime noises of the woods were beginning to come back. "Whoever it was, they're dead. Nobody could've gotten out of that car alive."

"Jesus Christ, Van. . . . What if it *was* Zark? If we just bumped him off, we're as good as dead. No one will have a thing to do with us."

"Hell, we'd be better off without him. I don't trust that guy. Never did."

"Well, we'd better check," said the Jackrabbit. He jumped nimbly to the ground. Homer followed slowly, brandishing the Tommy gun even though the drum was empty.

They each circled in front of the car, covering both passenger's-side windows. Inside, two slumped figures were riddled with bullet holes. One was fat and the other was skinny. The Jackrabbit reached into the driver'-side window and pulled back the hair of the fat man behind the wheel. Three bullets had crashed into his head, tearing off most of the left side of his face.

"I don't know who this is, but it ain't Zark," said the Jackrabbit.

Homer reached into the passenger's-side window and tilted the skinny rider's head back. It wasn't as grisly as the driver. He studied the dead man's features. "Hey, I think I know this guy," he said. "He's an East Chicago cop. I think his name's O'Brien."

"Shit!" shrieked the Jackrabbit. "*Shit!* Get back in the truck, now! We've gotta get out of here—fast!"

They sprinted back to the truck and hopped in, the Jackrabbit positioned behind the wheel and Homer in his normal tail gunner spot. The Jackrabbit peeled out and fishtailed the truck crazily down the country road.

"Christ!" cried Homer. "What the hell was that all about? Do you think it was a setup?"

"I don't know," said the Jackrabbit. "Maybe Zark told them where we would be, or maybe they tricked the information out of him. I don't know. I don't know!"

"Where are we going?" asked Homer.

"Back to the city. Where else? Indiana isn't safe for us anymore. I don't know why these guys were out here. All I know is that we can't spend another damn minute in Lake County or anywhere else this side of the state line."

"Suits me, pal. I was getting tired of the Gypsy life anyway." He peered out the rear window looking for more headlights.

"Just keep your head on straight," said the Jackrabbit. "We'll be back in Chicago soon enough."

# CHAPTER TWENTY-THREE

### Chicago, Illinois
### May 27, 1934

Jimmy Probasco sat in his kitchen with his morning eye-opener, Irish coffee. Jimmy mixed them with a whole lot of Irish and just a little bit of coffee—just enough to mask the flavor of the cheap booze. Quantity, not quality, was Jimmy's philosophy when it came to alcohol. From the Irish whiskey that spiked his morning coffee, to the beer that quenched his afternoon thirst, to the gin he started on when the sun was over the yardarm, Jimmy always bought—and consumed—in bulk.

As he sipped his drink, Jimmy's thoughts turned toward money. He was always working an angle to put a little more folding green in his pocket. At sixty-six, Jimmy was starting to think about retirement. He'd tried his hand at a number of jobs over the years: teamster, boxer, bootlegger, even jackleg veterinarian. Mostly, though, he'd worked as a fence. People brought him items that they'd "found," and Jimmy took them off their hands for a modest sum. He was then able to unload the found items for a nice profit through a network of pawnshops and shady jewelry stores.

It provided a modest income, but it was not without risks. Jimmy had been indicted a number of times for receiving stolen property but had managed to beat the rap each time. Having a slick lawyer like Louis Piquett definitely helped.

In the backyard, Jimmy's two German shepherds began barking. "Shit," he muttered, slamming his drink down. The dogs were skittish and would go off at the slightest provocation, despite all the "training" that Jimmy had tried to impose. This training mostly consisted of Jimmy standing on the rear porch and screaming at the dogs to shut up. "King! Queen! God dammit! You two shut the hell up! It's too early! SHUT UP YOU DUMB MUTTS!"

But the dogs kept barking. Jimmy shrugged and went back inside to freshen his drink. A short, dark-haired woman emerged from the back bedroom and went to the front parlor. It was Peggy Doyle, Jimmy's live-in companion. She was half his age, but it was hard to tell by looking at her. She had a dumpy figure and a plain face that could have been thirty or fifty. Peggy shared Jimmy's house and usually his bed. Mostly, though, she cooked and cleaned and generally tried to keep Jimmy from accidentally killing himself.

Peggy looked at Jimmy's morning pick-me-up and sniffed, "At it already, eh?"

"Sun's over the yardarm somewhere, darlin'," he replied. "Care to join me?"

"Of course not, you drunkard! I've got work to do. Today's my cleanin' day."

"Oh, yeah, great," said Jimmy. "That's perfect. I forgot to tell you that we'll be having some houseguests for a while."

"*Bejaysus!* Nice of you to let me know, Jimmy. It's bad enough keepin' up after the likes o' you, but now we're havin' guests as well?"

Jimmy took a swig of his drink and eyed Peggy warily. It was too early for a fight with her, so he decided to play it smooth. "Look, my Wild Irish Rose," he said. "I'm sorry I didn't tell you earlier, but I wasn't sure it was going to happen until last night."

"Well, you coulda told me then," she pouted. "I don't want anyone to think we're slobs, y'know. Why the hell are we puttin' people up, anyway? These some more lowlife friends of yours?"

"Look, Peggy darlin', these are paying guests. Get that? *Paying* guests. You've been after me to get out of the found-items business, right?"

"My goodness, yes!" exclaimed Peggy. "You're gettin' too old for that racket, you know that. What if you get caught? You're too old to do a stretch behind bars, even a short one!"

"Oh, come off it, woman," said Jimmy. "I can take care of myself." Actually, Jimmy wasn't so sure about that. When he was young, dumb, and full of spunk, he had spent a night or two in jail on a couple of low-rent charges. He'd worn that proudly—having some time in lockup was necessary for maintaining underworld credibility. Now, the idea of spending an extended period behind bars was frightening. He *was* too old for that, and he sure couldn't fight like he used to.

"Yeah, yeah, sure," Peggy said dismissively.

Jimmy ground his teeth and continued with his charm offensive. "Look, the only bars I want to spend time behind now are mahogany ones," he said.

"Har! You do enough of that as it is!"

"Will you just shut up and let me finish, woman? The owner of the Green Log Inn wants to sell the place and move to Miami. For five thousand dollars, I can buy it. No more fencing, just honest bartending. Doesn't that sound good, Peggy? We could really make a go of it, you and me."

Of course, even better, he could also use the bar to move the occasional piece of jewelry or expensive watch. Peggy didn't have to know about that, though, and as far as the rest of the world knew, he'd be just another law-abiding saloon proprietor.

"Yeah, and where are you going to get the money to buy the Green Log?" Peggy asked. "You don't have five thousand *pennies* to rub together!"

"That's where our guests come in. Lou Piquett set me up. They're just a couple of guys who need a place to stay while they get some medical work done. Nothing risky, and the payoff will be grand."

"Oh, this is startin' to smell like last week's fish," grumbled Peggy. "What kind of hoodlums is that shyster Piquett going to stick us with, huh? Some lowlife criminals, I'm sure."

"Just some friends in need, Peggy darlin'. Friends with *money*, understand? If this works out, it could be a whole new start for me—for us! Don't you want that?"

"Yeah, sure, I guess so."

"Good girl!" Jimmy hopped up and freshened his drink. "Then it's settled. So why don't you clean up for our guests, beautiful?"

Peggy complained but got up and cleaned the house. Jimmy drank some more.

About an hour later, the dogs started barking again.

"Jimmy!" Peggy called from the front room. "There's four men milling around out front. They look suspicious."

Jimmy topped off his drink with gin and hurried into the front room. "OK, Peggy, our guests are here. They don't want a bunch of people knowing that they're here, though, so you get back in the bedroom and stay there. I don't want you queering the deal."

Peggy gave him a nasty look but retreated from the front room without another word.

There was a heavy knock on the front door. Jimmy took a moment before answering. He didn't want to come across as too eager. When he swung open the door, Louis Piquett was standing there along with his investigator Art O'Leary. Behind them were two other men with straw boaters pulled down low on their foreheads.

"Hello, Jimmy," said Piquett. "You mind if we come in? I don't want to spend any more time out on the street."

Jimmy let them in, and, for a moment, the five men stood around in the front parlor. Jimmy looked from face to face as Piquett began the introductions. "Jimmy Probasco, these are my clients. The tall fellow is Homer Van Meter. I'm sure I don't have to introduce the other."

With a flourish, the other man removed his hat, and Jimmy gasped. Even though Piquett had told him that his client was well known, Jimmy was surprised to see the Jackrabbit standing in the front parlor of his house. It was like Clark Gable had stopped by to say howdy.

"Hiya, Jimmy," said the Jackrabbit. He grabbed Jimmy's hand and gave it a hearty shake.

"Yeah, hi," said Homer.

"Oh, yes, pleased to meet you both," said Jimmy. "You boys have a seat, OK? Make yourselves at home. Can I get you a drink? I got gin, rum, whiskey, beer, you name it. You thirsty?"

"Nothing for me," said the Jackrabbit.

"I think we can dispense with the refreshments for now," said Piquett. "Let's get down to business, shall we?"

"Yeah, sure, sure," said Jimmy. He was more than eager to get down to the details. He'd like to be able to swing by the Green Log Inn and tell the owner that he would soon be able to hand over a down payment.

"OK, we discussed this earlier," said Piquett. "The Jackrabbit and Mr. Van Meter need a place to stay while they undergo some minor surgery. We'll take care of the medical arrangements, as well as the postoperative care. We just need a safe place for the surgery and lodgings for while they recover. This may be two or three weeks."

"Yeah, sure," said Jimmy. "Fifty bucks a day—apiece."

"Jesus!" cried Homer. "That's highway robbery!"

"Say, pal," said the Jackrabbit. "Don't you think that's a little steep?"

"Hey, you're red-hot right now," said Jimmy. "Every cop in the country is looking for you. If they find you here, I'm not just looking at a harboring charge, you know? They'll probably just shoot me down along with you guys." He paused and eyed the Jackrabbit. Jimmy was a seasoned negotiator, and he could see that his argument wasn't flying. Better to go for a lower price than to blow the deal entirely.

"Look, I want you to think you're getting a decent deal," Jimmy said. "What do you think would be fair?"

"How about thirty-five a day?" said the Jackrabbit.

"Done," said Jimmy.

"Hell, that's still too high," said Homer.

Jimmy didn't like Homer Van Meter already. He looked like a stubborn yokel. Jimmy could see the look of suspicion on Van Meter's horsey face—it was the look of someone who thought he was being rooked at the livestock market. Jimmy knew better than to try and argue with one of his type.

"For you, twenty-five a day," Jimmy said. "As long as you pay up a week in advance."

The Jackrabbit and Van Meter dug out their wallets and handed over their rent.

"While you're at it," said Piquett. "There is the matter of the payment for the surgery."

The Jackrabbit pulled a large roll of bills from his pants pocket. "Here you go, Lou," he said. "Here's three grand. I'll pay you the other two once the surgery's over."

"Very good," said Piquett. "How about you, Homer?"

"Hell, no," said Van Meter. "I'm gonna wait and see what happens to *him* before I let anybody hack away at *my* face."

"Suit yourself," said Piquett. "Here's what's going to happen. Tomorrow night at eight, Art will bring Doctors Loeser and Cassidy over. Loeser will perform the operation with Cassidy assisting. Jimmy, you'll need to prepare a place for the operation; it needs to be relatively clean. After the surgery, Cassidy will stop by every few days to make sure you're recovering well. Also, the doc said not to have any food before the operation. Just stick with coffee, toast, juice during the day. Eat light."

"No problem, Lou," said the Jackrabbit. "I got it."

Piquett and O'Leary took off, leaving Jimmy to install his new boarders in their room. "I got one of them fold-out couches in the front bedroom," he said. "That'll be good for you, right?"

"You bet," said the Jackrabbit. "It sure beats that last couple of places we've stayed."

From the back bedroom, there was a loud crash. "Hey, what the hell's that?" asked Homer.

"Sorry, that's my, uh, housekeeper," said Jimmy. "I told her to keep to herself, but you know how women are. I can throw her out if you want."

"Is she a good cook?" asked the Jackrabbit.

"Best in Chicago," said Jimmy. "She can cook a meatloaf like you wouldn't believe."

"In that case, she'd better stay," said the Jackrabbit. "We haven't had any home-cooked meals for a long time."

Jimmy hustled back to the bedroom to let Peggy know that "Mr. Harrison" and his pal "Cletus" were going to be staying for a while and that she was not to disturb them in any way. She should stay in the back bedroom unless she was cooking.

"Bejaysus, you're treatin' me like a slave!" she groused.

Jimmy could see from the look in her eye that her dander was up. "Look, Angel, it'll only be for a week, maybe two. They're paying top dollar. Maybe enough to put a down payment on the Green Log. Just go along with me here, sweetheart. I'm practically beggin' you!"

"Oh, all right," she said. "But you'll be takin' me out for a night on the town when it's over. Got it?"

"Got it. You're a princess, Peggy."

The next day, the Jackrabbit and Homer relaxed at Jimmy's house playing cards, reading the papers, and listening to the radio. Jimmy spent the day drinking and thinking about money, as usual. He'd gotten 420 bucks in advance for one week's stay. If they stayed an additional week, that would be 840—not enough to buy the Green Log, but it was a good start. He figured there might be other ways he could make a few bucks off the gangsters' stay—like by running errands or something. There were always different angles for Jimmy to consider as long as he could drink and think.

Around eight o'clock, there was a knock at the front door. Jimmy admitted Art O'Leary and two men carrying leather satchels. The older of the two was Wilhelm Loeser. He was in his late fifties and had a round face and hooded eyes. He spoke with a German accent. Harold Cassidy was in his early thirties and had a high forehead and pasty complexion. Jimmy could tell that the man enjoyed his liquor because there was a slight tremor in his hand. Jimmy decided he wouldn't want Dr. Cassidy operating on him.

"Zo," said Loeser. "Shall ve get started?"

"I'm as ready as I'm gonna get, Doc," said the Jackrabbit.

"Right in here," said Jimmy. He led the men to the dining room, which he'd had Peggy clean out and scrub down. The dining table was covered with layers of clean white sheets.

"Where do you want me?" asked the Jackrabbit.

"Take off your shirt and lie down on zee table, please," said Loeser.

Jimmy backed out of the room, saying, "I'll stay out of your hair. Just let me know if you need anything." He went down to the kitchen to pour himself a stiff drink. Now that the operation was about to happen, he'd begun to feel distinctly nervous. He prepared a gin fizz without the fizz and went back to lurk outside the dining room door.

"Say, Art," said the Jackrabbit. "Are you going to stay here?"

"I'll stay if you want me to," said O'Leary.

"Yeah, I'd like that."

"I'm staying too," said Homer. "I wanna see what this is all about if I'm gonna let you guys do it to me." He pulled a chair into the corner and plopped down.

"Ve shall begin," said Loeser. "I trust you have not eaten in zeex hours as instructed?"

"Nothing but coffee all day, Doc."

"Good. Do you vant zee cheneral anesthesia or zee local?"

"The general is what knocks you completely out, right?"

"Zat ees correct."

"Well, if Art and Van are going to be here, I guess that's OK."

"Very good," said Loeser. "Dr. Cazzeedy, please administer zee anesthesia vhile I vash up."

Loeser disappeared into the washroom across the hall. Cassidy put a small towel over the Jackrabbit's mouth and nose and sprinkled a small amount of ether over it. After a minute, the Jackrabbit's eyes began to droop, and he started muttering indistinctly. Cassidy sprinkled some more ether onto the towel, but the Jackrabbit kept fighting it. Another sprinkling of ether had no effect—the Jackrabbit's eyes would close momentarily then snap back open.

"Jeez, he's a stubborn one," said Cassidy. He upended the ether bottle, soaking the towel with the powerful anesthetic.

The Jackrabbit's eyes snapped shut, and the muffled babble ceased. Then his face turned blue. He made a horrible gurgling noise and began thrashing on the sheet-covered table.

"Oh, shit!" exclaimed Cassidy. "Dr. Loeser? LOESER!"

Loeser bolted into the room, his hands still dripping from the washroom.

He quickly brushed Cassidy back from the table and assessed the purple patient. "He's svallowed hees tongue!" Loeser announced.

From his vantage point in the hallway, Jimmy craned his neck trying to get a better view. This was bad. If the Jackrabbit died, Van Meter would probably kill the doctors, and he might take out Jimmy and Peggy as well.

"Oh my God!" Jimmy moaned. "Oh my God!"

"You shut up!" commanded Loeser. "Give me zhose forceps!" he barked at Cassidy.

Loeser pried open the Jackrabbit's mouth and used the forceps to retrieve his tongue. He stopped thrashing and lay completely still on the makeshift operating table.

"There's no respiration!" said Cassidy.

"Ya, zhanks to your admeeneeztration of zee anesthesia," said Loeser. "You used haff zee bottle! Vhat vere you zeenking?"

Before Cassidy could reply, Loeser pointed at O'Leary. "You!" he said. "Open zee vindow! Ve must dizeepate zee fumes!"

Loeser grabbed the Jackrabbit's elbows and slammed them into his sides like he was pumping a bellows. On the third pump, the Jackrabbit coughed and struggled briefly then lay back. His chest rose and fell normally.

"Oh, thank you, Jesus," muttered Jimmy. "Oh, thank you, God."

"What's going on?" asked Peggy. She was standing right beside him, looking into the room. "Who is that?"

"Dammit, woman, I told you to stay away!" snapped Jimmy. "Why do you micks have to be so damn stubborn? You don't need—"

"Oh my God!" shrieked Peggy, her eyes growing wide. "That can't be . . . it's the Jack—"

Jimmy clamped a hand over her mouth and pulled her back to the kitchen. "Shhhhhh!" he hissed. "He was dead, Peggy! He stopped breathing for a minute! It's a good thing he started again, or we'd all be dead! So don't say anything! And stay in the bedroom when you're not cooking."

"I will," she pouted. "But you gotta buy me a new outfit—at Field's!"

"OK, OK! Just keep quiet and stay out of sight!"

Over the next three hours, Loeser cut and filled, pulled and sutured. The

Jackrabbit drifted in and out of consciousness and threw up three times. The dining room floor was awash in blood and vomit. At last, Loeser closed up the last stitch. Cassidy began bandaging the battered face.

"So . . . what did you do exactly?" asked Homer.

"Vell, first I cut away three moles," said Loeser as he began stripping off his blood-spattered gown and gloves. "Zhen I used zome kangaroo tendon to pull up hees cheeks and tighten hees face—a standard face-leeft. I removed zome teezue from around hees ear and used eet to feell zee breedge of hees nose and zee rather promeenent cleft on hees cheen. I daresay he vill look like a completely deefferent man once zee bandages come off."

"And when will that be?" asked Homer.

"Oh, four to zeex days, I should zeenk," said Loeser. "I vill check back on zee patient een a day or two. In zee meantime, I vill leave heem een zee capable hands of Dr. Cazzeedy. Don't bother showing me out; I know zee way."

Loeser pushed past Jimmy and walked briskly down the hall and out the front door. Jimmy couldn't blame him. He'd be in a hurry to cut out too if he'd come so close to losing such a famous and dangerous patient.

It took nearly an hour for the Jackrabbit to regain consciousness. By then, Cassidy had swaddled his head with bandages.

"You look like the Mummy," observed Homer with a laugh. "You'd probably scare Boris Karloff himself."

The Jackrabbit mumbled something that sounded suspiciously like "fuck you."

After ten more minutes, he was more articulate. "Uh, how'd it go, boys?" he asked.

"There were a few hitches," said O'Leary. "But overall, it went pretty well."

"Except for the part where you almost died," said Homer. "That was a little touchy."

"Quit clownin', Van," said the Jackrabbit. "Thash not funny."

"Um, there was a slight problem with the anesthetic," admitted Cassidy. "But Dr. Loeser was able to get you breathing again."

"We did think you were gonna die, though," said Homer.

The Jackrabbit emitted a croak that was probably meant to be a laugh. "Well," he said. "It might just as well have been then as any other time, I guess."

# CHAPTER TWENTY-FOUR

### Chicago, Illinois
### June 3, 1934

D oris was not happy about having to work on Sunday again, especially since she'd worked all day on Saturday. That had been bad enough because she'd spent most of the day dealing with a few unexpected arrivals. She'd been trying hard to catch up on some correspondence when three new special agents turned up unannounced. They were all from Oklahoma City and looked like cowboys. The leader of the trio, Clarence Hurt, was very polite, but he looked rough to Doris. There was a coldness in his eyes, as if he enjoyed the bloody part of the job. He was not at all like the earnest college boys that the Bureau typically recruited.

Doris knew there were freshly recruited agents on their way, she just hadn't expected them to turn up so soon. She had heard that they had been chosen based on their experience with firearms rather than the normal bureau prerequisites of law or accounting degrees. Still, Doris hadn't expected them to be dressed in real cowboy boots and ten-gallon hats. The only people she'd ever seen in such outfits were kids at Halloween.

As a result of their unexpected arrival, Doris had spent most of Saturday processing the new cowboy agents. Now she was back at her desk, muttering under her breath about bothersome cowboys. She was nonplussed when a dumpy man in an ill-fitting gray suit appeared before her desk. He had thinning hair and sad eyes, and his skin looked like oatmeal. His sudden apparition surprised her, as she normally kept part of her attention focused on the door to the hallway to make sure none of the press corps tried to sneak in. She hadn't noticed him enter the office or approach her desk; he just sort of materialized.

"Good afternoon, Miss . . . Rogers," said the man, looking at the nameplate on her desk. Maybe he was a reporter, but he didn't really look like one. He didn't look like an agent, either.

"Yes, sir?" Doris said stiffly. "May I help you?"

"I believe so," said the man. "My name is Inspector Samuel Cowley. Director Hoover has sent me to be of assistance in the Jackrabbit case. I have just arrived from Washington. Is SAC Purvis available?"

"Well, no, sir. You see, it's Sunday, and he usually—"

"Please call him at home and have him report immediately." Doris began to object, but Cowley continued, "In the meantime, there are other matters to attend to. I understand that this field office had the girlfriends of two of the Jackrabbit Gang under surveillance, and they got away. I would like to speak to the agents responsible for the surveillance. Immediately."

"Ah, yes, I believe I've seen both of them here today," said Doris. "Let me just see if I can find them for you." She eyed the inspector warily. She knew she should show this man respect; after all, he was a high-ranking member of the Bureau. However, his sudden appearance and domineering attitude, along with her own fatigue, made her short-tempered. Added to this was the fact that Inspector Cowley seemed to be a threat to her own boss, whom she respected and admired greatly. Shrugging this aside, she got up to comply with the inspector's request.

"No need for you to go," said Cowley. "I should start familiarizing myself with the office and the agents. I will find them myself."

As soon as Cowley had gone off to canvass the agents in the office, Doris got on the phone to call Mr. Purvis at home.

"What? He's here already?" asked Mr. Purvis. "What's he doing now?"

"He's interviewing the agents who were . . . uh . . . doing the surveillance on Helen Gillis and Jean Delaney."

"Holy Chr . . . moly! OK, well, I'll be there as quickly as possible."

The disappearance of Helen Gillis and Jean Delaney was the latest sore spot with the Jackrabbit investigation. The molls who'd been picked up at Little Bohemia had been released on probation at the FBI's suggestion. It was thought that they would lead investigators directly to the current whereabouts of the gangsters. Two of them—Gillis and Delaney—had promptly given their tails the slip and disappeared. It was the latest black eye for Mr. Purvis.

"Is there anything you need me to do . . . um . . . until you get here?"

"No, no," said Mr. Purvis. "Remember—Sam Cowley was handpicked by Director Hoover. You show him all the respect and deference he deserves. I'll be down there as soon as I can."

It only took Mr. Purvis ten minutes to get to the office. As with the day of the Little Bohemia raid, he was still putting on his tie as he rushed through the door. "Where is he?" inquired Mr. Purvis.

"In the interview room." Doris answered. Cowley and the two agents had been in there for twenty minutes. Their voices had gradually become louder and louder as the debriefing became more contentious. Mr. Purvis rushed into the room with Doris trailing discretely behind.

Mr. Purvis threw open the door to the interview room while Cowley was in the middle of berating the agents who had let Gillis and Delaney get away. "And who might you be?" Cowley demanded.

"Melvin Purvis. Pleased to make your acquaintance."

"Ah, Special Agent Purvis," said Cowley. "Glad you could make it. I'm Sam Cowley."

The two men stood and briefly shook hands. Doris noticed that Cowley had not addressed Mr. Purvis as special agent in charge. The two agents in the interview room exchanged a worried look. They must have noticed this slight as well.

"I was just having these agents explain to me why they let a common criminal, this . . ." Cowley flipped through his notebook. ". . . this Jimmy Johnson, take over the surveillance of these two women instead of doing the job themselves."

"Gillis and Delaney knew they were under surveillance," said Mr. Purvis.

"It was felt that having someone who was unfamiliar to the women keep close—"

"I understand the reasoning, Agent Purvis, but it was *faulty*," snapped Cowley. "The bottom line is that the subjects were allowed to escape surveillance. The mission was a *failure*. Is there any question of that?"

Doris could see a storm of emotions cross her boss's face: anger, embarrassment, uncertainty, resentment. After a pause, he said, "No, Inspector Cowley. Your assessment is absolutely correct."

"Good," said Cowley. "I want to make one thing perfectly clear to every member of the Bureau in this office: we *will* take down the Jackrabbit. In order to do so, we are going to have to make changes in the way this investigation is being run—*drastic* changes—starting right now. Any questions?"

There were none.

Doris followed her boss back to his office. He walked hunched over, looking beaten down. "Hold all my calls," he said without looking back. He went inside and pulled the door shut behind him.

Doris slumped down behind her desk and stared at the work on before her. There were only a few items there, but it just seemed too daunting to even start. She had no energy. Everything was miserable.

Ever since Little Bohemia, coming into work had been like visiting a morgue. The entire office had taken Carter Baum's death hard. For all the cops-and-robbers excitement of the FBI, Doris had never had to confront this ultimate risk of law enforcement. People got killed. Sometimes *good* people—people you knew and cared about.

As miserable as Doris felt, she knew that Mr. Purvis had to be in much worse shape. Not only did he have to carry the burden of Baum's death but also that of the poor lumberjack and all those who were wounded. Doris didn't know how he managed it.

On top of that, now Inspector Cowley had showed up and practically handed Mr. Purvis his walking papers. The official word from Washington was that Cowley was just in the Chicago office to "assist." But he had just made it pretty clear that he was now in charge and that Mr. Purvis was going to be playing a subordinate role. Doris felt horrible for her boss.

"Doris? Hey, Dore? You there?" Allan Lockerman had appeared in front of her desk without her seeing him. That was twice in an hour someone had snuck up on her!

"Oh, Agent Lockerman," said Doris. "I didn't see you there." She wondered what he wanted. He was probably going to ask her out again. Here was another typically tactless man, thinking with his wanger at a time like this. Dating was the furthest thing from her mind right now. She sighed.

"What's the matter?" asked Allan.

"What do you think?" she asked. "Things around here have been positively miserable. The whole mess in Wisconsin with poor Carter getting killed. And now this Cowley person shows up and starts upsetting the applecart!"

"Sounds like you could use a drink," said Allan. "Goodness knows I do. Say, I know a place that makes a terrific gin rickey. Let's go get one right now. We've both done our work for the week and then some."

Doris was all set to rebuff him. The last thing she wanted to do right now was complicate her social life. Her life was difficult enough as it was. But instead, she surprised herself by saying, "OK. Just let me go freshen up first."

"What the heck?" she thought. OK, maybe her life *was* complicated. Still, there was something reassuring in the thought of going out for a drink with Allan Lockerman. He was strong, polite, handsome, and could handle himself well. He seemed very stable. The idea of having a stabilizing influence in her life had a great deal of appeal to Doris right now.

Besides, she really liked gin rickeys.

# CHAPTER TWENTY-FIVE

### Chicago, Illinois
### June 4, 1934

"Zo, are you ready to zee your new face?" Dr. Loeser had the Jackrabbit in a chair in Jimmy Probasco's front room. He laid out some surgical tools on the mantelpiece.

"Hell, yes, Doc. I've been through hell to get this new mug. I want to see if it's worth it."

"Chust a moment now," said Loeser. With a few deft snips, the bandages fell from the Jackrabbit's face. Loeser handed him a mirror. "Zo, vhat do you think?"

"Jesus! It looks like I've been snorting wildcats!" He frowned at the reflection of his face. It was still bruised, puffy, and crisscrossed with angry red scars.

"Don't worry," Piquett told him. "All plastic surgery patients look like that at first. The swelling will go down soon. You'll look like a new man in no time. Right, doc?"

"Chust zo," said Loeser.

Sure enough, just a day later the Jackrabbit's face looked less like a horror show, and he declared himself pleased with the results. Jimmy Probasco thought he looked pretty much the same as he had before, but he decided that it was best not to say anything.

Based on the Jackrabbit's results, Homer decided to go under the knife as well. A few days later, Loeser and Cassidy returned to remap Van Meter's

166

mug. In addition to the facial surgery, they also removed a tattoo on his forearm that read "Hope." Jimmy thought that was bad luck, but again, he kept his opinion to himself.

They also performed a procedure on both the Jackrabbit and Homer to eradicate their fingerprints. This involved whittling off the skin of their fingertips with a scalpel and soaking the exposed flesh in hydrochloric acid. Loeser had developed the technique on himself to try to avoid his narcotics rap. "Zee?" he said, showing off his featureless fingertips. "Zmooz as a baby's bottom."

Regardless of its efficacy, the procedure was painful. The Jackrabbit endured it in silence, but Homer—who was still woozy from his facial surgery—hollered and danced around the room waving his hands as if they were on fire.

Loeser left a huge bottle of morphine tablets to help his patients deal with the pain. The Jackrabbit took them sparingly, but Homer ate them like Necco wafers. Jimmy didn't like how the dope made Homer moody and volatile.

On this particular morning, Jimmy was especially nervous because Loeser was coming back to remove Van Meter's bandages. Homer was popping morphine tablets every twenty minutes and alternated between sitting in a stupor and pacing the front room muttering, "This better be worth it."

When there was a knock at the front door, Jimmy sprang up to get it. But instead of Dr. Loeser, he was surprised to see the leering grin of Baby Face Nelson.

"Lester Gillis?" said Jimmy. "What the hell are you doing here?"

"I don't use that name anymore," said Nelson. "Just call me George."

"I hope you don't mind, Jimmy," said the Jackrabbit. "Our friend here was interested in the plastic surgery and wanted to stop by to see the results."

"Oh. . . . OK."

Jimmy Probasco and Nelson had known each other for a long time. Both had grown up in a tough Chicago neighborhood called the Patch, and both were very well connected in the city's underworld. They knew many of the same people, but they'd never worked together. This was just fine with

Jimmy since Nelson had a reputation for being violent and unpredictable. Having both Nelson and a drugged-up Homer Van Meter in his house made Jimmy very uneasy. The potential for violence was high. Jimmy thought he could take care of himself, but Peggy could get hurt. For the first time, he began to wonder whether the money he was making was worth the risk.

"So, uh, George, can I get you a drink?" asked Jimmy. He thought he could stand another one himself.

"Yeah, sure. Beer."

Jimmy hustled back to the kitchen and pulled a bottle of beer from the icebox. He also filled his coffee cup nearly to the brim with whiskey and added just enough coffee to give it some opacity. He took a long sip and tried to relax.

He thought about the money he was bringing in. His guests had already stayed for over a week and showed no sign of leaving anytime soon. He had already hit them up for another week's rent, which brought his total take to over $800. If the Jackrabbit and Van Meter stayed another three weeks recovering from surgery, it would be over $2,000! That would make a nice down payment on the Green Log Inn. With that happy thought, Jimmy took another knock of his fortified coffee and shuttled the beer out to Nelson in the living room.

"I dunno," Nelson was saying. "Maybe you should keep them bandages on, Van Meter. It's definitely an improvement."

"Aw, go pound sand, Baby Face."

"Hey, you know I don't like being called that!"

"Too bad," said Homer. He popped another morphine pill. "Maybe you can ask the doc to give you a new face. One that doesn't look like an eight year old."

"The doc's gonna have to give *you* another new face if you keep ragging me like that. I'll rip yours clean off!"

"Say, George," said the Jackrabbit, trying to diffuse the situation. "Are you really thinking of getting the operation done?"

"Not sure."

"Well, whaddaya think of *my* new mug?"

Nelson sipped his beer and eyed the Jackrabbit's face critically. "Well, it pretty much looks like you were in a dogfight," he said. "I mean, I can still tell it's you, you know what I mean? But you *do* look different. I guess I'll wait to see how much ugly the docs were able to cut off Van Meter's mug before I decide for sure."

They didn't have to wait long. Piquett and the two doctors showed up ten minutes later. With great ceremony, Loeser removed the bandages from Homer's face and handed him a mirror.

"Vell, vhat do you think?" asked Loeser.

"What do I think?" said Van Meter. "I think I paid five grand to let a butcher hack at my face!"

"Now don't vorry," said Loeser. "It takes a vhile to recover from zees zort of procedure. Zurely, you zaw zat veeth your companion here."

"All *I* see is my old face with a bunch of damn scars! It doesn't look any different!"

"Of course eet does," insisted Loeser. "Your nose ees shorter and more narrow, and your lower leep ees noticeably smaller, even veeth zee residual swelling."

Homer began pacing and swearing. "My face is a goddamn mess, you lousy quack! And it hurts like hell all the time!"

"It's sure killing me," laughed Nelson.

"I can't believe I let you fuck up my face like this! You miserable kraut son of a bitch! I'll show you what happens when you mess with me!" Homer ducked into the front bedroom and emerged with his Tommy gun.

"Whoa, now!" exclaimed Jimmy. He backed into a corner and tried to make himself look small.

Homer rushed up to Loeser and shoved the barrel of the gun in his face. "You think it's funny that you hacked up my face like this? You're gonna need a whole new head in about three seconds!"

There was a loud *clunk* from the other side of the room. Baby Face Nelson had dropped his beer. He rolled on the couch holding his stomach and wheezing with laughter.

"Just keep laughing, asshole!" hissed Homer. "You're gonna be—"

"Easy, buddy," said the Jackrabbit. He stepped in front of Homer and gently pushed the barrel of the Tommy gun down. "Let's just calm down now, OK? I know it doesn': look so good now, but you have to give it a little time to heal."

"That's easy for you to say! He did a good job on *you*! I look exactly the same except my face is covered with scars!"

"It's still an improvement," snickered Nelson.

"Stifle it, would you?" said the Jackrabbit. "Let's everybody take a deep breath and calm down. Van, I know it doesn't seem too good right now, but there are still things the doc can do. Right, doc?"

"Oh, ya, of course," said Loeser with an obvious measure of relief. "You haff to underztand zat Mr. Van Meter has a rather, um, deezteencteeve face."

"That's one way of putting it!" snorted Nelson.

"Dammit, Baby Face, quit stirring the pot!" snapped the Jackrabbit.

For a moment, an ugly look crossed Nelson's face, and Jimmy was certain there was going to be a gunfight right in his living room. Then Nelson shrugged, retrieved the fallen beer bottle, and took another sip.

"As I vas zaying," continued Loeser. "Mr. Van Meter has a much more deezteencteeve face, making eet more deefeecult to obscure. Mr. Chackrabbit, on zee other hand, has features zat are less pronounced, shall ve zay. Eet vas zerefore easier to alter zee appearance of zee latter zan zee former, eh?"

"Yes, but there's still some stuff you can do to help change Van's face, right?" asked the Jackrabbit.

"Oh, ya, certainly," said Loeser. "Chust looking right now, I can zee a few areas vhere ve can make zome improvements."

"And at no extra cost, right doc?" asked Piquett.

Loeser cut his eyes to Van Meter's submachine gun and said, "Of course not. I have my bag een zee car. Ve can operate eemeedeeately."

"Well, since you're going to set up shop," said Piquett. "Perhaps Mr. Nelson here would be interested in having his face done as well."

Baby Face Nelson polished off the dregs of his beer and jumped to his feet. He pulled out his wallet and thumbed through the bills inside. "Nah," he said. "I think I'm gonna keep my baby face just the way it is." He pulled out a five and stuck it in Loeser's breast pocket. "That's for you, doc. This was the funniest show I've seen since *Duck Soup*." He strolled out the front door and disappeared down the walk.

"Well, that's settled," said the Jackrabbit. "Jimmy, why don't you get the 'operating room' ready again?"

"Sure thing, boss," said Jimmy. He hustled to the back bedroom where Peggy was reading a movie magazine.

"Peg, go clean up the dining room and put some sheets on the table. The doc's going to do a touch-up job on 'Cletus.'"

"What . . . again?" she pouted. "You never said I was going to have to be an operating room nurse. I don't like this."

"Look, do you want that new outfit from Field's or not?" snapped Jimmy. Sometimes Peggy could really get under his skin. It was bad enough having three of the country's most notorious gangsters bickering in his front room. At least his woman could do what she's told.

"No, Jimmy, I'm really scared," she said. "These guys are dangerous. I don't like having them around."

"Hey, they get a little hot under the collar sometimes, but they're good eggs. They're not gonna hurt us."

"It's not them I'm worried about. If the cops or the Feds find out they're here, they're just gonna come in and shoot up the place. Little people like you and me don't make a difference to them." She looked at him imploringly.

Jimmy started to rebuke her, but something in her blue eyes made him hold his tongue. She *did* have a point. When Piquett first approached him about harboring the Jackrabbit and Van Meter, all Jimmy could think about was the money. Of course, he knew there was a risk involved, but there was always a risk if you really wanted to make some cabbage. So he'd written it off, mainly because he knew he could take care of himself.

But he had to consider the danger he was putting Peggy in. Sure, she wasn't the prettiest dame in town, but she took good care of him and put up with his drunken shenanigans when most women would have been out the door. She didn't deserve this.

"Look, baby doll, I've given my word here," he said. "I can't just turn them out now. Tell you what, though—why don't you go visit your mother in Sheboygan? I'll give you some cash for the train. You have a good visit for a week or two, and by the time you get back, they'll be gone." Actually, Jimmy hoped that wasn't the case. If the two gangsters stayed around for another month, he'd be pretty close to having his nest egg.

"I don't want to leave you," said Peggy. "I'm worried about you, Jimmy. This deal is getting more and more rotten by the day."

"It's the same deal it's always been, sweetheart. Things are a little rough right now, but it'll all work out. If everything goes according to plan, I'll have enough money to buy the Green Log, and we'll be on Easy Street. We just gotta hang in there."

"Well, OK," she said. "I'll go get the room ready. But then we're going down to Marshall Field's, and you're going to buy me that outfit—today."

"Of course, baby doll. I promise. But first we have work to do."

"I know," said Peggy with a sigh. "Again."

Homer Van Meter's follow-up surgery went smoothly, and the visibly relieved Doctors Loeser and Cassidy beat a hasty retreat as soon as it was done. For the next few days, things settled down a bit. Homer popped morphine pills constantly and dozed. The Jackrabbit seemed content to listen to baseball games on the radio and read the newspapers.

\* \* \*

Two days later, Jimmy went out to chat up the owner of the Green Log and have a drink or three. As soon as he stumbled back in his front door, he knew something was wrong. The Jackrabbit and Homer were hunched over the radio in the corner.

"Hiya, fellas!" called Jimmy jovially. "How's tricks?"

The gangsters looked over at him, and he could see murder in their eyes.

"Shut your face," hissed Homer. "We're trying to listen to this!"

Jimmy started to apologize, then he shut his mouth with an audible click.

The news announcer on the radio was saying: ". . . died in the hospital just hours after being shot by police in Waterloo, Iowa. Carroll was part of the deadly shoot-out in Wisconsin that resulted in the death of an FBI agent and an innocent bystander from the Civilian Conservation Corps. Once again, Tommy Carroll, member of the notorious Jackrabbit Gang, was killed by police today in Iowa."

"Shut it off, Van," ordered the Jackrabbit. "Jimmy, why don't you make yourself scarce?"

"Right," said Jimmy. "I'm just going to go change the sheets in your room, OK, fellas?"

They didn't respond. Jimmy disappeared into the front bedroom and busied himself tidying up. Normally, he would have had Peggy take care of it, but she was at her mother's. Besides, he wanted to learn more about what had happened. He kept the bedroom door open enough so that he could hear the conversation in the living room.

There wasn't much to listen to. The two gangsters were dead silent for nearly ten minutes. Finally, the Jackrabbit said, "Jesus, poor Tommy. He was a good egg. He didn't deserve to go out like that."

"Yeah," said Homer. "I'd hate for that to happen to me. Shot down in some dirty alley like a dog."

"First Eddie Green, then Red, now Tommy. Where's it going to end?"

"You sure you want an answer to that question, pal?"

"I know, I know," said the Jackrabbit. "This doesn't look good. But cheer up."

"Cheer up?" said Homer. "How the hell am I supposed to cheer up? The noose is tightening every damn day!"

"Well, we got these nifty new faces, for starters. We should be able to just blend in with the ordinary citizens now."

"Yeah, I guess so," said Homer doubtfully.

"Keep this under your hat, Van, but I've got an escape plan. I'm heading to Mexico."

"How the hell are you going to manage that?"

"Should be easy with my shiny new mug," said the Jackrabbit, patting his scarred cheek. "There's a nice retired couple who'll drive me down there and say I'm their son. I just have to pay 'em ten grand. So I just need a little more cash to finance things. All we need is one more job. A big one."

"Yeah, I keep hearing about that fabled big job," said Homer. "It never seems to come along, though."

"No, no," said the Jackrabbit. "I've been talking with Nelson. He says he's got something working in Indiana. Solid job, quarter of a million, easy. One last big score, then I'm done for good."

"Sure thing, pal," said Homer. "Sure thing."

# CHAPTER TWENTY-SIX

"Looks like the cat is out of the bag," said Martin Zarkovich.

"How's that?" asked Tim O'Neil.

They were sitting in their dingy office in the East Chicago PD headquarters, drinking awful station-house coffee. Zarkovich was looking through the personals section of the *Indianapolis Star*. He did this frequently, as many brothels advertised their services through coded ads there. He wanted to make sure there weren't any cathouses operating in the area without paying the requisite protection money.

"Check out this ad," said Zarkovich. He circled a listing on the page and shoved it across the desk to O'Neil.

O'Neil picked up the paper and read, "'Birthday greetings to my darling brother, the Jackrabbit, on his 31st birthday. Wherever he may be, I hope he will read this message. Sister Audrey.' Aw, ain't that cute?"

"It's not 'cute,'" said Zarkovich. "It's a pain in the ass."

"So what? It's a silly girlie birthday greeting."

"It means, partner o' mine, that everybody will know the Jackrabbit is still alive. They're going to be looking for him even harder. I haven't heard from him since those do-gooders Mulvihill and O'Brien got popped down in Munster. The Jackrabbit took off right after that."

"Yeah, I noticed that too," said O'Neil. "Say, pal, you didn't have anything to do with that caper, did you?"

Zarkovich laughed and tapped the side of his nose. "Don't worry about that, Timmy. What you don't know won't hurt you, right?"

"Hell, no. Forget I asked."

"Already forgotten. But speaking of forbidden knowledge, the Jackrabbit knows entirely too much for our own good. I was hoping I could find him first and sort of take care of the problem myself."

"Uh, are you sure that's such a good idea?" asked O'Neil. "A lot of our . . . um . . . associates know he's under our protection. If we turn around and 'fix' him, won't that hurt our reputation?"

"Our reputation won't mean squat if we end up in the Michigan City pen," said Zarkovich. "Besides, we're not the only ones who are worried about the Jackrabbit. Nitti and the Syndicate boys in the city would be plenty happy to see him out of the picture too. He's bringing too much heat down on their operations."

"Yeah, well, he's making me plenty nervous too," said O'Neil. "The sooner he's dead, the better. We're probably pretty safe, though."

"How do you figure?"

"Well, every damn cop in the country is looking for him, right? I figure that when the Jackrabbit pops out of his hole, they'll shoot first and ask questions later."

"Yeah, maybe," said Zarkovich. "On the other hand—"

"What other hand?"

"A lot of people are talking about what's happened to all the money he's stolen. They say there's some fabulous 'Jackrabbit Treasure' stashed away somewhere in the sticks. Some of the more literate cops might figure they could sweat that information out of him and either get a reward or pocket the money themselves."

"Ah, you know there's no damn 'Jackrabbit Treasure,'" said O'Neil. "The guy's payin' most of his money to keep himself safe. Hell, we got a big chunk of it ourselves."

"Yeah, you know that, and I know that, but J. Edgar Hoover doesn't know that. So we've really got to make sure no one else finds out. Christ knows what he'll spill if he gets captured alive."

"So what are we gonna do?"

"We've got to get to him first and make sure he goes down before anybody asks him a single question."

"How are we gonna do that?"

"Police work, partner, police work," said Zarkovich. "It's our sworn duty to uphold the law and protect honest citizens from evildoers like the Jackrabbit. Or have you forgotten?"

"Yeah, I guess I've been too busy working the whorehouses and gambling joints to remember," laughed O'Neil.

Zarkovich stared down at the personal ads. As soon as word got out that the Jackrabbit wasn't pushing up daisies or enjoying the sights of Old London Town, the heat would be cranked up even higher. "I'm going out to get another paper," he said.

"Another? You've already got three there, Professor."

"Yeah, but if I spotted darling sister's personal ad, then someone else has too," said Zarkovich. "I want to see if there's anything in the late editions about it. C'mon, Honey." He stood up, and the golden retriever sprang up from the corner where she'd been snoozing. She had proven to be a surprisingly good companion after Zarkovich offed the Fink.

Zarkovich and the dog left the station house to take a stroll to the newsstand. Along the way, Zarkovich was lost in thought. Things had gotten too complicated, and the situation was starting to get out of hand. He had always prided himself on his care and discretion in his extracurricular business activities. But in retrospect, he'd gone too far in setting up the Jackrabbit to bump off Mulvihill and O'Brien. He had let the two crusading cops get under his skin, and he'd made a bad call. There were more discrete ways he could have had the two White Knight cops taken care of, but he had gotten jumpy. "Shit, too late now," he thought.

"Paper, mister?" A grubby kid on the corner was hawking late editions of the *Indianapolis Star*. "Get the latest on the Jackrabbit!"

The headline on the paper read: "JACKRABBIT ALIVE! SISTER'S BIRTHDAY GREETING CONFIRMS GANGSTER NOT DEAD."

"Yeah, kid, give me the paper."

The kid handed him a paper, and Zarkovich gave him a nickel. "Keep the change, kid."

"Gee, thanks, mister!"

Zarkovich hustled back toward the station house, and it wasn't until he was almost there that he scanned the print below the headline. What he saw stopped him in his tracks: "$15,000 Offered for Capture of the Jackrabbit." He scanned the article. The Department of Justice had announced this huge reward for the Jackrabbit's capture. The article strongly hinted that the full reward would be given dead or alive.

Fifteen thousand dollars was an enormous bundle of money—you could buy a mansion for that sum and still have enough left over for a fleet of cars. Most of the people Zarkovich knew would murder their own mothers for fifteen grand. The competition to find the Jackrabbit would be intense. There was also the possibility that whoever bagged him might bring him in alive. That was an unacceptable risk.

There was only one solution: Martin Zarkovich had to be the one who brought the Jackrabbit down. He'd make sure the man did not live to tell any tales. There may be a lot of people looking for the fugitive bank robber, but few of them knew the guy as well as he did. Hell, the Jackrabbit might even become desperate enough to seek him out for help. That would simplify matters immensely, but Zarkovich doubted it would happen. The Jackrabbit also knew *him* too well.

He tucked the paper under his arm and hurried back to his office to fetch his partner. The hunt was on.

# CHAPTER TWENTY-SEVEN

**Palatine, Illinois**
**June 22, 1934**

It was nearly midnight when the last car approached the empty schoolhouse. It was a sultry night, and the full moon hung heavy in the new summer sky. Crickets and cicadas in the woods around the schoolyard sang in celebration of the solstice.

Baby Face Nelson, Homer Van Meter, and the Jackrabbit stood by their cars, shooting the breeze and waiting for the new arrivals.

Approaching headlights cut through the summer night's haze. "Is this them?" asked Homer. His hand crept toward his shoulder holster out of sheer habit.

"Yeah, of course it's them," said Baby Face. "Who else would it be, the Marx Brothers?"

"I don't know that," said Homer. "And neither do you. Someone might have tipped off the cops."

"You calling me a rat?" sneered Nelson.

"I'm not calling anybody anything. I'm just nervous, that's all."

Homer was more nervous about Nelson than anything else. Things had been pretty good when they'd started working together last year. Nelson had seemed like a stand-up guy when he helped Homer after he got out of Michigan City by cutting him in on some lucrative jobs. But ever since the Jackrabbit had joined the gang, Nelson's behavior was more unsettling. He was quick to anger and prone to vicious insults.

The Jackrabbit was good at fending off Nelson's jibes and slights, but they really got under Homer's skin. He especially hated the way Nelson had laughed at him after his surgery. It had been irritating and humiliating. Ever since then, Homer found himself disliking the impish young man more and more.

The approach of the car snapped Homer out of his introspection. The car's headlights dimmed and two men stepped out. "You there, George?" asked one of them.

"Yeah, I'm here," said Nelson. "See, I told you it was them," he said to Homer.

The new arrivals stepped up to the gangsters. In the moonlight, it was difficult to make out their features. One was short and round with a swarthy complexion. The other was tall with an athletic build. He had high cheekbones and a high forehead and wore his hair slicked straight back.

Nelson made the introductions. "These are my boys from Reno," he said. "J. P. Chase and Fatso Negri, meet the Jackrabbit and his dumb friend Homer Van Meter."

Homer gritted his teeth. He had the urge to pop Nelson one on the schnoz. Instead, he shook the guys' hands and kept quiet.

"All right," said the Jackrabbit. "It's good to meet you boys. I've heard a lot about both of you, and George here says you're stand-up guys. Glad to have you on the team."

"Hey, whose team are you talking about, pally?" asked Nelson. "*I'm* the one running the show here, and don't you forget it!"

Homer couldn't help himself. "That's not what the Feds say," he snorted. "You're only worth half of what the Jackrabbit is, according to what I read."

"God dammit!" spat Nelson. "Those fuckers don't know what's what! If it wasn't for me, there wouldn't *be* a gang! *I'm* the boss, see? I'M THE GODDAMN BOSS! I should be worth more than him!"

"Yeah, sure, George, of course," said the Jackrabbit. "Those Feds are dumber than a bag of hair, everybody knows that. You should be worth twenty grand, easy."

"Damn right," said Nelson. "Besides, Van Moron here doesn't even rate. You're worth exactly zero, shitheel!"

"Yeah, and I'll be alive a lot longer than you because of it, you punk."

"Hey, knock it off, both of you!" said the Jackrabbit. "We're here to talk business. Let's act like professionals. All right?"

"Yeah, sure, of course," said Homer.

Nelson just muttered under his breath.

"So what's the score?" asked Fatso. "George here says we're on to a big one."

"Hell, yes," said Nelson. "Merchants National Bank in South Bend. It's a fat jug. They receive remittances from the post office every Saturday morning. I figure it's worth two hundred thou, easy. Maybe a quarter of a mil."

"How's this going down?" asked J. P.

"You, Fatso, and the Jackrabbit will work the bank," said Nelson. "Van Meter will guard the entrance, and I'll be down the street a bit to make sure he don't screw it up too bad."

They spent another forty-five minutes going over the details of the job. Homer was assigned to draw up the git and figure out the best way for the gang to escape. He'd have to travel to South Bend tomorrow to start mapping out possible escape routes and come up with detailed getaway instructions.

He wasn't keen on leaving since he'd just gotten back together with his girlfriend, Marie. She'd been released from custody along with the other molls arrested at Little Bohemia. At first, he'd been reluctant to contact her because it was a certainty that the FBI was watching her closely. But after Jean Delaney and Helen Gillis had gotten away, he figured that maybe the Feds weren't paying too much attention.

After the plastic surgery, he thought it was worth the risk. He'd bought himself a dandy new suit with pince-nez spectacles. He made contact with his sweetheart by leaving coded messages with her parents. Since then, they'd been seeing each other several times a week.

Just then, Baby Face Nelson startled Homer with the comment, "Well, we should be OK if Van Meter don't spill the beans to that chippie of his."

"What?" snapped Homer. "What the hell are you talking about?"

"I'm talking about that wop bitch you've been porking," snarled Nelson. "She's a rat. She's been talking to the cops."

"Dammit, Baby Face, I've had about as much shit out of you as I'm gonna take!"

"I told you I don't like that name!"

"Too goddamn bad! You better be able to back up what you're saying about Marie!"

"Ooh, Marie!" mocked Nelson. "You're so sweet on her, you can't even see that she's selling you out, you lunk!"

"Hold on, George," interjected the Jackrabbit. "What are you saying? This sounds serious."

"It *is* serious," said Nelson. "That Comforti bitch is palling around with cops all the time."

"Quit saying that!" said Homer. "Sure, there's cops following her. There were cops following Jean and Helen too!"

"You leave my wife out of this, you son of a bitch!" yelled Nelson. His hand went to his shoulder holster. Homer's did the same. His head felt hot and stuffy, and the angry red ring was creeping in around his vision.

Fatso and J. P. took a few steps backward.

The Jackrabbit placidly held his ground. "Fellas, fellas, we need to calm down a bit here," he said, holding up his hands. "I don't think it's unusual that the law is following her around. We knew that was gonna happen when they sprang the girls."

"Yeah!" said Homer. "We're extra careful when we meet. There's no cops following her. I check it every time!"

Nelson seemed to relax slightly. "They're not just following her," he insisted. "She's been talking to them. I got witnesses, a bunch of 'em."

"What?" said Homer. "What the hell are you saying?" His head pounded even harder now.

"Yeah," said Nelson. "Jimmy Murray at the Rain-Bo Inn said he saw her talking to a Chicago cop named Wittiger. One of the Jackrabbit Squad—one of Stege's men."

"That's hardly 'a bunch,'" said Homer uncertainly.

"Oh yeah? Well, my old pal Clarey Lieder said he saw her talking to an FBI agent—a guy named McLaughlin. Said the two looked real chummy too."

Homer's head spun. Could it be possible that his Marie was selling him out? He didn't know what to think. She was always a bit of a flirt but singing to the cops didn't seem possible. Or was it? "What?" he said. "No . . . that can't be right. I don't believe—"

"You better believe it, buster," said Nelson. "Your little wop tramp is singing to the fuzz. Hell, she's probably screwing 'em too."

"Fuck you, Baby Face!"

Homer went for his gun again, but Nelson just laughed. "Get a clue, pal! She's playing you for a sucker! You don't believe me, you can talk to Jimmy and Clarey. Hell, I can probably find half a dozen other guys to back me up—without even trying hard!"

"That . . . little . . . bitch!" spat Homer. His vision swam, and his head thundered like a kettledrum. He wished he had some of his morphine pills. They always helped him calm down when he got tense, which seemed to be happening much more often lately.

"Finally!" said Nelson. "The lug nut sees reason!"

It made sense, in a way. Sure, Marie *said* she'd been at her parents' house, but what else had she been doing? She liked attention and liked showing off, especially for men. If all of a sudden there were a bunch of cops and FBI agents following her everywhere she went . . . well, wouldn't she *like* it in a way? Yes, of course she would. And sooner or later, wouldn't she strike up a conversation with one of them, maybe even start flirting with him? Sure, sure, that would be just like her. After that, who knows what she might say . . . or do. That two-timing little whore! How *dare* she sell him out like this!

The crimson veil descended over his vision, and Homer blew his top. "GOD DAMMIT!" he roared. "I'M GONNA KILL HER!"

"You'd better!" said Nelson. "If you don't pop a cap in her, I'll do it myself!"

"Oh, don't worry about that!" said Homer. "I'm gonna take care of it right now, believe me!" He turned and headed toward the car.

The Jackrabbit hurried after him. "Say, pal, why don't you let me drive? You seem a little worked up."

Homer was about to tell him to go screw, but then he thought better of it. The Jackrabbit was probably right. It wasn't a good idea to be behind the wheel when he was this upset. Reluctantly, he handed over the car keys.

"That's a fella," said the Jackrabbit. "We'll get this cleared up, I'm sure." He turned to Fatso and J. P. and said, "Say, it was nice meeting you boys. Looking forward to working with you." He started the car with a roar and pulled out.

They drove in silence for ten minutes. Finally, the Jackrabbit said, "You're not really going to shoot Marie, are you?"

Homer had been pondering that question the entire ride. Now that he was away from Nelson, it didn't seem so bad. Sure, the cops were following Marie. She might have even talked to one of them. If she did, it was probably just to razz the cop—to let him know that she was on to him. She could be a real firecracker that way. It was one of the things Homer liked about her.

He'd never been what you'd call a ladies' man. He'd always secretly envied the Jackrabbit's easy way with women. That had never been Homer's strong suit. He remembered a crush he'd had on a girl named Daisy back in the fifth grade. She called him "Homely Homer" and laughed in his face when he asked her to the picture show. Marie was never like that. She doted on him.

Besides, if she *had* spilled the beans to the cops, they would have already swooped in and nabbed him by now, tried to sweat him out to get to the Jackrabbit. No, there was no way Marie would ever sell him out like that.

He tried a lighthearted chuckle. "Ha! You believed that? I was just saying that to get Nelson to shut up."

His mood shifted again. That bastard Nelson had really gotten him worked up. Why the hell had he said those things? The guy was pretty paranoid. He'd probably just heard a rumor and immediately jumped to the wrong conclusion. It was also possible that Nelson was saying those things to wind Homer up just out of spite. Baby Face Nelson had no shortage of *that*.

# CHAPTER TWENTY-SEVEN

"That Nelson really gets my goat," said Homer.

"Yeah, I've just about had it with old Baby Face myself," the Jackrabbit said. "He comes up with good jobs, but he's too crazy. You never know what the little bastard is gonna do."

"You got that right," said Homer darkly. "I ought to pop a cap in *him*. That little psycho!"

"Just take it easy, pal. We've still got a job to do. This is *it*. This is the big one. Let's keep our eyes on the prize."

"Yeah, OK. But after this, I'm done working with Nelson. I can mark a jug just as good as him—maybe better."

"Yeah, sure," said the Jackrabbit. "And everybody knows that you're aces at putting together the gits."

"After this South Bend job, it'll just be you and me, right? The two of us taking on smaller jobs. No more Baby Face. Or any of his West Coast pals."

"Well, old friend, you're partially right," said the Jackrabbit. "I agree, no more Baby Face Nelson. After this, I'm getting out of here. Heading to Mexico, remember? I really mean it."

"You sound like you're serious."

"Of course, I'm serious. You should think about what you're gonna do too. Maybe you should take Marie somewhere out of the way. Find a nice little cabin in the Northwoods somewhere and have a long rest."

"Yeah, that sounds real nice. We'll clean out this South Bend jug and just relax."

"Absolutely," said the Jackrabbit. "That's just what we'll do. A quick, simple heist. It'll be a cinch."

# CHAPTER TWENTY-EIGHT

### South Bend, Indiana
### June 30, 1934

The stolen Hudson cruised slowly past the bank. "Christ, look at all the people!" said Baby Face Nelson. "Why didn't you tell us there'd be so many damn people, Van Meter?"

"What the hell did you expect?" replied Homer. "You picked the bank. You *knew* it was in the middle of town."

The Merchants National Bank was at the intersection of Wayne and Michigan, the busiest streets in South Bend. When Homer had been in town earlier in the week, he noticed how crowded the area was, but he figured it would thin out on a Saturday. However, just the opposite was true: there were even more people around now. Streetcars clanged down the tracks on Wayne every few minutes, and the sidewalks bustled with shoppers.

"You two hens quit squawking," said the Jackrabbit. "We've got a job to do. What time is it?"

"A quarter to twelve," said Nelson. "Almost closing time. They shoulda deposited the cash from the post office an hour ago."

"Perfect. Van, pull up right there," said the Jackrabbit, pointing to a spot down the block from the bank.

Homer pulled the Hudson to the curb where the Jackrabbit had indicated.

"OK, boys, let's make this quick," said Nelson, and they piled out of the car.

Right in front of them, a teenager in a red beanie was getting out of an old jalopy. He took a quick look at them and his jaw dropped. He must have noticed the odd way they were dressed. Despite the summer heat, most of the men were wearing long overcoats. The Jackrabbit was dressed even more conspicuously in overalls and a floppy straw hat. He had a handkerchief draped over his hand.

"You'd better scram, kid," the Jackrabbit said as he pulled away the handkerchief to reveal his .45 pistol. The kid scrammed.

Nelson stayed by the car while Homer followed the Jackrabbit, J. P., and Fatso down to the entrance of the bank. Under his duster, Homer had a heavy .351 automatic rifle strapped to the side of his leg.

While the Jackrabbit, J. P., and Fatso entered the bank, Homer stationed himself on the sidewalk near the entrance. A cop stood in the intersection directing traffic. Homer eyed him carefully. The cop didn't seem to notice the strangely dressed men entering the bank; he continued to toot his whistle and direct traffic. Homer touched the rifle clamped to his leg and tried to look casual.

For a moment, all was calm. Homer watched the cars in the street and the people on the sidewalks. A gaggle of college girls romped by on the other side of the street, talking and laughing. They stopped in front of Berg's jewelry store and oohed and aahed over the pieces in the window. Behind Homer, a young couple led their protesting toddler to a nearby shoe store. They promised him an ice-cream cone if he was a good boy and tried on some new shoes for church.

Homer sighed. He envied the South Benders enjoying their pleasant Saturday morning. He thought of them doing some shopping, visiting the park, then going home to their peaceful houses to savor a nice meal and listen to a program on the radio. If not for a few wrong turns, his own life might have turned out like that.

He looked back down toward their car, and his heart dropped into his stomach. The kid in the red beanie had come back and was reaching into the window of their Hudson. Baby Face Nelson appeared from behind the car and grabbed him. Homer winced, expecting Nelson to shoot the kid right then and there. Instead, he just gave the kid a shove, and the kid took off running.

From Homer's vantage point, it looked like the kid was heading straight for a telephone booth at the end of the block. He knew the Saturday morning calm of downtown South Bend was about to be shattered. He reached down and undid the strap on the rifle beneath his coat.

Before the kid was even halfway down the block, a burst of machine-gun fire came from inside the bank. Most of the people on the street looked around curiously but continued on with their business. A man behind Homer said, "Huh, firecrackers. Kids these days." After all, the Fourth of July was only a few days away.

The traffic cop in the intersection was not so blasé. The silver whistle dropped from his open mouth, and as he began to walk toward the bank, he released the snap on the holster of his service revolver.

In one fluid motion, Homer raised the rifle to his shoulder and put three rounds into the center of the cop's chest—*ka-chow! ka-chow! ka-chow!* The cop flew backward and landed square on his back. A red stain spread across his uniform as he continued to scrabble weakly for his gun. Then he was still.

Homer briefly wondered about the man he had just shot: "What kind of guy was he? Did he have a family?" Then his well-honed sense of self-preservation kicked in, and he turned and ran for cover.

The echoes of the gunfire reverberated off the downtown storefronts. People screamed and ran in every direction, unsure of where the shots were coming from. Homer crouched down behind a trash can, scanning the panicked mob for more cops.

He glanced back toward the car. Baby Face hefted his Tommy gun and was scanning the crowd for targets. The college girls saw him and screamed, shrinking back to the storefront of Berg's Jewelry. Ignoring them, Nelson walked around the front of the car and peered down the alley beside the bank.

Behind him, a bowling ball-shaped man came out of Berg's Jewelry holding a small pistol. The rotund man aimed the gun with both hands, closed his eyes, and squeezed the trigger. Nelson turned around just in time to catch the shot in his breastbone. Homer watched as the fabric of Nelson's coat burst outward as the bullet hit home. Nelson fell over backward. The round man slowly lowered his pistol. An expression of wonder and pride spread across his face.

It disappeared a moment later when Baby Face Nelson bounced back to his feet. He unlimbered his Tommy gun and sent a long burst of gunfire in the short man's direction. The shots sailed over the man's head and disintegrated the plate glass window of the jewelry store. The man shrieked and scuttled back inside.

Nelson scowled and rubbed his chest. The ever-paranoid gangster never went on a job without a bulletproof vest. Homer had ribbed him for paying $300 for it—enough for a decent used car. He could see now that it had been well worth the price, and now he wondered if he hadn't made a huge mistake in not getting one for himself.

He was still pondering this when a teenager came running from the crowd and jumped onto Nelson's back. Homer watched, his mouth agape. The citizens of South Bend must be out of their damn minds! He raised the rifle to try to pick off the kid, but he couldn't get a clear shot. Nelson swung around wildly, trying to dislodge his attacker.

Finally, the kid fell off Nelson's back but managed to land on his feet. Nelson slammed the butt of his Tommy gun into the side of the kid's head. The kid staggered sideways and fell over into the shattered display window of Berg's Jewelry. He didn't get up.

Nelson retreated to the car and crouched down behind the fender. A block down the street, Homer looked around. In the middle of the intersection, the cop was lying unattended in a pool of blood. Drivers, oblivious to the drama going on at the corner of Wayne and Michigan, sailed through the intersection, missing the officer's body by inches. The sidewalks were largely clear of pedestrians, although one or two still dashed madly for better cover. Sirens wailed in the distance and grew louder by the moment.

There had been no action from inside the bank since the initial burst of gunfire. Baby Face Nelson was out of sight behind the Hudson. Homer felt distinctly exposed and alone. He looked around wildly. Next to the bank he saw half a dozen people in the back of Nisley Shoes, peering out at the street. "A nice group of hostages," Homer thought.

Holding the rifle across his chest, Homer stormed through the door of the shoe store like a squad of marines. The customers shrank back against the rear wall. As he leveled his gun, two of the women screamed.

"Guess what folks!" he cried with demented joviality. "Today, we're having a sidewalk sale! Now get your goddamn asses out on the sidewalk! You may go home with the bargain of your lives!"

He hustled his hostages onto the sidewalk. Three cops converged on the intersection just in time to see Homer array the six shoe shoppers around him. They pulled their pistols but didn't fire.

Homer leveled his automatic rifle between two women and let loose a prolonged barrage that sent the cops diving for cover. One of the women in Homer's human shield began to sob.

Amazingly, cars were still puttering through the intersection, directly into the middle of the gun battle. A black Dodge sailed across the field of fire. As soon as it was clear, the cops across the street opened fire from behind the row of parked cars.

"What the hell's wrong with you cops?" yelled Homer. "You might hit someone here!"

Down the block, Baby Face noticed the cops and opened fire with his Thompson. A hail of gunfire raked across the parked cars and storefronts across the street, shattering glass and puncturing sheet metal. A silver DeSoto Airflow drove directly into the stream of Nelson's bullets. The driver jerked back, and the Airflow slammed into a light pole on the other side of the street. The driver started screaming. Homer figured the guy couldn't be hurt too badly if he had the energy to scream so loudly.

He scanned the sidewalk. Where the hell were the Jackrabbit and the two new guys? Homer felt like he was in the Battle of Gettysburg, and he wanted to get the hell out of town while he still could.

Finally, the door to the bank burst open, and the Jackrabbit, Fatso, and J. P. emerged. They were each clutching a bulging cloth sack and herding a hostage before them. Fatso and J. P. had terrified tellers leading their way. The Jackrabbit's hostage was a stuffy-looking man in a three-piece suit. He looked more annoyed than scared.

Seeing the police crouched behind the cars across the street, the Jackrabbit and his fellow robbers threw lead their way. The cops returned fire. One hit the Jackrabbit's hostage, and he fell to the ground as a gout of blood burst from his calf.

"I'm hit!" he screeched. "I'm dying!"

"You're fine," said the Jackrabbit as he hauled the injured man to his feet. He began frog-marching him toward the parked Hudson. Baby Face Nelson scurried around the front of the car and let loose another terrific burst of machine-gun fire at the concealed cops.

Homer decided to make a dash for it. He wasn't going to bother herding a hostage. He sprinted away from the shoe store toward the driver's-side door of the Hudson.

He had almost made it when he heard a terrific *bang*, and a sheet of white fire flashed across his vision. A silver spike of pain lanced into the side of his skull. Then the pavement rushed up and smacked him in the face. He was vaguely aware of a warm pool of liquid spreading around his head. From miles above him, he heard the Jackrabbit yell, "Get him in the car! Get him in the car!"

And then everything went black.

# CHAPTER TWENTY-NINE

**Chicago, Illinois**
**July 1, 1934**

Jimmy Probasco was not a churchgoing man. His mama had dragged him to Mass when he was a kid, but he hadn't gone inside one of those Gothic guilt-barns since he was twelve. Jimmy liked his Saturday nights too much to be up early on Sunday mornings.

For some reason, though, he was up early on this particular Sunday morning. His eyes came open at half past four according to the noisy windup clock on the bedside table, and he hadn't been able to get back to sleep.

Also, Peggy was snoring like a truck, which didn't help matters at all. She had recently returned from her mother's place in Sheboygan, and she was none too thrilled to see that their houseguests were still there. He decided to avoid rousing her—she had been in a horrible mood ever since her return.

Perhaps a little nip of something would help him doze off again. He slipped out of bed and padded down to the kitchen. A bit of Irish coffee would hit the spot, but he didn't really feel like making coffee. Instead, he filled a coffee cup with Irish whiskey and sat down at the kitchen table.

A few belts of his morning pick-me-up helped clear his head. Then he suddenly realized why he was so restless: his houseguests hadn't come home last night. Ever since they'd moved in, the Jackrabbit and Homer had spent most of their time around the house. After the round of surgeries, they didn't leave at all. Then, about a week ago, they started going out at night. They didn't usually leave until ten or eleven and were sometimes gone for several hours. Jimmy suspected they were planning something big, but he knew better than to ask. As long as they kept paying their rent in advance, Jimmy was happy.

He'd already made a good bundle by harboring the two gangsters. In fact, he had over two grand tucked away in his hidey-hole under the bedroom floorboards. It was a decent chunk of change, but it still wasn't enough to buy the Green Log Inn. Jimmy was in the habit of stopping by the Green Log every couple of days to chat up the owner, Murray Abelman. Jimmy let it be known that he was interested in purchasing the place, but Abelman was being stubborn about the price. He wouldn't budge from his five grand asking price; said he needed at least that much to make the move to Miami. "Typical Jew," thought Jimmy. They were bastards to bargain with.

Now his boarders had disappeared, and Jimmy began to worry about his cash flow. Sure, their stuff was still here, but that didn't mean they'd come back for it. Maybe he could make a few bucks selling it off. If it turned out that they'd left for good, he didn't know how he'd pull together the rest of the dough to buy the Green Log.

The dogs in the backyard started barking, and before Jimmy could go outside and yell at them, there was a commotion on the front porch. He hustled up to the front room to see the Jackrabbit and an unknown man dragging Homer Van Meter through the front door. Van Meter's face and clothes were matted with dried blood. A steady red trickle sprang from an ugly gash on the side of his head. The two men carried Homer to a horsehair chair in the corner.

"Holy moly!" exclaimed Jimmy. "What the hell happened to him?"

"He had an accident," said the Jackrabbit darkly. "We need to get a doctor."

For once, Jimmy was at a loss for words. He should have expected that something like this might happen, but having it unfold at five in the morning threw him for a loop. His reaction was pure instinct: he drained the whiskey in his cup.

"Hey, didn't you hear me?" said the Jackrabbit. "Get a doctor! NOW!"

"Huh? Oh, yeah," said Jimmy. "Uh . . . Cassidy left his number in case there were any problems after the surgery."

"This counts as a problem! Go call him!" ordered the Jackrabbit.

Jimmy hustled back to the hallway to call Dr. Cassidy. He came back a minute later. "No answer," he reported.

"Shit!" said the Jackrabbit. "We need to get him sewn up before he loses any more blood."

"I can do it," said Jimmy. "I got medical training."

"*You've* been to med school?"

"Uh, no . . . not exactly," Jimmy admitted. "Veterinary school."

"You're an animal doctor?"

"Yeah."

"Oh, for Chrissakes!" said the Jackrabbit. "Oh, go on then! I guess you can sew up Van just as easy as you could sew up a critter."

"I'll go find my tool bag," said Jimmy.

"*Tool* bag?"

"Yeah, with my medical tools. Instruments. My instrument bag. I'll be right back."

Jimmy took a detour through the kitchen to top off his cup before rooting in the bedroom closet for his little black bag. He hoped the Jackrabbit wouldn't ask to see his diploma because he didn't have one. It wouldn't have been that impressive if he did—the Midwest Veterinary Correspondence School was not a prestigious institution.

Jimmy had gotten most of the way through the vet-by-mail course back in the mid-20s. At the time, he'd been involved in a dogfighting ring and figured he could cut costs by stitching up the animals himself. But just as he was starting the next-to-last course, the ring was shut down by the vice squad and the ASPCA, and Jimmy lost interest in his studies.

In the bed, Peggy was still snoring. Jimmy grabbed her by the ankle and shook her hard. "Peg! Wake up!"

She mumbled.

"Dammit, Peg! Wake up! This is serious! 'Cletus' has been shot!"

She popped up from under the covers and asked, "Where is he?"

"Out in the front room. I'm going to take care of him." He held up the black bag and gave it a shake. The instruments jingled inside. "I need you to help me."

"Oh, no," she said. "Oh, *Bejaysus*, no! This has gone too far, James Dominick Probasco! I'll have no more to do with this, and if you had a lick of sense, neither would you!"

"Then just get out!" said Jimmy. "If you're not going to help me in my hour of need, just get your sorry Irish ass out of my house!"

Peggy threw on a housedress and began shoving clothes into a paper sack. "I'll do just that, you ungrateful, drunken wop! I'm going back to my mother's!"

"I'll show you who's a drunken wop!" said Jimmy as he took another huge gulp from his cup. "Move that fat ass of yours!" He threw a kick at her butt, but he lost his balance and fell backward on his own rear end.

"That figures!" said Peggy. "Those men must be crazy! I wouldn't let you get within five feet of me with a scalpel!"

Jimmy bellowed and scrambled to his feet. Peggy was already halfway to the back door. Jimmy almost ran after her but checked himself at the last moment. "Let her go," he thought. This wouldn't be the first time she'd taken an unexpected trip to Sheboygan to visit her old bat of a mother. It would be easier to deal with the situation without having her underfoot anyway.

He went back to the kitchen to top off his cup, and, as an afterthought, he started a pot of coffee brewing. He grabbed a handful of dish towels and went back to the front room to attend to his patient.

Homer was half-conscious, lolling in the horsehair chair. Jimmy dragged a floor lamp to the chair and angled the shade to aim a cone of light on Van Meter's head wound. Jimmy dabbed gingerly at it with a dish towel.

"Jesus Christ!" hollered Homer, who was now wide awake. "That hurts like a bastard!"

"Uh, maybe you should have one of your pain pills," suggested Jimmy.

"My pills!" said Homer. "Hell, yes! Give me one of my pills! Better yet, give me two!"

"I dunno, Van," said the Jackrabbit. "You've lost a lot of blood. Two might be—"

"Fuck that!" snapped Homer. "Two pills! NOW!"

Jimmy took two pills from the bottle in the bedroom and handed them over to Homer, who swallowed them immediately.

"Very good," said Jimmy, "We'll just wait a few minutes for those to kick in. I'll go see if Cassidy's back."

He wasn't. Jimmy put a touch of coffee in his cup and then more whiskey.

The Jackrabbit sniffed at the cup. "Hey, how mucha that stuff's booze?" he asked.

"Just a tot to steady my hand," said Jimmy. "How are we feeling, Homer?"

"Uh, OK, I guess," mumbled Van Meter. In less than a minute, his head slumped, and he began to drool.

"Finally," said Jimmy. He began to work on Homer, first cleaning the wound and picking hair and debris out of the gash left by the bullet. At first, he seemed uncertain, but as the morning wore on, he began to feel more confident about his medical skills. This was immensely bolstered by frequent trips to call Cassidy and top off his drink in the kitchen.

Then he started thinking about Peggy, and his good mood vanished. That ungrateful bitch! She walked out on him just when he needed her most! God dammit, he'd sure show her. Just wait until—

In the hallway, the phone rang. He put down his forceps and rushed to the phone in the hallway. "Cassidy?" he asked.

It wasn't Cassidy; it was an ill-tempered Polack named Casmir Doranski. Jimmy had sold Casmir's car for him but hadn't gotten around to giving him the $200 he'd gotten for it.

"Dammit, Jimmy!" came Casmir's crackly voice from the receiver. "You've been sitting on that money for two weeks! That's mine!"

"Screw you, bud," hissed Jimmy. He had enough on his plate without this bullshit. "I don't have time to mess around with this right now."

"You can't keep ducking me! That money's legally mine! You pay up or I'll be over with the cops!"

"Fuck you, Casmir! You just send the cops over here and see what happens!" he screamed and slammed down the phone.

The Jackrabbit appeared at his side. "What was that all about, Jimmy?"

"Nothing," said Jimmy. "Just this pesky Polack. I sold his piece of junk Durant, and he's been bitching ever since."

"What was all that about calling the cops?"

"That? Aw, that was nothing. The Polack said he's gonna send the cops over. He's just blowing smoke."

"I think you should call him back," said the Jackrabbit. "Call him back and apologize."

"Hell, no!" said Jimmy. But before he could blink, the Jackrabbit had his pistol out and was pointing it at his left eye.

"I wasn't asking," said the Jackrabbit. "I was telling you. How much do you owe this guy?"

"Two hundred."

"Jesus," said the Jackrabbit. He put his gun away and pulled out his billfold. "You were gonna run the risk of having the cops come here over a lousy two hundred?" He pulled two C-notes from his wallet and thrust them at Jimmy, who grabbed them reflexively.

"Now square things with the Polack," said the Jackrabbit. "Then get back to working on Van."

It took over four hours to clean the wound. He gave Homer another morphine tablet and stitched up the gash. It was a little uneven, but it would do. Actually, Jimmy was pretty proud of his handiwork, so he decided to have a little drink to celebrate.

"That's all I can do," Jimmy told the Jackrabbit. "Let's get him back to the bedroom."

"Any word from Cassidy?"

"No. I've called his number six, seven times. Nothing, the bum."

The two managed to half-drag, half-carry Van Meter to his bed. They accidentally knocked his head on the wall as they were hoisting him into the bed.

"Ow!!! Holy Christ that hurts!" Homer cried. Jimmy anxiously checked the sutures, but they seemed to be holding. It was quality work.

"Sorry, Van," said the Jackrabbit.

"Ah, it's all right ol' pal," said Van Meter. "Am I gonna be OK?"

"You are now!" said Jimmy. "That bum Cassidy ran off on you, but good ol' Jimmy was able to fix you up good. Isn't that right?"

"Yeah, sure, Jimmy," said the Jackrabbit. "You probably saved his life!"

"Yeah!" said Jimmy. "I sure did! You fellas might want to think about giving me a reward, huh?"

"Jesus, I just gave you two hundred dollars!" shouted the Jackrabbit. "Isn't that enough of a reward?"

"Say, speaking of rewards," said Homer. "How'd we make out on the jug?"

"Not as well as we'd hoped," said the Jackrabbit. "There were a lot of bills, but they were mostly ones and fives."

"Oh. So how much was it?"

"Thirty-eight grand."

"Apiece?"

"No, that was the whole take," said the Jackrabbit. "When we take off the expenses, it comes to just over seven grand apiece."

"Shit," said Homer dejectedly. "So much for the last big score."

The Jackrabbit laughed. "Yeah. I guess so."

"What'll you do now?"

The Jackrabbit grinned his lopsided grin. "I dunno," he said. "Maybe I'll go back to the farm."

Jimmy doubted it. He knew just as well as his houseguests that there was no going back now.

# CHAPTER THIRTY

**Indianapolis, Indiana**
**July 2, 1934**

A rt O'Leary cruised slowly through Indianapolis and turned left onto LaSalle Street on the tattered edge of downtown. The neighborhood was a mishmash of shabby two-story office buildings and tired wooden houses. The sagging buildings baked under the oppressive July heat.

The Jackrabbit had gotten in touch with him the night before. The fugitive had practically begged Art to accompany him to visit his father's farm, saying he wanted to pick up some cash that he'd stashed there. It struck Art as extremely risky. The gangster had already embarrassed the FBI by escaping after the shoot-out at the Saint Paul apartment then compounded the embarrassment by slipping under their noses to visit his family immediately afterward. It seemed like suicide to try it again. Art had talked him out of making the trip by promising to do it himself. He'd rather go alone than have the Jackrabbit get nabbed. Art had a lot of emotional investment in the Jackrabbit's freedom at this point. After all, it had been the entire focus of his existence for the last four months.

Art checked the address written on a slip of paper. He was looking for a service station that should be just ahead at 10th and LaSalle. Down the street he saw a sign reading "Big D Automotive Service." That was it. Art pulled around the corner and parked.

It was a slow Monday afternoon at the Big D. Out front, a guy leaned up against a stack of tires while reading a newspaper. Art could see someone moving inside the office, so he headed that way.

The guy with the paper didn't look up as Art strolled by. He was wearing billowing pleated pants and a dress shirt with the sleeves rolled up. He looked familiar, but Art didn't stop to ponder it. He went inside.

It was oppressively hot inside the office. A squeaky ceiling fan beat helplessly against the stagnant air, and a thin patina of dust covered the peeling furniture. A man in coveralls was idly flipping through an auto parts catalog. The name "Hubert" was stitched onto his breast pocket. Art could see a strong family resemblance between Hubert and the Jackrabbit. They were half brothers, but their faces were very similar—each sported a high forehead and rounded nose.

Art pulled a note from his jacket. "A friend sent me," he said. "I was wondering if you have this particular type of tire." He shoved the paper across the desk.

Hubert gave him a quizzical look and picked up the note. He frowned, read the note carefully, and tucked it into his pocket.

"I'm sorry, sir," said Hubert. "We don't carry that particular brand. Let me give you the address of a place that does." He scribbled something onto a scrap of paper and handed it to Art.

It read, "12th in 5 min."

"OK," said Art. "Thank you."

"Have a good day, sir. Sorry we couldn't help you."

On the way out, Art cast a sideways glance at the man reading the paper. He was still engrossed in his copy of the *Indianapolis Star*. Art was halfway up the block before it dawned on him. The man with the paper was Arthur McGuiness, a low-level crook in the East Indiana underworld who had run in some of the same circles as the Jackrabbit. About a year ago, word had gotten around that he was a fink for the Indiana State Police. After that, McGuiness's name was mud. A number of gangsters had threatened to shoot him on sight. Not surprisingly, he hadn't been seen much since—until now.

Two blocks away, Art waited at the appointed corner. Ten minutes later,

Hubert pulled up in a black Ford V8. "Get in quick," he said, holding open the passenger's-side door. Art ducked in and Hubert pulled away from the curb.

"How's my brother?" asked Hubert.

"Doing well," said Art. "He just had surgery on his face. Wanted to be less recognizable."

"Ha! Ha!" barked Hubert. He had the same laugh as the Jackrabbit. "That must be tough for him. He always loved attention, even as a kid."

"Well, he gets any more attention, it'll get him killed."

"Yeah," sighed Hubert. "Hell, it's just a matter of time anyway." He seemed resigned to his brother's fate. Art wondered what it would be like knowing that someone close to you was living on borrowed time.

"Say, was that Arthur McGuinness hanging out at your place?" asked Art.

"Yeah. He used to come poking around every month or so. Now that there's a big reward, he's there every day."

"Why do you let that rat stay around?"

"I like to keep an eye on him," said Hubert. "Doesn't matter if he's there or not anyway. The Feds rented an apartment two blocks down on Saint Joseph so they can keep an eye on *me*. Thing is, they really can't see the gas station from there, the dumb clucks. So I'm pretty sure they didn't see you or me leave, even if that fink McGuinness did."

"Don't you think he'll tell the Feds?"

"Maybe. But by the time they put two and two together, I'll be back, and you'll be long gone."

They drove through the suburbs of Indianapolis out into farm country. The houses became farther and farther apart, and cornfields lined the road. A sign announced they were approaching Mooresville.

"You better hunker down," said Hubert. "There's Feds in this house up here. Best if you keep down until we get to Dad's."

Art crouched down on the floorboard. Five minutes later, they swung right onto a dirt road that jounced him around like a kernel in a popcorn popper. When the car rumbled to a stop, he sat up.

They were parked in the dooryard of a well-worn white farmhouse. A large red barn loomed beyond the dooryard. Around them, fields of waist-high stalks of corn whispered in the summer breeze.

"OK, it's safe," said Hubert. "They don't have a clear view of us from here."

"Where are they watching from?" asked Art.

"Mostly from the woods over yonder," said Hubert as he gestured toward a small copse of trees on the far side of the cornfield. "They also rented a house down the road, but they can't see anything from there except the front of the driveway."

A man in coveralls and a battered fedora emerged from the barn wiping his hands on an old rag. His mouth curved up in the familiar lemon-twist grin. An amazing array of wrinkles surrounded his sunburned face.

"Dad, this is Art O'Leary," said Hubert. "He's trying to help."

"Hello, sir," said Art.

"I'm John," said the man. He took Art's hand in an oak-hard grip and gave it a single strong pump. "So . . . you've seen m'boy, then?"

"Yes, just this morning. He wanted to come down himself, but I talked him out of it."

John grunted. "Good thing y'did," he said. "'Tain't safe for him down here no more. 'Tain't safe for him anywheres. So what are ya after, O'Leary?"

Hubert pulled the Jackrabbit's note out of his coveralls. John scanned it, his lips moving as he worked out his son's message. He abruptly turned and walked back to the barn.

Five minutes later, he emerged with a large bundle wrapped in newspaper. He thrust it into Arts hands. "There y'go," he said. "That's the last of it. I reckon you best be goin' before they gets to missing Hubert at the fillin' station."

There wasn't much sentimentality in the old man. But then again, Art hadn't expected any. From what the Jackrabbit had told him, his father was a hard man. He hadn't spared the rod with his children, especially with his troublesome oldest son.

Art shoved the bundle into his coat. "Thank you, sir," he told John. "Don't worry about your boy. He can take care of himself. He's going to be OK."

"If you think that, then you're a fool," said John. "That boy has always been trouble. His days are numbered. I know that, he knows that, and I suspect you do too. You just see what you can do to keep that number as large as possible."

"I will, sir. Don't worry."

"I'm past worryin'," said John. He started to turn away then stopped. "Mr. O'Leary, I'd appreciate it if you'd do me a favor."

"Of course."

"The next time you see m' boy, you tell him . . . well, just tell him that . . . we're gonna miss him." The old man turned abruptly and shuffled back to the barn.

# CHAPTER THIRTY-ONE

**Chicago, Illinois**
**July 2, 1934**

H omer Van Meter took another morphine pill and relaxed in his chair. Almost immediately, he felt the calm warmth spread from his belly to the rest of his body. He sighed. It was a lot easier to relax with Jimmy Probasco out of the house. Jimmy had been drinking especially heavily over the last few days, and it made Homer nervous. The more nervous he got, the more morphine he took.

Homer nodded off for a bit, and when he came to, he found the Jackrabbit and Lou Piquett with him in the living room. Piquett had stopped by to pitch ideas about new ways to raise money. This was of particular interest since the South Bend job had not paid off as handsomely as they had hoped.

"So Counselor," said the Jackrabbit. "We could really use some more cash. Things didn't work out so well on our . . . uh . . . our latest venture."

"OK, boys," said Piquett. "I've got a couple of ideas about how we can raise some cash from our current situation. I've got a contact at the *Chicago American*. Now, this isn't official, mind you, but he thinks he can convince the paper to put up fifty thousand for an exclusive."

The Jackrabbit gave a long whistle. "Fifty thousand dollars? Just for an interview? That's nuts!"

"Well, there's more to it than that," said Piquett. "For a payday like that, they want more than an exclusive interview."

"What more could they want?" asked the Jackrabbit.

Piquett took a long moment to drain his beer. "Well, that's a lot of folding green, you understand. But they're willing to pay it—if they have exclusive rights to cover the story. They want to be there when you surrender."

"WHAT?" said the Jackrabbit and Homer in unison.

"Now hear me out, hear me out," said Piquett. "We're talking fifty *thousand* dollars here. That's a lot of money, and it will buy you a lot of good old American justice. With plenty left over for you to spend."

The Jackrabbit stared at the lawyer in disbelief. "It doesn't matter how much is left over!" he said. "You can't spend money when you're *dead!* As soon as those cops get their hands on me, I'm going to the chair!"

"Not necessarily," said Piquett. "I've already put out some feelers, and I'm pretty sure that I could negotiate surrender in return for a promise not to seek the death penalty."

"You're out of your fucking mind, Lou!" exclaimed the Jackrabbit. "They want me for killing a cop. There's no way you can negotiate that down. No way! You can take your 'feelers' and cram them up your ass!"

"There are worse things than life behind bars," insisted Piquett. "In case you've forgotten, you've got a $15,000 price tag on your head. Dead or alive. That's more money than most people will see in their entire lives. Most of the American public would be happy to shoot you on sight for that kind of money. If you ask me, you'd be better off copping a plea. Would you rather end up like Tommy Carroll?"

"Shit, I'd hate to wind up dead in some dirty alley," said Homer. The news of Tommy's death haunted him. The poor guy was just minding his own business, trying to get a sandwich, and the cops shot him down like a dog. Homer'd had an especially vivid dream that it had happened to *him*. He'd woken up in a cold sweat, the image of breathing his last on the grimy cobblestones of a filthy alley fresh in his mind. He'd doubled up on his morphine pills the day after that one.

"That's a rotten way to go," Homer continued. "Still, I'd prefer that to spending even one day in the Michigan City pen. There are some things worse than death."

"Damn right," said the Jackrabbit. "I don't want to hear another word about surrendering, Lou. You got me?" He shrugged open his coat, revealing his shoulder holster.

Piquett got the hint. "OK, OK, forget I even mentioned it," he said. "Here's another idea I think you'll find more appealing. How would you boys like to be in the movies? Not just a newsreel, mind you, but starring in a real Hollywood film about your lives, playing yourselves."

A huge grin spread across the Jackrabbit's face. Homer could see that the lawyer's suggestion had hit home. But Homer wasn't so sure about the idea. Piquett's talk about surrendering was unsettling. So was the talk about ending up dead in an alley.

He reached for his bottle of morphine and popped another pill. Everything quickly became much better, and the notions of dying in an alley or surrendering were like a half-remembered bad dream. No need for those bad thoughts, only good ones. For instance, he was going to be in a movie!

"A film, eh?" said the Jackrabbit. "Now you're talking! I've always wanted to be in films!"

"You already have been," Homer pointed out. "There were newsreel crews there when they brought you to Crown Point."

"That doesn't count," said the Jackrabbit. "I was in handcuffs. I want to be free to express myself. It'll be great! C'mon, Van, don't you want to be a movie star?"

"Yeah, that does sound pretty good," said Homer. It was actually a pretty neat idea. He'd always loved going to the movies, and it was a thrill to think that he might be in one. The Jackrabbit's enthusiasm was contagious—and certainly, the morphine helped with that.

"So how would this work anyway?" the Jackrabbit asked.

"Well, I've got a few contacts in Hollywood," said Piquett. "They understand the need for security—for anonymity. Basically, we would get a small filming crew and swear them to secrecy. Then I figured we'd find someplace up in Wisconsin or Minnesota, rent a cabin or a lodge. We'd get up there and film the whole thing, then they'd go back to California and edit it. And voilà! The Jackrabbit and Homer Van Meter on the silver screen!"

"Can we trust these guys?" asked the Jackrabbit. "Why wouldn't they just turn me in the first chance they got and claim the reward?"

"Are you kidding?" said Piquett. "Look, I know most people couldn't put together fifteen bucks, but for Hollywood fifteen grand is nothing. It's chump change for them. Last year, *King Kong* brought in nearly three million simoleons. A movie featuring the famous Jackrabbit could beat that, easy. They wouldn't risk screwing that up for a measly fifteen grand."

"Three million, huh?" said the Jackrabbit. "And we'd get a big cut of that?"

"You bet," said Piquett. "You'd probably pull in two, three hundred thousand. Van Meter, maybe a hundred grand. Sorry, but you're just the costar."

"Doesn't bother me," said Homer. "I don't mind being a costar."

"Yeah, I like this idea," said the Jackrabbit. "Do what you can to make it happen, Lou."

Homer's head was swimming with possibilities. "Yeah, I like it too," he said. "I have a message for the youth of America."

"Oh yeah?" asked the Jackrabbit. "What's that?"

"Oh, hell, I dunno. I guess I'd say that you have to stand up for yourself and take what you want if you want to get anywhere in this world."

"That's a horrible message, Van. We need to tell them that crime doesn't pay."

"Fine. I'll give *my* message to the youth of America, and *you* can tell them that crime doesn't pay."

"Boys, I think we'll let the scriptwriters handle the actual messages," said Piquett.

"OK, that's fine," said the Jackrabbit. "But we will be playing ourselves, right? We'll be the stars?"

"Of course," said Piquett. "We might need to find some actors to play younger versions of you."

"Ha! Ha!" barked the Jackrabbit. "I don't think that'll be a problem. Didja hear about the candy salesman they arrested in Kankakee? He looks just like me! Guys are getting arrested all over the place for looking like me! Ha! Ha!"

"Well, then, it's settled," said Piquett. He rose from the couch and put on his camel hair overcoat. "I'll call my friends in Hollywood. We'll get this in production."

"Excellent, Lou!" said the Jackrabbit. He slapped the lawyer on the back and pumped his hand heartily. "You're the best lawyer a guy could want!"

Piquett left, and Homer took two more morphine tablets to celebrate. He could feel the narcotic start to sink its velvet claws into his nervous system. He chuckled at the thought of being on the big screen. "Heh. Gonna be in the movies," he said to himself.

"There ain't gonna be any damn movie," the Jackrabbit said.

"What? Why not?"

"I don't trust Lou Piquett no more. Surrender? He must be out of his mind!"

"Yeah, I didn't like that very much, either," said Homer. He remembered being pissed about it earlier, but now that the morphine was kicking in, everything was wonderful.

"He's started holding out on me," said the Jackrabbit. "I gave him two grand to pay Handsome Harry's lawyers. They never got the money. His execution date is gonna be set soon."

"Goddamn," said Homer mildly.

"If he needs money bad enough to steal from us, then he's probably willing to rat us out for the reward money."

"Oh, yeah," said Homer. "I hadn't thought of that."

"Well, buddy, I think it's time we took our leave from the hospitality of Mr. Probasco. I'm finally going to get out of here for good. Do you have someplace you can go?"

"Well, I thought I could take Marie up to Wisconsin or to Ohio," said Homer. "Maybe Indian Lake. Rent a lakeside cabin. How about you?"

"Like I said, I'm going to Mexico," answered the Jackrabbit. "For ten grand, a nice old couple will drive me to Tijuana and swear that I'm their son."

"Wow! Do you have that much?"

"I have enough. I was hoping that we'd get enough from that South Bend job to retire in style, but no dice. That's OK, though. After I see Art tomorrow, I should have enough to get down there and get settled. I'm gonna need your help with something first, though. A little diversion."

"Whatever you need, pal," said Homer. "I'll help you get down to Mexico, amigo. But what will you do then?"

"Oh, I don't know," said the Jackrabbit. "I'm pretty handy, y'know. I should be able to find honest work in a mill or machine shop. Besides, if that doesn't work out, Mexico has banks. Right?"

"Yeah, I guess so," laughed Homer. "But what about Billie?"

The Jackrabbit slumped. "I really don't know, Van. She's in that federal pen now, so there's nothing I can do. Maybe if I can lay low for a year or so, I can hook up with her after she gets out." He sighed. "Or maybe she's just better off without me. I don't know."

"Well, either way, you're not going to be able to do any good for her if you're dead or in jail," said Homer.

"That's right. I gotta get out before I can do anything." The Jackrabbit paused and gave Homer a long look. "Before I go, I've got a big favor to ask, Van."

"Shoot."

"I need you to cover my back one last time."

"Really?" said Homer. "Are we going to take down one last jug?"

"Nope, we're just going to take in a ball game or two, maybe a few movies. Or at least *you* will."

"What? I don't get it."

The Jackrabbit scratched his chin. "Well, buddy," he said. "Lately, it seems like there's a lot of stuff you don't get. You've been pretty damn foggy."

"Huh?"

"It's those pills, Van. You need to quit poppin' those pills all the time!"

"What? Hell, no! I'm still hurtin' from where that quack cut on me!"

"You can't be hurting that bad," said the Jackrabbit. "I feel fine, and I had the same operation you did."

"I don't care," said Homer. "*You* didn't get shot in the head. I need those pills!"

"Like hell you do!" The Jackrabbit's face was twisted in an uncharacteristic mask of anger. "I've seen too many guys go down that road and never come back. I know that dope helps you feel better, but you're losing your edge. We need to stay sharp, especially now. Things are coming to a boiling point—can't you feel it?"

Homer could feel it very well—it was one of the reasons he was taking so many pills. Ever since Tommy had been killed, it seemed like there was an hourglass with all their names on it, and it was almost out of sand. The morphine slowed down the sand's flow.

Still, he hated to think he was turning into some sort of junkie. He had seen too many of them in the pen and on the outside. They were pretty much worthless. He knew it would never happen to him, though. He could handle it. In the meantime, he'd just have to keep things on the down-low. He didn't need the Jackrabbit riding his tail about the pills.

"Yeah, you're right, pal," Homer fibbed. "I'll keep my head clear. I know it's the only way that we're gonna get out of this mess."

# CHAPTER THIRTY-TWO

**Chicago, Illinois**
**July 3, 1934**

Art pulled up to the entrance of Humboldt Park. The Jackrabbit was sitting on a white rock next to the arched entryway. He was attired in a natty gray suit, straw boater, and shaded glasses. When he saw Art's car, he stood up and climbed into the passenger seat. He tossed a burlap sack into the back seat.

"Hiya, Art! Got a little souvenir for ya."

"What's that?"

"A Tommy gun," said the Jackrabbit. "Practically brand-new. Only ever used by a little old lady to shoot up the church on Sundays."

"Whoa!" said Art. "I'm not sure I want to deal with a piece of hardware that can be linked to a crime."

"Nope, like I said, it's never been used," said the Jackrabbit. "Sell it, mount it behind your desk, throw it in the river—I don't care. Just take it as a little memento."

Art glanced at the lumpy parcel in the back seat. The way things were going, the gun would be a memento mori.

"Now, do you have something for me?" asked the Jackrabbit.

"Sure thing. Here's the package your dad gave me." Art handed over the newspaper-wrapped bundle he'd picked up in Mooresville. He had peeked inside, just on general principles. Sure enough, it was stuffed full of cash.

The Jackrabbit opened the package, thumbed through the contents, and nodded.

"Your dad wanted me to tell you something," said Art. "He said he was going to miss you."

"Really?" The Jackrabbit genuinely sounded surprised. "That's a pretty amazing thing for the old man to say, especially to a stranger." He sighed. "For what it's worth, I'm going to miss them too. Maybe not the old man so much, but definitely Hubert and my sister and her kids."

Art didn't know how to respond. He didn't know how the Jackrabbit was going to miss anybody unless the gangster believed in an afterlife. It didn't seem like a good topic of conversation.

"Say, I happened to stop by Probasco's on my way over," said Art.

"Yeah? How drunk was he?"

"He was boiled as an owl."

"Figures," said the Jackrabbit. "I guess he's always been a heavy drinker, but lately he's just been schnockered all the time. It's starting to make me nervous."

"It's not him you should be nervous about," said Art. "He was talking some crazy stuff—"

"About Piquett?" the Jackrabbit interrupted.

"Yes. How did you know?"

"Look, Art, I know Lou Piquett is your boss and that you two go back a ways. Fact of the matter is that I don't trust him anymore. Can I trust *you*?"

"Pal, if I were in your shoes, I wouldn't trust *anyone*."

"Ha! Ha!" laughed the Jackrabbit. "Good answer, Art! Maybe *you* should be a lawyer! Look, I know Lou's been skimming. If he's willing to steal from me, well, what else is he willing to do?"

"I dunno," said Art. He didn't know what to think about Piquett stealing from the Jackrabbit. He knew that his boss was a man of flexible morals. Also, Piquett had bitched a great deal about how little he was getting paid for his efforts to represent the Jackrabbit. It came as no surprise to learn that Lou had been holding something back for himself. Still, it seemed foolish to steal from a man who traveled with multiple submachine guns and hung around with the likes of Baby Face Nelson. "So what are you going to do?"

he asked.

The Jackrabbit shrugged. "I'm going to pay a visit to his office and leave my calling card. What else?"

"Jesus! You can't be serious!"

"You need to leave town, Art. Tonight. You got someplace you can take your family?"

"Really? I can't just up and take off—"

"Sure you can. Take an impromptu vacation. Relax for a week or two." The Jackrabbit delved into his father's package and came up with a fistful of twenties. He quickly counted them out and thrust them at Art. "Here's five hundred bucks. Take your family someplace nice for a couple of weeks. Or go to Toledo and spend it on hookers. I don't care. Just get out of town, Art. OK?"

Art reluctantly accepted the cash. He knew there was plenty more in the package. Plus, he had been putting in long hours over the last four months and didn't have much to show for it. He wondered if Piquett was holding out on him too. "I don't know what to say, except thanks," he said.

"It's you I've got to thank," said the Jackrabbit. "You've been a good friend, Art. I don't have many left, especially now that there's a price on my head."

"Hey, that's not true. You don't know that—"

"Don't be an ass, man. We both know it. Things are going to start getting very heavy, very fast now. Do you doubt it?"

"No."

"Then take the money and make yourself scarce. You've got a good life, Art. A job, a family, a nice place to live. Respectability. There's nothing I wouldn't do to have what you have. You've stuck your neck out for me plenty of times, and it's been more than enough. Now just take a powder, man. You can read in the papers about how it all comes out, OK?"

"Yeah, sure thing. We'll go tonight."

Art had always thought of himself as a tough customer. In this line of work, you had to have a hard edge. Still, he felt a lump in his throat at hearing the Jackrabbit's words. He coughed and gave his head a shake.

"Well, I guess I'd better shove off," said the Jackrabbit. "Places to go and people to see, y'know?"

He slipped out of the car and started to walk away then turned back and stuck his head in the window. "You're a good man, Art O'Leary," he said. "Have a nice life."

Automatically, Art said, "You too."

The Jackrabbit looked at him for a long moment and then barked his staccato laugh, "Ha! Ha! That's a good one, Art!" Then he turned and strolled off into Humboldt Park.

# CHAPTER THIRTY-THREE

### Chicago, Illinois
### July 3, 1934

Jimmy Lawrence sat down in his living room and opened the paper to the sports section. His apartment on North Sheffield was small and cluttered with furniture and knickknacks. He hadn't had many possessions growing up—their house had been a barely furnished shack. Now that he had the means to buy nice things, he did so. He was partial to stylish clothes and furniture, so his cozy apartment was stuffed with high-fashion items. He considered himself one lucky son of a bitch.

Jimmy had once been a small-time crook in the Patch, the tough Northside neighborhood where he'd grown up. Even though he'd dropped out of school at eleven, he was smart and had a good head for numbers. Someone like him would be an asset to any ambitious criminal enterprise. He had the potential to be a top-notch bookmaker or gang accountant.

But those career options had pretty much ended for Jimmy after a jewelry store robbery had gone wrong. When the elderly store owner foolishly tried to defend himself with an ancient lupara shotgun, one of Jimmy's companions put two slugs in the old fool's head. In the confusion that followed, the gang fled the store without taking anything of value. Almost as an afterthought, Jimmy smashed a glass display case and grabbed a large onyx ring that had caught his eye. It was a cheap ring, but he liked the way it looked. It was the only reward for that day's work.

The fact that he was now an accessory to murder made him reassess his career path. Maybe there were better ways to use his smarts than in a violent criminal gang. A fence he knew named Probasco had introduced him to a drinking buddy who worked at the Board of Trade. The buddy offered Jimmy a job as a clerk, and he eagerly accepted.

The job wasn't very exciting, but the pay was decent and, above all, steady. Jimmy realized he had once again lucked into a good thing. A year after the botched jewelry store job, the rest of his old gang were either dead or in jail. Clerking was a much safer profession. Whenever Jimmy was bored at his desk or started to miss the excitement of running with a gang, he considered the onyx ring he still wore on his left hand. It reminded him that he had the smarts to make the right decision.

Besides, the Board of Trade job had its fringe benefits. Early on, Jimmy realized that many of his coworkers had a very loose grasp on how money was moving in and out of the Board. It was an easy matter to skim off a bit here and there without anybody noticing. He was very careful not to appropriate large amounts or do it frequently enough to attract attention. It satisfied his taste for a bit of that old larcenous thrill and made for a nice supplement to his salary.

He also made a few bucks on the side betting on sporting events. Not too many, not too large—just enough to keep things interesting. Mostly he stuck with baseball, a sport he knew well. He could always make money betting on the Cubs—or against the White Sox. That wasn't luck, that was just common sense.

He'd made a bit of a mistake recently, though, betting heavily on the Carnera-Loughran prizefight. A buddy of his had told him that the fix was in and that Tommy Loughran was a sure bet. Indeed, Loughran had gone the distance, but Carnera was declared the winner in a unanimous decision.

Jimmy was now 800 bucks in debt to his bookie, and he was starting to get a little worried about how he was going to pay. He sure didn't have that kind of money on hand, and it was too risky trying to skim that much at work in one go. He tried not to sweat it, though—these things always had a way of working themselves out. His luck always came through in the end.

When Jimmy heard a knock on the door, he smiled, thinking that it must be Polly coming to pay him a surprise visit. They'd only been on two dates, but he was ape about her. She seemed to feel the same way about him too. Things were good.

"Hello, baby!" he said as he opened the apartment door. But instead of his petite girlfriend, there were two men standing there. One was about his height. He was wearing a straw boater and dark glasses and held a small suitcase. Behind him lurked a taller man. He was hard to see in the dim light of the hallway, but he looked to be wearing pince-nez glasses and a vest.

These guys looked like bad news. They were either gangsters or cops, and Jimmy wanted nothing to do with either. He tried to slam the door, but the guy with the shades got his foot in the way.

"Hiya, pal," said the man. "There's no need to be rude. Are you Jimmy Lawrence?"

"Depends on who's asking. Who the hell are you?" Jimmy had to fight to keep a quaver out of his voice.

"We're friends of Billie Frechette."

"Huh?" This answer threw him for a loop. He and Billie had had a fling a few years back, but he hadn't seen her in ages. He had no idea why friends of hers would be interested in him now. "Ah, so how's Billie?" he asked.

"She's in prison," said the taller man. "Can we come in?"

"Um . . . Sure, I guess," Jimmy said tentatively.

Jimmy held the door open, and the two men came into the living room. He stepped to the window and raised the blinds to let in more light.

"Don't do that," said the man with the shades. "Best we keep things dark."

"Well, I'll be damned," said the taller man. "He really *does* look like you. Same size and everything."

The shorter man removed his shades and gave Jimmy a crooked half smile. Jimmy's eyes widened as he realized that two of the most wanted criminals in the world were standing in his living room.

"Jesus Christ!" exclaimed Jimmy.

"Not quite," said the Jackrabbit. "But nearly as famous. Ha! Ha!"

"You mind if we sit?" asked Homer Van Meter. He removed the pince-nez glasses and tucked them into a pocket in his vest.

217

"Yeah, have a seat," said Jimmy. "So, uh, what do you want?"

"Got a job for you," said the Jackrabbit. "An easy thousand bucks."

"Whoa, fellas!" said Jimmy. "I don't know what you heard, but I'm not in that racket anymore. I got a nice straight job going, and I don't want to blow it. It's a pretty sweet deal."

"No, it's nothing like that," said the Jackrabbit. "Nothing criminal."

"Then what do you want me to do?" asked Jimmy.

"Simple," said the Jackrabbit. "I want *you* to be *me*."

"Come again?"

"Look," said the Jackrabbit. "Surely you've noticed that you bear more than a passing resemblance to me. Billie showed me a picture of you two together at the beach. You look just like me. Nobody's ever mentioned that?"

"Yeah, all the time," said Jimmy. "Hell, one time this cop grabbed me on the sidewalk when I was coming home from work and started giving me the business. Fortunately, one of the guys from work happened along and vouched for me. Man, did I ever hear about *that* the next day!"

"There's guys being picked up all the time for looking like me," said the Jackrabbit. "One poor slob's been arrested eight times. Can you believe it? Eight!"

"I'd hate to be him," said Jimmy. "But what's it to me? It was just one nearsighted cop. It's not like we're identical twins or anything."

"Doesn't matter," said the Jackrabbit. He rubbed his scarred cheek. "I just got my mug fixed. Word's starting to get around that the Jackrabbit's got a new face. I need you to be that new face around town while I slip out the back door. Get it?"

"Yeah, I think so." Jimmy scratched his head. This was definitely weird. He wasn't sure what to say, but there was a little thrill of excitement in the pit of his gut. To be honest, part of him missed the thrill of running with a gang. This wouldn't be the same thing, but it might be fun for a while. Besides, he could really use the cash. "OK, count me in," he said.

"Good man," said the Jackrabbit. "Just be careful. This thing is going to be dangerous."

"I can handle a little danger," said Jimmy. "A thousand smackers is worth a little risk," he thought. He could take care of his betting marker and show his new sweetie a real good time.

"Just play it cool," said Homer. "Remember: there's a $15,000 reward, dead or alive."

"Yeah, yeah," said Jimmy. "What's the worst that can happen? They pick me up, check my fingerprints, let me go, right?"

"That's right," said the Jackrabbit. "No need to stick your neck out. I just want you to hang around the city, go to a few ball games, wear some of my clothes." He hefted the suitcase.

Jimmy took the suitcase and popped it open. There were a bunch of nice clothes in there. A snappy gray seersucker suit caught his eye. He tried on the jacket. It fit perfectly. "So do I get to keep the clothes too?" he asked.

"Yeah, that's part of the deal," said the Jackrabbit. "Like I said, just play it cool. If anyone asks you if you're the Jackrabbit, don't deny it, but don't confirm it, either. Be coy, you know?"

"I can do that," said Jimmy absently. He pawed through the suitcase. It was full of top-quality garments.

"OK, great," said the Jackrabbit. "You and Homer here can hit a few clubs where somebody might think they recognize me—or you. Maybe go on a double date. You got a girl?"

"Yeah," said Jimmy. "Her name's Polly. She looks a lot like Billie, actually."

"What's she do?" asked the Jackrabbit.

"Well, um, she waits tables at a diner downtown," said Jimmy. "But also—"

"What 'also'?" asked Homer.

"Um, she's also a B-girl," admitted Jimmy. "Works at some of the clubs, gets men to buy her expensive drinks, you know. Sometimes other stuff. Is that a problem?"

"No," laughed the Jackrabbit. "She sounds like my kind of gal! Ha! Ha!"

"How long have you been going out?" asked Homer.

"Not long. About a week. I'm going to see her tonight."

"Perfect," said the Jackrabbit. "You get her to think you're the Jackrabbit. Dames can't keep their traps shut about stuff like that. Pretty soon, it'll be all over town that the Jackrabbit and his new girl Polly are out and about in the city. In the meantime, I'll be gone like a cool breeze." He pulled a wad of fifties from his jacket, counted out ten, and handed them over to Jimmy. "Here's half up front. Homer here will give you the rest at the end of the month."

"What happens then?" asked Jimmy.

"Nothing," said the Jackrabbit. "I'll be long gone, and you can tell your new girl you were just funning her or something."

"I'm really sorry to hear that Billie's in stir," said Jimmy.

"Not half as sorry as I am, pal," said the Jackrabbit. "Believe me."

"Will you be able to help her?" asked Jimmy.

The Jackrabbit's grin faltered. "Not as much as I'd like," he said. "I've got my lawyer trying to help her out. I don't know what good that's doing, though. I'll do what I can once I get out of town, but right now, I'm just trying to save my own hide. I can't help her much if I'm cooling on a mortician's slab. And neither can you, remember?"

"You're just being paranoid," said Jimmy. "I'll be OK. This is easy money. A quick grand and a new wardrobe to boot. Fat city!"

"I'm glad we were able to come to an agreement," said the Jackrabbit. "Just don't do anything stupid."

"I won't," said Jimmy. "At least not until I've got that other five hundred in my pocket."

"By that time, it won't matter," the Jackrabbit said as he rose to leave. "You can be as stupid as you want then."

"I'll be in touch in a few days," said Homer. "We'll have a nice double date, maybe go to a Cubs game or something."

"OK, swell!" replied Jimmy. "The Cubbies are doing great this season!"

The Jackrabbit was almost out the door when he spun and said, "Here, kid," and he tossed his boater to Jimmy. "I'd give you the shades too," he said. "But I'm going to need them where I'm going. I suggest you get yourself a pair. Be careful, Jimmy."

"You bet," Jimmy said distractedly. He was busily investigating the hat as the two men let themselves out. It came from Brooks Brothers—a quality lid.

Jimmy grinned to himself. Without him even trying, Lady Luck had marched into his apartment and dropped five hundred bucks and a new wardrobe right into his lap. He'd get a big chunk of that to his bookie then show his new girl a good time tonight. He just knew it would all work out for him. It was another lucky day for Jimmy Lawrence.

# CHAPTER THIRTY-FOUR

### Chicago, Illinois
### July 4, 1934

Jimmy Probasco and Louis Piquett had set up camp at a corner booth in the Green Log Inn. They'd been drinking for three hours, celebrating Independence Day with style.

"Hey, Murray!" Piquett called to the bartender. "How 'bout another round here? Drinks for me and the future owner of the Green Log!"

The proprietor of the bar came over with two mugs of Old Style lager. "So you've scraped up the cash to buy the place, eh?" he asked as he thumped the beers onto the scarred wooden table.

"Not yet, not yet," said Jimmy. "But I'll have it soon enough. Just you wait!"

"Ain't gonna wait too much longer," said Murray. "I swear I've spent my last winter in Chicago, Jimmy. If you don't come up with the money soon, I'm gonna put it on the market. There's a couple of guys from Cicero who're interested in the place. *Real* interested."

"Don't worry, don't worry," said Jimmy. "I'll figger somethin' out."

Murray shrugged and went back to the bar. The place was crowded with holiday revelers celebrating the birth of the nation with legal booze for the first Independence Day in fourteen years.

Piquett drank deeply and regarded his glass. "Y'know, Jimmy," he said. "I know of a way we could get that money pretty quick. If you're interested."

"'Course I'm innerested. What is it?"

"Well, you got a gold mine sittin' right there in your house," answered Lou.

"A gold mine?" said Jimmy. "What're you talkin' about? All I gots is a run-down house and a backyard full of dog shit."

"Don't be a dunce," said Piquett. "You know who I'm talkin' about. Our friend, 'Mr. Harrison.'"

"Oh, yeah!" said Jimmy. "Yeah, maybe he can lend me some money!"

"No, no, no, no," said Piquett. "You're not following me." He leaned in close and hissed, "We turn him in for the reward. Fifteen thousand."

Jimmy was uncertain. That was a lot of money, all right. But he didn't feel right getting it by ratting out a man who had paid him for protection. "Uh, I don't know, Lou," he said. "That just don't seem right."

"Right?" said Piquett. "Right? I'll tell you about right! If a man does a job for another man, isn't it right that he should be compensated for his endeavors?"

"Yeah, I guess so."

"Of course!" roared Piquett in his best courtroom baritone. A number of other customers looked over at their table. "It's only right! I've been representing that man since February, and he's only paid me a fraction of what he owes me—a miniscule fraction! I was at his beck and call around the clock ready to charge off to God knows where at the drop of a hat. Sleepless nights without count! Isn't it right that I'm rewarded for my tireless efforts?"

"Damn right!" shouted Jimmy. He was caught up in the spirit of Piquett's oratory.

"Damn right!" echoed Piquett. He leaned in and whispered, "Now, just how much longer do you think our friend Mr. Jackrabbit is going to be hopping around out there?"

"Jeez, Lou, not long. I mean, he goes out all the time. I know he had that surgery, but I don't think it really changed his face that much. With a $15,000 price tag on his head, it's only a matter of time before he slips up and someone gets him."

"EXACTLY!" shouted Piquett. "And after all I've done—after all *we've* done, Jimmy—why should someone else get that dough? Right?"

"Right! We both deserve a share of that reward!" Jimmy exclaimed, slapping the table in front of him.

"Absolutely," said Piquett. "And we'll split it fair and square—seventy-thirty."

"Wait," said Jimmy. "Who gets the seventy and who gets the thirty?"

Piquett leaned in, snarling, "Who do you think?"

"I think that whatever you think is good."

"Then we have come to an understanding," intoned Piquett. "Let's celebrate our agreement with a drink!"

Many drinks later, Jimmy and Piquett loaded into the lawyer's massive Lincoln and rolled unsteadily back to Jimmy's house. All over the city, people were celebrating the nation's independence with fireworks. As the late afternoon faded into a warm, purple dusk, minor explosions and fountains of fire blossomed in the evening air.

"When are we gonna, y'know . . . ?" asked Jimmy.

"'If it were done when 'tis done, then 'twere well it were done quickly.'"

"Huh?"

"Shakespeare," said Piquett. "*Macbeth*. It means we should do it without delay. We'll swing by your place and make sure he's around, then I'll go make a call. The police will be there in minutes, and the reward will be ours!"

"What about me?" asked Jimmy. "Shouldn't I come with you?"

"No, I need you to stay at the house to make sure they don't leave."

"I don't know. There's liable to be shooting!"

"Then keep your head down," said Piquett. "Don't worry—you'll probably be fine. Well, here we are." He parked the Lincoln clumsily with two of the fat whitewalls propped up on the edge of the curb. The drunken conspirators stumbled up the steps and into the house.

"Yoo-hoo!" called Piquett. "Boys? Where are my favorite clients?"

"They're not here," said Jimmy. He darted into the front bedroom and emerged a moment later. "All their stuff's gone! Completely cleared out! Hey, you OK, Lou?"

Piquett had suddenly gone pale, and a thin sheen of sweat sprang up on his forehead.

"Whassa matter, Lou? Say, you don't think they figured out that we're gonna—"

"I don't know what they figured," snapped Piquett. "And I don't care. All I know is that I'm going to take a last-minute Fourth of July vacation, and you might want to do the same."

"What . . ." began Jimmy, but Piquett was already on his way down the walk. He jumped into his enormous Lincoln and sped off into the twilight.

\* \* \*

Homer van Meter threaded his car through the traffic on West Adams Street. As he crossed the bridge over the South Branch of the Chicago River, the cluster of cars got even thicker. He cut around a bus and slid neatly into a space in front of a produce truck.

"Well, here we are," he said. "Where do you want to go?"

"Just drop me in front of the main building," said the Jackrabbit. "Ma and Pa will pick me up soon enough."

"What about Jimmy?" asked Homer.

"What *about* Jimmy?" repeated the Jackrabbit. "He's gonna be OK. He's got you to look after him."

"I can't look after him all the time," said Homer. "It just feels like, I dunno . . . like we're setting him up or something."

"Setting him up?" scoffed the Jackrabbit. "C'mon, Van. He's no babe in the woods. He knows the risks."

"He sure didn't seem like he did."

"What are you talking about? You heard him say that the cops already put the arm on him for looking like me. He walked away from it, no problem."

"Yeah, well it's one thing to have some dumbass flatfoot grab you by mistake," said Homer. "It's another to go around *telling* people that you're Public Enemy Number One."

"Yeah, it's a risk," agreed the Jackrabbit. "He takes the risk, he gets a reward. That's the point. He gets a thousand bucks. Pretty nice payday for wearing my clothes to a couple of ball games."

"I dunno," said Homer. "It just feels weird." Lately to Homer, it seemed like everything felt weird. He'd cut way back on the morphine pills, and that made him feel tense and nervous all the time.

Even more disconcerting was the notion that his pal was leaving for good. He knew he'd never see the Jackrabbit again. This was really it—the end of an era. The Jackrabbit had been the closest friend he'd ever had, and now he was going away for good. That was bad enough. Even worse, he'd now be spending time with some dandified clerk who was pretending to be that best friend. It seemed disloyal somehow.

Homer cut a hard left onto Canal Street, narrowly missing a streetcar. He pulled to the curb in front of Union Station. "Here we are," he announced. "Say, do you remember the day we met? I was out in the yard at Pendleton, and you—"

The Jackrabbit bounded out the passenger's-side door, a small suitcase in his hand. "Of course, I remember," he said. "Look, Van, I hate long goodbyes. You've been a great friend to me, and I appreciate that more than I can say. Goodbye and good luck, Homer Van Meter."

He turned and disappeared into the eddying crowd of rail passengers. Across the river, a great salvo of skyrockets shot up from the riverbank and burst into red, white, and blue bouquets.

Homer sat and watched the swirling crowd for a minute then put the car in gear and drove away.

# CHAPTER THIRTY-FIVE

**Chicago, Illinois**
**July 12, 1934**

T he tension on the nineteenth floor of the Bankers Building was
nearly overwhelming.

Doris had felt the pressure building ever since the Jackrabbit had
escaped from Crown Point. It had gone up exponentially with the arrival
of Inspector Samuel Cowley. He was supposed to be there in a support
role, but everyone knew that Director Hoover had sent him to take over the
Jackrabbit investigation. The agents had resented it—at least at first.

Cowley was not a bad boss as far as Doris could tell. He was very polite to
her and was generally respectful to Mr. Purvis and the agents in the office.
He demanded a lot of hard work, but he put in even more work himself.
He was always at his desk when Doris arrived in the morning and was still
there when she left in the evening. She had helped him find a room in a
residential hotel, but it didn't seem as if he ever used it. Doris suspected
that he just slept at his desk most nights.

Cowley had managed to achieve at least one thing since his arrival: he had
lit a fire under the agents in the Chicago field office. Through intimidation
and his own tireless work ethic, the agents were working harder and with
more intensity than Doris had seen in a long time. Despite the initial
resentment, there was also a sense that the Bureau was finally making
headway in the case. More than anything else, the agents wanted to nail the
gangster who was responsible for the death of one of their own.

Every morning, Mr. Purvis and Mr. Cowley met in Purvis's office, reviewing recent activity and planning for the day. Doris always sat in to take notes. The two men rarely paid her any attention when she was in the room; it was as if she was just part of the furniture.

"Well, we have some good news today," began Mr. Purvis.

"That's a welcome change," said Cowley. Doris couldn't tell if he was making a joke or rebuking Mr. Purvis. The man's droopy face never changed.

"Yes," said Mr. Purvis. "We've finally got an informant in place in the office of Louis Piquett."

"Piquett?" said Cowley. He shuffled through a pile of notebooks on his lap and flipped one open. "Ah, yes, the Jackrabbit's crooked attorney."

"Yes, yes," said Mr. Purvis. "After a strenuous effort, we have finally convinced his secretary to keep us informed of the activities going on in his office. It's only a matter of time before he makes contact with the Jackrabbit. If he's still alive, that is."

"Mel, I keep hearing these rumors about the Jackrabbit having perished after the gun battle in Wisconsin. They are entirely unfounded. Until someone can show me his corpse, I will consider the Jackrabbit to be alive and well. Until that time, I don't want to hear another word from you or any of the agents in this office about the Jackrabbit being dead. Understood?"

"Perfectly, sir."

"So tell me more about this informant in Counselor Piquett's office."

"Her name is Margie Baker; she's Piquett's secretary. Apparently, the day the Jackrabbit broke out of jail in Crown Point, Piquett showed up on her doorstep with the crook in tow, wanting her to hide him for the night. Of course, she refused. She's been upset with her boss ever since then, although it did take a bit of convincing to get her to cooperate. However, I'm pleased to say—"

"Hold on," said Cowley, raising his hand. "So how long have you known about Piquett helping this criminal find a place to stay after he absconded from justice?"

"Just since we were able to talk to the secretary," said Mr. Purvis. "It's hardly surprising, though. We've long suspected that Piquett had a hand in the Crown Point escape. Clearly, the Jackrabbit had outside help in that affair. Piquett seemed a likely suspect."

"In that case, you would most certainly have had Mr. Piquett tailed and watched, of course."

"Well," said Mr. Purvis. "Not as such, I'm afraid." He looked nervous. Doris felt a funny feeling in her stomach. Once again, her boss had been caught out.

"What?" spat Cowley. "You *knew* this crooked shyster was in league with the top criminal in America, and you didn't have him followed? You didn't have his house watched? Mr. Purvis, I certainly hope this is some sort of sorry joke you are telling me!"

"I couldn't!" blurted Mr. Purvis. A thin sheen of sweat had popped up on his forehead. "I just didn't have the resources!"

"I'm going to have to report this to the director," said Cowley. "I don't expect him to be pleased."

A deep flush settled over Mr. Purvis's face. His voice took on an exaggerated southern drawl. "Frankly, Inspector Cowley, Ah no longer give much of a damn if the director is pleased or not!" Doris suppressed a gasp. She had never seen her boss this upset.

"Mr. Purvis—" Cowley began.

"'Mr. Purvis' nothin'. Ah'm not sure if you realize the demayunds this field office has been under for the last yeuh. In addition to this whole Jackrabbit situation, we've been tasked with solving the Kansas City killings, the Bremer kidnapping, and the Hamm kidnapping. *All* of them have been deemed highest priority. In order to put surveillance on ever' person of interest on ever' case, Ah would need the entire staff of the Bureau and then some. Ah've been working mah tail off, and so has ever' single agent in this office! So you can go ahead and tell Director Hoover whatever you want, suh!"

"So noted," said Cowley dryly.

Mr. Purvis took a deep breath, and his face began to return to its normal color. He looked shamefaced about his outburst. He said, "Inspector Cowley,

I mean no disrespect to you or Director Hoover. It has been an exceptionally trying year for this field office. As special agent in charge, I, of course, take full responsibility for its shortcomings. I'll be the first to admit that we—that I—made mistakes, and I'll gladly atone for them. In the meantime, however, I wish to focus on the matters at hand."

"That's a laudable approach, Mr. Purvis," said Cowley.

Doris shrank back in her seat. She hated seeing Mr. Purvis being put on the spot this way.

"Regardless of what did or didn't happen in the past," continued Mr. Purvis. "We now have a line on Counselor Piquett, and it has already paid off. Several days ago, our informant suggested we follow Mr. Piquett to a meeting. We did so, and he met with a gentleman on a street corner, where they had an animated argument about money. The agents followed this man to a building, where he entered an apartment listed as being rented to a Ralph Robeind. We have had that apartment under observation ever since."

"Well, that's all well and good," said Cowley. "Now bring him in for questioning."

Mr. Purvis said, "Doris, please connect me with Agent Lockerman at the Robeind stakeout."

Doris went to her desk. Just the mention of Allan Lockerman's name made her stomach feel funny. She had gone out with him twice, and she had certain *feelings* about him. Feelings that she hadn't had in a long time. Too strong to be a crush, but not strong enough to be love. Well, not really. Not yet.

With Allan, it was different than the other agents she had dated. There was something about him that was more . . . substantial. He was strong and steady, as well as funny and kind. His strength had been a great comfort to Doris after the Little Bohemia fiasco. She felt secure when she was with Allan, and that meant a great deal right now. Still, she was deliberately taking things slow with him. She didn't want to make the same mistake she had made with John McLaughlin by rushing into a physical relationship.

She dialed up Allan at the stakeout apartment.

"Hey, Dore!" said Allan, clearly pleased to hear from her. "I've just been thinking about you, and how maybe we—"

"Agent Lockerman," said Doris abruptly. "Mr. Purvis wishes to speak to you immediately on a most pressing matter." It was difficult to speak to him this way, but she had to do it. With Cowley in the office now, she knew she had to be discreet. Mr. Purvis might look the other way, but Inspector Cowley would surely disapprove.

"Of course, Miss Rogers," said Allan. "Please put me through."

Doris connected the call and went back into Mr. Purvis's office.

"Has the subject been exhibiting any suspicious behavior?" asked Mr. Purvis. "Really? When? . . . Then bring him in! . . . Why? Suspicion of narcotics trafficking, that's why! . . . Agent Lockerman, that is a direct order! I want to see this Robeind character in this office in thirty minutes, understood?" He put down the phone.

"Apparently, Mr. Robeind was out late last night," said Mr. Purvis. "When he returned, he was carrying a black leather Gladstone bag. That sounds like probable cause to me. The agents will have him here shortly."

"Very good," said Cowley. "In the meantime, we can go over the reports about the money-laundering operation that was linked to the Bremer ransom money."

Twenty minutes later, there was a commotion at the entrance. Agents Lockerman and Suran dragged a protesting man in handcuffs through the front door. "Zees ees an outrage!" the man cried in a thick German accent. "I haff done nozzing to varrant zuch treatment!"

"We'll just see about that, Fritz," said Lockerman. Mr. Purvis and Mr. Cowley emerged from the office to watch the proceedings.

Doris felt a bloom of pride and . . . something else—perhaps desire—watching Allan handle the suspect. "Where do you want him, boss?" Lockerman asked.

"In the interview room, please," said Cowley. "I will conduct the interview personally."

The agents dragged the protesting man into the small interrogation room. Doris winced—it was not going to be a pleasant experience for the man.

At least it was quick. Cowley, Purvis, Lockerman, and Suran piled into the room, and soon the interview was in full swing. Doris could hear questions being shouted then the flat, meaty thuds of punches being thrown. The man cried out, protesting his innocence, but this merely increased the intensity of the "interview." Finally, the man broke down sobbing, and the sound of beating diminished.

After ten minutes, Mr. Purvis threw open the door to the interview room. "Someone run a check on the name 'Wilhelm Loeser,'" he said, spelling the last name. "Listen up, gentlemen! Despite rumors to the contrary, the Jackrabbit is alive and well! And he has a new face!"

# CHAPTER THIRTY-SIX

### Chicago, Illinois
### July 20, 1934

T he car pulled up in front of an apartment building on North Halsted Street, and Jimmy Lawrence stepped out, followed by a short woman with dark, bobbed hair. He leaned into the front window where another couple was sitting. "Thanks for the ride, Van!" Jimmy said. "That was a sockdolager of a game! The Cubbies really showed those Philly jerks how to play!"

Jimmy stepped back and the car pulled away from the curb with two cheery toots from the horn as it merged into traffic.

He turned to his companion. "Whaddaya say, Polly? Have a good time?"

"Yeah, Jimmy," she replied. "It's like I can't *not* have a good time with you. I just wish it wasn't so hot today."

"Yeah, it's been a real scorcher." Jimmy scanned the brick apartment building. "You think she's home?" he asked.

"Yeah, probably. What's the matter? Are you having second thoughts about staying here now?" A week earlier, Jimmy had moved out of his place and into the apartment of Polly's friend Anna Sage. Sage was a middle-aged Romanian woman who had run a string of brothels in Chicago and nearby towns, although she was now semi-retired. She had a large apartment with more than enough room for herself, Polly, Jimmy, and her son, Steve. Even though it meant a little less privacy, Jimmy had jumped at the chance to move in with his new flame. He was nuts about her.

"Hey, doll, if it means I get to spend more time with you, it's all right by me. I just don't want to think that I'm, y'know, imposing or anything."

"What do you mean?"

"Well, I know what Anna's business is."

"I bet you do!"

"Yeah, OK, I do. I'd be lying if I said otherwise. You know I used to go to places like that. I also know that you used to do a little work like that on the side too."

"Does that bother you, Jimmy? Because if it does, you'd better let me know right now—"

Jimmy leaned in and gave Polly a loud kiss on the lips. "You know it doesn't bother me a bit, princess. What kind of heel would I be if it did?"

"You'd just be a guy, is all. All guys are hypocrites when it comes to sex."

Jimmy chuckled. "Yeah, I guess we are," he said. "But that doesn't mean that I'm gonna be one now. I'm just goofy about you, Pol. I don't care what you used to do in the past, as long as it stays in the past."

"OK, good. I'll stay out of the cathouses as long as you do too."

"It's a deal," said Jimmy. "I'm just worried about Anna. Have you told her that you're not going to be working for her anymore . . . like that?"

"Of course, you big silly. I told her that right after our first date."

"And she doesn't mind?"

"We're both paying rent, so no. Why would she?" Polly grabbed Jimmy's hand and pulled him toward the building entrance. "Anna's been more like a mother to me than my own mother ever was. She doesn't care that I'm not working for her anymore. She's my friend, not my boss."

They went into the big brick building and up to the apartment on the third floor. When they got there, Anna Sage was on the phone. She was 45 years old, thick-waisted, with dark hair and even darker eyes. Those eyes were red-rimmed, and her round face was twisted into a scowl. She was barking into the telephone in her Slavic accent.

"Vat do you mean zhere ees no ozzer recourse? Martin, I zhought you said you could take care of zees! . . . No, no . . . OK, I'll zee vat I can do . . . Time ees short. Do vatever you can." She slammed the receiver down.

"Anna, what's wrong?" asked Polly.

Anna looked up, surprised. "Oh, I deedn't hear you come een!"

"Aw, sorry if we startled you," said Jimmy. "Say, you look a little rough around the edges."

Anna sighed deeply. "Zhey zay zhey are going to deport me now. Zhey zay I am 'undesirable alien.' Chust because I am running a brothel. Vat's wrong vith zat? I'll bet haffa zee cops and prosecutors een zee area are my customers."

"What's the problem?" asked Jimmy. "Just slip an envelope with a few big bills into the right hands, and your problem will go away."

"Not too long ago zat vould have vorked," sighed Anna. "Een fact, eet has many times een zee past. But ever zince those damned Democrats got eento power, nothing ees zee same. Eet's a dirty, dirty shame!"

She turned quickly and gazed out the window at the traffic passing below. When she turned back, it was as if she were a different person. The worry lines on her face had disappeared, and her eyes were clear and sparkling. "Who vants zome cheecken and dumplings for dinner?" she asked merrily. "Vith strawberry shortcake for dessert!"

"Put me down for both!" exclaimed Jimmy.

While Anna bustled about in the kitchen, Jimmy and Polly relaxed in the living room and listened to the radio. Jimmy read the sports section of the paper while Polly worked on some knitting.

When the radio began to play "All I Do Is Dream of You," Jimmy jumped up and began crooning along. He pulled Polly out of her chair and danced her around the living room. "All I dooo is dream of yooou, the whole night throoooough . . ."

"Oh, look at zee two lovebirds," said Anna. She stood in the doorway to the kitchen, wiping her hands on her apron. She smiled widely as Jimmy and Polly sashayed around the living room.

After dinner, Jimmy shooed the women out of the kitchen and did the dishes. He didn't mind rolling up his sleeves, putting on an apron, and just spending a little time cleaning up. His buddies would rag him if they knew about it, but Jimmy didn't care. He found it relaxing. Besides, after the wonderful meals Anna had prepared for them, he felt it was the least he could do.

When he finished, he went back to the living room and sat down by Polly. "So princess," he said. "Did you enjoy the ball game today? Those Cubs sure are hot this year!"

"Aw, honey, I enjoy anything as long as I'm with you. I've got to admit, though, that I didn't care too much for your pal Van at first. He just seemed . . . weird, especially with all his silly wisecracks. I think he's OK now, it just took a little while to warm up to him. You have to admit he's a little goofy-looking."

"Vhy do you say zhat?" asked Anna. "Vat does he look like?"

"Oh, he just has this funny face," said Polly. "It's sort of rubbery and horsey. He looks like a country rube."

"And you zay hees name ees Van?" asked Anna.

"Well, that's what Jimmy calls him. His girlfriend Marie calls him Homer."

"Homer Van Meter?" asked Anna. "Eet has to be."

"Do you know him?" asked Jimmy. He wasn't particularly surprised. Even in a city the size of Chicago, the criminal element was a tight fraternity. All the professional gangsters and hoodlums knew each other, at least by reputation.

"I may have met heem," said Anna. "Zertainly, he has dated some of my girls. Zhey zay he ees a good teeper."

"That's Van," said Jimmy. "Generous to a fault."

"Have you known heem long?" asked Anna.

Jimmy decided it was a good opportunity to play his role. After all, he was being paid handsomely to pretend to be the Jackrabbit; he might as well earn it. "Oh, yeah," he said. "Me and Van go way back."

Anna stared at Jimmy, looking intently at him as if she was seeing him for the first time. "You know, Jeemy," she said. "Eet has chust occurred to me zhat I don't know very much about you."

"I'm just Jimmy Lawrence, and I work at the Board of Trade."

"You must make good money zhere," said Anna. "You always zeem to have plenty of money to zpend on clothes and going out."

# CHAPTER THIRTY-SIX

"Buy low, sell high. It's pretty simple when you get down to it."

"Right," said Anna dismissively. "Vhere deed you say you vere from?"

"Oh, I'm just another Indiana farm boy who washed up in the big city. Chicago is full of guys like me. Even Van is from some dirt farm outside Fort Wayne."

Anna continued to stare at Jimmy. It was starting to make him uncomfortable. "Is there something wrong, Anna?"

"Zo, 'Jeemy,' I am going to ask you a queztion, and I vant you to be completely honest vith me."

"Shoot."

"Are you zee Jackrabbeet?"

Jimmy laughed. He had been expecting this question. A seasoned operator like Anna was bound to pick up on the clues he'd been dropping. He tapped the side of his nose and said, "Ask me no questions, Anna, and I'll tell you no lies."

"Zhat's vhat I thought," said Anna. She shrugged and picked up the newspaper.

"Is it true, Jimmy?" asked Polly. "Am I really going around with the Jackrabbit?"

"Well, if it were true, I'm not sure I'd want you to know. The Jackrabbit is a hot ticket—every copper in the country is looking for m . . . him. The last thing I want is for you to get hurt, princess." He thought that the fake stutter step was a nice playacting touch.

"Oh, I know, Jimmy," said Polly. "I don't care about your past. I just think you're dreamy." She turned to Anna. "Where's Steve?" Steve Chiolak was Anna's twenty-three-year-old son. He also stayed in Anna's apartment, although he was frequently gone.

"Oh, Steve's got a softball game tonight, zhen he's taking hees girl to a picture show. I vouldn't be surprised eef he zpent zee night at her place."

"Oh, that's good," said Polly. "Excuse me, won't you?" She got up and stepped briskly from the living room. She paused at the doorway to give Jimmy a long look over her shoulder before she disappeared.

"Look, Anna," said Jimmy. "I don't want to cause any trouble for you, either."

"Oh, zhere's no trouble. Birds of a feazzer must flock togezzer, right?"

"Absolutely."

From back in the bedroom, Polly's voice drifted out. "Jimmy? Could you come back here?"

When he stepped into the bedroom, Polly greeted him in a pair of stockings and garter belt—and nothing else. Her olive skin glowed with a sheen of perspiration. There was a high flush on her cheeks and chest, and the nipples of her small breasts stood hard and dark.

"Oh, wow, princess!" he said. "You really know what I like." He was still wearing the Jackrabbit's clothes, and he could feel his wanger stiffening in his pants.

She stepped to him and pressed her body tight against his. He could feel her heat radiating through his clothes. "I know what you like, all right," she said. "And I know what I like too. I like you, lover, a lot!"

She knelt down and unzipped his trousers then let them slide to the floor. Normally, Jimmy was fastidious about hanging up his clothes, but now was not the time. In a moment, his cock was in her mouth.

"Oh, my God . . ." he sighed. Not for the first time, he realized there were some advantages to dating a professional woman.

"That's right, baby," she purred. "Crack your marbles, baby. I want to taste your jizz."

It didn't take long. Jimmy shuddered all over; it felt like a million volts were shooting through his spine and out his penis.

Polly looked up at him, eyes shining. "Now what, big boy?"

"Now this," he said, and pulled her to her feet. He wrapped his arms around her narrow waist, picked her up, and tossed her onto the bed. "One good turn deserves another. I'm going to give your twichet such a tongue-lashing!"

She giggled, spread her legs, and slid up on the mattress to make room for him.

"Aren't you even going to take off your shirt?"

"Hell, no!"

He knelt down between her thighs and let his tongue luxuriate in the exotic taste of her cunt. She was ready to go; it only took a few seconds of licking before she got off. Jimmy kept going and got no complaints. He couldn't believe how hot Polly was. It was possible that day's high temperature might have had something to do with her ardor; some women seemed to get randy in the heat. However, Jimmy suspected Polly's enthusiasm had a lot more to do with the "revelation" that he was the Jackrabbit. He grinned to himself. In a few days, he could hit Van Meter up for the rest of the money he was to receive for playing this role. He'd have to tell Polly that he wasn't really the Jackrabbit then too. In the meantime, he was going to have as much hot mattress polo as he could manage.

Soon, he felt his wanger standing at attention again. He sat up, removed his shirt, and tossed it in the middle of the floor with the rest of his clothes.

"Oh, yesss," she murmured. "You've got quite the kidney-prodder there, Mister. What ever will you do with it?"

"This," he said, and with one decisive motion he was inside of her.

"Oh, yes! Oh, Jimmy! Oh, Jackrabbit! Jackrabbit! OHHH GOD!"

Out in the living room, Anna Sage listened with a disinterested ear. She had been in the sex business for a long time, and this was nothing new to her. Polly had always been one of her noisier girls. A lot of Johns liked that.

Anna picked up the newspaper and turned it to an article about Public Enemy Number One. It featured a photograph of the Jackrabbit, one that had been taken during his incarceration in Crown Point. There certainly was a great deal of similarity between him and Jimmy Lawrence. Darken the hair a bit and add a pencil mustache, and the resemblance was uncanny. It *had* to be him.

Anna carefully folded the paper and reached for the telephone.

# CHAPTER THIRTY-SEVEN

**Chicago, Illinois**
**July 21, 1934**

artin Zarkovich looked at his watch. It was just after nine o'clock, and Anna Sage should have been there by now. He pulled out a crisp linen handkerchief and carefully blotted his forehead. Even though the sun was down, it was still sweltering in the city. The heat wave that had started three days earlier showed no signs of letting up.

Zarkovich waited in a car on a tree-lined street near Children's Memorial Hospital. Melvin Purvis sat in the driver's seat. In the car behind them, Tim O'Neil waited with Sam Cowley.

After Anna Sage had called him with the tip about the Jackrabbit, Zarkovich wasn't sure how to proceed. He hadn't been especially surprised when the Jackrabbit and that idiot Van Meter disappeared after the murders of Mulvihill and O'Brien. Even if they hadn't suspected Zarkovich of setting them up, it would have been suicidal to stick around Lake County. Of course, he was sure the Jackrabbit *knew* he'd been set up. It worried him because that was yet one more piece of information the gangster could hold over Zarkovich's head.

Consequently, Zarkovich had been amazed—and quite relieved—when Anna Sage contacted him about trading the Jackrabbit for her freedom. Now he could finally take care of the big loose end that had been bothering him. He just had to make absolutely sure the Jackrabbit wouldn't live to tell any tales.

He first tried contacting the Chicago police. But they didn't want anything to do with his offer. That wasn't surprising given the long-standing animosity between them and the East Chicago PD. After that, Zarkovich had taken his tale to the FBI. He had no love for either the Chicago PD or the FBI. The Chicago PD was nearly as bent as Zarkovich and was a threat to his profits. The Feds were too white hat and were a threat to his freedom.

However, he figured he could play the FBI do-gooders, so he'd brought his tale of Anna and her Jackrabbit snare to the nineteenth floor of the Bankers Building. The Feds snapped at it like a hungry trout. The only hitch was that they wanted to meet with Anna Sage in person to determine if she was the genuine article.

Purvis checked his watch. "Your contact should already be here by now," he said.

"She will be," assured Zarkovich. "She's reliable. I've known her for quite some time." Zarkovich had met Sage in 1920 when she was running a brothel in Gary. He'd gotten to know her quite well—so much so that she was named as a respondent when Zarkovich's wife filed for divorce a year later. Zarkovich hadn't kept in close touch with her afterward, so he was surprised when she had suddenly popped up asking him to help with her deportation problem. He hadn't been interested in doing so—until she had offered him information on the Jackrabbit.

"I'm still curious about one thing," said Purvis. "I don't fully understand why you don't want the Chicago Police Department to be involved in this."

"I'm surprised you have to ask," Zarkovich said. "Surely, you've been in town long enough to know that the Chicago PD is as crooked as a dog's hind leg."

"I admit that the FBI has . . . concerns about the Chicago police. On the other hand, the East Chicago police don't exactly enjoy a stellar reputation."

"Lies!" spat Zarkovich. "Lies and innuendo, mostly spread by those rotten Chicago cops. Sure, there were a few bad apples in the past, but that was a long time ago. We've cleaned house, Agent Purvis, and we mean business. It's the dirty Chicago cops that you have to look out for."

"I see," said Purvis. "And why exactly are you and Captain O'Neil so insistent that the East Chicago force be along when we confront the Jackrabbit?"

"A matter of pride, mostly. Even though we didn't have direct jurisdiction at Crown Point, the Jackrabbit's escape was a real black eye for Lake County and Indiana. All those Chicago PD jokers have been calling us hicks and Keystone Kops ever since. I want to show the world that we can clean up our own messes."

"And of course, there *is* the matter of the reward," said Purvis.

"Sure. I've got a family to support, just like anybody else." This wasn't even close to being the truth. Zarkovich's wife had divorced him over ten years prior after she'd found him in bed with Anna Sage. He never remarried, figuring that there was no point in buying the cow when you could extort the milk for free.

"To be truthful, I don't really care who gets the reward," said Purvis. "Right now, I only care about one thing: catching the Jackrabbit."

"Believe me, Agent Purvis, I feel the same way," said Zarkovich. "All I'm interested in is killing the Jackrabbit."

"I said 'catch' the Jackrabbit, not 'kill,'" said Purvis. "Director Hoover is especially insistent that the Jackrabbit be captured alive."

"This is a dangerous man we're talking about here," said Zarkovich. "I have no intention of putting my men in jeopardy just so your director can grab another headline."

Purvis looked at him sharply. "If you're so worried about the danger of this operation, maybe you and your men should stay home."

"Hell, no!" said Zarkovich. "That was the deal: we'd give you the Jackrabbit and the East Chicago PD would be there to help take him down. If you have a problem with that, I'll leave right now. I'm sure your smart college boys will be able to handle it without us."

"No, no," said Purvis hastily. "We still have a deal. I respect your concern for your men's safety. We just need to try to take him alive, if at all possible."

"And if it's not possible, then we are free to defend ourselves, right?"

"Yes, of course."

"Good enough," said Zarkovich. He should have figured these FBI twits would go all white hat on him. No matter—he would make sure that he would have to "defend" himself once the deal went down. Hoover might be mad about it, but probably not very much.

Zarkovich blotted himself with his handkerchief again. He could feel the sweat running down the back of his shirt collar. He hated hot days like these—it made it hard to keep looking sharp. He'd already changed his shirt three times today.

The trees surrounding Children's Memorial Hospital obscured the streetlights, making the area shadowy and gloomy. Outside the car, a dim figure scurried by. It went to the end of the block and looked carefully up and down the street. Apparently satisfied, it turned back and walked quickly toward the car where Zarkovich and Purvis sat. Zarkovich leaned over and pushed open the rear door, and Anna Sage jumped inside.

"Are you Anna Sage?" asked Purvis.

"Yes, yes," she hissed. "Ve can't stay here. Drive over to Lincoln Park."

"We're perfectly safe here," assured Purvis.

"Don't you underztand?" asked Anna. "Thees ees the *Jackrabbeet* ve're talking about here. Eef he even *suspected* I vas doing thees, he'd keell me cold."

"OK," said Purvis. He started the car and pulled out. Behind them, the other car did likewise.

"Who's zhat behind us?" asked Anna.

"Calm down," said Zarkovich. "It's just Captain O'Neil and Bureau Inspector Samuel Cowley." Normally, Sage was as cool a customer as you'd find. He had never seen her this jumpy. He took that as a good sign—she must be on to the real thing.

As they drove, Zarkovich gave instructions to an out-of-the-way spot near North Avenue Beach. There were still a number of people at the beach trying to beat the oppressive heat, but their parking spot was relatively isolated. A low haze hung over the lakeshore, reflecting the glow from the city lights. The swampy air seemed to amplify the fishy smell from the lake.

"OK, Ms. Sage," said Purvis as he turned to face her in the back seat. "We want the Jackrabbit. Detective Zarkovich says you can give him to us. Is that true?"

"Of course, eet's true!" said Sage. "Do you zhink I made zees up chust for fun? I'm already een enough hot water. I don't need any more trouble vith zee government!"

"How do you know the Jackrabbit?" asked Purvis.

"He's dating one of my girls . . . my friends. I vasn't sure eet vas heem at firzt, but zee ozzer day, he zaid zomezing zat raised my zuzpicions. When I asked heem, he admeeted zat he vas zee Jackrabbeet."

"And you're sure about this?" asked Purvis.

"As zure as I can be. Zee man's peecture ees een every newspaper. I know vhat he looks like. Everybody knows vhat he looks like."

"Word on the street is that he had his face changed," said Zarkovich.

"I deedn't zay he looked *exactly* like zee newspaper photos. Hees face ees a leetle deef'rent, hees hair ees darker, and he has now a leetle mustache, but zo vhat? He *admeeted* he vas zee Jackrabbeet. Why vould anybody lie about being zee most hunted man een zee vorld?"

"Well, that sounds convincing to me," said Purvis. "Now how will you be able to—"

"Vait!" interrupted Sage. "Before I talk about vhat I'm going to do for *you*, I vant to know zhat you vill be able to help *me*. Zhey are going to deport me. I have received final noteece. You must help me stay een zee country. Otherwise, no Jackrabbeet."

Purvis pushed his straw boater back from his forehead and wiped it with a soggy handkerchief. "You have to understand that this is outside my jurisdiction. The Bureau is part of the Department of Justice. Immigration matters fall under the Department of Labor."

"Vhat? Vhat ees zees?" wailed Sage. "Martin, you zaid zees man vould be able to help me!"

"Easy now, Ms. Sage," said Purvis. "I'm just trying to be honest about the situation. As I said, I can't promise to have your deportation order revoked because it is a different branch of the government. However, I can promise you that I will do everything in my power to keep you from being deported. Director Hoover has a great interest in apprehending the Jackrabbit. I'm certain he'll be able to convince the Secretary of Labor to rescind the deportation order. The director swings a great deal of weight in Washington."

In the back seat, Anna mulled over this information. Zarkovich was certain Purvis wasn't being as honest as he claimed. Just one telephone call to the right Assistant Attorney General should be enough to make the deportation order disappear. Zarkovich really didn't care what Purvis would do. Anna was an old friend and lover, but *his* neck was on the line now. It would be tough if she got deported, but it would be much worse for him if the Jackrabbit were captured alive and spilled the beans.

"It's OK, Anna," Zarkovich said. "These guys are on the up-and-up. If J. Edgar Hoover is on your side, you're sure to get that deportation order quashed."

"OK, OK," said Anna. "I don't like eet, but I guess eet veel haff to do."

"Don't worry," said Purvis. "We're as good as our word."

"I zure hope so," she muttered.

"On to the business at hand," said Purvis. "We'll keep you in the country, but first you have to deliver the Jackrabbit."

"Like I said, he's been dating my . . . friend. Ve veel often go out to zee movie shows. I have invited zhem both for deener tomorrow night. After zat, ve veel probably go zee show at zee Marbro Theatre."

"So he's coming to your place for dinner?" asked Purvis. "What's your address?"

"Nuzzing doing," said Anna. "I veel not have you teeping heem off veeth your clumsy agents stumbling around my home. He veel know for zure zat I ratted heem out."

"It would be an easy matter to find out where you live," said Purvis sharply. "We could have you tailed."

"Ah, hold on there, Agent Purvis," said Zarkovich. "She has a point. The man is extraordinarily wily. He seems to have a sixth sense for spotting tails and traps. I'm certain I don't have to remind you of how easily he got away from Little Bohemia."

"No, you certainly don't," snapped Purvis. He pushed back his hat and mopped his forehead again. "OK, Ms. Sage, we'll do things your way. What time will you be going to the theater?"

"I don't know yet," she said. "Probably late. After eet's cooled down."

Purvis pulled a notepad out of his jacket and scrawled a number with a stubby pencil then handed it back to her. "This is my direct line. It will ring directly to my office. Call me as soon as you have more information."

Anna scowled at the phone number then carefully put it away in her purse. "I veel let you know as zoon as I know more. Zees ees very deefeecult for me, you underztand. I am taking my life een my hands! You promise zhat I veel not get deported?"

"I promise that the Bureau will do everything in its power to make sure you stay in America."

"Good enough," Anna grunted. She opened the car door and disappeared into the steamy evening.

# CHAPTER THIRTY-EIGHT

### Chicago, Illinois
### July 22, 1934, 10:00 a.m.

D oris had been enjoying a lazy Sunday morning in bed when another urgent call came in from the office. She was told to drop whatever she was doing and rush into work right away. She was not pleased to be working on Sunday—again—but neither was she surprised. She had already worked a full day on Saturday, and she would probably be in for a long stretch today as well. She grumbled as she dressed and hustled downtown to the Bankers Building.

For the last two days, Mr. Purvis and Inspector Cowley had been conferring on an urgent matter. From what Doris could tell, it had something to do with a confidential informant who might know the whereabouts of the Jackrabbit. The day before, two unfamiliar men had come in to meet with Mr. Purvis. One had been very well dressed. In his spotless linen suit, he looked like a millionaire or a movie star. After a hushed conversation in Mr. Purvis's office, all three had departed to visit Inspector Cowley in his hotel room.

As soon as she arrived at the office, Mr. Purvis took her aside. "I am expecting a very important call on my personal line," he told her. "Any calls that come in on that line, please come find me if I'm not at my desk. Even if I'm in the washroom, y'hear? This is very important."

"Yes, Mr. Purvis."

Mr. Purvis leaned in and spoke almost in a whisper. "Look, Ms. Rogers, I know that you sometimes . . . uh . . . monitor my telephone conversations."

Doris was taken aback. "Mr. Purvis, I don't—"

He cut her off with a wave of his hand. "There's no problem," he said. "My faith in your loyalty to me and the Bureau is absolute. However, right now things are a little bit touchy. We have an informant who claims to be able to provide us with the location of the Jackrabbit. We are attempting to set up a trap to catch him tonight. We will be in regular contact with our informant throughout the day. Do you understand?"

"Yes, sir." Doris was still unnerved by the thought that her boss knew about her eavesdropping. If things went badly, she might not only lose her job but also face criminal proceedings.

"You don't have to worry," Mr. Purvis reassured her. "I know you are just looking out for me, and I appreciate it. However, Inspector Cowley would not understand. At this point, it would not be productive to have any misunderstandings. So, until the current situation is resolved, please just forward my calls and trust me to take care of myself, OK?"

"Yes, sir." Doris could feel a deep flush heating her face. She turned away quickly and went back to her desk.

At half past one, a call came in on Mr. Purvis's personal line. He was in his office and answered it directly. It was a short conversation. Shortly afterward, Cowley came out and told her, "Call every agent in the office. Tell them to get here by three. We need every available man here as soon as possible."

Doris started dialing. Dozens of agents were assigned to the Chicago office, so it took her a while to work through the list. By the time she was done, they had begun to arrive.

A handful of reporters were still camped out in the hallway. Not nearly as many as when Billie Frechette had been arrested, but it still seemed as if each newspaper in town had assigned a cub reporter to maintain a vigil. She could faintly hear the *ka-ching, ka-ching* of coins being dropped into the pay telephones down the hall as the reporters called into their editors to say that something was going on at FBI office.

As more agents arrived, Doris began to feel uneasy. The scene was reminiscent of the day of the Little Bohemia fiasco. The atmosphere was filled with nervous tension and unanswered questions. Everyone knew something big was about to happen but had no idea what it might be.

Doris was relieved—and a little frightened—to see Allan Lockerman come through the door at a quarter to three. After Carter Baum's fatal shooting, she was afraid that the same thing might happen to Allan. The notion made her stomach knot up.

Something strange happened to her then. The nervous bustle of the office seemed to fade into the background, as if she were viewing it from far away. All the circumstances that led to this moment—throughout her entire life and especially since she began working for the Bureau—had led up to this point. She saw Allan Lockerman walking toward her desk, a smile spreading across his all-American face. He seemed suffused with a brilliant glow that came from within. Alongside that was the feeling of loss and grief that had accompanied the death of Carter Baum. Doris knew that if something happened to Allan, her heart would break.

Suddenly, she realized she was in love with him.

"Hey, Dore," he said. "Hello? Anyone home?"

Doris felt a flush spread across her face as her heart hammered harder. Her mouth worked soundlessly for a moment, then she managed to croak out, "Hi, Allan . . . um, Agent Lockerman."

"Hey, are you OK? You look a little . . . I dunno . . . distracted."

Doris composed herself, trying to get her fluttering stomach under control. "I'm just fine, Agent Lockerman," she said stiffly. It was difficult to keep her voice from trembling. "As you can plainly see, there is quite a lot to command my attention in the office today."

"Whoa, sorry! I didn't mean to—" Allan said, taken aback.

"No, no, don't mind me." She reached out to touch his arm and felt a burst of electricity shoot up her arm and through her body. "I don't really know what's going on, although I'd guess it has something to do with the Jackrabbit. I'm just having a bad memory of what happened in Wisconsin. I don't know what I'd do if something happened to you, Allan. I'd go completely to pieces."

"What are you saying, Doris?"

This innocent question flustered her even more. "I . . . I don't . . . It's just that, look, Allan—I just want you to be safe, OK? Just come back in one piece. Promise me."

Allan laughed, and, for a moment, it took all of her self-control to keep from slapping him.

"OK, I promise, Dore. I'll come back in one piece, no problem. After that . . . maybe we should have a long talk over a nice dinner, eh?"

"Yes. Oh, yes!" A wave of emotions churned through her: frustration, hope, love, fear. She opened her mouth, feeling like she had to say *something* but didn't know what to say. She was spared the decision by an incoming phone call. "Excuse me, Agent Lockerman. This is a very important call I must take. I look forward to our upcoming discussion."

She snatched up the receiver as Allan walked away with a bewildered smile on his face. She watched him go as she fielded yet another call from the director's office in Washington. They had been coming frequently all day. She patched the call through to Mr. Purvis.

Shortly afterward, Mr. Purvis called her into his office. Inspector Cowley was there, and they were poring over a map of downtown Chicago spread out on the desk.

"Ah, Ms. Rogers," said Mr. Purvis. "I'll need you to . . ."

Just then, the phone on the desk rang. Purvis and Cowley exchanged looks. Purvis snatched up the receiver. "Melvin Purvis speaking."

He listened intently. At last, he said, "Well, I understand. You do realize it's important that you get me the information as quickly as possible? . . . Yes, yes, of course. . . . Please call me as soon as you do. . . . Thank you."

He hung up. "That was our informant. She now says that she's not sure if they're going to the Marbro or the Biograph."

Inspector Cowley gave Doris a dark look. "Agent Purvis, do you think it's wise to be discussing this in front of a mere secretary?"

"I trust Ms. Rogers implicitly," said Mr. Purvis. "Anything you can tell me, you can tell her." A burst of pride and affection welled up in Doris. Just a few minutes earlier, she was afraid of losing her job, and now Mr. Purvis was paying her the highest compliment of her career.

Inspector Cowley looked at Doris skeptically. "I will defer to your judgment, Agent Purvis," he said. "Now to the matter at hand: where is this Biograph Theater?"

"It's up on Lincoln, a few blocks from the park," said Mr. Purvis.

"We'd better get information about this theater as well," said Cowley. He stuck his head out the door and corralled four agents who were standing nearby. He gave them instructions to head over to the Biograph and make detailed diagrams of the theater: all entrances and exits, all the surrounding streets and alleyways, and anything else that might be of importance.

The agents departed hastily, further exciting the reporters who were congregating in the hallway outside. One or two peeled away from the pack in an attempt to follow them.

"Goodness gracious," said Cowley. "Is this never going to end? Now we don't know where he's supposed to be going. I swear the man's as slippery as an eel."

"We'll get him, Sam," said Mr. Purvis. "We're close this time; I can really feel it."

"This is not the first time we've been 'close.' You know that."

Doris saw her boss wince. She knew he still carried the shame and horror of the Little Bohemia disaster with him every waking moment. She wouldn't be surprised if it haunted his dreams as well.

"We're ready this time," said Mr. Purvis firmly. "We'll have enough men with enough training, and we'll know the layout of where we're going too. We didn't have that luxury at Little Bohemia."

"We don't even know *where* he's going," Cowley pointed out.

"Has anybody checked to see what's playing?" Doris asked.

The two FBI men looked at her in surprise. Inspector Cowley looked annoyed, but Mr. Purvis just seemed amused. It occurred to her that she might have just overstepped her bounds. Perhaps Mr. Purvis's vote of confidence had emboldened her. Perhaps her thoughts about Allan were coloring her actions as well. She'd do anything she could to make sure all the agents—especially Allan—made it back safely.

"What was that, Ms. Rogers?" asked Mr. Purvis.

"Has anybody checked to see what's playing at the theaters?" she repeated.

"An interesting idea," said Inspector Cowley. "Why don't you do that right now?"

Doris dashed into the bull pen and snatched a copy of the *Tribune* from one of the desks. She returned to the office and thumbed through the paper to the movie listings.

"Tonight, the Marbro is playing *Little Miss Marker* with that cute little Shirley Temple," said Doris. "At the Biograph, they're showing *Manhattan Melodrama* with Clark Gable."

"I don't get out to the movie shows very much," said Mr. Purvis. "What's the Clark Gable picture about?"

"Oh, a girlfriend of mine saw it last week," said Doris. "It's about two friends who end up on different sides of the law. One becomes a district attorney and the other a notorious gangster."

"So the choice is between a show about a cute little girl or one about a gangster," said Inspector Cowley. He nodded to Doris. "I think even our junior G-man here could deduce which movie the Jackrabbit would prefer."

# CHAPTER THIRTY-NINE

### Chicago, Illinois
### July 22, 1934, 5:00 p.m.

Jimmy and Polly had been playing pinochle all afternoon, and he was getting tired of the game. However, it was too hot to do anything else. They'd propped a fan in the open window, desperately seeking relief from the triple-digit temperature.

Jimmy put down his cards. "I don't want to go to a stupid Shirley Temple picture," he complained. "That little tyke makes me sick!"

"Oh, but she's so cute!" said Polly.

"I know—that's the problem. She's just so cutesy-sweet, it just makes me want to heave!"

"Vell, zhen, vhere do you vant to go?" asked Anna. "I veesh you vould make up your mind!"

Jimmy glanced up at her. She was standing in the doorway to the kitchen, twisting her apron back and forth. Jimmy noticed that she'd been very jumpy lately, but he figured it was because of the impending deportation order. Anna's accent was more pronounced when she was nervous.

"Wow, you sure are keyed up," said Jimmy. "What's the rush?"

"I don't know. I'd just like to know where ve're going."

"Ha! Ha!" said Jimmy. "You sound just like Bela Lugosi in *Dracula!*"

"Vhat, ees zat zuppozed to be funny? You zheenk eet ees funny for me to be vorried about being deported all zee time? I don't vant to go back to Romania! Have you ever been to Romania? Eet ees not a nice place to be,

253

trust me."

"Hey, hey, I'm sorry!" said Jimmy. "Look, I could talk with some of the lawyers down at the Board of Trade. I'm sure they could recommend someone who can help you out."

"No, no," muttered Anna. "No lawyers. I have a friend who ees helping me out. I can't vait until zees eemeegration people finally *lasama in pache*."

"What?"

"Leave me alone!" Anna cried. "I chust vant zhem to leave me alone!" She looked down at her apron, which was wadded into a tight knot. "I'm sorry, I chust vant zees to be over. Zo, vhich film are ve going to zee, zhen?"

"I'd like to go see *Manhattan Melodrama* at the Biograph," said Jimmy. "It's a lot closer than the Marbro, and they've got better air conditioning too."

"But we've seen that already," said Polly.

"So what? I liked it. That Clark Gable is great as Blackie. Myrna Loy too—she's easy on the eyes!"

"You like her better than me," pouted Polly.

"Nothing doing, baby." Jimmy leaned in and gave her a smack on the lips. "You're better than a hundred Myrna Loys."

"Vell, I'm glad zhat's zettled," said Anna. "Now vhat do you vant for deener, Jeemy? I can make vhatever you like."

"You know I can't resist your fried chicken, Anna."

"Veeth rhubarb pie for dessert?"

"You bet!"

Anna disappeared into the kitchen and reappeared a moment later. "I'm out of butter," she announced. "I must go down to zee market now. I shall return shortly." She hustled out the front door and gave Jimmy a quick look over her shoulder before she slammed the door behind her.

"She sure is nervous," he observed.

"It's this deportation order," said Polly. "It's really got her worried. I'm sure she'll be much better once her friend helps her get it cleared up."

"I sure hope so. How about another game?" He began dealing another pinochle hand and whistled merrily as he dealt the cards. He would get his favorite dinner and then go to a good movie with two pretty women. It would be a perfect evening.

# CHAPTER FORTY

**Chicago, Illinois**
**July 22, 1934, 7:00 p.m.**

It was early evening, but on the nineteenth floor of the Bankers Building it was still sweltering. The agents were all in their required dark suits and ties. They milled around the bull pen or sat at their desks, fanning themselves with newspapers and grumbling about the heat.

Doris had been busy all day connecting calls between their office and Bureau headquarters in Washington. Despite the oppressive heat in the office, the atmosphere was electric. There had been no official announcement, but the word had spread: they had a line on the Jackrabbit, and something was going to happen soon.

Shortly before six o'clock, four men came into the office. One of them was the well-dressed man who had showed up the day before demanding to speak with Mr. Purvis. Doris thought they were the police officers responsible for setting up the operation—whatever it may be. She scrutinized the sharp dresser—he was supposed to be a police officer, but he looked like a mob boss.

Shortly after the four officers arrived, another call came in on Mr. Purvis's personal line. This had elicited a great deal of excitement among the group huddled in Mr. Purvis's office. After an intense discussion, Inspector Cowley came out and instructed all the agents to come into Mr. Purvis's office. "You too, Ms. Rogers," he told her. "I would like you to take notes."

"Gentlemen!" said Mr. Purvis. "Gentlemen, your attention please!" The crowded room immediately fell silent.

"Undoubtedly, you are wondering about the nature of this evening's operation," said Purvis. "To explain the details, I present Detective Martin Zarkovich of the East Chicago Police Department."

The well-dressed police officer squeezed his way to the front of the room. He removed his natty homburg hat and fanned himself briefly. "All right!" he announced. "Tonight, we will nail the Jackrabbit!"

An excited buzz ran through the room. Most of the agents already suspected the fuss was about the Jackrabbit, but hearing confirmation made it that much more exciting.

Zarkovich continued, "We have an informant who is providing us with information on the Jackrabbit's activities. Our informant tells us that she and another lady will be accompanying the Jackrabbit to a movie at a local theater this evening at eight o'clock. However, we still don't know whether they will be attending the show at the Biograph Theater or the Marbro."

"How are we going to identify him then?" asked one agent. "I heard the Jackrabbit had his face changed surgically."

"Our informant will be wearing a bright orange skirt in order to aid in identification. She is in her mid-forties, heavily built—about 160 pounds—and has black hair. The other woman who will be with him is in her mid-twenties, slim, with a dark complexion."

Zarkovich leaned back on the desk with a smile. Doris thought he looked like a cat contemplating the flavor of a nearby canary.

Inspector Cowley stood up. "As I'm sure you are aware, Director Hoover is closely following this operation," he said. "He is quite anxious to avoid repeating any of the . . . uh . . . missteps of the past. We do not want to endanger any member of the public, which is why we will only be carrying sidearms. In order to minimize the hazard to the public, we will wait until the picture show is over before we make the apprehension. Also, Director Hoover has made it abundantly clear that he wants the Jackrabbit taken alive, if at all possible."

This seemed to startle Zarkovich. He stood up abruptly and leaned over and said something into the ear of one of the other East Chicago police officers, who frowned and shook his head.

"Excuse me," said Allan Lockerman. "You mentioned that the suspect will be in the company of two women. Is there any chance that his gang members will be with him?"

"Excellent question," said Mr. Purvis. "We have no information that the Jackrabbit will be accompanied by anyone other than the two women. Of course, our information may be incomplete. Even if it isn't, you are to regard the Jackrabbit as armed and dangerous. You men should use your best judgment and do what you need to do to protect innocent bystanders and yourselves."

At this pronouncement, Zarkovich relaxed. Doris watched him lean back on the desk as the lazy smirk returned to his face. He turned to his companion and drew his thumb across his throat.

Inspector Cowley looked at his watch. "OK, gentlemen, the time is seven fifty-five. It's time to move out."

The men quickly filed out of the cramped office. Allan Lockerman was one of the last to leave. Before he stepped through the door, he turned to Doris and frowned, giving his head a little shake. She felt the bottom of her stomach drop out. Something was wrong.

She hustled out of Mr. Purvis's office and grabbed his shoulder. "Allan, what's wrong?" she asked.

He scowled and shook his head again. "I don't know, Dore. Nothing. . . . Everything. . . . Something's wrong here, but I can't put my finger on it."

"I understand," Doris said. "I think it's these East Chicago officers. They seem a little . . . off. That Detective Zarkovich—"

Allan rolled his eyes. "That guy's as crooked as the day is long," he said. "Him and his pals are up to something. I think they've sold the Bureau a bill of goods. Something's not right."

Doris felt her breath catch in her throat. She flashed back to just before the Little Bohemia raid and the way Cater Baum had seemed childishly excited before heading off to his death. The thought of something like that happening to Allan was unbearable. "Allan, don't go!" she begged. "Tell them you're sick or something!"

"You know I can't do that. I have my duty."

A wave of panic washed over her. She couldn't bear to have anything happen to this man. She began to babble. "No . . . wait. . . . I'll talk to Mr. Purvis. . . . He'll understand. . . . Please, Allan!"

Allan pursed his lips and shook his head. He leaned in and gave Doris a brief but fierce hug. "Look, sweetheart, I have to go out and do my duty. That's all there is to it. But I'd be lying to you if I said I liked it. In fact, I think it stinks to high heaven. These East Chicago cops have dangled something in front of the Bureau, and they snapped at it like an alligator. I think the Bureau's making a big mistake trusting these crooked cops. They're too desperate to catch the Jackrabbit, and they don't care what they have to do."

"Then don't go!" Doris cried.

"That's not an option. I tell you what, though: once this thing's over, I'm going to sit down and think long and hard about my future, and whether there's a place in it for the Bureau."

"I hope there's a place in it for me," Doris whispered.

"Yes," said Allan. "I'd like to think you and I have a great future together. As for my future with the Bureau . . . well, that remains to be seen. But in the meantime, I have a job to do."

Around them in the bull pen, the rest of the agents prepared to move out. There was much less exuberance than when they were preparing for the Little Bohemia raid. Doris's head felt light. The idea of a long future together with Allan Lockerman made her heart sing, but she had not given any thought to the possibility of leaving the Bureau. The thought had just never occurred to her. It seemed disloyal somehow. After all that Mr. Purvis had done for her, it didn't seem right to go off and leave him in a lurch. On the other hand, if it came down to choosing between Allan and her career at the Bureau, Allan would win hands down.

First, however, they had to make it through tonight. She just wanted it to be over—and to have Allan back safe. She grabbed both his hands and stared him straight in the eyes. It didn't matter who saw her do this or what they might think. This was more important than a bunch of stupid bureaucratic rules. "Just promise me you'll be safe," she said. "I . . . I don't know what I'd do if something happened to you out there."

She expected him to laugh off her concerns with typical male bravado and tell her that she was being silly. Instead, he squeezed back. "Don't worry, Doris. Knowing that I've got you to come back to, I will be extra careful."

Doris dropped his hands. "OK, go," she said. "Do it now and come back safe." She turned from him and walked stiffly back to her desk. She kept her back turned until she thought that he'd gone out the door. Her mind was awhirl, but she just couldn't stand to watch him leave. If she never saw him again, she wanted her last image of him to be his deep brown eyes, not the back of his coat.

# CHAPTER FORTY-ONE

**Chicago, Illinois**
**July 22, 1934, 8:15 p.m.**

"We should be going soon," said Anna Sage.

"What's the rush?" asked Jimmy. "The theater's right down the street."

"No rush. I'm chust ready to get out of zhees heat and eento some air-condeetioning." The Biograph was cooled with huge blocks of ice in the basement. A fan blew air over the ice and up beneath the seats in the auditorium.

"I can understand that," said Jimmy. "It's been a scorcher all day. Just let me get a few things, and we can be off."

He went back to the bedroom and opened the top drawer of the dresser. He took his lucky onyx ring and slipped it onto his left hand then fished out a large roll of bills. One of his scams at the Board of Trade had just paid off, and he was nearly $4,000 richer because of it. But he hadn't had time to distribute the cash to his various hidey-holes. So, in the meantime, he preferred to keep the cash with him—along with a little extra protection.

From the dresser drawer, he also removed a Colt .380 hammerless pistol. Jimmy didn't carry a gun often, but he liked to make sure he was covered when he was carrying a large sum of cash. The .380 was a good little gun—lightweight, but it packed a punch. He worked the slide and made sure a round was in the chamber.

"Do you really need to take that thing with you?" Polly had slipped into the bedroom unnoticed.

"Huh?" said Jimmy, startled.

"Do you really need to take that gun with you?" Polly repeated. "I don't like guns."

Jimmy shrugged. "I'm sorry, princess. I just got paid on Friday, and I haven't had the chance to put it in the bank. I don't like walking around with a lot of cash without my popgun for protection. It's nothing, really."

"Oh, OK," said Polly. "I guess when you're Public Enemy Number One, you need to have a little protection."

"Huh?" said Jimmy. "Oh, yeah. Right. You don't need to worry about that." He slipped the Colt into his trouser pocket. "See? You can't even tell it's there."

Polly stepped to him and rubbed the front of his trousers. "Say, big boy," she purred. "Is that a pistol in your pocket, or are you just glad to see me?"

"Um, both."

She rubbed harder. "Maybe we should just skip the picture," she said. "We've seen it already, anyway."

"Well, I can easily be convinced—"

From the living room, Anna's voice pierced the thin plaster wall. "Vill you two hurry up? Ve are going to be late!"

"I think the landlady is getting impatient," said Jimmy.

"Oh, OK," pouted Polly. "But when we get back from the show—"

"Don't worry," said Jimmy. "We'll have a fine time later."

"I'm not sure I can wait that long," said Polly. "You might just get a bit of a surprise *during* the show if you know what I—"

"Vhat ees taking you zo long?" grumbled Anna. "Let's go!"

Out in the living room, Anna paced back and forth, her bright orange skirt billowing out whenever she reached the end of the room and turned.

"Eet's about time!" she said when Jimmy and Polly appeared from the bedroom. "The movie starts een feefteen minutes!"

"It only takes five minutes to walk there," said Jimmy. "Besides, we'd only miss the newsreels."

"I don't care," said Anna. "I've been bakeeng like a potato all day. Let's go cool ourselves off!"

"All righty," said Jimmy. "Let's go then."

There were a lot of people out and about for a Sunday night. Even though the sun had almost set, it was still very hot—nearly 90—and the people in the crowd seemed restless and irritable. In the few blocks between the apartment and the theater, they saw three fistfights. "This heat's making everyone nuts," thought Jimmy. He just wanted to get a box of popcorn and relax with his best girl in the air-conditioned theater.

While waiting in line at the Biograph's box office, Jimmy felt himself getting a little restless. He noticed a man lounging by the box office who seemed familiar. He was short and wore a straw boater and a blue blazer. Jimmy thought he might have seen the man's picture in the newspaper. It was probably some political hotshot. Well, it didn't matter much now. Jimmy bought three tickets and went inside.

By the time he'd bought a box of popcorn and a package of Necco wafers, the theater was almost full. They couldn't find three seats together, so he and Polly sat with each other down front while Anna settled for a solitary seat near the back.

"Psst," said Jimmy. "C'mere."

Polly leaned over and asked, "What?"

Jimmy gave her a loud kiss. "That's what!"

"You big . . ." began Polly. "Oh, wait—the show's starting."

The lights inside the Biograph dimmed, and Jimmy Lawrence sat back to enjoy the show.

# CHAPTER FORTY-TWO

### Chicago, Illinois
### July 22, 1934, 10:00 p.m.

"Those smart college boys are going to spoil the whole setup," said Martin Zarkovich. He and O'Neil lounged in a doorway smoking cigarettes across from the Biograph Theater. The entire operation had been tense and confused, but now it was just down to waiting.

Earlier in the evening, Zarkovich had gone with Inspector Cowley to keep an eye on the Marbro, while Purvis and another agent covered the Biograph. The rest of the team sweated it out at the Bankers Building until the determination had been made as to which theater the Jackrabbit was patronizing.

There was no sign of the Jackrabbit at the Marbro, and Cowley had called in to headquarters to get an update. Sure enough, the Jackrabbit and the two women had been spotted entering the Biograph shortly before the beginning of the show. Zarkovich and Cowley had sped across town to join the rest of the team in front of the theater.

After they arrived, there was a hurried conference to finalize the agents' positions. Melvin Purvis would wait right outside the theater doors when the crowd exited the theater. When he spotted the Jackrabbit, he would signal the others by lighting a cigar.

Zarkovich and O'Neil, along with two FBI agents named Hurt and Hollis, would wait in front of the theater and move in once the signal was given. The rest of the team was divided up and assigned to positions on either side of the theater and near the emergency exits in the back.

Now they waited.

Zarkovich pitched his butt and lit another one immediately. He normally didn't chain-smoke like this, but he was nervous. He'd spent a lot of time worrying about getting the Jackrabbit out of his hair, and now it was time to wrap things up. He'd be glad to have the troublesome gangster dead and gone—provided these FBI nitwits didn't screw things up.

"They're gonna blow the whole deal," stated Zarkovich. "Look, he's doing it again!" He jerked his chin toward the box office, where Purvis was talking with the ticket seller.

"Jeez, that's the third time," said O'Neil. "If he keeps pestering them about when the show's going to let out, they're gonna get suspicious."

"The show's still going to let out at ten forty, just like it has all night."

"Those other guys aren't helping, either," observed O'Neil. Besides Purvis bothering the ticket taker, other clumps of agents were loitering around the building in a suspicious manner. To Zarkovich's eye, they looked like a gang of robbers casing a joint.

One of the FBI agents, a man named Clarence Hurt, walked up to Zarkovich and O'Neil. He wasn't like most of the other agents Zarkovich had encountered. Most of them were soft, snotty college boys who overthought everything and probably couldn't shoot for shit. Hurt, on the other hand, was older and had a tough, weathered look to him. Zarkovich could tell that this man was a killer.

Zarkovich noticed the pointed cowboy boots sticking out from underneath the man's suit trousers. On anyone else, they would have seemed like an affectation, but Hurt wore them naturally. Zarkovich was impressed; the boots were hand-tooled ostrich skin, and they looked sharp. He thought he might pick up a pair for himself.

"Hey, fellas," said Hurt. "You should probably get back on station with us. They might come out any time."

Zarkovich consulted his watch. It was a few minutes past ten. "We've got over half an hour before the show lets out," he said. "Cool your heels, Hopalong Cassidy. We won't miss anything."

Hurt gave Zarkovich a flat look and turned back to join his partner in front of the theater. Zarkovich watched him go. "Those guys make me nervous," he said. "We can't have them going white hat on us, Tim."

"Don't worry," said O'Neil. "If we don't nail the Jackrabbit with the first shot, I'll make sure you can finish the job."

"Good man. I'll be glad to have this problem out of the way. Even more so than Hoover."

"Yeah," laughed O'Neil. "He don't know it, but we've got a lot more at stake than he does. Oh hell, wouldya look at that!" He pointed to the front of the theater.

A large Lincoln sedan had pulled up to where the largest group of agents were milling around. Four men jumped out of the sedan with guns drawn.

"Holy shit!" exclaimed Zarkovich. "I knew those dumb bastards were going to ruin the setup."

"Who is it?" asked O'Neil.

"Chicago PD."

"Nothing we can do about it now."

They watched as the Chicago cops waved their guns around and shouted. Passersby on the street looked on with interest. Finally, one of the agents pulled out his wallet and showed a badge to the lead cop. After some more bad noise, the cops climbed back into their Lincoln and sped off.

"Dumb Feds," said Zarkovich. He took a drag from his cigarette and tossed it into the gutter. "Well, let's go back and join ol' Hopalong and his sidekick. The bad guys should be coming through the pass pretty soon now."

They crossed the street and rejoined Hurt and Hollis. The minutes dragged by. Zarkovich could feel the familiar adrenaline rush building. This always happened when he knew he was about to engage in gunplay. It started in his solar plexus and radiated out to his limbs. To be truthful, he really got off on it—especially when he capped things off by blowing away his adversary. It was a rush that couldn't be matched.

O'Neil elbowed him and said, "Look alive . . . Here they come."

Zarkovich straightened up. People were starting to come out of the theater—just a few at first then a rush. He checked his revolver. He was ready.

By the main doors, Purvis toyed with a cigar. He looked nervous as hell. His knees were practically knocking as he stood scrutinizing the departing theatergoers. "He's going to fuck it all up," thought Zarkovich.

As people continued to come out of the Biograph Theater, Zarkovich took a few deep breaths then shook his shoulders to stay loose. The adrenaline rush smoothed out like a sea of glass. It was there, brittle and smooth, and all he had to do was ride it to the end.

More people came out of the theater but still no Jackrabbit. Purvis looked like he might wet his pants. The departing crowd started to thin out. Had the Jackrabbit sensed a trap? Had he slipped from the theater unnoticed? That would be just like him. Still, Zarkovich wouldn't let his guard down until the last patron had exited.

"There!" hissed Hurt. "That's the signal!"

Purvis stuck the cigar in his mouth and tried to light it with a shaky hand. It took three tries for him to get the match going. Before he could light the cigar, Zarkovich saw their quarry. Anna Sage was on the outside, wearing her orange skirt. In the neon lights of the theater, it looked blood red. Next to her was the Jackrabbit, fashionably dressed in a straw boater and white buckskin shoes. On the other side of him was a younger woman in a green skirt.

Zarkovich, O'Neil, Hurt, and Hollis moved in to intercept their target. Nobody said a thing.

The Jackrabbit must have sensed something was wrong. Without saying a word to his companions, he hunched over and took off running. He sprinted toward the alleyway to the south of the theater entrance, scrabbling at his pocket.

"He's going for his gun!" cried Hollis.

"Halt!" yelled Hurt. He raised his pistol and fired. Blood splashed from high up on the Jackrabbit's right shoulder. He staggered but made the turn into the alley.

Zarkovich ran at full speed after him. Behind him, he heard a thud of colliding bodies. "Hey, watch it!" said someone. It sounded like Hurt. O'Neil had "accidentally" run into both of the pursuing FBI agents.

Now unaccompanied, Zarkovich turned into the alley. The Jackrabbit stumbled again and went down hard on his face. The glassy feeling of elation peaked inside Zarkovich. This was it—the ultimate moment. Zarkovich stepped up behind the fallen man, leveled his revolver at the back of his head, and calmly pulled the trigger.

The Jackrabbit shuddered violently and lay still. A pool of blood poured out from beneath his head. Almost without thinking, Zarkovich reached down and checked the man's pockets. There was a small semiautomatic pistol and a roll of bills. He pocketed the cash. There was also a large onyx ring on his left hand. He thought about grabbing that too, but there wasn't enough time. He shook his head and stood up.

Behind him, Hurt, Hollis, and O'Neil pounded into the alley. "We got him, boys," said Zarkovich. "Agent Hurt got him good, I just finished the job."

"I could have finished him myself if it weren't for your clumsy partner!" spat Hurt. He looked furious. O'Neil tipped Zarkovich a quick wink.

Cowley and Purvis rushed into the alley with the other agents close behind. They stood in a circle around the body. "Well, let's see what we've got here," said Cowley. "Somebody turn him over."

A dozen hands flipped over the limp body, and someone used a handkerchief to mop the blood from the dead man's face. Zarkovich's bullet had exited beneath the left eye, but the exit wound wasn't particularly large.

"That's him, all right," pronounced Purvis. "I'd recognize him anywhere. The Bureau has finally gotten its man!" He looked immensely relieved.

Zarkovich stood looking down at the dead man's face. He was undeniably dead, but there was one problem: the dead man wasn't the Jackrabbit.

His stomach dropped. All this work for nothing! He'd been running around like a one-armed paperhanger for the last week to make sure he could strike the Jackrabbit from his list of problems, but the bastard had slipped away—again! He felt a headache blossom from the base of his neck. His stomach felt like it was full of battery acid.

"What's wrong, Zark?" asked O'Neil.

Zarkovich grabbed his partner by the shoulder and pulled him away from where the federal agents were congratulating themselves.

"That's not him!" Zarkovich hissed.

"What the hell?"

"That's not the Jackrabbit!"

"But the facial surgery—"

"Surgery, my ass! Look at his face—there are no scars. That man hasn't had any plastic surgery!"

"But—"

"But nothing, Tim! Of all the people here, I'm the only one who's ever seen the Jackrabbit in person. And I'm telling you, that's not him. Sure it looks like him . . . a little. But that's *not* the Jackrabbit."

"But—"

"There's that word again! Shut up and let me think!"

Zarkovich could feel the exhaustion stealing up—a heaviness filled his arms and legs, his eyelids felt leaden. It was the adrenaline letdown that came after every big shoot-out or takedown. He shook his head—he couldn't afford to slow down now. There was still important work to do.

He didn't know how the hell it happened, but the Jackrabbit had given everybody the slip once again. He knew now that he shouldn't have taken Anna at her word; he should have checked the target out himself before going to the Feds.

It didn't matter now—Zarkovich had to focus on saving his own ass. He watched the crowd of FBI agents standing around the body. Would they figure out that they'd killed the wrong man? More importantly, would they do anything if they did?

"Fingerprints," said Zarkovich.

"Huh?" said O'Neil. He was aggressively puffing a cigarette and staring intently at the crowd that was growing outside the alley. It was like a living animal—a monster. It was talking to itself. The words *Jackrabbit* and *dead* and *got him* were emanating from the crowd-beast. It eddied and pulsed and grew around the alley and the street in front of the theater.

"Fingerprints," Zarkovich repeated. "That's the weak link. As soon as they fingerprint the corpse, they'll realize they got the wrong guy. We've gotta do something about that. Tim, do you know anybody at Records & Identification here in Chicago?"

"Yeah, sure, I have a couple of R & I contacts. I don't think they're gonna be talkin' to me after tonight, though. They're gonna be pissed when they find out how we cut the Chicago PD outta the action."

"Well, they'll just have to get over it," said Zarkovich. "I need the Jackrabbit's print card from Chicago R & I. We can pull the old switcheroo with the prints they take from the corpse."

"That'll probably take a little grease," said O'Neil.

Zarkovich patted the roll of stolen bills in his pocket. "Don't worry, partner; I've got that part covered."

"Then maybe you can slide a little grease my way to help me soothe the hurt feelings of my R & I friends."

Zarkovich shrugged and peeled off $300 from the roll. "That should take care of it," he said. "I can use the rest to pay off the coroner's assistant." To himself, he thought, "And maybe get me a pair of those ostrich-skin boots with what's left."

"Do you think it'll work?" asked O'Neil.

Zarkovich looked over to the front of the theater. Purvis and Cowley were talking to a small knot of reporters. Purvis was strutting around like a barnyard rooster—quite a change from the man who ten minutes earlier was so nervous that he could barely light a cigar.

"Yeah, I think it'll work," said Zarkovich. "Even if we don't switch the prints, I think it'll work anyway."

"Really? Why?"

"The Feds and Hoover have too much at stake. By midnight, there will be extras on the street blaring about how the Bureau got its man. It'll be all over the country by morning. I think Hoover would let everybody think that poor dead sap is the Jackrabbit rather than admit his boys screwed it up again."

"I hope you're right," said O'Neil.

"I'm sure I'm right. We might as well hedge our bets, though. We've got some work to do. Let's get going."

Zarkovich spun and walked away with O'Neil close behind. Behind them, the crowd continued to grow around the corpse cooling in the alley.

# EPILOGUE

## McNeil Island Federal Penitentiary
## January 1969

W ell, friend, that's pretty much the end of the ball game. The public story of the Jackrabbit came to an end on a hot July night outside a theater in downtown Chicago. The case of mistaken identity was never found out—or if it was, it was kept under wraps.

Zarkovich and O'Neil managed to make the switch with the fingerprint cards. In the public record, the corpse behind the Biograph was that of the Jackrabbit—at least according to his fingers. However, the crooked East Chicago cops couldn't do likewise with his eyes. The corpse of Jimmy Lawrence had brown eyes; the Jackrabbit's were blue. This is documented from the Jackrabbit's short stint in the US Navy back in the '20s —his medical records clearly indicate blue eyes. By the time some smart researcher discovered this fascinating contradiction thirty years later, it was ancient history as far as the FBI was concerned.

I'm sure the Jackrabbit's family knew their kin hadn't really been killed. His sister, Audrey, was brought in to identify the corpse. At the morgue, she asked to see the legs. She stared for a long time, then said, "There is no question in my mind. Bury him." Then she quickly left the building. Word on the street was that she wanted to see if the corpse had a scar on his right leg, a memento from a childhood injury. There was none.

The Jackrabbit's old man was in on it too. After the funeral, he had the casket reburied underneath four thick slabs of reinforced concrete. He said

272

it was because he didn't want anyone tampering with the grave or looking for souvenirs. He probably just wanted to make sure that the Feds could never verify their mistake.

The hubbub over the "death" of the Jackrabbit died down in time, as these things always do. Still, the Jackrabbit remained a fixture in the public's imagination, and a few folks were even able to profit from it.

Billie Frechette, the Jackrabbit's true love, did her time at the federal detention farm in Milan, Michigan, and was released in 1936. She disappeared for a little while then turned up a few months later with a deep tan and a gig with a traveling road show. She and the Jackrabbit's old man told audiences about their adventures with the legendary robber and reenacted dramatic moments in his career. The name of the show was "Crime Does Not Pay!" It didn't pay in the long run for the Jackrabbit, but at least his dame and his dad made a few bucks off it.

Personally, I think she slipped across the border once or twice to be with the Jackrabbit after she got out of prison. But I guess things just didn't work out between the two of them. Maybe she missed the wild, impetuous Jackrabbit and was bored with the new man he'd become. She moved back to Wisconsin and married a man named Arthur Tic, and lived near the Menominee Reservation where she grew up.

Not everyone else was as fortunate. A few days after the events at the Biograph, the FBI picked up Jimmy Probasco for harboring the Jackrabbit. Jimmy took a dry dive out the nineteenth-floor window of the Bureau's interview room. The Feds fobbed it off as a suicide, saying that Probasco was distraught at the idea of going back behind bars. I doubt this story very much.

A few months before Jimmy's death, the Feds hauled in a member of my gang and gave him the third degree, trying to get him to spill the beans about the Bremer kidnapping. At one point, they dangled him out of the same window Jimmy Probasco fell from, trying to scare my guy into snitching. It's a safe bet that the agents were giving Jimmy the same treatment and their hands slipped—or maybe they dropped him on purpose. Regardless of the reason, the result for Jimmy was the same—a helluva big mess in the alley behind the Bankers Building.

Thanks to Dr. Loeser's squealing, the FBI was able to quickly sweep up Louis Piquett and Art O'Leary on charges of harboring the Jackrabbit. Piquett put on an impassioned defense, claiming that the attorney-client relationship obligated him to provide shelter and comfort to the Jackrabbit by way of Jimmy Probasco's hospitality. The jury bought the argument, and Piquett was acquitted.

However, that argument didn't work regarding Homer Van Meter since he was never officially Piquett's client. Consequently, the *next* jury found Louis Piquett guilty of harboring Van Meter and sentenced the lawyer to two years in Leavenworth along with a $10,000 fine and disbarment. Not surprisingly, the bombastic Piquett appealed it all the way to the Supreme Court, but in the end he did his time.

Art O'Leary managed to get away with a suspended sentence in return for his testimony against Piquett. Ordinarily, that would make him a fink in my book, but there were extenuating circumstances. Piquett's defense had been that O'Leary was responsible for most of the crimes. Given that cheapjack behavior, I can't blame O'Leary for testifying against him. Besides, Piquett was all ready to sell out the Jackrabbit anyway, so to hell with him. He's lucky he didn't get shanked in Leavenworth.

O'Leary was a good guy, and he got what he deserved: a long, successful career in business. Far from being a liability, his association with the Jackrabbit provided him with an air of mystery and celebrity. He never really talked about it, but, at the same time, he managed to keep people from forgetting about it. Maybe the Tommy gun mounted on the wall of his office had something to do with that. Art very wisely faded from the public eye, and as far as I know, he's still alive and well.

The same can't be said about Baby Face Nelson. He died a violent death, and, of course, the bastard took a couple of people with him. A few months after the Biograph incident, Nelson narrowly managed to skip out of a trap the FBI had set for him in Wisconsin. At first it seemed like he'd made another clean getaway, but two carloads of agents quickly picked up his trail. Soon, a running gun battle developed on the highway to Chicago.

Inspector Sam Cowley and Agent Herman Hollis cornered Nelson, his wife and J. P. Chase just outside of Barrington, Illinois. Hollis disabled Nelson's car with a shot to the radiator. Nelson and Chase jumped out and a furious gunfight erupted in a cornfield outside of town. Cowley and Hollis pumped lead into Nelson with little effect. Like a nightmarish movie monster, the gangster continued lurching toward the agents, firing his .351 automatic rifle. He killed Hollis outright and fatally injured Cowley before stealing their car. However, Nelson had been hit seventeen times— *seventeen!*—and he didn't get far. The next morning, his naked corpse was discovered wrapped in a blanket on the edge of a cemetery 30 miles away in Niles Center.

The hapless Homer Van Meter didn't fare much better. About a month after the Biograph shooting, Van Meter strolled out of a Chevrolet dealership on University Avenue in downtown Saint Paul. Four cops were waiting for him. Van Meter got off two shots and sprinted across the street—right into a dead-end alley.

The cops blew him apart.

They dug over fifty slugs out of his body. Later, one of Van Meter's relatives complained that the Saint Paul police had "used him for target practice." The funeral was closed casket. Poor Van Meter died the way he feared most—shot down like a dog in a dirty alley.

Melvin Purvis did OK, at least at first. He became the public's darling after the events at the Biograph, especially after he made a number of other high-profile arrests later that year. However, he'd also made a powerful enemy—J. Edgar Hoover. Purvis was blind to the seething jealousy that his fame generated in his boss. Hoover felt that Purvis was stealing glory more rightfully deserved by the Bureau, and by extension, J. Edgar Hoover himself.

Over the next year, Hoover made Purvis's professional life a living hell. He left him out of choice assignments and forced him to conduct boring and demeaning "inspection tours" of far-flung Bureau offices.

Humiliated by Hoover's treatment, Purvis resigned from the Bureau in 1935. He went back into law and served in the Second World War. Even then, years later, Hoover dogged Melvin Purvis by blocking him from choice federal appointments and jobs.

In 1960, Purvis shot himself in his study in Florence, South Carolina. Some say it was an accident; others say it was suicide. I say it was about fifty-fifty.

Anna Sage fared better than she should have, but not by much. By the time the reward money was divvied up, Sage got $2,500. She also got a one-way ticket to Romania. To his credit, Purvis did keep his word and tried to prevent her deportation. No one else in the government was as honorable, though, and Sage was deported a few months later. It was better than that fink deserved, if you ask me.

Of course, Martin Zarkovich came out of the whole mess smelling like a rose, as all true bastards do. And Zarkovich was one of the truest of true bastards. He ended up pocketing the lion's share of the reward money, and he didn't seem too sorry that his old flame got deported in the process. Basically, he went back to running rackets and taking bribes in East Chicago. As far as I know, he's doing it still.

There were a few people in this story who deserved the happy ending they got. A few months after the Biograph shooting, Doris Rogers and Allan Lockerman both resigned from the FBI. They got married the next day. They're still married, and I hope they're still in love. Last I heard, they live in Atlanta, where he's a lawyer and she writes froufrou ladies' columns for the newspaper.

As you can tell, things didn't end that great for me personally. I ain't complainin', though—at least I'm still sucking wind. By the time the Battle of Barrington took place, my gang was all but finished. Even worse, with Baby Face dead, the title of Public Enemy Number One passed to yours truly. Unlike that vain little psycho, I didn't want it. It just meant that the whole law enforcement world was after my hide.

They finally nabbed me in New Orleans in 1936. Someone tipped them off, and as I was getting ready to leave town, a bunch of Feds surrounded me. After they had all but booked me, J. Edgar Hoover himself scuttled out from behind a bush to slap the cuffs on me. But here's the kicker: none of those dumb Feds had brought a pair of handcuffs! They ended up tying my hands together with someone's necktie.

Hoover had been itching to play the hero for a while. Some senator had criticized him for never having made an arrest, so he engineered the whole bust to make himself look like a tough crime fighter. He's not, though—he's a coward and a liar, and it aggravates me to no end that the bastard is still in power today.

I was sentenced to a good long stretch in prison. Most of that stretch was at Alcatraz. By the time it closed in 1962, I was the longest-serving con in the joint, with twenty-six years under my belt. That was nearly seven years ago, and I'm still serving time. I've got a parole hearing coming up soon, and this time they might actually let me graduate from Con College.

As much of a soul-crushing bore the last thirty-three years have been, I do realize that it beats the alternative. A lot of friends and associates who were big news back in the summer of 1934 didn't live to see 1935. I remind myself of that almost daily—it's one of the things I do to keep from going stir-crazy.

So what about the Jackrabbit? That's the million-dollar question, ain't it? Last we saw, he was strolling into a crowd at Union Station on the Fourth of July. Surely, there's more about him.

Yeah, there's a thing or two about the Jackrabbit that only I know. I've been sitting on this information for years now, but I guess there's no harm in telling it now. I doubt anyone's going to read this mess anyway.

Nobody really ever heard another peep out of the Jackrabbit after he disappeared into the crowd at Union Station—except for yours truly. I don't know if he planned on having dumb Jimmy Lawrence take the fall for him or not. I'd like to think the Jackrabbit just wanted Jimmy to play decoy until he was safely in sunny Mexico. But when Jimmy got mixed up with Polly and Anna, his goose was cooked. It wasn't the Jackrabbit's fault, really. If anyone's to blame, it's the rats Sage and Zarkovich.

Anyway, the Jackrabbit must have known to play it cool while he was south of the border. Yeah, like he said, there are banks in Mexico too. However, if he knocked off any, he kept a low profile. Maybe he just turned a wrench in an auto shop. It doesn't matter. As far as the rest of the world knew, the Jackrabbit died on that hot night outside the Biograph Theater.

I wouldn't be the least bit surprised if the FBI knew they'd shot the wrong man. Even if Zarkovich hadn't managed to switch the fingerprint cards, I'll bet that dirtbag Hoover would have let it slide. It would have been too embarrassing to admit that, once again, the Jackrabbit had gotten away and another innocent civilian had been killed. I sure wouldn't put it past the bastard, especially after the bullshit about how he had "arrested" me.

I'm sure Hoover saw it as a calculated risk. He could go along with the cover-up and just pray that the Jackrabbit didn't turn up again later on. I wonder if the Jackrabbit was ever tempted to break cover just to embarrass Hoover. God knows I would have been tempted quite a bit.

I think about things like that. Like I said, thirty-three years in prison gives you a lot of time to think. It gives you a lot of opportunities to hear things too, like the pieces of the story I've been telling you. All these pieces were common currency, easily available in the yard if you could spare a couple of smokes. Anyone could have told you this tale if they had done a little digging. Although they would have to dig pretty deep for some of the Jimmy Lawrence stuff, let me tell you.

However, I still have two pieces to the puzzle that nobody else knows about. One is something I had, and one is something I saw.

Both these things happened six years ago, shortly after I got off "The Rock." When they shut down Alcatraz in '62, I got shipped here to McNeil Island Federal Penitentiary in Washington State.

McNeil Island is just as dismal and run-down as Alcatraz, but at least there aren't as many damn rules here. We can send and receive mail from people other than our lawyers, and there is a commissary and occasionally a movie night.

In the spring of '63, I got a very unusual piece of mail. The envelope was a normal business one postmarked Los Angeles. Inside was a page torn from a *Playboy* magazine. Normally, this would be contraband that never would have made it past the guardhouse. However, there were no naked women on the page. One side was the continuation of some wordy blah-blah interview with a famous writer. The other was a full-page ad for Camel cigarettes.

On the cigarette ad, someone had circled the cartoon image of the pack of Camels in heavy red ink. Underneath was written, "You O me 1." And below that, there was another small circle around the magazine's logo—the famous rabbit logo.

My mind flew back to that night in Aurora and the conversation I had with the Jackrabbit right after Red Hamilton's rough end. I guess the son of a bitch really pulled it off. He not only got out but stayed out for nearly thirty fuckin' years. Hell, that was worth a pack of cigarettes. That was worth a whole damn truckload!

I stared at that cigarette ad for a long, long time. Then I chewed it up and spit it into the toilet.

I wondered about it a lot, though. The way I figured, the Jackrabbit made it across the border with his rented parents and made a life for himself in Mexico. Maybe his money held out for a bit, or maybe he was able to find honest work in a machine shop or something.

He probably came back across the border during the war—or if he was smart, shortly before it. Still, it probably wasn't too hard for someone who spoke English and had an all-American grin to make his way to Los Angeles and find work with the booming defense industry. Especially if he was good with his hands.

I would have left it at that, but then a few months later, the *second* weird thing happened. They were showing a western called *Hearts Aflame at the Old Corral* in the rec hall. About halfway through the movie, during a fight scene, I started laughing and couldn't stop. A bunch of the other guys got really pissed that I was ruining the movie, and I knew it, but I just couldn't stop laughing. Soon, a fight broke out, they stopped the movie, and I got tossed in solitary for a week.

What happened was that I was watching the movie sorta half-heartedly, not really paying attention to whatever plot there may have been. A standard barroom brawl scene broke out, which was always a high point for an audience full of cons. Suddenly, it was as if the film slowed down. In the background, I saw a cowboy standing by a window. I squinted at the cowboy, who was barely in focus, and I swear, *it was the Jackrabbit!* Then another cowboy stepped up and socked him, and the Jackrabbit-cowboy crashed backward through a plate glass window.

It was all over in less than three seconds, but I knew in my heart of black hearts that it was him. There was something indefinable—something about the way he held himself, the tilt of his head, and the shade of a lemon-twist grin underneath the shadow of the cowboy hat. It was him. I'm *absolutely sure* of it. And for the first time in three decades, I felt a ray of hope.

And I needed it because right now, I'm a little afraid. You'd figure a tough yegg like me who's been inside for over three decades would fear nothing. But for the first time I can remember, I'm afraid. I'm afraid they're going to let me out of here, and that idea is more terrifying than it is wonderful.

I like thinking that the Jackrabbit is still out there getting his adrenaline fix by working in the movies as a stuntman. He's faceless, but he attracts all the attention. It's the perfect role for a man like the Jackrabbit. I'm glad he found a way to get his fix and still keep his ass from getting shot off.

Who knows, he may have appeared in dozens of movies—maybe hundreds. Ever since then, whenever there's a movie night, I'm there early to get a front-row seat, and I carefully scrutinize all the bit actors and stuntmen. There have been maybe half a dozen times when I spotted someone who might have been him, but nothing approaching the certainty from that first cowboy film.

So I think he's out there, and I find that a comfort. Even though I'll never see him again—and I'd be an idiot to try and find him—it's still nice to think that he's out there. And that under different circumstances, I could go visit him in California.

He'd live on a ranch somewhere out in the wilderness beyond the city. We'd sit on a patio and drink large drinks and talk about the old days. There'd be a lot of vines and fruit trees around the ranch and also animals—especially animals. The Jackrabbit was a good guy, and he always liked little kids and animals.

**THE END**

# About the Author

Crawford was born and raised in York, Pennsylvania. He has received degrees in engineering and architecture, which of course led to an interest in writing novels. His first novel, *Jackrabbit* (2019), was a retelling of the career of Depression gangster John Dillinger. His writing frequently concerns crime and history, with dark humor used to highlight the foibles of human nature. He currently lives and works in Portland, Oregon.

**You can connect with me on:**
🌐 http://sweetweaselwords.com
f https://www.facebook.com/CrawfordSmithAuthor

**Subscribe to my newsletter:**
✉ http://sweetweaselwords.com/contact

# Also by Crawford Smith

**Powwows**

Deep in the woods lives a wizard called the Professor. In the depths of the Depression, the residents of Fester, Pennsylvania call on "powwowers" such as the Professor to heal ailments, tell fortunes . . . and exact revenge. When an upstart powwower threatens to horn in on the Professor's business, he starts making plans for his own revenge. The sinister forces he sets in motion spiral out of control, and soon threaten to consume the leading citizens of the town.

sweetweaselwords.com/powwows/

### Fester

Welcome to Fester, Pennsylvania. Population: weird.

Inspector Martin Prieboy is a good cop in a bad town. The Batman-obsessed inspector now has to contend with two big cases: a murder/suicide at the local college and the mysterious disappearance of a well-respected nurse. Further complicating matters are the machinations of a drug-pushing clown, a group of inept Satanists, a family of crazed hillbillies, and an old-school Germanic witchdoctor.

When two love-struck teens make a fearsome discovery in the woods, the volatile mixture of mystery and greed begins to burn, threatening the future of Fester!

sweetweaselwords.com/fester/

### Laughingstock

Chuck Marshall has the stand-up comedy world in the palm of his hand – big-time gigs, streaming specials and his own network TV show.

Then he mysteriously disappears.

Duckie Dunne, Chuck's original comedy partner, sets out to locate his old friend. To help his search, Duckie enlists the aid of Cheryl, daughter of the late comedy legend Mickey Gross. However, Mickey may not be quite as dead as everyone thinks. At the end of their long, strange trip is a secret comics' retreat and an explosive comedy showdown!

sweetweaselwords.com/laughingstock